OHIO COUNTY PUBLIC
WHEELING, W. VA. 26003

S0-BIM-337

Praise for *Just Visiting*

"Just Visiting is about more than a college campus tour—
it's a glimpse into a rite of passage that, ultimately,
teaches the reader a thing or two about love, friendship,
and what it means to commit to one's own future."
—*Kelly Fiore, author of* Just Like the Movies

"Hilarious and heartfelt, Dahlia Adler's *Just Visiting* is
a story about breaking out of your small town, falling
in love, road trips with your best friend, and figuring
out who you're supposed to be. Reagan and Victoria's
friendship is nothing short of magic."
—*Rachael Allen, author of* The Revenge Playbook
and 17 First Kisses

"Adler gives you a story filled with road trips, hardships,
unanticipated love and a pair of best friends who want
to find the perfect college to escape their disruptive
pasts. You will laugh, cry and feel utterly torn in two,
all at the same time. A fascinating and authentic take
on friendship and following your dreams, however far-
fetched they may seem."
—*Natasha Minoso,* Book Baristas

"Reagan and Victoria's friendship is one most teenage
girls dream of—but what happens when the two
halves of a whole no longer want the same thing? *Just
Visiting* is an exploration of heartache, growing pains,
frustration, love, and forgiveness. It's filled to the brim

with everything YA fiction is missing, satisfying that gap while causing demand for more."
—*Gaby Salpeter,* Bookish Broads

Praise for *Under the Lights*

"In a sharp narrative...Adler tackles important issues, such as race, coming out, and bisexual erasure... Recommend to readers who like their romances a little more thoughtful."
—*Booklist*

"Summer reading at its finest."
—RT Book Reviews

"So much fun and so satisfying."
—Teen Librarian Toolbox

"Adler explores coming out and being a minority in a cutthroat industry, deftly weaving both threads together to show their intersectionality. A positive, empowering coming-of-age that lifts the veil hanging over queerness in YA."
—*Leah Raeder,* USA Today *bestselling author of* Unteachable *and* Black Iris

"*Under the Lights* is hilarious, sassy, and has many scenes with hot girls kissing, so yeah you want this."
—*Christina Franke,* Reader of Fictions

Praise for *Behind the Scenes*

"[A]n enjoyable pick that merges a handful of topics— family, illness, friendships, and relationships— successfully."
—*School Library Journal*

"*Behind the Scenes* keeps the promise of its title, ushering readers backstage in a Hollywood romance they won't want to leave. I loved this book every bit as much as I expected."
—*Jennifer Echols, author of* Biggest Flirts *and* Dirty Little Secret

"*Behind the Scenes* is sweet, sexy, and satisfying. Once you start reading, you won't want to stop!"
—*Trish Doller, author of* Where the Stars Still Shine

Copyright © 2015 by Dahlia Adler
First Edition

All rights reserved. No part of this book may be
reproduced or transmitted in any form or by in any means,
electronic or mechanical, including photocopying, recording, or by
any information storage and retrieval system, without the express
written permission of the publisher, except in cases of a reviewer
quoting brief passages in a review.

This book is a work of fiction. Names, characters, places, and incidents
are used fictitiously. Any resemblance to actual persons, living or dead,
business establishments, events, or locales is entirely coincidental.
Use of any copyrighted, trademarked, or brand names in this work of
fiction does not imply endorsement of that brand.

Library of Congress Cataloging-in-Publication Data
available upon request

Published in the United States by Spencer Hill Press
www.SpencerHillPress.com

Distributed by Midpoint Trade Books
www.midpointtrade.com

This edition ISBN: 9781633920538

Printed in the United States of America

Design by Michael Short
Cover by Maggie Hall

OCLC

OHIO COUNTY PUBLIC LIBRARY
WHEELING, W. VA. 26003

DAHLIA ADLER

JUST VISITING

YA
Fic
Adle
2015

Spencer Hill Press

1270304003   JAN 1 1 2016

*To best friends come and gone
and especially those who've stayed*

CHAPTER ONE

REAGAN

There comes a crossroads in every great friendship in which one of you has to tell the other a painful, ugly truth.

For Victoria Reyes and me, it seems that day is today.

"Vic, if you buy that shirt, forget rooming with you in college. I will get an actual restraining order against you."

She laughs and holds the leopard print...thing against herself. "Rae, my dear, you—"

"I know, I know," I say, examining one handwritten price tag after another dangling from flowy garment after flowy garment at Babette's, the only clothing store in the entirety of Charytan, Kansas. We'd never venture in here at all if the next closest one weren't the Walmart in Dodge City. Not that I care much either way; that's exactly where the jeans I'm wearing right now came from. "I have no 'vision.'"

A slow smile spreads across Vic's face as she snatches a belt from a display on the wall and wraps it around what's either a shirt, a dress, or a weirdly sheer bathrobe. "Exactly. Don't worry—we will totally style you up for our visit to Southeastern this weekend. This is exactly why you have a fashionista as your bestie."

"You know you're my best friend *despite* being a fashionista, right?"

She sighs. "Sometimes I think you are beyond hope." She puts back the belt, replacing it with a glittery silver one instead. "So, lemme guess. For our first road trip up to college, and basically your first trip out of Charytan *ever*, you're gonna wear...those jeans and a hand-me-down flannel from your dad."

"I can afford my half of the gas for this trip, or I can afford to buy a Vic-approved outfit from Walmart," I remind her. "Those are the options."

"Fair enough!" She hangs up both the belt and the top, and does a quick glance around the store before leading me out into the late-summer sunshine. "God, that store is depressing. What I wouldn't give to take it over, fill it with Victoria Reyes originals, pump T. Swift over the speakers…"

"Yeah, that all sounds great, except that it's *here*." I sweep my arm in the direction of Charytan's sad-ass lone strip of shops, capped off by Joe's Diner, where I work way too many hours a week, including today—my shift starts in five minutes. "By the time Babette gives that place up, you and I will be long gone. We'll be college girls, living on our own, learning actual things and not the racist revisionist shit they try to teach us at CHS…"

"Certainly sounds like paradise when you make it all about education," she says wryly as we make our way down to Joe's, walking slowly to soak up the last bits of sunshine before I'm stuck indoors for eight hours, serving eighty-seven kinds of grease to locals I don't like and passing truckers I'll never see again. "If you're going to amp me up about college, at least focus on the important things, Rae."

"Boys and sororities?"

"Boys and sororities."

I shake my head and glance through the front door of Joe's, immediately assessing the crowd. It looks pretty quiet for a Saturday afternoon, which isn't great for tips, but is excellent for my sanity and squeezing in some quality time with my AP Chemistry textbook.

"You sticking around for a bacon tuna melt, or heading home?" I ask, pulling my blond curls into a bun.

"Gotta go home," she says ruefully, checking the time on her cell phone. "My parents agreed to let me go next weekend on the condition I finish my English assignment before then, and I'm not even done with the book."

"*The Sun Also Rises*? Spoiler alert: it's more of Papa Reyes's favorite genre—White Man Lit."

"Oh yay, can't wait. My dad keeps asking when we're gonna see Gabriel García Márquez or Julia Alvarez as summer reading. I told him not to hold his breath." She shoves her phone in the back pocket of her jean skirt and hitches her bag—a colorful cloth thing of her own creation—up on her shoulder. "Wanna come over when you're done? Watch a movie?"

By the time I'm done with an eight-hour shift, I know all I'll want to do is shower and pass out, but both of those things are a whole lot more comfortable at Vic's house than in the trailer I share with my parents. "Sure. It'll probably be, like, ten."

She doesn't so much as blink at the late hour, just like I won't when she devours the bacon tuna melt I bring her in exactly five bites, but absolutely *will* when she tries to make me watch an old episode of *Project Runway*. And then we'll settle on *Law & Order: SVU*, as we always do, because I love the legal stuff and she loves the drama and Benson's leather jackets. Basically, we've got co-habitation down to a science; how could we ever even think about living with anyone else next year? "Don't forget—"

"I let Hector put pickles on it *once*, Vic. I wasn't paying attention, and I'm still sorry. It'll never happen again."

She grins. "Cool. I'll see you later." Then she blows me a kiss and flutters her fingers in a good-bye wave as she turns to walk home, and I push open the door to the diner, ready to begin that day's descent into madness.

My shift goes even later than usual, thanks to a record number of spills and crashes that take forever to clean up. By the time I finally leave Joe's, it's too late to head over to Vic's, and I'm bone tired anyway. I text her that I'm going home instead, and get in the car it took me years of taking orders, juggling plates, and wiping up spills to buy.

It's a short drive, but at this hour, it's far better to just hop in the car and suck up the little bit of wasted gas than walk through the streets, subjected to the beer-breathed leering of the Charytan menfolk who populate the local bars. It's worse now that my father's one of them far more often than he used to be, and bad enough I'll still have to walk past way too many creeps in our trailer park once I get there.

I park in my usual spot in the makeshift dirt lot in the center of the park—my dad's truck gets the spot in front of the house—and brace myself for the fifty-foot walk to our trailer. The stench of bad weed is heavy in the air, and I can feel it clinging to me the instant I slam my car door.

"Hey, Forrester," Tommy Witson calls as soon as he spots me from the gathering of lawn chairs where he and a few others are passing around a joint and chugging from silver cans I can't read in the dark. "You bring us back some cheeseburgers?"

"Sure smells like it." Britney O'Connell wrinkles the nose I know she'd fix in a heartbeat if she had the money. "Jeez, don't they let you shower off the stink?"

I snort. "I realize you've never held down a job in your life, Britney, but where exactly do you think they hide the showers in diners?"

By the time she comes up with her undoubtedly super-clever response, I'm too far to hear it. I used to be friendly with that crew, once upon a time, back when we used to play tag around the park and I actually loved living here. But they turned against me when everyone else in town did, and now they think I'm a snobby bitch, and I think they're wastes of space, and here we all are.

But not for long.

The TV is blaring through the wall of the trailer and I let myself in quietly, thinking maybe I can avoid my parents entirely. Sure enough, they're wrapped up in each other on the couch, watching some cop show they've apparently deemed worth the money they throw away on satellite TV every month but won't put toward getting our stove fixed.

"Are you just getting back from work, Rae?" my dad

asks gruffly.

"Yeah. Lot of cleanup tonight."

"Joe's keeping you too late."

It's an empty statement; expressing four seconds of bullshit concern is Bill Forrester Parenting 101. Sure enough, he re-focuses on the TV without waiting for a response, and I trudge off to my room. There's no point in sticking around to see if my mother will acknowledge my presence. My dad got paid yesterday, which means she doesn't need anything from me.

Just as well; I've got the early shift at Joe's tomorrow, and plenty of homework to squeeze in around it. I pull my Chem textbook back out of my bag to resume the reading I didn't get to finish up at the diner.

It's hard to stay focused, though, especially with the TV blaring from the living room and my feet aching something fierce. After ten minutes, I resign myself to the fact that this is gonna have to wait until tomorrow's shift, where there are far more windows of quiet than in this trailer. I put the notebook back down and pick up the booklet next to it, a course catalog for Southeastern Kansas University, where Vic and I are headed this weekend.

I've read through this thing so many times, there are smudges on the pages with the majors I keep flipping between. English. History. Sociology. So many windows into a world that isn't here; this little booklet is practically a breathing tube. Just touching the glossy cover calms me.

This weekend will be Vic's and my first visit to a college, but we've been planning it for so long, I feel like I already know the campus backward and forward. I know what class I'll be checking out when I get there, which freshman dorm is closest to the library, and where to get the best coffee near the quad. Vic's scouting may have much more to do with sorority houses, but I love that she's every bit as excited as I am. Though we may not have tons of the superficial stuff in common, we've been united by our desire to get out of Charytan for bigger and better since the day we met in the nurse's office back in sophomore year—both of us feigning illness to escape the rest of the student body. Charytan was brand-new unpleasantness for her, and sadly old-hat for me, but it's amazing the way a strong distaste for the population around you can bond friends for life. By the time I went to her house that weekend for the very first time, we were already making future plans.

And now the future is almost here.

Finally.

I close the catalog and take a deep breath. I don't want to put too much pressure on one visit; hopefully it'll only be the first of many trips we'll be taking out of town to scout out our home base for the next four years. I only get four application fee waivers, so I'll have to choose the final picks wisely, and staying in Kansas is a must for in-state tuition and hopefully a scholarship, but anything that isn't Charytan Community College seems like a pretty glorious option. And just getting out to visit them feels like its own kind of magic.

The smell of fried food still clinging to me, I head into the shower, which is icy cold as usual and makes me wish I'd gone to Vic's after all. Then I climb into bed, reaching blindly for one of the three books that never stray far from my nightstand. I only manage one chapter of *Howl's Moving Castle* before I slip under the veil of exhaustion that's been hanging over me for hours, but it's exactly what I need to remind me of what gets me through the day.

There is more beyond this.

VICTORIA

I am literally surrounded by clothing right now, and I do not have a single thing to wear.

On a regular day, I love my clothing. I love that I don't dress like anyone else at CHS; it goes along with the fact that I don't look like anyone there, either. I love how much of it was made by my own hands, and that I get to show off my skills, even if no one really appreciates them except my parents and Reagan. But a college visit isn't a regular day, and right now I'm feeling totally out of my realm.

Would shorts be too childish? Are jeans too boring?

Does a dress look like I'm trying too hard? This is the problem when your best friend couldn't care less, your only sibling is thousands of miles away in the Peace Corps and doesn't know a thing about women's fashion other than what bikinis he likes, and your parents cringe just a little more with every extra inch of skin you show.

You end up talking to your clothing in the mirror a lot.

"That is not the right belt for this skirt," I murmur at the glass, untying the cloth sash I embroidered myself under my abuela's careful observation the last time I visited her and my abuelo in Mexico City. "You need something leather. Or metallic. Or both." I know I had something like that, somewhere, at some point, but after ten minutes of riffling through my stuff, it's clear it's not in my closet. Which means my mom definitely helped herself.

I sigh and go downstairs, knowing I'll find her in one of two places—the kitchen, attempting to cook something with a fifty-percent chance of success, or in her office. She turns out to be in the latter, typing so rapidly I know it's an e-mail to either my brother or one of my thousand cousins she keeps in touch with regularly. I reach up a hand to flicker the lights to get her attention, but she spots me before I can, waves, and smiles.

"What's up?" she signs.

"Do you have my silver belt?" I sign back.

"In my closet." She circles her fist in front of her chest, thumb straight across the top—*Sorry*—one of the first signs I ever learned.

"No problem." I start to turn back, but then she gestures with a flattened hand for me to hold up; the conversation's not over.

"I thought you were doing your homework now?"

Oh, right. That's what I'm supposed to be doing; not packing for a trip I'm not taking for another six days. "I am. Just taking a little break to pick outfits for the weekend."

"You know that to get into college, you have to actually do your work, right? No point in visiting otherwise."

It's clear from her smile that she's teasing, but I know it's no joke that she or my father will check at the end of the week to make sure it's been done before they let me get in Rae's car. My parents met in grad school, where they were both getting teaching degrees—his roommate was my mom's interpreter—and they're so obsessed with education, I swear, if my abuela weren't so into needlework, I'd be sure I was adopted.

"I know, Mom." But nausea creeps up my throat as I sign it. Truth is I'm barely three chapters in to the book, and the thought of picking it up again puts me to sleep. It's not that I have trouble reading or anything, it's just... I'd so much rather *do*.

I am so, so ready to *do*.

"I'll get back to it. I promise."

She smiles softly. "I know you will, sweetheart. We trust you. You know that."

I do know it, and the last thing in the world I want is to let my parents down. Every single day I wake up in Kansas I remember what they've sacrificed for me to be happy and I really do want to make them proud, I just... can't quite seem to do it this way.

But I have to try.

I excuse myself back upstairs, retrieve the belt from her closet—even when she forgets to return stuff, she's always good about hanging it up—and get back to my work, pushing my clothing aside to make some space on my bed for me to curl up with Hemingway. *Just nine more months of this*, I remind myself as I slog through more white man problems. *After that, it'll be summer, and then...*

I glance back at the pile of clothing I've shoved to the edge of my bed and smile. I may not have enough of the right clothes to be a sorority girl just yet, but I can fix that. I love dressing up, but neither in Tucson— where I spent the first fifteen years of my life—nor here in Charytan has my unparalleled fashion sense stopped people from making gross assumptions about me and my family based on the skin underneath.

It's the total opposite of how most people think, I know, but I'm excited for the superficial stuff to make a difference. I'm excited for how I dress, how I look—how I *make* myself look—to matter. I'm proud of being Mexican; I'm just tired of it being *all* I am. And it was, to the girls in Tucson like Ashley Martin, who spoke English to me at a snail's pace and made "jokes" about my family jumping the fence, despite both my parents being documented, and me and Javi having been born in the U.S. It is, to the other girls here, who pretend I don't exist except when they wanna moan about affirmative action. It is, to the guys who holler "Caliente!" and "Mamacita!" at me. (Most of whom are definitely failing Spanish.)

But out there it won't be. It can't be.

We moved here for something different, and while it's better here than it was in Tucson, it's still not enough. I need to be more than this, and I'm not letting college be anything like high school.

Reagan and I are gonna rock Southeastern, and Ashley Martin and all the rest will be nothing but a bad memory.

"Victoria?" A hand gently nudges my shoulder, and it takes me a few seconds to realize I've fallen asleep and drooled all over Hemingway. "I'm guessing homework isn't going very well?"

Whoops. "Guess not," I say, shifting over in my bed so my father can sit down. "You're a literature professor—can you just tell me what happens? Maybe write my paper for me, if you're feeling especially generous?"

"I will never feel that generous, mija." Still, he frowns at the book. "Hemingway. Always with the white men, that school."

"Exactly! See? You understand why I can't get through this thing."

He chuckles, looking around at the piles of clothing heaped everywhere, the mess of my sewing table, and the sketches of my designs hung up on the walls. "Somehow, I don't think that's the problem." He pats my hair and moves the book to my nightstand. "Did you call Abuela tonight?"

"Oh, no, how long have I been asleep?" I pick up my phone to check the time, and see that it's after eleven. I also have a text from Reagan, apologizing that she's skipping out on coming over. "I'll have to call her tomorrow." I hate to be late. I know she and my grandfather wait by the phone, and it's hard enough for them having to coordinate with my brother, who's halfway around the world (like, literally—he's in the Peace Corps in Fiji); it shouldn't be difficult with me, considering Charytan and Mexico City are in the same time zone.

Thankfully, Papi knows how bad I already feel, and he doesn't dwell on it. "I'm sure she'll be happy to hear from you. I know she wants to hear all about your fancy college visit plans with Reagan."

Pretty sure my abuela doesn't want to hear my *real* plans for this weekend, unless she's magically changed her stance on boys, drinking, and parties. But I just say, "Not much to report until we actually go."

"Are you looking forward to it?"

"Very much," I say with a smile I hope is just the right size to convey that he's not misguided to be letting me go on my own with my best friend instead of him and my mother taking me, as they'd originally wanted to do. "Reagan has big plans for us to spend hours memorizing every inch of the library."

"I knew I liked that girl." He kisses my cheek and stands up. "Get some sleep, mija. You know the rule—if you're not caught up by the weekend…"

"I know, Papi. Trust me, I know."

"I know you know." He lets himself out, closing the door gently behind him. I collapse back on my bed, send a quick reply text to Reagan to make sure she got home okay, and pick the book back up.

Six days. Six days is all I have to get through, and then I'll get my first hint of proof that all of this is worth it, that there's a point to Hemingway and Trig and Physics and hours spent studying for the ACTs with Reagan at the Joe's counter, when I already know what I love to do and it doesn't involve any of it.

Six days, and I'll finally see what's beyond this.

Chapter Two

Reagan

It's a lot easier to pack quickly when everything you own fits into a six-by-eight room in a double-wide. If I repeat that to myself enough, maybe I'll grow some patience with Vic instead of getting tempted to drive off to Southeastern without her. Much like my best friend, the sun is taking its sweet time showing up that morning. The clock on my dashboard hits 6:29, making it fifteen minutes since I pulled up in front of the Reyeses' two-story, twice as long as it took me to throw a few things into a bag and drive over here.

My palms are itching to jam the horn, but it's way too

early and Vic already knows I'm out here; she's given me the "one more minute" gesture from her window twice already. I can only hope visiting a college for a weekend will provide her with some much-needed counting skills.

Finally, her front door swings open and there stands Vic, laden with more bags than I even own.

"What the hell could you *possibly* need that much crap for?" I demand as soon as she gets close enough for me to pop the trunk. "Do you understand what a weekend is?"

"Do *you* understand what college is?" She tosses a huge purple monstrosity of a bag in the trunk and then yanks open the passenger door and slides in next to me. Yet another bag is tossed onto the floor and two others into the backseat. "Besides, you told me to bring snacks." She waves a hand behind her. "Voila. Snacks. And…," she says slowly, as if drawing out some kind of torture, "you wouldn't want me to leave this behind, would you?" She reaches into her bag and brandishes the one thing she knows I couldn't make the trip without.

"Gimme gimme gimme!" I reach out and yank her phone from her hands. She promised she'd fill it with music for our road trips, and I'm relieved to see she made good on that. "Does this actually have good music on it now or am I going to be listening to boy bands the entire way to Southeastern?"

"First of all, One Direction *is* good music," she declares, buckling herself in as I scroll through the playlists, "and second of all, I told you I would throw on some of your screaming banshees and I did."

"I dare you to call Janis Joplin a screaming banshee to her face. Metaphorically speaking, of course." I live without plenty of things most consider essential, but music for a road trip isn't one of them. Since buying a car wiped out every dollar that wasn't earmarked for the Reagan Forrester College Fund, and the radio is nothing but country music and political talk shows about how Vic's fellow Mexicans are ruining the country, I'm sadly reliant on someone who thinks Rihanna is the greatest lyricist of our time to provide it.

"I'm not afraid of any chick named *Janis*," says Vic, yanking down the sun visor to expose the mirror and pulling lip gloss out of her bag. "I'll gladly say it to her face."

"She died in 1970." I pull away from the house just sharply enough to make her draw a jagged line of Petal Pink on her face.

"Then she's probably not going to argue with me, is she?" Vic says sweetly, wiping the gloss from her cheek. "Unlike a certain someone, who is going to lose her best friend status realllly quickly if she tries that again while I'm doing my eyeliner."

"You do your eyeliner in a moving vehicle and you deserve whatever's coming to you."

She sighs. "You are a sadist."

"If I were a sadist, I would keep driving right on past Joe's and deprive you of the sugary goodness I know you've been craving since you woke up this morning."

"You wouldn't dare."

"No," I admit, "I wouldn't. No chance I'm making the two-hour drive to Southeastern without a super tall black coffee in my system." I pull into the parking lot at Joe's two minutes later, feeling almost guilty at the number of cars already there, belonging to customers I won't be serving today. While Vic rims her eyes with black pencil, I scan the parking lot, looking for the dirty navy-blue pickup truck with a "Kiss Me, I'm Irish" bumper sticker I know won't be there.

I do, however, see an equally familiar and very unwelcome junker a few spots down, with some even more unwelcome bodies emerging. If Vic doesn't hurry the hell up with her eyeliner…shit. Too late.

"Boys, look who it is! Ragin' Reagan, the killer lay!" Sean Fitzpatrick's voice is nails on a chalkboard, magnified by a PA system.

"Are you sure she's any good?" Drew Ballard brays, and for the first time in my life I'm relieved that when Vic applies eye makeup, she gets into a zone, especially pre-coffee. The shit from these guys has gotten way worse in the past few months, and I hate, hate, hate the idea of the only person in this town I actually respect hearing it. When she first moved here, she used to ask why people gave me such a hard time; I said they were just giving me shit because I'm on food stamps, knowing bringing money into it would make her uncomfortable enough to stop asking. Which she did soon after. "Wouldn't your brother have stuck around if she was?"

The guys crack up into laughter, finally drawing Vic's attention, but before she can take stock of names, faces, or the fact that I'm their target, I tell her we have to go.

She whimpers and tosses the pencil back in her bag. "We can't leave yet. If I don't get a coffee right now I will literally die."

"I really hope they teach you the meaning of 'literally' in college too," I mumble under my breath as I drag her into the diner. We force ourselves to smile brief greetings at everyone present because in a town like Charytan, nearly every face is a familiar one, especially when your dad's been a day laborer here for twenty years. I'm relieved to see Steve—aka Freckles, for reasons that are obvious if you've ever so much as caught a glimpse of him—behind the counter; the guys never dare to be dicks to me when he's around.

I glance behind me before we dodge around a passing trucker to get in line. The boys are still shooting the shit in the parking lot, and thankfully can't be heard through the glass. Finger-combing her long brown waves while she scans the pastry racks, Vic remains blissfully oblivious. "So what is it *you* hope to get out of visiting Southeastern, seeing as you have zero interest in parties, sororities, or anything else that actually sounds like fun?"

"They still have that nunnery, right?" She sticks out her tongue at me, and I return the gesture before resuming the age-old quandary of a banana-nut muffin or a somewhat more well-rounded-sounding egg 'n cheese. Hmmm… "I'd love to sit in on a class," I answer, sniffing to see if I can determine which is fresher. "There's an Intro to Sociology lecture that meets at one today, if you're interested in joining."

"Are you kidding? First of all, I don't even know what Sociology is, and don't pretend you do. Second of all, why would you want to hang out with a bunch of kids who were crazy enough to take class on a Friday?"

Before I can respond, Freckles motions for us to step up.

"Hey," I greet him with a smile that requires a whole lot more effort now that I've started my morning off with a Sean Fitzpatrick sighting. "How's it going on the early shift?"

"About a thousand times slower than when you're working," he teases, though he's probably lying. Freckles is the morning-est morning person I know. It's sick, really. He pulls out the old-school pad he loves to use even though he has a crazy memory for orders. "Lemme guess. Super tall black coffee and a banana-nut muffin?"

"You think you know me so well." I sniff. "I'll have

you know, I was considering an egg 'n cheese instead of the muffin. Care to be the deciding vote?"

"Tell you what. How about I slip you the egg 'n cheese on the side? You deserve it for all your years of dedicated service."

I should say no. Not that Freckles is a thief—Joe's totally down with us helping ourselves occasionally. (I'd say we were the kids he never had, except he has two kids; he just doesn't like them.) I just don't like the idea of being someone's charity case.

But today, I'm so wired with excitement, I decide to take him up on it. "Freckles, my man, you are the greatest co-worker a person who generally hates co-workers could ever ask for."

He grins and calls back my sandwich order to Hector, the line cook, while he gets to work making my coffee. Next to me, Vic heaves a dramatic sigh. "Hello, I'm here too," she mutters. "Yeah, skim milk, please. Thanks."

"Hey, Freckles, can we also get a large coffee with skim milk and a powdered sugar donut?"

"You got it, Pepe." Pepe, as in cartoon skunk Pepe Le Pew, for the white streak (actually a lack of pigment) that runs from my front-most curl down in a stripe through my right eyebrow and lash, which I guess is obvious if you've ever so much as glimpsed me.

"Tia Maria, he has such a crush on you," she huffs, examining the ends of her own glossy hair. "It's like no one else is even here."

I can't help cracking a smile, though Vic's way off base. I used to think Tia Maria was such a charming substitute for a swear word…until I met Vic's Aunt Maria. Now I want to cover children's ears when she says it in their presence. "He does not; he just knows me because we've worked together for three freakin' years. He's a nice guy."

"Whatever." She leans against the counter and taps her foot impatiently while we wait for our order. A couple of minutes later, we have our drinks and assorted sugary, fatty goodness and we're back on the road.

"Do you think whatever college guy I hook up with tonight will make it impossible for me to ever go back to high school boys?" Vic asks dreamily as she swipes a bit of powdered sugar from her lip.

"I was just wondering the same thing about the library." I fiddle with the phone, clicking triumphantly when I discover she's actually put the Runaways on it. "Do you know that the Southeastern library supposedly has over fifteen thousand books? Fifteen thousand! Can you imagine if the Charytan High library had fifteen thousand books?"

"You are such a nerd." Vic examines her cuticles. "How are we friends?"

The actual answer is that Vic had arrived at Charytan High at the beginning of sophomore year, exactly when I desperately needed a new friend who knew nothing about me and had no attachment to the ex who'd ruined my life. I didn't have much competition for the role of her BFF because people were too scared of her—*gasp!*— brown skin and Hispanic last name to get to know that she's a fiercely loyal, eerily resourceful fashion savant who's so damn full of positive energy it actually manages to infect *me* of all people on occasion.

There's no need to say it, though, and I simply roll my eyes and turn up the volume.

Two hours, several bathroom breaks, infinite rest-stop selfies, and lots of bickering about music later, we arrive at the gates to Southeastern Kansas University. "Holy crap, this place is huge," I observe immediately, and Vic nods in silent agreement. We emerge slowly from the car, staring up in awe at the huge buildings and lush green lawns. Compared to the scraggly grass and dirt roads of Charytan, Southeastern may as well be the most beautiful place on earth.

"This is so ridiculously gorgeous." I inhale deeply, taking in the tall, leafy trees, just beginning to change; the beautiful white-trimmed red brick; and colorful banners proclaiming everything from upcoming blood drives to general welcomes. Everything just looks so... bright here. Breathing in fills my lungs with the scent of freshly cut grass rather than cooking fumes and truck exhaust. Part of me is nervous to set foot on the campus, like the second I do, everyone will see just how drab I am against the vibrancy of real life. But then Vic hooks an arm through mine, and I remember that I'm walking in with plenty of vibrancy by my side.

"*So* gorgeous," Vic agrees, squeezing my arm. When I follow her line of vision, she's looking at a hulking blond guy wearing a deep-green T-shirt that spreads three Greek letters across his broad chest.

"Jesus, Vic. You have such a one-track mind."

"I do not; I'm interested in girls too. As in, which girls wanna be my future sorority sisters." She runs her fingers absently through her hair while her warm brown eyes scout the campus, and I pretend my stomach's not twinging at the thought of all the new friends she's gonna make at college while I'm hanging out with books every night. "And I think I'm gonna try going by Tori in college. It sounds so much more adult than Vic, no?"

Adult. Is that a thing I'm supposed to feel? Because I so totally don't. But I'm gonna have to start if I wanna be a college girl, and if there's one thing I'm sure of on this planet—other than my friendship with Vic—it's that I do. So I shrug as if the idea of her being an adult doesn't freak the shit out of me and say, "Sure, I guess. So am I supposed to call you Tori here? Are we taking it for a practice run?"

"What better time?" She stops looking around and I know she's found herself something tall, dark, and handsome. She smooths down the tiers of her pink miniskirt, presses her lips together, and rubs the little stripe of a scar on her forehead for luck—Vic's prep-for-battle stance.

Suddenly, I cannot wait for class.

VICTORIA

It takes me thirty seconds to fall in love with college.

Sure, maybe I don't love it for the same reasons as Reagan—I'm not quite as psyched about the "classes" part of college, and I don't get a thrill out of musty old buildings like she does—but all the same, I know that the Victoria Reyes and Reagan Forrester College Tour Bonanza is the most brilliant idea I have ever had. What better way to spend time with my BFF and escape Charytan to see the real world at the same time? Great parties, hot guys, and no classes are just huge bonuses.

Well, there's class for Reagan, I guess. Having fun isn't exactly at the top of her priority list. Obviously there are things I want to learn too—I *am* excited to finally take fashion classes from someone other than my abuela—but right now, all I can think about is how much bigger this world is than the one I've been in for the last two years.

It feels like I finally have the space to breathe.

"Ooh, I think that's the library!" Reagan gushes, pointing out a brick building that looks just like all the other brick buildings. "And there's a map next to it." She grabs my arm and pulls me in that direction. "Let's see if we can find the social sciences building where the class is later."

"You wild thing," I tease, but I let her drag me along, since I fully plan to do some dragging of my own when the parties start up later that night. Sometimes getting Reagan to have any fun is like trying to teach a dog how to read. "Has anyone ever told you you're a total nerd?"

"You. Every single day." But despite my teasing, the excitement brightening up her pale cheeks doesn't lessen one bit. Despite being super tiny, not even five feet, Rae can be the most determined force in the universe when she wants to be.

It's a big part of the reason I want to visit schools together. I might be excited about college, but unlike Reagan, I'm not completely fearless at the idea of going. Also unlike Reagan, I actually like my parents; the thought of leaving them, especially with Javi in Fiji, hurts more than I want to think about. It's not like I can just call up my mom to talk whenever I feel like it; making sure we catch each other when we can both video-chat is worlds away from being able to tell her every detail of my life the way I do now. What's it gonna be like when I can't talk to her fifty times a day?

You don't need to chat with your mommy fifty times a day, I remind myself as I watch Reagan eagerly devour the map with her huge brown eyes shining so brightly, she looks like a cartoon character. *You're almost a hot, sophisticated college woman. No hot, sophisticated college woman needs to talk to her mom every day.* Of course, even as I lecture myself, I find myself pulling out my phone to send my mother a text. Just to tell her we made it safely.

My phone beeps a minute later with her reply text. *Glad you survived Reagan's music choices ;)*

Just barely!! Might have to accidentally delete a few things before the ride home...

Reagan's amused voice breaks in. "You're totally texting with your mom, aren't you?"

I blush and tuck my phone back into my bag. "Of course not."

"I don't know why you bother trying to hide it." Reagan switches to signing. "You know I love your mom."

It's true, she does, and the feeling is mutual for obvious reasons—as soon as Reagan found out that my mom's deaf, she immediately started to teach herself ASL. She's still rusty, but that first time she surprised both me and Mom by expertly signing "Nice to meet you," I knew without a doubt she was going to be the best friend I ever had. Even if she thinks sororities are "stupid, sexist, probably racist, and definitely pointless." Direct quote.

Two guys jog by just then, one in a plain blue T-shirt and the other with no shirt at all, and I swear they both check me out as they pass. "Rae!" I whisper fiercely. "Did you see those guys? They were so freaking hot."

"No, I did not see those guys, *Tori*," she says dryly, glancing at her watch. "We only have one afternoon to actually go to classes and stuff. Are you sure you don't want to come with me?"

"Positive. Anyway, your class isn't for a while. Should we go check into our motel or just leave our bags in the car and give ourselves a self-guided tour?"

"I think it's probably too early to check in, but I'm all for a tour. What did you want to see?"

Now it's my turn to grab her hand and yank her away. "Greek Row, of course!" I reply cheerfully, dragging her along as quickly as my fantastic studded cowboy boots can carry me.

My feet are aching and my caffeine buzz is wearing off, but after half an hour of getting lost, I couldn't be happier to have arrived at our destination. "Do you see how gorgeous that house is?" I stab a glittery purple fingernail in the direction of a huge, stunning sorority house the color of snow with regal pillars to match. I've never been to Washington D.C., but it's pretty much exactly how I imagine the White House to look in person.

"It is beautiful," Rae agrees, and I pretend not to hear just how hard it is for her to say it, like I'd just told her we'll need to use her beloved copy of *Harry Potter* for firewood. "But Vi—*Tori*—are you seriously sure you want to join a sorority? They're so…"

"*Yes*," I say firmly before she can fill in her own blank. "And you should at least think about joining with me. We'd have such a cute room in a gorgeous house, and they totally help you network and stuff so you can get a job after graduation."

"I can't even think about the 'after graduation' part yet," admits Rae as she pulls her white-streaked blond curls into a bun on top of her head. "I'm dying to leave Charytan and all, but…baby steps. Let's get *into* college before we talk about leaving it, shall we?"

It's so rare to hear Rae acknowledge even the tiniest hint of nervousness about all this that I can't help but smile and give in. "Deal."

We continue to walk around for a while, looking at the awesome houses while I size up the inhabitants of Greek Row to get an idea of how our maybe-future-classmates are dressing. I'm glad to see that I fit in perfectly with my miniskirt and cute sweater, though it doesn't seem like anyone else has studded her own boots or embroidered a funky sequined bow *on* to said sweater. I make a mental note to look into the Greek-letter pendants I see a few girls wearing and take on a couple of extra babysitting jobs so I can buy the super cute boots that seem to be the sorority girl footwear of choice.

And then I see it. It's massive but not scary, a beautiful tan stucco trimmed in dark, chocolate brown, standing atop a lawn that's impossibly, perfectly green. It has a huge wraparound porch on which a bunch of girls are sitting around, talking and laughing, reading magazines while they polish their nails. Everything about it screams "We have more fun on an average Friday than you do at your best parties!" and I'm dying to race up the flagstone path and join them.

I must be staring way too obviously because suddenly a friendly, high-pitched voice chirps from behind me, "Hey, are you a freshman?"

I turn to face a tall blonde who's even paler than Reagan, with perfectly curled hair and one of those Greek-letter pendants hanging around her neck. She looks so perfect, the epitome of college-girl sophistication, I wish I could take a picture of her for Javi; my brother would flip. "High school senior," I admit, standing up just a little taller. "Just checking out the campus, trying to figure out where to go next year."

"Thinking about pledging a sorority?"

"Definitely!" I force myself to ignore the sound of Rae laughing into her hand at my enthusiasm. "Is this your house?"

"Lambda through and through," says the blonde, which I guess is a yes, although the letters posted over the entrance of the house don't match the ones on her necklace. "You wanna come see the house?"

Um, yes?! my mind screams, but for once, my mouth plays it cooler. "Sure," I say with a shrug, "that'd be great."

I shoot Reagan a pleading look behind blondie's back, but she stabs a finger at her watch and I realize it's almost time for her class.

The sorority girl doesn't even seem to notice Rae, who gives me a little wave, mouths "have fun," and dashes off to find the building. Without Reagan by my side, I'm getting a little anxious. I'm about to tell Lambda that I actually have to go with my friend when she cheerfully says, "Awesome, let's go! I'm Sasha, by the way."

Sasha. I have never, ever in my life met anyone named Sasha. Except for, like, Reagan, I feel like everyone I know is "Mary" or "Annie" or "Katie." How could I *not* follow a Sasha?

"I'm Tori," I reply, and as I do, I can already feel everything start to change.

CHAPTER THREE

REAGAN

I sit in the back of the class and do not get called on once, which is simultaneously a relief and hugely disappointing. As I file out among the Southeastern students, I check my phone, which I'd silenced for the class, but there are no messages from Vic. Guess she and Lambda are still bonding over the fine arts of eyebrow waxing and lip gloss selection. I send her a text to let her know that I'm done and then head out of the building and back toward the large column on the edge of the quad bearing the map I'd seen earlier that morning. Might as well take advantage of Vic's being occupied to check out the library, since she'd made it clear she was about as interested in seeing it as she was in studying nuclear physics.

When I get to the map, I see that someone's already standing there studying it, and I wonder if I should wait my turn or just squeeze in. He mumbles something aloud as I'm still trying to decide, although I can't see his face and I don't know if he's trying to talk to me or just muttering to himself.

I don't want to be rude in case it's the former, so I just say, "Sorry?"

He jumps about a foot in the air; guess he wasn't talking to me after all. "Jesus," he mutters, and he whirls around to face me, then looks startled when he doesn't see anyone. It takes him a second to look down. I'm at least a foot shorter than he is, maybe more. He's holding a hand to his chest, like I freaked him out by interrupting his concentration. Or maybe it's my white streak—it tends to have that effect on people. "I didn't realize anyone else was out here."

"Class just ended," I explain. I think he might be blushing, but with his skin tone—a deeper, toastier shade of brown than Vic's—it's hard to tell. "There will be a lot of people around now, probably."

"Good," he grumbles. "Maybe one of them can tell me how to find the stupid library."

"I was just coming to the map to look for the library

myself." I'm annoyed to hear the words come out of my mouth sounding as if I think it's the world's most brilliant coincidence, like I've just uncovered that we both hail from the same tiny Martian colony. "Are you a prospective too?"

"Yup." He furrows the thick black eyebrows that arch just slightly over his dark eyes. "I thought you just came from a class."

"I went to check out Intro to Sociology."

"You can do that?"

"Sure, I just walked right in with my visitor's pass."

"Dammit! I wish I'd thought of that."

I smile sympathetically, or at least I hope it's sympathetically. Not that I'm worried about how some boy feels. But I still like that he wishes he'd been able to go to a class. "Well, at least you got some time to check out the campus, which is more than I've done. All I've gotten to see so far is Greek Row."

One of those eyebrows rises ever so slightly. "You're planning to rush a sorority?"

The sheer image of me in a sorority is so absurd, it nearly cracks me up. "God no. I was just going with a friend." Then I realize I might be offending him. "Are you planning to rush a fraternity?"

"God no." He echoes my horrified tone. "I'm not exactly the 'frat bro' type."

"Well, in my mind, 'frat bros' don't make it to class, so

maybe you're more the type than you think," I tease. His laugh is a great sound and when it stops I immediately want to hear it again. "So, any luck tracking down the library?"

"No, I suck at maps. Maybe I can catch Intro to Geography later this afternoon." He sweeps a hand toward the directory. "Have at it. If you can point me in the right direction, my firstborn child is yours." I must have a funny look on my face because he immediately says, "I feel the need to state here that I do not actually have any children."

"Phew!" I say, and we both smile again, even though whether or not he has kids is of no consequence to me, this stranger whose name I don't even know. Right?

Right.

Looking at the map, it takes me all of five seconds to find the library. "Got it." I wipe my forehead as if I've just run a marathon. "Man, you're right. That was a serious mental workout."

"Are you always this difficult?"

"My parents would tell you this isn't even the tip of the iceberg."

The corners of his lips slide upward, and it's cute enough to remind me why I *don't* flirt with guys anymore. "Ready?" I ask as brusquely as I can considering that even forcing my eyes back to the map isn't making that smile disappear from my brain.

"You seriously found it?"

"I seriously did." I adjust my oversized bag on my arm so the spiral-bound notebook inside will stop jabbing me in the ribs. "What kind of school do you go to that you can't read a basic map? You know, so I can *not* send your firstborn there when you eventually hand it over."

He smiles, a full one this time, and his teeth are almost blindingly white against his skin. "Chaplin Prep is excellent, thank you very much," he informs me. "My firstborn would be lucky to go to my alma mater."

"Your firstborn would be lucky to find his way out of the womb," I retort as we start on our way to the library.

"So many preconceived notions and you've only just met me." He shakes his head in disbelief, though the visible dimple in his cheek suggests he's not all that disappointed.

"Actually, I haven't," I point out. "I don't even know your name."

"All part of my being an international man of mystery."

I snort. Not the prettiest sound, but I can't help it. "Oh, yes, I got that whole mysterious vibe immediately."

"Ah, what can I do?" he beseeches the sky, which is gray with the suggestion of impending rain. "She sees right through me." He slows his pace and turns to me. "Dave Shah, but if they ask, I revealed that information only under extreme duress."

"Obviously. I'll just stick with 'Bond' to be safe."

He nods, a serious expression on his face, but his eyes are twinkling and I'd be lying if I said it wasn't the tiniest bit cute.

"I feel you're not taking me seriously," he says.

"I also feel I'm not taking you seriously."

"Fair enough. Does my revelation earn me a similar one, at least?"

I debate both holding out a little longer to prolong our conversation as well as whether or not I should pause and extend a hand. It's too much thinking at once, and "Reagan Forrester" slips out of my lips, though my hands stay in the pockets of my navy-blue windbreaker.

"Pretty," he says, and I can feel my cheeks heating up. "Your name, I mean. Not that you're not," he adds quickly, obviously flustered. Now he's blushing too; this time, I'm sure I see it. "Jesus, I'm awkward."

I can't help grinning, which only makes things worse for him, so I decide to cut him a break. "Thanks," I say. "My dad was pushing for DJ after some old TV show character, but my mom's best friend told her it was 'super fancy' to give a kid your maiden name as a first name."

My mom has a burning desire to be a "fancy person," which is utterly ridiculous given our surroundings, but at least her whole delusion works in my favor. The only reason she doesn't bully me into working full-time when I graduate in June is because to her, there's nothing fancier than going to college, except maybe a bag by an Italian designer whose name she can't pronounce.

"So this is me, being fancy." I stop walking to gesture down at my frayed jeans and a worn "Muck Fizzou" shirt handed down by one of the older boys in the trailer park that's so huge I'm basically swimming in it. "I know, I know. I'm intimidating."

"Oh, no, this isn't my 'intimidated' face. It's my 'envious' face. To think I could've been Fancy Gujarati Shah. How intimidating would *that* be?"

"So intimidating that I'm wearing my envy face." I make a serious expression with furrowed brows and pursed lips. "Don't worry, I will reveal this secret only under extreme duress."

He cracks up, and my expression gives way as I do the same. Like that, all awkwardness is gone, and we continue the rest of the way to the library, keeping an eye out for spies all the while.

It's both nice and strange joking with Dave as we walk up the stone steps of the library. With the exception of Vic and maybe Freckles, I don't think I've actually enjoyed a conversation with anyone since freshman year, before everything happened with Fitz. Once we show our passes and get into the actual building, however, I go completely mute. My mouth is too busy dropping open at the sight of what looks like millions of colorful spines, all waiting to be cracked open by yours truly.

I'm so impressed by it all that I don't even realize Dave is watching me gape like a dork until he says, "You look like you just entered a museum of chocolate and someone told you that you could lick the entire thing from floor to ceiling."

My cheeks prickle, though whether it's because I'm embarrassed at being a geek or because Dave is talking about licking things, I'm not sure. "I really like books," I say meekly, tearing my eyes away from the stacks and attempting to meet his like a normal person.

His lips curve up in one corner. "Yeah, I got that. So what's your favorite?"

I drop my eyes to the little insignia on his rugby shirt, afraid the blush I can feel his smile inducing is gonna sell me out. I'm not used to talking about books; Fitz used to make fun of my "girly princess books" so much I started hiding them from him. But I can already sense Dave wouldn't be like that, so, screw it. "You can't possibly expect me to pick just one. But if it was written by Tamora Pierce, Diana Wynne Jones, or Terry Pratchett, chances are it's near the top of my list."

"Good choices," he says with a smile. "No love for Tolkien?"

"Haven't read him yet," I admit shamefully. "He's on my to-read list, though, I swear. Those books are just *always* checked out of the library."

Dave stares at me with a dumbfounded expression.

"What kind of self-proclaimed book lover—a high fantasy lover, no less!—has never read Tolkien? He was only the most incredibly brilliant writer *ever.* The things that man invented! Seriously, he'd better jump to the very top of your to-read list immediately. I'll be quizzing you on him tomorrow."

Tomorrow. No, it isn't possible that the mere suggestion of seeing Dave tomorrow—even one made as a joke—is the reason I suddenly feel like doing a touchdown dance. Clearly, the smell of old books is getting to me. "Okay, *Lord of the Rings* is like a thousand pages," I inform him, trying to keep my thoughts on a sane track. "I'll need at least a weekend."

"A whole weekend? But—"

He's cut off by the sound of a ringing cell phone. *My* ringing cell phone, I realize, utterly mortified as every single person in the library turns to stare and shush me. I reach into my bag for my phone as I dash out into the entrance. Of course, it's Vic.

"Hey," I whisper as I start to walk toward the exit onto campus, only to realize that it's suddenly started pouring...and I've left my umbrella in the car. The librarians are glaring at me, but there's no chance I'm stepping out in that. "I'm in the library and I can't stay on the phone. What's up?"

"I'm coming to get you with Sasha and Kelly. They're gonna take us to this coffee shop everyone goes to and then we're gonna go to the mall so we can get you a hot outfit for the Gamma party tonight. Be ready in two!"

"The what?" I ask, but I'm talking to nothing; she's already hung up.

I can feel my stomach start to churn and I know I don't want to spend the afternoon with Sasha and Kelly, whoever they are. I definitely don't want to go shopping and I *really* don't want to go to whatever a Gamma party is. What I *really* wanna do is stay in the library, especially if it means spending a little more time with—

Okay, no. I am not tailoring my college visit around a guy, no matter how much my best friend would probably approve. How could I even think of prioritizing some random boy I just met over getting the basics of the college experience with Vic—sorry, *Tori*—the very person I'd come to Southeastern to do those things with? She's been dreaming of going to a Greek party forever, and as horrifying as I find the idea, I want her to have this.

"I have to go," I tell Dave before I can make any excuses *not* to tell Dave. "Apparently I'm going to something called a Gamma party, and judging by the friend who just informed me of this fact, it's not a physics-themed thing."

"Alas, what man can compete with a keg and a toga?" He smiles ruefully, and is it my imagination or does he look the tiniest bit wistful that I'm leaving him? "It was nice to meet you, Reagan. Thanks for helping me find my way."

"Right back atcha," I reply, wishing I had more—and more intelligent—things to say. When I come up with nothing, I turn and start to walk out, but just as I'm about to pass through the doors, I turn back around and see that he hasn't moved. In fact, I could swear he's watching me leave. I take that as a sign that it's okay to say, "Hey, if you're feeling up for a party later…" I let it trail off, completely unsure how I could possibly end that.

He flashes those perfect, blinding teeth again. "I'll check and see if my toga's back from the dry cleaners."

VICTORIA

I can't believe I'm here. I'm at a frat party. *I'm at a freaking frat party.* I feel like I've "arrived," and it doesn't hurt that I'm wearing an awesome dress I found at the mall. Nothing makes me feel better about the nasty girls who've hated on the color of my skin my entire life than looking superhot in white. Not that anyone here has been anything but super nice to me; every single girl I met on the tour of the Lambda house was a total sweetheart. And yeah, okay, maybe I'm still the only brown chick walking around, but if anyone's noticed, they certainly haven't said anything to me.

For once in my life, I think I actually manage to blend.

Even now, my new dress is a little quieter than the stuff I usually wear—okay, a *lot* quieter—but it helps me fit in perfectly and I've already figured out how I'm going to turn it into an awesome outfit with some pinking shears and leather cord when I get home.

Next to me, Rae is all fidgety, and I practically have to hold her down. She keeps rising up on her toes, as if that'll help the fact that she's barely taller than the couch. It's like she's looking for someone, except she doesn't know anyone there but me.

She *does* look super cute. I still can't get over that she actually bought a top at the mall, a cute halter thing that shows off the muscle in her scrawny arms from years of carrying heavy trays. I've never seen her spend money on *anything* non-essential, though of course she and I have totally different ideas of what falls into that category. She's still wearing the plain old jean skirt she always wears when she's not wearing jeans, or jean shorts, or something in corduroy that may as well be jeans. But still, it works.

"Are you looking for somebody in particular?" I tease her, since she seems so antsy. I'm obviously kidding, or at least I mean to be, but then she starts blushing, and I realize she *is*. "Did you meet someone?" I know I sound every bit as stunned as I feel, but I can't help it. I have never seen Reagan look twice at a guy—or girl. What exactly did I miss while I was checking out the Lambda house?

"Nobody really," she says dismissively, but then she bounces up again on her toes to catch a glimpse of the door, and her blond curls bounce right along with her. "I told this guy I met for two seconds to come to the party and I don't know what I was thinking but now I'll feel bad if he shows up, completely lost."

"If he goes to Southeastern, I'm sure he knows his way around a frat party," I assure her, still trying to wrap my brain around the fact that Rae's not only met a guy in our short day here but has gone as far as to invite him to the party. Like a *date*. How on earth did she do that already? I still haven't even found a guy willing to bring me a beer.

"He doesn't." Her gaze is still fixed on the door. "He's a prospective, like us."

My nose wrinkles without my even thinking about it, and I'm glad she's not looking at me. "Why would you waste your time with a high school senior when you could get with a college guy?"

Now she does look at me, and she rolls her eyes. "I'm not *getting* with anyone," she says flatly, and I recognize the tone and expression from a million similar conversations before. It's her response to my "Rae, Jason Brailey totally wants to bang you" (which was absolutely true) all over again, or to "Lance Oosterhouse has been checking you out for the last hour" (which was true, but apparently only because he wanted to copy her white streak for a rave that weekend, not realizing it was natural).

I don't know why she's so resistant, but I have my suspicions. I've seen and heard guys around school harassing her—the same guys who were doing it at Joe's this morning—though I usually pretend I don't, because it's so clear she prefers it that way. I found a picture once, though, when we were digging around her closet for Halloween costume ideas. When I asked who the blond guy in it was, she insisted he was nobody and snatched the picture out of my hand to toss it in the trash, but I saw "I love you" chicken-scratched on the back. She's never mentioned him, and I never ask. I feel like I owe her that, even though at times like this, my restraint totally kills me.

I'm still watching her watch the door when Sasha comes over with a super cute guy in tow, and I quickly smooth down my dress and press my lips together to make sure they're evenly glossed.

"Mark," she says, looping her skinny arm through his massive one, "this is the girl I was telling you about. Tori, this is Mark. Mark, Tori is *very* new here"—her tone is so suggestive, I can *feel* Rae mock-vomiting at the back of my head—"and needs someone to show her a good time. Get her a drink, will you?"

Instead, he turns to Rae. "And you are…?"

I pray she won't respond with her patented nasty "Not interested." Fortunately she just says her name, although she ignores the meaty hand he's holding out to her. Then, suddenly, I see her freeze, and my eyes immediately cut to the door.

I was sure that look meant The Guy had arrived, but

all I see are a redheaded chick in braids and cutoffs and a lanky Indian guy in a *Battlestar Galactica* T-shirt. I'm about to ask Rae where her guy is when *Battlestar* looks in our direction and flashes the brightest, whitest smile I've ever seen. He's obviously her man, and even kinda cute now that the smile's replaced his look of terrified confusion.

He starts to make his way over and I feel an overwhelming urge to give Rae her privacy. I turn to Mark, and for what I'm pretty sure is the first time in my entire life, I ask, "Do you wanna dance?"

"How about we get a drink first?" His voice is low and manly, as if to serve as an extra reminder that I'm not playing with high school boys anymore, and it makes my toes curl in my stilettos. The last thing I see before I close my eyes and let Mark pull my hand through the crowd is Sasha, smiling at me with approval.

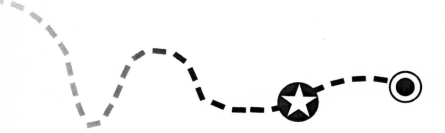

CHAPTER FOUR

REAGAN

"That's not a toga," I inform Dave as he winds his way over, his shaggy black hair falling in his eyes.

He shrugs. "Still at the dry cleaners."

"So hard to find good help these days."

"Too true."

We're both quiet for a long enough moment for me to ponder how weird this is, that I met a guy and mentioned this party and now he's here, and it seems like he's here for me, and I'm wearing a new shirt, and I never buy a new shirt.

"So this is what the kids are doing these days, huh?"

Dave scans the room, and I take advantage of the fact that his eyes aren't on me by glancing at his butt. His jeans hang low on his non-existent hips, which I find sexy for no reason I can possibly explain. I even love that he's wearing a *Battlestar* T-shirt. There's just something about the way he owns his nerdiness—

"Deciding how you feel about being seen with a guy in a *Battlestar Galactica* T-shirt?"

Oh God, I've been caught staring. I'm about to insist that I was looking at something else—I have no idea what—when he adds, "Your judgment wounds me."

"No judgment," I say, holding up my hands. "No frakking way."

His face lights up like the hideously tacky inflatable Santa this one family at the trailer park always puts out around Christmas and leaves outside until around St. Patrick's Day, when one of the six boys who crams into that tiny trailer inevitably knocks it down in a drunken stupor. It's covered in duct tape and bandages, but somehow, it always seems to shine even brighter the next year. "A fan!"

"Not fan enough to own a T-shirt," I admit, "but I've seen a few episodes. Shockingly, there's never a waitlist for those DVDs at the library."

"Well, it's hard to beat a true superfan," he says with a cocky grin that so doesn't belong on his face that I can't help but laugh. The grin turns into a frown. "I sense you're mocking me again."

"Your powers of intuition are only getting stronger, Clark Kent."

He wrinkles his nose. "First of all, Superman doesn't even *have* powers of intuition; he's a guy who changes in a phone booth. Second of all, my fandom is a DC-free zone, thank you very much. Thor or bust."

"I think you're going to need to work your way up to Thor," I inform him, nodding my head toward arms so thin I could probably wrap my thumb and middle finger around his biceps.

"What?" He flexes his arm muscle, and although there is indeed a little bulge when he does, he's nowhere near godlike territory. Elementary school basketball player, maybe. "Not impressed by my superhuman strength?"

"Well, I'm sure weighing under a hundred pounds helps you get around faster than the average guy," I offer helpfully. "Less bulk to carry around and all that."

"I can't believe I'm being picked on about my size by a twerp who's probably not legally allowed to ride Space Mountain."

"Now that's just mean."

"And making fun of my manhood isn't?"

"I did *not* make fun of your, uh…" My eyes flicker downward, and in an instant I realize I've just pointedly glanced at his crotch. There's so much heat emanating from my face right now that I'm afraid getting too close to the tequila would make me spontaneously combust.

He purses his lips, which quirk up at the corners. "You were saying?"

"Oh, shut up."

"Hey, we can't all look like X-Men," he says, folding his arms over his chest.

"Are you saying *I* look like one of the X-Men?" I'm not sure how to take that.

"Duh." He reaches out and flips up the one white curl that hangs in my face. "Rogue, obviously."

"Oh, yes. Her. Obviously."

He gives me a *you must be kidding* look. "Please tell me you know who Rogue is."

"Hey, I knew 'frak.' That has to count for something."

The head shake reeks of disappointment. "Absorbs powers and memories? Not ringing a bell?"

"Nope, but I'm guessing she has a freak-of-nature white streak in her hair too."

"Indeed she does. And it's not freaky, it's cool. Or at least it's freaky in the coolest possible way."

I tuck my mutant hair back behind my ear, trying to ignore the weird flip thing my stomach's doing right now. "So if you have X-Men envy, I take that to mean you *don't* have weird spiky things hiding in your hands?"

He sighs. "You know Wolverine. Of course you know Wolverine. Why do the chicks always know Wolverine?"

"'The chicks'? I think I've been insulted."

"It's because of Hugh Jackman, isn't it."

"Duh. So hot."

He grins, and I can't help smiling too, and the two of us are smiling like idiots when Vic strolls up to us, a "WTF" look on her face and the guy I'd met earlier—a much closer fit for Thor—in tow.

"Having fun?" she asks with a knowing smile, eyebrow raised in a perfect arch I just know she's practiced in the mirror.

"It's not the worst party I've ever been to," I concede.

"I think it's the *only* party I've ever been to," Dave says, scratching his head, and Mark looks so perplexed by him that I just laugh again.

"Yes, well, you chose a good one," I say. "What with my being here and all. Not to mention my absolutely best friend in the entire universe. Dave Shah, this is Vic—" She jerks her head slightly and I remember the whole "Tori" thing. For some reason, I don't want to introduce her to Dave that way, but I obviously have no choice right now. "Um, Tori Reyes. Tori, Dave. And this is Mark," I add quickly.

"Hey." Dave flashes a smile at Vic and goes to shake Mark's hand, which I can see he regrets a few moments later when he retrieves slightly crushed fingers from Mark's iron grip. "You're a senior too?" he asks Vic.

"Freshman," she replies, her voice so loaded with meaning that I know even Dave can tell she's lied about being a student there to Mark. "But I'm flattered you think I'm legal to drink."

"Maybe that's because you smell like a distillery." As soon as I say it, I know I probably shouldn't have. Behind me, Dave stifles a laugh, but Vic is not amused. It's true, though—I can tell she's had a couple already, and we've barely been at the party twenty minutes. Still, I recognize that I should probably rectify my comment immediately.

"So where's the good stuff?" I ask as if I care. "The line for the kegs is so long I figured I'd be better off just waiting until I turn twenty-one."

"I can help you guys out with that," says Mark, and although I wish he wouldn't, it seems to mollify Vic, so we follow them to the kitchen. Trays of Jell-O shots line the counter and a huge bowl of hideously green punch sits on a small square table. He hands each of us a Jell-O shot, and then hands a few to some stragglers hanging out in the kitchen, and together we toast college, and then his frat, and then we switch to punch and things get a little fuzzy.

"You have a *what?*" Dave blurts before cracking up laughing again. It's nearly 2:00 a.m. and we're sitting in the backyard of the house. We've both switched to water, but the smell of the meat grilling on the barbecue is still enough to make my stomach turn ever so slightly, thanks to the little drinking marathon earlier.

"A steam 'n mash," I repeat, and just hearing the words out loud makes me explode into giggles. "We can't buy food to put *in* the damn thing, but of course that doesn't stop my mother from buying it just because 'Oh my God, Reagan, sugar!'"—I put on my mom's incredibly over-the-top southern accent, which she's carefully cultivated because she thinks it makes her sound like some sort of wealthy belle—"'We *have* to have this! Think of how quickly Ah could make mah mashed potatas!' Never mind that the woman has made mashed potatoes approximately once, ever. And they were disgusting."

Dave laughs again. "Man, I thought southerners were supposed to be great cooks."

"Oh, that's the best part." I lean back on my elbows. "She's not even from the South. She's never been there. She just has this delusion that she's some sort of Mississippi debutante or something. For my last birthday, she got me a *parasol.*"

He shakes his head in disbelief. "What the hell is a seventeen-year-old supposed to do with a parasol?"

"Don't ask me. I pawned it and bought myself a couple cans of tuna instead."

"Man, this kills me. My mom would *love* to cook for you. How do you feel about khandvi and samosas?"

"Like I need a dictionary to know what you're talking about," I admit, looking away from him and up to the stars instead. "I'm guessing that's Indian food?"

"You've never had Indian food?" He sounds like his eyes are bugging out of his head. "Man oh man, this world of yours just gets crazier and crazier."

I laugh, and though I'm still tipsy—tipsy enough to be sharing these embarrassing details of my life, which means *very*—even I can hear the edge of bitterness to it. "My world of poor white trash?"

"That's not what I mean," he says stiffly. "Just, you know. Small-town life and everything."

"It's not small-town life that's the problem." I wish I knew the constellations so I could find the Big Dipper or something. Without a focal point, my eyes are starting to blur. "It's me. It's me and my stupid, shitty, white-trash life. I bet Vic's had Indian food."

"Vic?"

I roll my eyes, knowing he can't see from that angle. "Tori. I forgot she's a different person this weekend."

He's quiet for a moment, and I think he hasn't heard me, but then he says, "Well, it's a good weekend to be a different person, isn't it?"

I want to see his face right now, but I can't bring myself to look in his direction. "Are you a different person this weekend? Because I'm sure as hell not." I glance down at my outfit—my brand-new shirt which now looks to me like $12.99 in wasted gas money, my Walmart jean skirt, my tennis shoes with their tiny hole poked in the toe. "Except for the fact that I'm telling shit about my life to a total stranger, there's nothing different about me at all."

"I'm guessing telling shit about your life to a total stranger is *very* different for you, actually." Now I do glance at him. His gaze is traveling in the same path down my body mine just did, though the look in his eyes is nothing like the disgust and resentment and frustration I imagine are in mine. Goose bumps rise on my legs and I wonder if he can see them. "Telling shit to anyone, probably."

Anyone but Vic, I mentally correct him. Who else would I even tell? The whole town of Charytan has already heard enough. "You think you know me already, huh?"

"I think…" He inhales deeply. "I think you don't really feel like a total stranger anymore." His eyes flutter shut, his long lashes brushing his cheekbones. "You never really did," he says, so quietly I can tell he couldn't really decide if he wanted me to hear those words or not.

I don't understand what's happening here, only that I feel the same way, and that my entire body is fizzing with it. But I don't know how to say that. In fact, I'm pretty sure I shouldn't. But he's right that somehow I have a comfort with him I haven't experienced with anyone but Vic in a long time. It's so much easier to let your guard down around someone who doesn't seem to have any guard at all.

It gives me an indescribable urge to get to know him for real. "I think it's time you tell me something about yourself, then. I refuse to be the only one whose shitty life is on display here."

His lids flutter open, slowly, and he turns to me with a confused look. "Who says I have a shitty life?"

Silence hangs between us, and an inexplicable feeling of betrayal fills my stomach with acid I can feel climbing into my throat. Somehow I'd thought we were the same, but we aren't, not at all, and suddenly, I'm filled with an intense urge to throw up. Without so much as a glance back at him I run to the bushes that separate the frat house from the next one over and I hurl the most hideously colored vomit in existence.

"Nice one!" some asshat yells out, and I can hear people laughing behind me, not the pleasant laughter of Dave's crack-ups but cruel, mean laughter that takes me back to a time and place I never, ever want to revisit. I'm not sure I'm done, but the urge to run away is almost as strong as the urge to throw up again. I contemplate dashing off into the street until a hand grasps my hair firmly, and with that, I bend forward and expel the rest until I'm heaving nothing but air.

Finally, I turn around, ready to beg Vic to go to the motel, but the words die on my lips when I see she's not the one standing there; Dave is. One warm brown hand gently releases my hair while the other one offers me a cup of water. I can't even meet his eyes long enough to say thank you as I rinse my mouth out.

I've taken a couple of sips by the time Vic comes rushing out of the house. "Rae!" She throws her arms around my waist, which nearly makes me spill my water. "Are you okay? Sasha just told me you were out here, throwing up."

"Sasha was correct," I inform her, stepping out of her grasp. "It's fine. I'm fine. I just…" I'm about to say *don't want to be here anymore,* but I can tell she's still into this stupid party, and Dave is looking all concerned, and I don't want to seem like an irritable baby, even though that's exactly what I feel like. "Need to keep drinking some water," I say meekly, taking a dramatic sip as if to prove H2O will cure *everything.*

"Why don't we just go to the motel now?" Vic tweaks one of my curls, which are vomit-free, thanks to Dave's quick action. "This party's getting old anyway."

She's lying. I know she's lying. Both are reasons why I love her. "It's okay," I say, because I can lie badly too. "I don't want to disappoint Mark or anything."

She waves her hand dismissively. "Lousy kisser. Come on." She links her arm through mine and starts to pull me away, and I let her, because I can't even bring myself to look at Dave, though I can still feel a tingling in my scalp left by his firmly holding back my hair.

We're a safe distance away from the party by the time either one of us speaks again. "Are you okay?" Vic asks, obviously trying to keep her voice down such that I can barely hear her question over the clacking of her obscenely impractical heels.

"I'm fine," I mutter, going for another sip of water, only to find that my cup is empty. My mouth is dry, but I feel stone-cold-fucking-sober, like I could've driven us back to the motel instead of making us take the campus drunkmobile, which is waiting at the corner. I crush the empty cup in my hand, and it cracks and slices into my skin.

"Are you sure? You didn't even say goodbye to that Dave guy. Did you get his number, at least?"

"No, I definitely didn't."

She stops in her tracks, which I only realize after I've walked a few yards without her.

"What the hell?" I demand when I turn and see her just standing there, hands planted on her hips.

"My question exactly." She walks up to me slowly, her heels somehow giving her a menacing vibe. "You like your first guy in the entire time I've known you and you don't even get his number?" She yanks my wrist and jerks me forward. "We're going back to the party."

I snatch my arm back with a force that makes her wobble on those crazy stiletto things. "Oh no, we're not. You said we could go, and we're going."

"Not without his number, we aren't!"

I grit my teeth. "When will you get it through your

head that I am not like you?" I seethe. "I don't *need* a guy around. I don't *want* some stupid distraction getting in my way. And I *certainly* don't need someone like Dave fucking Shah who probably thinks I'm some sort of fascinating sociological study of the fucking Kansas trailer park population now."

Vic's eyes flash with fire, and suddenly I wish I could take back every word that's just come out of my mouth. "That's a really messed-up thing to say. I don't *need* a guy around, and I'd think you'd know—"

"I do," I say quickly, feeling the heat ebb out of me as guilt over being shitty to Vic takes its place. "I'm sorry; that was a really dick thing to say. I just…need you to let this go, okay? I know you're trying to help, but this isn't gonna happen."

I watch her jaw for a minute until it unclenches, which is always the sign she's forgiven me when I lose my shit. But then it sets again, and I prepare myself for an angry response, but this time, her ire's not directed at me. "Was he a jerk to you?" she demands, sounding so protective I wonder if she's been taking actual lessons on how to be a big sibling from Javier.

"I'll jam a stiletto up his butt if he was. Just so you know."

And just like that, I fall apart laughing, and so does she, and for a moment I think about how many times I've done that in the last twenty-four hours. Okay, so maybe the fun I had with Dave was a wash, but I still have Vic—will *always* have Vic—and right now, as we stumble to the Drunkmobile under the weight of laughter, residual alcohol consumption, and uncomfortable shoes, I think that really could be enough.

VICTORIA

I've been sitting awake so long that I can feel the alcohol wearing off, especially now that I've made about a zillion trips to the bathroom, and I can't help watching Reagan sleep. She is so darn tiny. I forget that sometimes because she packs a lot into one little person, but sometimes, like tonight, I can't help feeling like she's this baby sister I have to watch over, because no one else will.

I'm dying to speak to my mom, but it's too late to text her—she's the epitome of "early to bed, early to rise"—and while I love my dad, he's not really the chatty type. He mostly does his scatterbrained-professor thing and nods and says, "Hmm, very nice, mija," when I show him a bag I've stitched or a skirt I've made out of his old neckties. I picture telling him, "I went to a really weird party tonight where I pretended to be someone else and it made me feel really, really lonely," and him saying, "Hmm, very nice, mija," and it makes me snort. I quickly clap a hand over my mouth to shut myself up so I won't wake Reagan, but another giggle escapes.

She sleeps through it anyway. She always sleeps like

a rock, except when she's at home. When we have rare sleepovers in her trailer, I can feel her toss and turn on her bottom bunk and I wonder if she literally feels the itch to get out of Charytan when she's in those sheets. Mostly, though, we sleep at my house, and when we do, I practically have to throw a bucket of water on her face to get her out of bed.

It hits me then that while it's too late to call home, it's actually perfect timing to Skype with Javi…provided he has Internet access, which is never a given. I duck into the bathroom and call him, and I'm so surprised he picks up that I actually jump a few inches in surprise.

"Bula!" he greets me, his deeply tan skin and bright white smile lighting up the screen. "You OK, hermana? You look a little freaked out."

"I just can't believe you picked up!" I say, feeling my stupid-huge smile nearly split my face in two. "I'm at Southeastern with Rae and I—"

"One second!" he yells to someone off on the side, then turns back to me. "Sorry, you caught me on our way out to dinner, and the guys here are not patient about their food. How's college?"

I know I only have a minute before he runs off, so I quickly give him the basics, but I only get as far as mentioning the frat party before he groans and tells me he'll have to e-mail me when he gets back. I swallow back the little lump forming in my throat and nod, but I don't want an e-mail; I want to *talk* to my big brother, this stupid thing I used to take for granted until I could barely do it anymore. But it's clear that isn't an option right now, so I just tell him to have fun and he says the same—"but not too much"—and then I'm alone again.

I'm not sure why I can't sleep. I don't drink often, but when I do, it usually puts me out like a light. Tonight, though, I feel like my brain is buzzing. I need to talk about college, about the future, about how weird and uncertain everything feels. I want to wake Reagan up and hear her promise again that we'll be roommates wherever we go.

After driving for two hours that day and having to do the same again tomorrow, though, I can't bring myself to disturb her beauty sleep. So I leave her alone and instead help myself to the lone sheet of ugly motel stationery so I can spend the next twenty minutes sketching out exactly what I'm gonna do to the dress I wore tonight. Then I flip the page over and sketch a cute new skirt for Reagan so I can get her to wear something other than that jean thing that's practically falling apart.

When I've etched in every detail possible and am still no closer to sleep, I decide to venture outside, just to stretch my legs with a walk up and down the path in front of the rooms. I grab a sweatshirt from my bag and zip it up over my pajamas, then tuck the room key in a pocket. There aren't many times I'll venture outside without a cute outfit and makeup, but I'd say 4:00 a.m. at some random motel off the edge of the Southeastern campus is one of them.

I regret it the second I close the door behind me; there's someone standing outside at the vending machine, similarly bundled in pajamas and sweats. I think about going back inside, but decide any nut job who's outside at 4:00 a.m. in his pajamas, trying to decide whether Coke or Pepsi would make a better midnight snack, probably isn't someone I care about looking my best in front of. I jam my hands into my pockets, toss my hair back, and walk past, immediately appreciating the stretch of my poor muscles.

"Tori?"

The weird realization that the guy is talking to me happens in two phases: One being "Who the heck is Tori?" and two being "Do I know this person?" It all smacks me in the face at once when he smiles slightly, revealing teeth that glow ultra-bright in the moonlight, and I realize I'm looking at Dave. Reagan's Dave.

"What are you doing here?" I ask when I've once again found the power of speech.

"I'm guessing the same thing as you." He glances at the vending machine. "Or maybe not."

"You're not seriously about to drink one of those things, are you?"

"Nah, just something to keep me busy." He rocks on

his heels. "Can't sleep."

"Me either," I say, though as I do, I yawn.

He cracks one of those blinding smiles. "Show-off."

"That was my first one, I swear."

We're both awkwardly silent after that, both of us obviously holding back questions relating to a certain blonde. We find our courage at the exact same time, me asking, "What exactly did you say to her?" at the same time he asks, "Is Reagan okay?"

We both laugh uncomfortably, but his question for me is a little easier to answer, at least in the physical sense, so I say, "Yeah, she's fine. She's sleeping."

"I didn't mean to upset her," he says quietly, his eyes watching his toes trace lines on the cement.

"What'd you say?"

"I don't even know." I can tell from the frustration in his voice that it's mostly true. "Is she always so..."

"Impossible?"

He smiles, just a tiny bit. "I was gonna say volatile."

I laugh. "Doesn't matter—the answer is yes. But you have to understand, her life is pretty awful. You'd be... volatile too."

"Yeah, I got that sense." He scratches the back of his neck. "But does she...?"

"You're not so awesome at finishing your sentences, kid," I tease him, because it's easy to see that after only one day of knowing Reagan, he legit cares about her, and it makes me want us to be friends.

He doesn't smile. Instead, he blurts, "Does she need everyone else around her to be miserable too?"

The way he immediately presses his lips together makes it obvious he regrets the words as soon as they're out of his mouth, but it doesn't matter.

I can feel myself harden in response. "You've known her five seconds."

"No, I know, I just—"

"I'm not talking about her with you. You want to ask Reagan something, you can ask her yourself." Inside my sweatshirt pockets, my hands squeeze into fists. "Have a good night." I turn on my heel and walk back, and as I slip back inside, I can't help feeling guilty for snapping. He may only have known her for a day, but again, I can tell he inexplicably cares.

He just doesn't know how much it hurts to hear him say aloud after one day of knowing her what I've wondered alone for the past two years.

I write Javier a quick e-mail, just to say hi and that I'm thinking of him, and then I actually manage to fall asleep. When I wake up, I'm pretty surprised at how well-rested and refreshed I feel, considering it's only seven thirty. Then I look over at the cheap old alarm clock and realize it's three hours later than it should be and we've completely missed the breakfast.

"Reagan!" I whisper fiercely, throwing my pillow at her sleeping face. "Do you know what time it is?"

"Time for you to *stop* throwing pillows at my head?" she responds groggily, lifting her head up just slightly. "I shut off the alarm before we went to sleep."

"*Why?*"

"Did you really want to go to that pancake breakfast thing?"

"Didn't you?"

She ignores me and burrows back under the covers. Which is normally *my* move.

I roll out of bed, stalk over, and yank the blanket off her. "This is pathetic, Rae."

"Not everybody likes pancakes," she snaps back, sharply enough so that I know she's plenty awake now.

"No, but *you* do, *and* I know you wanted to make the most of these college visits." *And you've never passed up a free meal that wasn't actual charity in your life*, I think but obviously don't say. It's certainly not her fault that food in the Forrester house is somewhere on her mother's priority list between getting weekly manicures and buying furry cell phone accessories from the Home Shopping Network. I exhale sharply. "Is this about Dave?"

She sticks out her tongue. "Dave who?"

"Come off it, Rae. And skipping the breakfast to avoid him is just sad."

"Oh, shut up."

I sit down on the edge of her bed, even though she won't make eye contact with me, and stroke her hair. "He was here last night, you know."

She flips over so suddenly I don't even have time to move my hand and it nearly pokes her in the eye. "*Here*, here? Like he stalked us to the hotel?"

"Tia Maria, Rae, no. He was staying here also. I ran into him outside at 4:00 a.m." I bite the insides of my lips, wondering if I should be telling her this at all. "Anyway, I'm sure he's not here anymore."

She's quiet for a moment, and then she says, "Yeah. Well, funny coincidence." Then she sighs and sits up. "So, what do you want to do for breakfast?"

My eyebrows shoot up of their own free will. "That's it? That's all you have to say?"

"What do you want me to say? 'Did he ask about me? Did he pledge his undying love?'" She rolls her eyes. "Will you stop making this into more than it is? I hung out with a guy at a party. That's all."

There's no clear evidence that she's lying, but I *know* she is. I've seen Reagan talk to other guys and it's never like this. I can't help but wonder if she cracked up this easily with Secret Blond Guy, if she bought new shirts for him that showed off her arms. But fine, if she won't ask what I know she's dying to know, then I'm not going to tell her.

"If you say so," I allow, standing up and stretching.

"And I have no idea what there is to do for breakfast around here. Shall we go explore? Give ourselves that self-guided tour you were all gung-ho about?"

"You mean there are things you want to see outside of Greek Row?"

"Keep that up and your tour will be *really* self-guided, if you know what I mean."

She grunts but finally drags herself out of bed and heads to the bathroom to wash up. I follow her lead, and an hour later we're showered, dressed, and ready to take on our second day of college.

As soon as we track down some coffee.

After following the aroma of warm vanilla latte to a coffee cart on campus, we grab maps from the welcome center and start our trek around. To the surprise of absolutely nobody, there are approximately four hundred places on Reagan's "must-see" list, ranging from the gym with its indoor swimming pool to the statue of Charles L. Robinson, who Reagan informs me was the first governor of the state of Kansas. I'm exhausted after fifteen minutes, even though I've taken Reagan's stupid advice and worn stupid sneakers today instead of my super cute studded cowboy boots *or* my hot, over-the-knee leather boots that admittedly make me sweat like a pig after thirty seconds.

Finally, after we've seen every single building, sculpture, field, and cafeteria on campus—and refueled with cheeseburgers and fries—I convince Reagan to chill for a minute on one of the benches on the massive quad. We flop onto green-painted wood, put down our bags, and drink in the scenery—people studying under the shade of enormous oak trees, couples making out in plain sight, a bunch of guys in cargo shorts and sweatshirts tossing around a Frisbee. It's exactly how I pictured it, all of it, and suddenly, *finally*, I can see it, me and Reagan, doing the college thing.

I grab the bulletin she nabbed from the welcome center and flip through it. It's the first time I've seen one of these, and it's even scarier than I imagined it would be, but at least I know right where to go. Or at least I think I do. But it's not there. No matter how many times I flip the pages, I see it's still missing.

"Everything okay there, Vic? You're going nuts on that thing like it's a double issue of *Vogue*."

"It's not here," I say, handing it over.

"What's not?" She takes the catalog from me and looks down. "I see Environmental Studies and French."

"And what *don't* you see?"

She frowns and her forehead wrinkles as she reads the page yet again. Then, finally, her entire face softens. "Fashion design. Oh, Vic, didn't you check if they had it as a major before you planned out the Reagan and Victoria College Visit Bonanza?"

I feel a weird lump in my throat, as if someone's just

ripped out this perfect quad of my future from underneath my Pumas. "How could they *not* have it?" I ask, hating how defensive I sound. Of course I should've checked. I feel so stupid that it didn't even occur to me. "Even CCC has a fashion design major."

"CCC also has an auto repair major," she points out, gently closing the catalog. I stare down at her ragged, bitten nails. "It's Charytan Community College, Vic. They basically have whatever they can find someone to teach, and Miss Lucy's an institution in that place."

It's true. No one has any idea how old Miss Lucy is, but she's been designing the most fun and awesome clothes in Charytan for-freaking-ever. Her hair is super-shiny silver except for one streak in front that she keeps bright ketchup red. I don't think she has a single article of clothing that doesn't have enormous fake jewels stitched onto it somewhere. And, she went to the Fashion Institute in New York City, which basically makes her the coolest person ever to step foot in our little town.

She's basically my idol.

She's taught fashion design at CCC for as long as I can remember; I've spent many an afternoon peeking into her classroom while waiting for my parents to finish up their day. CCC is actually what brought us to Charytan of all places, once we left Arizona. Finding teaching positions for not one but both of my parents was a bigger challenge than any of us expected it to be, and they lucked out when an old grad school friend who ended up at K-State directed them there. Or at least it seemed lucky at the time, anyway. I was so excited about leaving Arizona, I didn't even really consider whether Kansas would be any better.

Now it's been my home for two years, and it will be for another five. But at least I won't be alone.

We're both quiet for another few minutes, just watching everyone having fun, enjoying their lives as philosophy majors or frat bros or whoever they are. Finally, Reagan says, "I think we passed an ice cream place a few blocks ago."

I can't help smiling, which is a nice change from being on the verge of tears. "I think so too." I hop up onto my feet and grab her hands, yanking her up with me. "We have a zillion other places to visit. Who cares about this one, right?"

"Right." She picks up the bulletin and makes to rip it in half, though it takes all of two seconds for us both to realize she has no shot. We both laugh, and then she says, "or maybe I'll just bring it back to the welcome center."

"Later," I insist. "First, I think we both need something with a *lot* of sprinkles."

Man, ice cream is good at fixing everything. One chocolate chip cookie dough sundae with fudge, sprinkles, and whipped cream on top later, we've moved on from boys and majors to movies we want to see, music we're going to listen to on the drive home, and what undoubtedly disgusting things took place in the history of our motel room.

"I mean, you saw that wallpaper," says Reagan, swirling her spoon in the remaining whipped cream. "That just screamed 'I take my maid here on the weekends.'"

I roll my eyes. "As *if* someone who knows *anything* about cleanliness could stand to be in that cesspool for more than five seconds. Please."

She grins and digs out a chunk of cookie dough, which she pops in her mouth just as her eyes dash to the plate-glass window and back to me so quickly I wouldn't have noticed if I hadn't been looking for it. But I did, because I was, and I roll my own eyes practically out of my head.

"What?" she demands.

"You're looking for him."

"Looking for who?"

"What is it you always say to me?" I yank the cup of ice cream away from her and dig in my spoon. "Oh yeah. 'I am not going to dignify that with a response.'"

She sighs. "You're impossible."

"I'll leave you alone as soon as you admit that you're hot for *Battlestar Gallactica*."

"He *has* a name."

"Am I allowed to say it or will that get me some sort of glare of doom?"

She yanks the ice cream back. "Still not talking about this."

"Of course you're not," I mutter, thinking about the mystery boy from Reagan's signed picture again.

"What's that supposed to mean?"

"It means for some reason, you cannot acknowledge that you have hormones like the rest of us," I declare, drawing stares from around the ice cream shop. "So you have a crush on a guy you met. Was that so terrifying that you just *had* to run away from him?"

"You pulled me away!"

"You let me!" I counter, trying to keep my voice down to limit the spectators. "I thought I was rescuing you from a lousy party and we'd see him this morning. I didn't know you picked a fight with him and then purposely made us miss the breakfast."

She narrows her eyes and I realize I've given away more than I'd meant to. "What makes you think I picked a fight with him? What did he say to you when you saw him last night?"

"Enough for me to know you picked a fight with him, which wasn't much, because I *know* you. Why do you do this, Rae? We're *supposed* to meet guys and have fun. That's the point!"

"No," she says slowly, her voice dripping with ice, "we're *supposed* to see what the classes and campus are like so we can figure out how to get actual decent college educations so we can get out of that sinking ship of a town for good."

Suddenly, the ice cream isn't sitting so well in my stomach. It's always been fun, if a little frustrating, how different Rae and I are, but for the first time in our friendship it hits me what those differences could mean for our future together.

Picture Boy Who Once Loved Reagan is on the tip of my tongue, and I desperately want to tell her that whoever he is, I think he's somehow holding her back, but I don't want to fight anymore. All I want is to get home, hug my mom, and lose myself in my sewing machine for a few hours.

"I think I'm done," I say weakly, pushing the cup away.

"Yeah, me too." Her voice is hollow as she digs her spoon back into the ice cream and leaves it there, sticking up out of the surface like an American flag on the moon. "Let's go get our stuff and get out of here." She grabs the cup—she is physically incapable of throwing out food and I've learned well enough never to do it in front of her—and we head out, back to the hotel with the horrid wallpaper, back to the old Nissan, back to "that sinking ship" that also happens to be home.

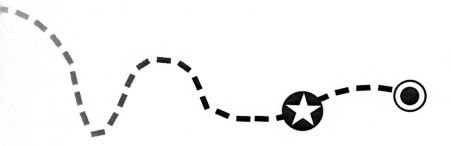

CHAPTER FIVE

REAGAN

The ride home is a whole lot quieter than the ride there. Things feel weird, and for the first time in a long time, all I want is to be home in my crappy little trailer. I can tell Vic's just as eager to get back to her cozy house so she can get into a signing frenzy with her mom over cups of hot chocolate with cinnamon and chili powder.

We hug goodbye as usual when I drop her off, and I head back home, dreading following up that awkward ride with some even more unpleasant Forrester Family Fun. When I pull into my spot in the lot, though, I realize there's no sound coming from inside.

I'm so excited at the potential for some uninterrupted time at home that I almost fall on my ass in my rush to scramble out of the car. I grab my stuff from the trunk and run inside, holding my breath until I can confirm that my mother is indeed *not* parked on the couch, watching our far-too-nice-for-our-trailer TV and ordering ridiculous things we can't remotely afford. It feels like a holiday, like freaking Christmas, and considering I've barely started my history paper—and that my mom usually gives me things like socks with fur around the ankles—it's probably the best gift I've ever gotten.

I squeeze past my mom's hoarded piles of junk into the tiny cell of my bedroom, flip on the light switch, and toss my bag on the bed. It takes me a few seconds to realize that the light hasn't turned on. I walk back to the switch and flip it a couple more times. Nothing.

A quick check of the rest of the trailer, including the TV, reveals that we're totally electricity-free. No wonder my mother's not home. If she can't watch TV, what good is this place?

Unfortunately, with only one tiny window that barely gets any light, my room's not a whole lot more useful without power. I know my mom just paid the bill last week—I gave her the money from my tips, even though I'm supposed to be saving it for gas money—but when I stick my head out the door and look from side to side, it's obvious both the Jamesons to the right of us and the

Karowskis to the left have power.

"Hey, Reagan." Jake Karowski waves from the lounge chair that's permanently parked in front of their trailer, rain or shine. Though most of the guys in the Myrtle Grove Trailer Park are in some sort of construction, Jake's in the tight-knit group of farmhands, and it shows on his lined, sun-browned skin. "You looking for your mom?"

"Guess I am now." I lift a hand over my eyes to shield them from the sun; our awning's been broken for-freaking-ever and my dad's never home long enough to fix it. "She in with Molly?"

"Nah, Molly's out at the school." Molly Karowski's a custodian at the middle school I went to as a kid. I know it kills my mom to be friends with a janitor, even more than it kills her that her daughter respects the hell out of said janitor for having a damn job in a trailer park where laziness and entitlement run rampant like shingles. "I think she's at the Blacks."

I purse my lips while I wait for him to elaborate, since sadly, at Myrtle Grove, there are two options—the actually-named-Blacks, a.k.a. Sheila and her son, Jimmy, and the lone black family in the entire white trash park, a.k.a. Beverly and Isaiah Pope and their two kids, whom people have unfortunately taken to dubbing "the blacks," because apparently that's easier than "the Popes" and also easier than not being an asshole.

He doesn't say anything more, but I decide that

despite being fairly old school, Jake's a decent guy and therefore probably means the actual ones. Which is a shame, because Isaiah Pope is the only electrician in the entire park full of construction workers and farmhands, and had she been there, I might've been able to believe she was actually trying to do something about our powerlessness. Instead, she's with another one of her lazy-ass friends, probably watching crappy TV.

"Thanks, Jake," I say with a sigh, trudging over to the Blacks' trailer. Before I can even make it halfway to the door, my mom comes bursting out.

"There ya are!" she cries out, fake southern accent and all, as if she's sent out some sort of search party for me. She jiggles on over—something that'd be far less noticeable if she didn't insist on wearing hot-pink spandex—and grabs me by the arm. "We've been waiting for you forever. You need to take Jimmy to his dad's."

I dig my heels into the dirt, halting both of us in our tracks. "What? No."

"I'm not asking you, I'm telling you," she says with a tightly set jaw, her voice losing a bit of its charm as she tries to tug me back toward the Blacks' trailer.

I yank my arm out of her grasp. "You can *tell* me things like that when you or Sheila starts chipping in for gas money," I hiss. "Hank Black lives twenty minutes away and these rides add up. Plus, I have work to do for school and we don't even have any power!"

"Oh, stop being a brat. Twenty minutes is nothing, and when a neighbor needs your help, you help."

"It's forty there and back," I point out, "plus Brenda always makes me stay so she can feed me whatever she's baked and burned that day. Why can't *she* drive Jimmy in her own damn car?"

"Don't you swear at me."

Oh God. I can't. I just can't. "I'm going to the library." I wrench my arm away for good and stalk back to the trailer, when suddenly I hear a familiar high voice behind me.

"Rae-Rae! Are you bringing me to my daddy'th?"

Christ. They sicced the kid on me, cute little lisp and all. I should've seen it coming. I take a deep breath and paste a smile on my face before turning around, even as I can feel my head work up a steady throb at the thought of losing an hour on this paper. Not to mention that I've literally just come back from driving for two hours and have no desire to do it again.

"Actually," I say sweetly, pointedly avoiding both my mother's and Sheila's eyes from where they both now stand, leaning against the trailer and watching what appears to be an amusing show to them, "I think your mommy's gonna take you this time! Isn't that fun?"

Judging by Jimmy's frown, it's not fun at all. "My mommy thays she'th not going near that thlut ever again," he informs me, scratching at his scalp. "Rae-Rae, what'th a thlut?"

I bite my lips from the inside, especially when I see my mom and Sheila smothering laughter behind their hands. "It's nothing, Jimmy. I'll take you. I just need to talk to your mom for a sec, okay?"

"Okay! I'll get my backpack."

He runs back into the trailer, dashing past both women in their nauseating spandex and cheap bleached hair, and I wait until he's out of earshot before I march up into Sheila's face. Only then do I notice the familiar gold band glinting on my mother's hand, and whatever reserves of control I might've had snap completely.

"One of these days," I tell Sheila in a voice of steel, "you're going to have to grow the fuck up. And take my mother with you. Now give me some gas money, or your kid can walk."

They both gasp, and I can hear the lecture my mother wants to give me bursting out in splutters, but there's no way in hell I'm listening to it today. Instead, I hold up my palm until Sheila reluctantly retrieves a five from her bra and slaps it in. Then I rap my knuckles on the trailer, which is even crappier than ours, and yell, "Let's hit the road, Jimbo!"

"Coming!" he calls back, and he sounds so close to joyful that it almost breaks my heart, knowing the happiest moments of his six-year-old life are the ones in which a near-stranger takes him out of this godforsaken town for twenty-four hours.

Knowing he'll spend the next twelve years the same way I did: letting this place consume him in a slow, torturous burn, gasping for air, until the opportunity to leave and never look back is so close he can taste burned rubber on his tongue.

VICTORIA

I spend most of Saturday filling my mom in on the past twenty-four hours, watching football with my dad, and working on this shirt I've been trying to sew for weeks, but which is taking me forever because I'm terrible at sleeves. (Which is what happens when the only "sewing classes" you've taken come from your grandmother…who lives in Mexico and visits once a year.) I know I should be working on my history paper, but after my first college visit was a total bust, I'm having a hard time finding the motivation.

It's only been a few hours since I got back from Southeastern, but I'm already going kinda stir-crazy. Charytan's as boring on Saturday nights as it is every other night. I mean, maybe it's fun if you have a boyfriend or whatever, but considering every guy in this town is either scared of my skin color or thinks I'm hot because I'm "exotic," I'd rather spend every weekend playing Scrabble with my mother or giving myself and Reagan manicures.

If Javier had come with us to Charytan instead of

doing a year at ASU and running off to Fiji, he would've laughed his butt off at this town. As Reagan pointed out to me almost immediately when we met, Charytan is a town without choices. There's one of everything—one school, one restaurant, one movie theater that plays exactly one movie…The only thing there's more than one of is bars, but in a town where everyone knows everyone, good luck using a fake ID at either of them.

I have no interest in the shoot-'em-up playing at the theater—not like I'd go to a movie myself anyway, and good luck getting Reagan to spend ten bucks on that. As I pull on jeans and a sweater—because I know I have to get out of this house, whether I have a destination or not—I think about the party last night. Okay, so in some ways it was a bust, but in other ways, it was *so* much fun and exactly why these college visits are completely necessary.

I wonder if there are any parties happening tonight. Not that I'd be invited if there were one. Being a social leper gets really boring sometimes. Ordinarily, I'd just stay home, but I'm all keyed up to get out of the house, and there's only one place I'm always welcome. Which means I'm headed out for a night of watching Reagan work while I pick at a tuna melt and fries at Joe's.

I pack up a bag with my history notes and my laptop, just in case I'm inspired to actually get things done, and start mentally planning my next trip with Reagan out of this place.

My parents are adorably curled up on the couch downstairs, watching a movie. They seem so content, always, just being with each other; I wonder if I could be happy here if I had the same sort of thing. Too bad I'll never know.

"Can I borrow the car?" I sign once I've caught their attention for long enough for them to pause.

"Where are you going?" my dad asks, disentangling his arms from around my mother for long enough for him to sign back as he speaks.

"Joe's. Where else?"

My parents exchange a glance. I know they're embarrassed for my lack of social life, and hate that they don't know how to make things better. But it certainly wasn't any better in Arizona, as they know, and at least they adore Reagan.

"Keys on hook," my mom signs after a minute. I walk over to kiss them both goodbye, grab the keys, and head out.

I can tell from the second I enter the parking lot that Joe's is pretty empty for a Saturday night, meaning there definitely *is* a party happening somewhere, which I know nothing about, of course. I pull up to a spot opposite the huge plate glass window and am about to get out of the car when I realize I've got a clear shot of Reagan standing behind the counter, arguing with a small group of guys.

Well, *they're* arguing; she's doing her best to ignore them. I can see her jaw clenching from here as she busies herself doing anything she can to avoid them.

Most, if not all, of these guys are the ones I pretended not to see in the parking lot on Friday morning. I don't really know them; they go to my school, but they're not in any of my classes. Younger guys, maybe. In the past, when they've pulled this stuff, I've always been at her side, pretending not to notice and letting her distract herself by talking so she doesn't have to acknowledge them. But now…now one of the guys is stepping forward—Sean something—and he looks so ready for battle that for the first time, I actually fear for her.

I get out of the car and head toward the diner, my eyes fixed on Sean. But just as I'm about to let myself inside, I freeze as I realize there's another reason he looks so familiar: he's a dead ringer for the guy in the "I love you" picture. Except I found that picture months ago, and it was a little yellowed even then. This kid is definitely too young. A brother, maybe.

Either way, it doesn't look like anyone else is around to save her from these guys, so I push inside and march straight through the obnoxious little group up to the counter. "Hey, Rae!" I say sunnily, hoping the guys will get the hint and GTFO. Confrontations aren't my strong suit, as the scar on my forehead—and the girl who gave it to me—will attest. "Got a bacon tuna melt and fries back there for me?"

I expect to see some gratitude on her face, or relief, or anything other than the flash of horror I get. "What are you doing here?"

Um…what? "Getting a bacon tuna melt," I repeat a little more slowly. I look around at the group of guys, who are all standing around and snickering. "Oh, sorry," I say sweetly to the boys. "Are you guys waiting? I didn't mean to cut the line."

"We're just having a chat with your girlfriend," the slimiest-looking one says, his stupid smile so wide it makes his acne bunch up in clusters on his cheeks.

"Haha!" I bark-laugh obnoxiously loudly, as I've seen Rae do in response to this tired line a zillion times. "Lesbian jokes! Those are funny! You and your friends are so clever!"

I wait for Reagan to jump in—ripping tormentors a new one is her specialty, not mine—but she's weirdly silent on the opposite side of the counter, scratching at something that's crusted on the Formica. Guess I'm on my own. I look pointedly at the acne-scarred kid's round belly and say, "Pretty sure you don't need any more fries, so maybe you should head outside and get some exercise or something."

Sean snorts but is otherwise silent, and I know, I just *know*, that this has something to do with him and the picture and Reagan's stupid, stupid secret. Suddenly, I regret that I ever walked inside Joe's tonight.

"I think we'll just stick around and watch you two make out," says Derek Laughlin, who I recognize from the basketball team and who'd be kinda cute if he weren't obviously a jerk.

"Sounds like you're the one who needs to get laid," Reagan mutters, quietly enough that I can tell she's still uncomfortable but loud enough for the guys to hear it.

"Wanna help me out?" Derek returns smoothly. "You must be *really* good if—"

"Just get the fuck out!" Reagan snaps, loudly now, her huge brown eyes flashing fire. She usually reminds me of an anime character come to life with those eyes, but right now, the intensity in them combined with the thin white line through her brow and lash makes her look more like a tiny blond Cruella de Vil.

Next to me, Acne Boy breathes a "holy shit" and steps back. Derek utters a "Dude, she's fucking crazy" to Sean, whose entire face has hardened.

"You *are* fucking crazy," Sean spits at her. "Wish my brother would've realized that before you sent him off to die." He narrows his eyes. "You hear from him lately?" At her silence, his lips twist into a triumphant but bitter smile. "Didn't think so." And with that, he and his stupid friends turn and walk out, leaving me gaping at Reagan, who watches them go with her jaw set so tight I'm half afraid it's going to crack.

Finally, she turns to me, the fire in her eyes dimmed considerably, and mutters, "Still want that bacon tuna melt and fries?"

I'm speechless at that point, so I just nod and take a seat at the breakfast bar, watching as Reagan calls the order back to Hector. Then she busies herself with wiping down counters that are already clean while pretending not to notice that I'm glaring at her.

Finally, she exhales and her shoulders slump. "He's nobody. I used to date his brother. It was nothing."

"Sounds like nothing."

"It was a bad breakup. And I didn't…" She sighs and ties her hair up into a tiny ponytail. "I mean, obviously."

"So where is he now?" I ask carefully, because though she seems to have no desire to talk about this, there's no way I'm letting *that* part go; there's only so much privacy a best friend can give a best friend. "Sean's brother, I mean."

She shrugs, which makes her look extra young, but it's more than that. She looks…lost, somehow. "Afghanistan, I think. I mean, I know. We just…we don't talk anymore. But he did join the army. After. And he's not dead; Sean's just a dick."

She goes back to busying herself, this time with filling salt shakers, but her shoulders are still up under her ears, like she's on high alert for more questions she doesn't want to answer. I decide to leave them for now. I've wondered for years why Reagan is just as friendless as I am, but I always made my own assumptions.

"So Sean's his little brother?"

"One of them." She scowls at a smudge on the counter. "There are five Fitzpatrick boys, and one girl. None of them like me very much. Shocking, I know."

"How come I don't know them?"

"Three of them are still pretty young, not even in high school yet." She licks the pad of her thumb and starts vigorously rubbing the spot. "Quinn's in eighth grade now. We used to be like sisters, and now she won't even look at me. Danny graduated two years ago, right after Fitz. He used to give me plenty of shit, but not as much as Sean."

Fitz. Finally, the boy in the picture has a name.

"Seems like you're better off without them," I offer, because I've got nothing else. My brain's too busy processing all this new information. All those times Reagan's made fun of me for having boys on the brain, and it turns out she used to have a *very* important one of her own. What else hasn't she told me about him? About herself? For the past two years, I've let myself remain ignorant about this stuff, figuring if it was really important, she'd tell me.

She exhales sharply but says nothing.

I watch her clean for another minute, swallowing down a million questions. I don't want to fight with

Reagan right now, not when she's all keyed up from those jerks, and I know from past experience when she's in this bad a mood, an argument is all that'll happen if I push. Finally I switch the topic to the history paper, and tell her I'm glad it's quiet at Joe's tonight, so maybe we can both get some work done.

She tips her head curiously. "What's wrong with your house?"

I shrug. "Nothing. Just getting a little stir-crazy in Casa Reyes."

She laughs shortly, just a little bitter puff of air through her nostrils, enough to let me know whatever's up at my house, something at hers is worse. My stomach tightens.

"Let me guess," I say. "Your mom set fire to the toaster oven again?"

She laughs again, a real one this time, which sounds a whole lot better. "Nah, that would involve her actually cooking. This time she just neglected to pay the electric bill, so we've got no power. Makes it a little challenging to get work done."

"Didn't you just tell me you gave her last week's tips to pay that bill?" I ask.

"My fault for thinking she'd actually *use* them to pay the bill and not conveniently forget *that's* why she had extra cash burning a hole in her pocket, just when cubic zirconium earrings that look *so* real popped up on the Home Shopping Network."

I just shake my head. I've met Reagan's mom a handful of times, but as a general rule, both Reagan and I prefer I keep my distance. It's obvious that every time I'm in that house, she's watching me like a hawk, as if I'm about to steal her precious, non-existent silver. As far as I can tell, she's a delusional gold-digger. On the bright side, she's probably a great essay topic for college applications.

"Oh, yeah, definitely your fault," I say sourly.

Reagan starts to answer but it's swallowed up in the sound of the bell Hector's ringing to let her know that my dinner's ready. She grabs the plate and slides it in front of me.

"Have you had anything to eat?" I ask, snatching one of the bottles of ketchup she's been filling and squeezing a blob onto my plate.

"Yeah, one of Brenda's bricks. I think she was calling this one biscotti."

I dip a couple of fries into the ketchup, and then push the plate toward Rae while I stuff them into my mouth. All of a sudden, I'm starving. She takes only one and nips it delicately before pushing the plate back. "Guest room's all yours if you want it," I say, but I can already tell she won't take me up on it tonight.

"Thanks, but I think I need to intercept my dad tonight before he hands off any more cash. She's out of control lately, and you know how he can't refuse her anything." Rae takes another fry, but it's obviously just to keep her hands busy; she doesn't even really eat it, just rips it into pieces that she pops into her mouth as an afterthought. "Anyway, I'm working a full shift here tomorrow, so I can get some stuff done when it's slow or I'm on break. Freckles will be here too, and he's cool about covering."

"Oh, yes, Freckles." I swirl another fry around in ketchup. "Yet another boy you insist is not interested."

She raises her striped eyebrow. "Trust me, Freckles and I are *just* friends, and that is *very* mutual."

"Why?" Taking a huge mouthful of sandwich, I realize I forgot to order a drink, and Rae turns to fill a cup with whatever generic cola they've got on tap. I swallow what was definitely too big a bite before accepting the cup and washing it down. "He's kinda cute."

"You really can't go five minutes without discussing guys, can you?" she teases, nabbing another fry.

I resist the urge to bring up the guy we went two years without discussing. "Hey, at least I didn't mention Boy from Last Night Who Must Not Be Named."

"Until now." She rolls her eyes and puts back the fry.

"Oh, that doesn't count." I take a noisy sip of pop. "So, is Fitz the reason you won't even give Dave a chance?"

"Vic!"

So much for resisting that urge. "What?" I say innocently, though even I'm surprised the words actually came out of my mouth; I thought I'd just been thinking them really intensely.

"Don't 'what' me. Stop pretending I had some chick flick moment with a stranger and eat your damn tuna melt."

I smile smugly but obediently take another bite. For a totally backwater diner in a gross town, Joe's food's not all that bad. Enough oil to fix all my split ends, probably, but not that bad.

"What about you?" she asks, just as the bell over the door dings and a whole new crowd pours in.

"What *about* me?" I ask, but my question simply hangs in the air for a while until it's eventually swallowed up by the noise.

Chapter Six

Reagan

Okay, so I may have lied to Vic; I have no intention of seeing my dad tonight. I know full well it's like talking to a brick wall, the way my mom has him completely hypnotized. But I need to get home, electricity or not. After a run-in like that with Sean Fitzpatrick, I need to break into my secret stash.

I know I'm weak, but nights like tonight, the need overpowers any sense of self-control or sanity I might've once possessed.

The trailer is completely dark when I get home, and it's quiet, which means my parents are out; if they were asleep, I'd be able to hear my dad snoring like a chainsaw. The power's still out, so I take out the flashlight I borrowed from the utility closet at Joe's and find my way to my room, to my closet, to my tippy-top shelf where I keep the box I am *never* supposed to touch. It takes some maneuvering with furniture and flashlight but eventually I grab it and yank it down, allowing myself to crumble to the linoleum with it clasped firmly in hand.

I tuck the flashlight under my chin and paw through the envelopes, trying to tell their respective ages by their yellowing. However, in the artificial battery-powered light, I can't tell a damn thing. I finally give up and open one, saying a little prayer as I remove its contents. Though I've saved each and every one, there are certainly a few I'd rather not see again. I look, and breathe a sigh of relief. Perfect.

> *Dear Ragin',*
> *It's hot as balls here. Sorry, that's kinda gross, but...* *it's hot as balls. Everyone here reeks so bad and I keep* *thinking I'll get used to the smell and the heat and I never* *do. At least I'm not sunburned all the time anymore. I* *can hear you flippin out at me to put on sunscreen but I* *don't even need it now, my skin's gettin so used to it. My* *ma probably wouldn't even recognize her little Irish boy* *right now.*
> *How's it over there? You still see my family around?* *I know Ma misses you, and so does Quinn. I hope my*

brothers aren't being dicks to you. ~~I know you'd never say anything but Quinn told me she heard Seany~~ I gotta go and I don't wanna waste space on my family. Just wanna let you know I'm thinkin of you. I know you're probably still too pissed to write, but I hope one day you won't be. I wait for letters from you every day, ya know. We even have e-mail here. So, yeah. Someday, I hope.

    I love you.

    Johnny

It's dated nine months ago, making it one of the newest letters in the box; they stopped coming entirely about three months later. I read it over and over again until my eyes blur, place it carefully back in the envelope, and then cry myself to sleep.

I wake up a few hours later, still on my floor, curled around the box. There's just enough light peeking through my window for me to guide myself back to the tippy-top shelf and put it back. Once it's been safely replaced, I turn and look longingly at my bed; all I want to do is drag my butt under the covers and sleep for eternity. Unfortunately, I have an all-day shift that starts in an hour and I need to stir up every ounce of energy I have to deal with both the hung-over and church-going crowds. The overlap is the absolute worst.

I resort to my never-fail trick for getting myself motivated to move. *All right, Reagan—five reasons to go to work today. One, because a full day's shift plus tips at Joe's pays for at least one textbook.* I uncurl from the fetal position and stretch my limbs with a yawn. *Two, even I'm not cruel enough to leave Freckles alone with the crazed waffle-seeking hordes. Three, free coffee, which I desperately need right now.* The thought of a tall, steaming cup of caffeine is enough to make me rock onto my feet and stand up. *Four*—I peel my disgusting, stinky clothes from my body and toss them onto the floor—*I reek of grease and need to shower more than I need to breathe right now.*

I can hear my dad snoring through the walls, so I go ahead and dash into the bathroom to turn on the shower without bothering to cover up. Instinctively, I go for the light switch. Twice. *Five—Joe's actually has power.* After five minutes of standing with my hand in the trickly shower stream, I add, *Six—and hot water.*

Finally, I jump in anyway—the stink of French fries is just too much—and scrub off what feels like an entire layer of skin while icy water drips in slow torture down my back. My teeth are chattering so hard it's compounding my crying-hangover headache, and as soon as I've got the shampoo rinsed clean, I jump out of the shower and bundle myself up as tightly as possible in the bathroom's only threadbare towel.

On the bright side, I'm certainly awake now. On the less-than-bright side, I feel like a cat that's been through a cycle in the dishwasher. I throw on my jeans, my last remaining clean Joe's Diner polo, and a sweatshirt, and grab my knapsack before bolting out to my car before my parents can wake up.

I'm early, but Freckles is even earlier, brewing coffee and setting out the morning's display of fresh bagels. I drop my stuff under the counter and pour myself a massive cup with one hand while trying to make neat rows of pastries with the other.

"You can give yourself an extra minute to make sure you don't spill scalding liquid all over yourself, Pepe."

I prefer Rogue. I brush the unwelcome thought from my mind as quickly as it comes. "I'm an excellent multi-tasker, thank you very much."

"Frighteningly so," he concedes, leaving the bagels to me while he goes back to the walk-in refrigerator for the huge tubs of cream cheese that reside there. I take a long, hot sip and then put down the cup to finish arranging baked goods in time to turn the "Sorry, we're closed!" sign around to "Come on in, we're open!" at 6:00 AM on the dot.

The first wave comes almost immediately, mostly truck drivers getting their caffeine fix before driving out to Dodge or Wichita, and each one makes brief, gruff conversation with "Bill Forrester's kid" while I pour endless refills of black coffee strong enough to peel paint off the walls.

Eventually, my dad comes in too, and says, "Thanks,

Pumpkin," with a wink when I shake cinnamon into his mug, exactly how he likes it.

Freckles handles the food, shuttling plate after plate of bacon, eggs, and sausage. We are a well-oiled machine for the next hour and a half, barely exchanging any words, and then business slows considerably. It will stay that way for another hour or so until the farmhands taking a break from field work start pouring in. Then there'll be another short lull before we get the post-church crowd, during which I'll actually get work done.

Charytan, Kansas: The most predictable city on the planet.

For now, the diner is literally empty except for us, Hector, and Charlie, the dishwasher, and we clean up a bit with our handy-dandy rags and settle down with some fresh coffee and bagels paid for from the tip jar.

"How'd it go last night?" he asks, pulling a couple of chairs behind the counter and dropping into one with a sigh of relief. "I heard Eddie bailed on you."

"Yeah, whatever, no big deal." The fiery look in Sean Fitzpatrick's eyes flashes through my brain for a second, but I push it back out just as quickly. I wonder if they knew somehow that I'd be working alone last night and that was why they'd come in to harass me. Sean's an asshole, no question, and he makes no secret of the fact that he thinks I drove his big brother to certain death. Still, he usually keeps his distance, preferring to glare at me from across the hallway. Last night was unsettling, to say the least, and having Vic see it all go down was the icing on the crap cake.

I can't even imagine what she's thinking after last night. I should've just told her myself, during one of those early conversations we must have had about boys and fooling around, so distant that my mind has turned its lies into truths. I can't blame her for feeling like she can't trust me right now. I barely trust myself to function in this town.

"So where's your other half?" Freckles asks, breaking into my thoughts.

"Still sleeping, I'm sure." I glance down at my watch. "It's only ten. Patience, boy." I smile slowly. "She'll be here at some point, don't you worry."

His skin reddens considerably beneath those freckles, his fair skin matching the crusty ketchup stain on the empty stool next to him. He mumbles something under his breath that I don't catch but I'm sure isn't flattering.

"Relax, I haven't said a thing to her about your little crush, much as it pains me."

"I don't—"

"Oh, save it." I roll my eyes as I take a big bite of my cinnamon-raisin bagel. The coffee I wash it down with scalds my throat just slightly in the way that I love. "Don't worry, she has no idea. She thinks I'm the one you want."

He wrinkles his nose. "Really?"

"Ouch!"

"You know what I mean." He swipes at a smear of cream cheese on his upper lip and misses.

"I'll have you know, some guys think I am wonderfully desirable." Without warning, I can feel Dave's hand, flipping up my white curl, see his eyes slowly making their way down my body. I stiffen, trying to combat the chills running down my spine, and refocus on the conversation. "Anyway, you should ask her out."

"Why?"

"Um, to go on a date? Isn't that generally the end game?"

He laughs shortly. "Come on. You don't actually think she'd go on a date with me. Who the hell wants to go on a date with the waiter living with his parents while he goes to community college?"

"It's not like the rest of the guys in Charytan are any more impressive." My coffee's no longer hot, but pleasantly warm as it goes down. "Anyway, you're not gonna be stuck here forever, Freckles. Not unless you wanna be."

"Ya think?" He rips off another piece of bagel and stuffs it into his mouth. "I'm starting to think no one ever really gets out of here."

"Bite your tongue."

"Just look at the Sunday crowds," he continues as if I haven't spoken, sweeping a hand around the empty diner.

"The construction workers? Every single one of those guys—including your dad—is a Charytan lifer, even though it means driving hours every day to find work. The farmhands who'll pour in soon? Ditto. Even Joe is like four-hundredth generation. Face it—this place is quicksand."

I stuff my bagel into my mouth to stop myself from responding, because I know that if I do, I'll rip poor, unsuspecting Freckles a new one. He doesn't mean to piss me off, and I know it, but this is probably my least favorite line of conversation.

A part of me is afraid that he's right, that I'll never really get out of this place. Every time a shift's worth of earnings has to pay for a new plumbing part or extra gas that doesn't fit into my careful budget, that's more money I need to dig up to make tuition and dorm fees. As if coming from a school with no newspaper, no debate team—almost no extra-curriculars at all except for sports—isn't bad enough, I can't allow myself to be at any other disadvantage.

This cannot remain my life.

VICTORIA

Monday mornings suck. And they suck double when you have to drag yourself out of bed extra early, but today, I'm on a mission. I hitch a ride to school with my dad on his way to teach his 7:00 a.m. class to whatever literature lovers are crazy enough to sit through a lecture that early (I've already told Reagan—if she takes any classes before noon she'd better tiptoe to them) and my butt finds its way into a seat in the college guidance office the minute it opens.

"Miss Reyes." Mrs. MacKinnon, the wrinkly counselor who probably went to college during World War I, looks at me over her half glasses. It should be weird that she knows my name considering we've met exactly once and there are a hundred kids in the class, but when you're the only Latina in a sea of Whitey McWhitersons you get used to people knowing who you are without your having to tell them. "Did we have an appointment?"

"We didn't"—I force as much apology into my voice as humanly possible considering her death stare—"but I was hoping that if I got here early, you might be able to squeeze me in."

She obviously doesn't want to, and when her eyes shift to the empty mug on her desk, I realize one crucial mistake. "After you have your coffee, of course," I add quickly.

Her shoulders relax a little, but she moves over to the coffee machine without another word to me. I assume that means I'm in. It's another few minutes before the smell of freshly brewed coffee fills the room, making my stomach rumble, and she pours herself a mug and then shuffles back to the seat across from me. "So," she says after she's taken her first sip. "You're thinking of going to college."

"Well…yeah. Of course."

"Of course?"

"I mean, isn't basically everyone? At some point, anyway." Obviously there are always people like my brother, who wanna travel or do do-goodery things before finishing, but it's where everyone ultimately ends up. Isn't it?

A weird smile distorts her mouth, and in her narrowed eyes I can plainly see "not people like you," but then it all disappears behind her mug as she takes a long drink. "Well then. Do you have a list of places you're considering? There are some wonderful minority scholarships available."

My lips stretch tightly over my teeth. *She's just trying to be helpful*, I remind myself. "That's great, thanks. And actually, making a list is what I wanted to talk to you about. I've started to visit schools and I realized that I don't really know which ones have the program I'm looking for."

"And what's that?"

"Fashion design." I sit up a little straighter in my chair so she can get the full effect of my outfit today, which consists of an asymmetrical sashed knit skirt I made out of two of my dad's old sweaters and a T-shirt onto which I've copied that Picasso dog sketch with what are impressively tight stitches, if I may say so myself. "I went to Southeastern this past weekend and they didn't have it in the catalogue, so…"

Her bushy eyebrows furrow. "Well, I can't say I'm surprised. I can't imagine Fashion Design is a popular course of study. It's more of a…" She waves a hand around in the air while she contemplates which offensive answer she's going to pull out of her butt. "A hobby, I suppose."

I grit my teeth and say nothing; I'm not sure what I *could* say that wouldn't land me in the principal's office. But considering there's an entire amazing school dedicated to fashion design in New York City, you'd think she'd realize how ridiculous she sounds, acting like it doesn't exist as a major.

Then again, with the exception of Miss Lucy, what are the odds anyone from Charytan High has ever attended FIT, or even heard of it?

"Have you considered studying Spanish?" she suggests. "Perhaps you could become a…translator."

In my mind I can hear Javi telling me to take deep breaths when I encounter ignorance this stupid, so I take three, slowly, until I feel calmer. "That's not really what I had in mind."

"Well, if you're interested in a more…practical major, you might find that something in business or accounting is right for you." She spins in her chair and gathers a few things, which she hands over as if she's giving me the keys to Sephora after hours. They turn out to be course catalogs from different schools, which I guess is as helpful as she's likely to get.

I take them and thank her, then leave as quickly as humanly possible. According to the cheap-pocketwatch-wrapped-around-a-scarf on my wrist, I've still got a few minutes before class, so I head into the library, hoping for an available computer so I can read my newest e-mail from Javi on a bigger screen.

Bula, little sis!

Glad to hear that you and Reagan are having a great time at college! Or at least that you are—yikes on the whole throwing-up thing. Good thing I know that my underage sister would never be dumb enough to drink at a college party where there were a whole bunch of horny frat guys around, right? RIGHT?! Getting to the more important part, though, I'm gonna need some pictures of these hot sorority girls you mentioned, stat.

Speaking of people having a lil fun this week, guess who decided to take a vacation and is currently e-mailing you from an Internet café in Sydney? Decided I needed a breather and was inspired by you and Reagan planning your own little trip. (Though mine's a hell of a lot cooler, obviously.) I came with Chase and Sam and we're having an awesome time, though the kangaroos seem less than amused by us and one almost kicked Chase's ass the other day.

We're only here another couple of days and then we head back to Fiji, but another one of the volunteers here is headed to the States soon, so keep an eye out for a real, old-timey letter. And you better keep writing even though you're soooo busy now, because you know I need to live vicariously through your whole college experience! You should probably delete this after reading it because I'll deny to the death that I ever said it, but I'm really proud of you, hermana. I know college is weird and scary on top of all the fun stuff and it's awesome that you're doing it.

Now enough sappiness—time to get plastered while I still can!

Love,

Big Bro

Just seeing his words on the screen makes me tear up. He's attached a photo, which I nearly open until I see "NSFS" in the file name, which means he's definitely plastered in it and probably double-fisting beers. I'm sure he's on some gorgeous beach, though; he always is. For all that I think Javi's crazy for going, I envy him too, and the experiences he's getting, the beautiful places—and clothes—he's seeing.

A lot of people were shocked when Javi decided to join the Peace Corps, thinking he was nothing but a party boy who went through girls at our high school like candy, but there's so much about him that nobody knows. Thinking about it makes me miss him so much at times my heart literally aches.

I decide that's about all I can take of my emotional roller coaster of a morning and close out of Javi's e-mail, but when I do, I notice another familiar name in my inbox and immediately click on the message.

Hey Tori!! Sorry I didn't get to see you again before you left! It was sooo nice to meet you and I hope you come back to Southeastern—and to Lambda!! If you have any questions about the house or anything, lemme know!! Xoxo Sasha

My stomach gets all flippy when I read it, like I've just been asked to the prom. Next to me, the pile of catalogs from Mrs. MacKinnon beckons. I riffle through them until I find the one from Southeastern and go back to the "F"s. The page looks just as I remember it— Environmental Studies followed by French—but with Javi's words still fresh in my brain, Sasha's e-mail still on the screen in front of me, and Mrs. MacKinnon's nasty expression looming behind my eyelids, suddenly that looks less like a gaping hole and more like a sign.

I flip around, and sure enough, they've got an Accounting major. And an Economics major. And a Literature major, which would basically make my dad's life. Okay, so maybe I can't make *my* dreams come true there, but what about everyone else's?

My mind is still a raging blur of contradicting thoughts by the time Rae drops me off at home on her way to her shift at Joe's. All I want is to go up to my room, blast some music, and think about nothing, but the most delicious smell in the world has me drooling the instant I open the front door, and all thoughts of doing anything other than stuffing myself into a kitchen chair disappear.

The first thing I see when I enter the kitchen is my mom standing over the big pot she uses any time she's cooking something that gets drowned in oil. Judging by both pot and fragrance, she's attempting churros for the four-millionth time, in an effort to perfect the recipe and impress my abuelita.

I wait until she looks up from the island in the center of the kitchen and notices me, and then sign, "Smells good. What's wrong with them?"

She makes a face at me, then puts down the bird's nest ladle. "Shape. They're blobs. And the shape was so perfect last time!"

"You also burned them last time," I remind her, then give her a kiss on the cheek. It's always something, to the point where we're both convinced my abuelita put a curse on the pot. I love my father's mother, but I wouldn't put it past her, honestly. The plate of glistening blobs sits on a paper towel next to her on the counter, and I pop one in my mouth, instantly regretting it when I burn every surface of my mouth.

My mom lightly whacks my wrist. "You don't have patience." She picks up the ladle again to lift more steaming churros out of the oil.

"Nope," I sign back, then settle into one of the tall chairs across the counter from her. "Javi e-mailed me today. Did you know he's in Australia?"

She nods, finishes spooning out the rest of the blobs, and turns off the flame. "He e-mailed me too. The cleaner version, I assume."

I grin. "I cannot confirm or deny."

"And now I have to worry about both my children, with you and Reagan and your college visits. How much are you leaving out about your trips?"

"I'm hurt that you think that." I puff my lower lip out in a dramatic pout. "Anyway, maybe Reagan's the one you should worry about. She's the one who met a boy."

"I thought you met a boy too."

"Mark?" I wave my hand dismissively and then reach for a churro. One nice thing about signing—you can mostly talk with your mouth full. "He's nice but he's nobody. Reagan actually likes this boy."

"Reagan?" Her eyebrows shoot up as she makes the name sign she assigned Reagan, the sign for "white" with the "R" handshape for her name—what Reagan laughingly calls her "white girl name" even though it's for the streak in her hair and lacks the gesture that turns "white" into "Caucasian" in ASL. "I didn't think she knew boys existed."

"Me neither, but she was totally—" I don't know how to sign "smitten," so I fingerspell it instead. "Not that she'll admit it. Then we left that morning without his phone number or e-mail address. I want to make sure she sees him again, but I don't know how."

I can see my mother's brain working, and I eat another churro while I watch her process her thoughts. Then she grins. "This is like that famous riddle. A woman sees a man at her mother's funeral and falls deeply in love at first sight, but when the funeral ends, he's nowhere to be found. The next day, she kills her sister."

I make a face at the bizarre and morbid non-sequitur. "That's terrible."

My mother rolls her eyes. "You've never heard this? Why does she kill her sister?"

"Because she's a psycho?"

"Yes, and…"

"Seriously," I sign. "No idea where you're going with this. But if you're planning to take out Tia Maria, I'm in."

She huffs out a sigh. "She reasons that if he was at the funeral of one of her family members, he'll show up at the funeral of another one. So she kills her sister so she can see the guy again."

I narrow my eyes. "Are you suggesting that I let Reagan kill me?"

She laughs, which is one of my favorite sounds in

the world. It's kind of goose-like, which isn't her fault, of course; she's never heard it. "No, my simple child. I'm suggesting you see if any other colleges nearby are hosting a prospective students' weekend, which is the most obvious way you might bump into him again."

"Why didn't you just say that?" I demand, my hands flailing wildly. "You and your creepy metaphors."

"It's not a metaphor," she signs back, but I've already moved past that point and am thinking about how obvious an answer that is. We hadn't planned to go on another college visit for another couple of weeks, when Barnaby State College is having a special prospective-student weekend, but now that my mom's planted her idea in my brain, I know I can't wait that long to try to hook Reagan and Dave back up. Especially now that I know about the misery Fitz is still inflicting on her from thousands of miles away.

"You're brilliant!" I wrap my arms around my mother in a massive hug and kiss her on the cheek with a loud smack. I disentangle myself long enough to sign, "I'm going to find another college to visit for next weekend. Thank you!" Then I give her another hug, grab another churro, and scamper upstairs to plan our next move.

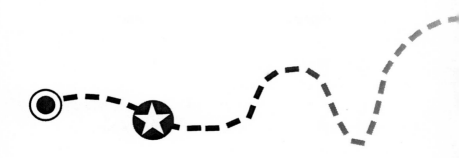

CHAPTER SEVEN

REAGAN

"This doesn't even make any sense." I hand the Halsing College catalog back to Vic, using my other hand to muffle a yawn. It took me for-fucking-ever to finish writing my history paper after work yesterday, and having to work by flashlight—only *after* my parents were done using it, of course—did not help. "They have no Greek life, no fashion design program—"

"I don't *need* those things," she interrupts, which is obviously a lie. I saw her at the sorority house at Southeastern; it was as much fun as I've ever seen her have. And fashion design is her *life*. Even now, on a random Tuesday at school, she's wearing an awesome outfit of her own design, a dress she's patchworked out of random fabrics. "Besides, they're having a prospective weekend, and look! There's a hayride!"

I'm pretty sure my best friend has been taken over by aliens. "A hayride, which I would think would be your worst nightmare. That's your big sell on this tiny, random college that's in the middle of basically nowhere?"

"This is Kansas. Everywhere is the middle of basically nowhere, with the exceptions of KU and K-State, both of which you refuse to consider."

My stomach tightens at the mention of the two Kansas schools big enough to be their own cities. I haven't been able to explain to her why those are non-options much better than I've been able to explain it to myself, but Vic being wonderful Vic, she hasn't pressed. "Cheap shot."

"And speaking of cheap…" She flips to the back of the catalog to point out the tuition. Sweet Jesus. With my savings and a minimum-wage paying job, even *I* can afford that with minimal loans.

"Fine," I grumble in concession. "Twenty-four hours. I have the four-to-close shift at Joe's this Saturday." Plus, cheap tuition or not, I'm not dying to spend too much time at a college whose motto is, "If at first you don't succeed."

She smiles broadly, and it's so glaringly obvious that

something is up, but I have no idea what. "It's only an hour away, so we don't even have to skip any school. The perfect plan!"

I calculate in my head. If we leave at three thirty, we should be there by five, with traffic. That should give us plenty of time to drop our stuff off at our hosts before the prospective students' dinner. According to Vic, the college will put us up as long as we register, which—surprise!— she's already done for us. After dinner is the hayride, which actually does sound sort of fun, especially when I take into account how much I know Vic will hate it. Between getting an unanticipated break from Charytan and hopefully getting to use a decent shower, it actually doesn't sound all that bad.

Still, I suspect something's up, and I'm not getting excited about this trip until I fish out what it is. "What aren't you telling me?"

"What do you still want to know?" she asks, fluttering her eyelashes the way she always does when she's purposely misunderstanding a question.

Fine, if that's how she wants to play it. "Gas for this unbudgeted-for road trip?"

"On me, of course."

This mystery is going to kill me, but if I know Vic, she won't be able to keep it a secret all that long. "I choose the music the entire way there."

"Deal."

I narrow my eyes. "You're making it impossible for me to say no. You realize that."

"You already said yes," she points out with a gleeful smile, tugging my white curl. "You're easier than you think. Whoops! Gotta go to Spanish. Hasta la vista, darling!"

She twirls on her jewel-studded cowboy boots and disappears down the hall with a flutter wave, leaving me wondering what in the hell I just agreed to.

Of course, the time I've spent contemplating what I'm being set up for has made me slip into English at the very last second, and Mr. Phelan's not a big fan of lateness. I'm pretty sure I've made it in under the bell, but I get a "Miss Forrester, please see me after class," as soon as I slide into my seat anyway.

Paying attention after that is a struggle, especially since I'm still fighting to stay awake on three hours of sleep, and the knowledge that I have an eight-hour shift at Joe's after school today isn't helping. I make it as far as three reasons I have to force myself to stay awake and then I drift off, which I know only because I'm awoken by an especially sharp "Miss Forrester?"

Shit. My eyes quickly dart around, looking for some guidance. I sit next to Phil Yardley, who basically idolized Fitz when he was a basketball star and therefore despises me, so I know he'll be no help. On my other side is Jessica Bartel, who tried and failed to get with Fitz pretty much the entire second year we were together, so, yeah, not much hope there. Ginnie Tucker sits in front of me and isn't entirely a bitch, but certainly isn't the type to risk pissing Mr. Phelan off by being obvious with her guidance of a wayward student.

Which basically means I'm screwed.

"I'm sorry, I was so focused on the use of a spectrum of criminals and the variety in their upbringings in *Great Expectations* that I completely missed your question." I say a silent thanks to Vic for that move—pick the one thing you know about a book and use it. "Would you mind repeating it?"

His jaw tightens. "That *was* the question, Miss Forrester."

Praise the freaking lord. It's literally the only thing I've studied about the book I've read maybe two chapters of in between writing my subpar history paper and cleaning out the soda fountain at Joe's. Mr. Phelan doesn't seem entirely pleased that I actually have a response for him, but the words themselves seem to satisfy him enough, and he nods and then moves on to bugging Jessica instead.

For a minute I actually imagine I might be able to get out of this whole "See me" thing, but as soon as the bell rings, I get my third "Miss Forrester" of the day and I trudge over to his desk at the front of the room, knowing I'm going to end up in similar trouble next period when this little meeting inevitably makes me late to AP Chemistry.

"I'm sorry I was late...ish." Mr. Phelan has always responded best to immediate apologies, in my experience, though I've never been one to apologize for something I didn't actually do.

He smiles wryly and gestures for me to take a seat. This is a definite first, and it's making me want to hurl all over his scruffy loafers. "It's not strictly about the tardiness, Miss Forrester." He opens his grading book and traces his index finger down the page. "Are you aware that you're bordering a B+ average in my class?"

Shit. Shit shit shit. "Are you sure? I could swear I've gotten A's on both quizzes you've given so far this year."

"Yes, but your homework has been late—"

"Twice!" I cry, knowing it's a mistake to interrupt him the second I do it but unable to stop myself. "Once because my mother accidentally threw it out!"

"And has arrived multiple times in unacceptable condition," he continues as if I haven't spoken.

"What does that even mean?"

"Assignments are expected to be typewritten, Miss Forrester. You know this."

"I don't have a personal computer, let alone a printer," I manage through gritted teeth. "Right now, I don't even have electricity. If the library was open later—"

"Excuses do not interest me. Getting your work done on time and in proper condition is what interests me. I know you are heavily reliant on academic scholarships to attend university, and I highly suggest you get your act together if you still hope to receive one."

A million profanities are screaming inside my head but I force a jerky puppet nod and a thank-you for the warning and slip outside, allowing myself just one deep breath before I dash over to AP Chem, praying I'll make it in time and avoid a similar lecture from Dr. Cole. I do, but it doesn't matter. The panic has already set in deep in my gut. Without an academic scholarship, I am screwed, doomed to a life of waitressing at Joe's while maybe, *maybe* squeezing in one class per semester at CCC, since first priority would be paying for a place of my own and getting the hell out of that trailer park.

Already, I can feel everything slipping away, and suddenly it's hard to breathe. *Calm the fuck down*, I order myself, counting to ten slowly in my head. *This is an AP class. You ace enough of these exams, you have one less semester to pay for. Calm. The fuck. Down.*

It doesn't work, and then I'm inhaling in loud, horrible gulps while sweat streams down my forehead. I'm screaming at myself to stop but it does nothing other than reverberate in my own skull while my body shakes with the force of it.

"Reagan, are you all right?"

I can't say anything in response. My throat has invisible hands wrapped around it, squeezing it...

"Becky, take Reagan to the nurse."

"But—"

"Quickly, Becky!"

I'm powerless to stop Becky Holtzmann from pulling me by the arm and practically dragging me down the hall, and believe me, I would've done anything to stop her—as Sean Fitzpatrick's girlfriend, she hates me about as much as anyone else in the school. She's told me more than once that Ma Fitzpatrick doesn't trust a single girl that goes near one of her boys, not since "Reagan Forrester done broke her boy's heart and then he broke his ma's." Even now as she takes me to the nurse, it's clear she hopes whatever's afflicting me is fast-acting and terminal.

"There." She practically shoves me at the door to the nurse's office and leaves me, her long brown curls swinging behind her as she marches back down the hall to class.

Great! I'm all better now! I want to shout after her, but duh, can't breathe, so instead I lurch toward the door, nearly knocking over Nurse Hocking in the process, and then promptly pass out.

"Reagan!"

My eyes fly open to see Vic standing over me. She must have rushed somehow, because there's no way I was out more than a minute or two. Was I? I put my hands down at my sides and grip the frame of the cot. What the hell is wrong with me?

"I'm not feeling so well," I mumble, closing my eyes again. The light is too damn bright.

"What happened to you? I heard Becky Holtzmann saying you passed out."

"Becky Holtzmann is a class-A bitch."

There's a loud coughing sound, and I realize Nurse Hocking is still in earshot. I squint and sit up slowly, accepting the cup of water Vic holds out to me. As I take a tentative sip, I'm not thinking at all about how Dave handed me a cup of water just a few days ago. Obviously.

"I don't know." I take another little sip and then hand the cup back to Vic so I can regain my balance on the cot. "My chest just got all tight and then my throat...I couldn't breathe."

"Rae! That sounds like a panic attack."

"How do you know?"

She rolls her eyes. "Because I *know*." She sits down next to me, her butt shoving me over a few inches. "Did something happen?"

I nibble on the inside of my lip while I replay the conversation with Mr. Phelan in my head. Finally, I tell her, "I might lose my chance at a scholarship."

"What? Who told you that?"

"Phelan. Apparently my homework is inappropriate

because I don't own a fucking computer." Another loud cough, and I lower my voice. "I'm screwed without a scholarship, Vic. I can't take out massive loans; I'll *never* be able to pay them off."

I don't even realize she's taken my hands until she squeezes them so hard I think the bones might break.

"I promise you, we're gonna fix this." Her voice is fierce, and it doesn't allow for a single shred of doubt— my very favorite Vic mode. "For one thing, you're staying at my house tonight, and every night until you get your power back and you're all caught up on everything." She pauses, and I can tell she doesn't want to say whatever she's about to say next. "Do you want to cancel on the weekend?"

I shake my head defiantly. "I want to go. I need to get out of here again." I need to be far, far away from the world of the Fitzpatricks and Becky Holtzmann and Mr. Phelan. "Seriously, this weekend can't come soon enough."

"Wow." She purses her glossy lips into a smug smile. "I think this might be the most determined I've seen you about anything in a while."

"Just make sure the trip doesn't suck, okay?"

She waves her hand dismissively. "Oh, please. It's college, and it's an hour away. What could possibly go wrong?"

VICTORIA

Here's what could possibly go wrong. We could get a flat tire halfway there and be forced to pull over to the side of the highway. (Fortunately, Reagan is seriously awesome with a jack and whatever that other thingy is called, and she has us back on the road in ten minutes.) Then I could realize I've left my emergency credit card in the back pocket of the jeans currently on my floor, and am currently carrying exactly five dollars, forcing us to beg the guy at the gas station replacing the spare to accept the thirty dollars in Reagan's wallet and bill me for the rest. Then we could get to Halsing and see that they've set us up in entirely different dorms, Reagan with a girl who opened the door in bunny pajamas and headgear despite it being seven thirty and me with a girl sporting enough black eyeliner and hair dye to suggest Satan is her stylist.

And best of all, Dave could not be there. Which I'm starting to suspect he isn't.

"I can't believe *you* want to go to the library," Reagan teases me as I drag her in the direction of the brick building. "What kind of apocalypse occurred on the car ride over here?"

I stay silent, knowing there's nothing I could come up with that would convince her. By the time we'd put our stuff down, showered, and gotten dressed, we'd missed the prospectives' dinner. We got there just in time to see the other high school seniors spilling out of Halsing Hall, and not one of them was a tall, skinny Indian kid with slightly shaggy black hair and what even I can admit is a pretty killer smile.

If Reagan's given Dave a second thought since the previous weekend, I haven't heard about it, but I can't give up. I've dragged our butts all the way to this ridiculously tiny campus that smells of manure and dry grass, and I'll be damned if I've done it for nothing. Dave's gotta be around here somewhere, and my first thought after he wasn't outside the hall where dinner was held is that maybe he's in the library, the same place he first bonded with Rae.

But no. It's closed. I look at the sign on the door. It closes at eight. Nightly.

What kind of college library closes at eight? If Reagan had been remotely considering Halsing before, I know this will kill its chances.

"What's the matter?" she asks from the base of the stairs.

"Closed," I admit. I'm out of ideas. I don't know where else Dave would be or how to find him. Heck, I know he's not even there, that it was a stupid choice to begin with. I just wanted to do something nice for Reagan, and instead I've dragged her out into the middle of nowhere for no reason.

I turn and sit on the steps, feeling like an idiot. "I'm

sorry, Rae. This was a stupid idea. Do you want to go home?"

She surprises me by walking up the steps and taking a seat next to me. "Vic?" she says, putting her head on my shoulder.

"Yeah?"

"What are we doing here?"

I exhale slowly. There's no point in lying. I don't like doing it anyway, especially not to Rae. "I thought we might find Dave if we went to another prospectives' weekend at a school with aprogram," I admit quietly, and wince in anticipation of a freak-out.

But there's no response. She's quiet, and one minute of silence stretches into two. Finally, she asks, "What'd you think would happen if we did?"

I shrug, just slightly so as not to displace her head. "I don't know. You just seemed happy with him. You never seem happy with anyone."

"I'm happy with you."

"I don't count."

She loops an arm through mine and squeezes. "Of course you count, Vic," she says softly. "More than anybody."

A lump forms in my throat, and I realize we've already moved off the topic of Dave. But she hasn't actually said it was a bad idea, or that she doesn't care about seeing him again. I decide to let it go, but I haven't given up on finding him. Not yet. Instead, I glance at my watch. "Hey, the hayride doesn't leave for another ten minutes. You wanna go?"

She laughs. "May as well, right?"

I give her arm one last quick squeeze and stand. "Definitely."

An hour later, we teeter up the hill back toward the dorm where Rae's staying, cracking up at nothing and everything and picking straw out of our hair. It sort of blends in with Rae's sunshine-colored curls, and I crack up all over again at the thought of it just hanging out in her hair until her next shower.

She makes a face as she yanks out yet another piece of hay. "This is so gross," she moans. "I feel like I'm covered in horse dung."

"You're not," I assure her. Then I grin wickedly. "You just reek like it."

She yelps and tosses the hay at me, and I toss it back, and we run like that up the hill, so wrapped up in our little straw war that I don't even notice when I practically trample on a guy playing Frisbee with his buddies in the fading light of the sunset. "Whoops!" I blurt, jumping away. It's easy to see from the smile on his face that he's not exactly upset to have been interrupted by two cute girls. "Sorry about that," I say, instantly slipping into flirt mode.

"No apology necessary," says another one of the guys, even cuter than the first. "You ladies wanna join?"

Reagan just looks at me and laughs, so I shrug and say, "Sure!" After all, we have nothing else going on that evening, so we may as well take whatever comes. If that means Frisbee with a cute male trio, so be it. This super-random weekend is all about saying yes!

Three hours later, we've said yes not only to Frisbee, but to joining the guys and their neighbors for a late-night barbecue in their shared yard, followed by beer, ice cream, and a game of tackle football in the bright lights of the quad. The others were mystified by Reagan's and my ability to communicate plays to each other via sign language, and that little advantage went a long way.

"Okay, you have to admit," I say to Reagan as we wash the mud from our faces and arms in the bathroom of the house the guys—Lawrence, Robbie, and Tyrique—share. "This weekend isn't a total wash."

"My knees hurt," she grumbles in response, but she can't help smiling as she presses a wet napkin to them. "I can't believe we just played football. I thought Robbie was going to actually kill me."

It *was* brave of her, considering he's about twice her size. "He totally wouldn't have," I say, examining myself in the mirror one last time. I need a shower. Badly. "He clearly thinks you're cute."

She rolls her eyes. "You think everyone thinks I'm cute."

"Well you *are*," I point out, wiping at a stray fleck of dirt on my collarbone.

Her silence makes me smile. Reagan Forrester is so incapable of taking a compliment, it makes me want to shower her with them, just to watch her cringe.

"I mean," I add, because I can't leave well enough alone, "Dave obviously thought so."

"You're obsessed," is all she says in response. Disappointing. Maybe it's because I'm feeling extra positive about our friendship tonight and how we've turned a night that could've sucked into one of my favorite ones in recent memory, but I feel the urge to get more out of her. So I go back to that place I know I shouldn't.

"Fitz obviously thought so too." I sit down on the edge of the tub and peer at her in the mirror as she dabs a spot of mud from her cheek.

There's a tic in her jaw at the sound of his name, nothing more. "Fitz had a lot of thoughts that were stupid."

"He loved you."

She closes her eyes, her knuckles going white as she grips the tissue in her hand as if it'll hold her steady. "Yeah," she says on an exhale. "In his way. Which was a little too much."

She doesn't offer any more, and I don't ask. I can see

her physically bracing herself for more questions, and her obvious discomfort is enough to shut me up…for now.

"Tori!" a voice hollers down the hall, and I'm pretty sure it's Tyrique. When I hear it again, I know for sure.

"We're coming!" I call back.

"We're going to the lake to set up a bonfire. You guys in?"

I glance at Reagan. She seems lost in thought, but then all at once, she sees me looking, and she snaps back into herself. "Yeah," she says with a slight smile. "I'm in."

There's no being polite about it—the next morning, we look like complete and total horse dung, and we still smell like hay. We're not even hungover, unless still feeling the weight of three hot dogs in my stomach counts. We'd stayed at the guys' house until well after three, then gone back to find ourselves locked out of our guest dorms. We ended up returning to the guys' house and sleeping on their couches. If you can call tossing and turning while looking for lice and cockroaches "sleeping."

"I'm scared to ask for my stuff back," Reagan confides as we approach her guest dorm room the next morning to change our clothes before the campus tour.

"Oh, don't be silly. Are you sure this is the right room?" She nods, and I rap on the door, my chunky rhinestone flower ring making an extra-loud knock that echoes down the hallway, causing Reagan to wince.

A minute later, Brittany—Bethany, maybe? Bella? Isabella?—comes to the door, scowling behind her headgear. "You," she says in a voice dripping with acid. She steps back and points to Reagan's bag in the corner, as if it's a puppy who's been bad. Then she turns on the heel of her bunny slipper, leaving Rae to slip in, grab the bag, and run out like the wind.

Fortunately, my hostess seems a lot less pissed off that I never showed up, and it's a slightly less painful process retrieving my stuff. By the time we grab breakfast for some much-needed caffeine and sugar before heading out to meet the rest of the prospectives for the tour, we're both cracking up laughing at Brittany-Bethany-Bella and her bunny slippers.

Then, abruptly, Reagan's laughter stops.

I follow her gaze, but I have no idea what she's looking at. "Rae?" I wave a hand in front of her eyes. "Everything okay there?"

"Yeah, yeah." She waves her hand dismissively and tries to refocus on our conversation, but it's way too late; I obviously have to know what captured her attention. It takes me another minute, but finally, I see it too.

The high-school sweatshirt Dave was wearing the night I saw him by the soda machine at the motel.

Being worn by a stocky blond kid.

Dave wasn't wearing the sweatshirt to the party, so either he was wearing it when he and Reagan first met or she recognizes the name of his high school on the back. Regardless, although Dave's obviously not the one wearing the navy-blue hoodie, it's the best lead we've had so far.

"Just admit that you want to find out if that kid knows Dave, and I'll do it," I say, keeping my voice low.

She presses her lips together and says nothing, just like I knew she would. Sometimes I think there's stubbornness in her actual bloodstream. But this time, I plan to be just as stubborn.

"You have thirty seconds to take me up on my offer, and then you're on your own."

"*You* are a horrible excuse for a best friend."

"Oh, please. This is the best thing I could possibly do for you and you know it."

She twists her white curl around her finger, yanks it straight, and lets it bounce back. "Fine."

"Fine what?"

"Fine, I wouldn't mind if maybe you found out if that kid knows Dave," she mumbles, so incoherently that if I hadn't been waiting for exactly those words, I wouldn't have understood a single one. I'm feeling nice, so I don't give her the smug smile that's practically forcing itself onto my lips, and instead I simply waltz over to navy-hoodie boy and ask if he indeed goes to Chaplin Prep.

"I...sorry, what?" He looks back and forth between

me and Reagan, then returns his eyes squarely to my boobs.

I reach out and snap my fingers in front of his face. "Up here, Chaplin. Do you go there or not?"

"Uh, yeah." His eyes slip back to checking me out, but I can tell he's trying really hard not to, so I let it go.

"Do you know a guy named Dave Shah?"

"Dave?" His blond brows furrow. Well, it's more like one brow.

"Tall? Skinny? Indian?" Reagan offers.

"Ohh, Dev, yeah." Chaplin looks proud of himself. "I know that kid. Little goofy, ain't he? You could do better. A *lot* better."

As if I would touch that—or him—with a ten-foot pole. "Say I wanted to get in touch with Dave—uh, Dev. How would I do that?"

Chaplin shrugs. "I dunno. I don't have his number or anything."

"What about an e-mail address?" I press. "Do you have school e-mail addresses or something?"

"We're all first initial, last name at Chaplin Prep," he says. "Like I'm SPowalczyk at Chaplin Prep because my name—"

"I got it," I say, reaching into my purse for a gum wrapper or receipt. I fish one of the former out just as Reagan hands me a pen and then I turn Chaplin around and use his back as a surface to write down Dave's e-mail address. "Thanks, S."

"It's Scott."

"Of course it is," Reagan says sweetly. "Goodbye, Scott."

He mutters something under his breath and walks off with a scowl, but I couldn't care less.

Mission accomplished.

CHAPTER EIGHT

REAGAN

I swear, I can still smell that goddamn hay in my hair when my internal alarm clock wakes me up at five on Sunday morning. It's taunting me, trying to shove someone in my brain who wasn't even there for the stupid hayride. It wafts into my nose in curly wisps that read, "E-mail him, Reagan. You know you want to." It converts into sound midair, and it sounds an awful lot like Victoria freaking Reyes, whose snoring is thunderous in my ear right now.

"Damn you, Vic," I mutter aloud, reaching onto the

nightstand next to my side of her bed and crumpling up the gum wrapper with Dave's e-mail address on it in a pathetically false act of defiance to nobody, as I've already got it completely memorized. "You're the one who got it into my head that there's even anything there. He's going to think I'm insane."

I know as soon as those words leave my mouth that I'm going to do it, though *why*, I still have no idea. I need something—anything—to distract me. Unfortunately, after a week of steady computer access at Casa Reyes, I'm actually caught up on work, including the extra assignment Mr. Phelan grudgingly gave me to allow me to pull my grade back up to a solid A. My shift doesn't start for another hour, and nothing on this planet could wake up Vic for another three.

I groan and swing my legs over, sliding out from under the covers to pad over to her computer and boot it up.

Deep breath. Compose new e-mail. *Dear Dave.*

Dev. Why had that kid called him Dev? Is that his real name? Did I even have the right guy? Was it possible this was all a weird coincidence?

Shut up, Reagan. Ugh, Inner Vic Voice. I hate that voice.

"Dear Dave." Or Dev. No, Dave. Why would I call him Dev if he called himself Dave? He *had* said Dave, right? Yes, definitely. Probably. I'm almost sure.

Backspace backspace backspace.

Hey.

Perfect.

You probably don't remember me, but... Pathetic. Backspace backspace backspace. *I met someone who knows you this weekend at Halsing. Thought I'd say hi.*

Now that I've had my best friend freakishly pry your e-mail address from a total stranger.

I take a deep breath and force myself not to delete; I know I'll be there all damn day if I do, and I have corned beef hash to sling to construction workers. *Also, I'm sorry if I was kind of a bitch.*

I contemplate my next line for twenty minutes, and after endless deleting, I just sign my name, click Send, and promptly hate myself.

It's hard to wash off the grime of self-loathing without using all the hot water, but I do my best and then get dressed for work. It's only after I pull my newly washed Joe's polo over my wet hair that I realize there's a new e-mail in my inbox.

From Dave.

Holy shit.

I check my watch, certain that it must be later than I think, but nope, seems he gets up ass-early too. I click open the e-mail.

Hey! Definitely did not expect to hear from you, but glad I did. I was gonna apologize for...whatever I did at breakfast the next morning, but then you weren't there, so…anyway, hi. And sorry. For whatever it is I did. You being pissed at me didn't keep you from reading Lord of the Rings, *right? There's a quiz attached to this e-mail.*

I glance at the header to the e-mail; there's definitely no attachment. I go back to the message.

Please tell me you actually looked. That would make my day.

Dave

Oh, crap. I can *feel* myself smiling uncontrollably. How does he *do* that?

I hit reply.

Of course I looked. And no, for your information, I have not *read* Lord of the Rings, *because it is a massive, stupid book.* And also because I've been spending every waking minute either working at Joe's or trying to keep my GPA at scholarship level, but he doesn't need to hear that. *How do I even know you have decent taste?* Send.

His response comes less than two minutes later. *What,* Battlestar Gallactica *didn't do it for you? My fancy clothes? My taste for fine beer? Man, you are an impossible woman to please! I had a feeling when we met that you were one of those ;)*

My fingers fly across the keys as I write back, and by the time I catch a glimpse of my watch again, I'm twenty minutes late for my shift. I type a frantic explanatory goodbye and race out the door, praying I haven't totally screwed Freckles.

As if enough people in this town don't already hate me over a guy.

"You can stop going insane now, Pepe. I got it. You're sorry you were late. You don't have to scrub down every single table and refill the salt shakers every time someone uses a few grains to prove to me you're a decent worker." Freckles smiles as he points out a spot I've missed, and I immediately attack it with the mildew-y rag in my hand. "Simply giving me half your tips would be plenty."

"Dream on." I toss the rag at his face and then move over to the big sink to wash my hands with soap. I hate that mildew smell; it smells far too much like the trailer after a storm. "But I really am sorry. It won't happen again."

"I know it won't, because you've said that thirty times. I appreciate it, but seriously, covering for you occasionally really isn't that big a deal. Lord knows you've done it for me enough times."

Have I? No instances comes to mind. Regardless, it does help to put my mind at ease.

And with my mind at ease, I start drifting into… thoughts.

And then, without warning, that stupid, stupid smile.

I immediately push past Freckles into the kitchen to get more lettuce for the salad tub, hoping he missed any show of happiness I might've expressed, but the knowing grin on his stupid face when I return tells me A) he definitely did not and B) I'm about to pay for my comments about him and Vic last week.

"*Somebody* looks mighty cheerful all of a sudden," he notes, hefting the bowl from my hands onto the counter. "Does this have something to do with why you were late this morning?"

"I have no idea what you're talking about."

"Oh, I think you do. Did you really think we needed more lettuce? When's the last time anyone in this town ate the side salad? You're trying to avoid my eagle eyes."

"Your eagle eyes see nothing. I had a good weekend away, that's all. It's nice to get out of this place sometimes. Not that you would know."

"Hey, I happen to like this town, thank you very much."

"The town where no one eats a salad?"

"The town where everyone knows me, I have the most chill employer ever, and I'm getting a decent education fifteen minutes from home."

"Did you even look at any other schools besides CCC?"

He opens his mouth to answer, but the bell over the

door dings and cuts him off. The farmhands have arrived. For the next two hours, we serve hash browns and sausage and bacon to leather-skinned men who smell of sweat and cow patties and grunt their thanks between cups of black coffee. My father comes in for an egg 'n cheese to go, and mentions that the power's back on in the trailer, but doesn't ask a thing about my weekend before he takes off with a couple other guys from Myrtle Grove. It's business as usual, and we wipe down tables sticky with syrup and confectioners' sugar and marry bottles of ketchup and mayo in preparation for the lunch crowd.

"No," Freckles says out of nowhere as we're refilling sugar-packet holders.

"No, what?"

"No, I didn't check out any other schools. I knew I didn't want to go anywhere else."

"How?" I stuff in the last packets and cross my arms over my chest. "Tell me. How could you *possibly* want to be in this place for another two years, or however long you're gonna be at CCC?"

He shrugs. "What do you want me to tell you? I know you hate it here; it's basically the worst kept secret in the history of Charytan. But I don't. I may not want to be here forever, but I'm happy to be here right now."

He doesn't sound pissed, just…firm. It makes me sort of jealous, that he likes our hometown enough to be defensive of it. I hope I feel that way about wherever I end up.

"That's cool," I say, and I mostly mean it. I still don't get the Charytan love, but I respect Freckles. "Is it everything you thought it would be?"

"And more," he responds with a grin. The bell tinkles over the door and we both look up and get into "service" mode, but it's only Vic.

"Hey, sunshine," I greet her. "Just saying hi or suddenly desperate for a bacon tuna melt?"

"Can't it be both?" She hops onto a stool at the counter and pulls a menu from the pile. "Or maybe I'll get something more interesting today. How's the…" She scans the menu. "Bacon tuna melt it is."

"Fries on the side?" Freckles double-checks.

"Obviously."

Freckles calls back the order and I pour Vic a fountain cola. "Hey, you do that art project yet?" I ask her as I slide the cup over the counter and toss her a straw.

"Most of it. Still annoyed I can't use any fabric. What am I supposed to do with a painting?"

"What would you do if it had fabric?" Freckles asks.

"Make it cool enough that it's actually worth hanging up." She sucks the pop up through her straw, then caps the top with her finger, admiring the way the bubbly brown liquid settles in the clear tube before she sucks it out the other end. I glance at Freckles; he's watching her lips purse around the straw, and I'm pretty sure he's about to go into conniptions. "So, what'd I miss?"

I wait a moment for Freckles to respond, but he appears to be a little tongue-tied at the moment. "We were just talking about how Freckles didn't visit any schools other than CCC."

"Really? How come?"

"Just knew what I wanted," he mumbles.

The bell dings again, and this time, it actually requires attention; Old Mrs. Webber is impossible when we don't get her standard order of fried catfish, white rice, and steamed string beans exactly right. If you're more than thirty seconds late to bring her a menu—even though it takes her five minutes to wobble to her seat on her ancient cane—she asks to speak to the manager.

Usually, Freckles deals with her, because he's the one who remains impossibly sunny no matter how unpleasant the customer, but now that he's got Vic's attention, I decide to cut him a break. I grab two menus—one for Mrs. Webber and one for her aide-of-the-week, whom she'll inevitably fire for "stealing"—and dash over to greet them.

Behind me, I can hear Vic peppering Freckles with questions, and I love that she's humoring him, even though I know she's not remotely interested in CCC. I doubt she's interested in Freckles, either, and while I'd love for him to get the girl, I can't help being glad for that.

Attachments only make it harder to leave, and when we finally get the hell out of here, it's gonna be on a one-way ticket.

VICTORIA

I've never seen a person with as many freckles on his entire body as Freckles seems to have on just his nose. It's kinda cute. I don't think I actually know any other red-haired guys. There's something so...warm about it all. Safe.

"So, that's it?" I ask, fiddling with my straw as I continue to look at Freckles until he once again meets my eyes. "You just knew what you wanted, and it was CCC, and you didn't even look to see if there was anything else out there?"

"Why does it surprise you so much that I only checked out one option? Aren't *you* only considering one option? College with Reagan or bust?"

My skin grows warm. "Yeah," I respond, hating how stiff I sound, "but we're checking out different schools and stuff. Anyway, college is just one path. People do other things, even if I'm not planning to."

"Of course. Right. Reagan told me your brother's in the Peace Corps, or something like that. Some island?"

"Fiji." I wonder if he's heard of it. I didn't know anything about it until Javi went. Of course, no one in

Charytan has met Javi, either—not even Rae, except on video chat. Sometimes it feels like he only exists in my head.

He doesn't ask where it is, just nods and says, "That's cool. I might like to travel someday."

"Oh yeah? That doesn't interfere in your Charytan-for-life plans?"

I expect him to snipe back, make some sort of joke, but instead he blushes, a deep watermelon pink that makes his freckles stand out like spots on a Dalmatian. Immediately I feel guilty for teasing, but he opens his mouth before I can say so.

"I don't know if I'll be here for life," he mumbles. "I just know I like it right now. Anyway, don't your parents teach at the college?"

"They do."

"So, don't they want you to go there? Obviously they think it's a good enough place to teach."

Anything's good enough when you're just desperate to move somewhere new. The thought immediately makes me feel disloyal, especially since it's certainly not my parents' fault we left Arizona. Not to mention that if Freckles believes CCC is a draw, I don't want to take that away from him. After two years of Reagan's jadedness and my parents' complacency-turned-contentment, it's nice to see actual pride and joy in this town.

"Do you think it's a good school?" I ask instead. "Are

you happy with your classes and stuff?"

"Sure." He shrugs. "I get to take a whole variety of stuff, and it helps a whole lot more with real life than the stuff they make you take in 'real' colleges." The finger quotes are kinda weak, not really angry, just making clear he's heard this argument before and it rolls off his back. "I can already do the books for this place, and as soon as I'm done with this semester, I'll have taken enough business classes for Joe to make me assistant manager. I've even taken a knife skills course so I can help with prep."

"Wow," I whistle, which is literally my only musical skill. "You really do have a lot invested in this place."

His cheeks start to show that tinge again. "Yeah, this place," he mumbles, "or maybe one like it."

And that's when I realize it. Freckles isn't this stay-at-home, happy-to-have-everything-remain-the-same-forever guy. He's got an actual dream, a plan. I suspect even Reagan doesn't know this, and I wonder what she'd say about it if she did. "So, you want to open your own restaurant someday?"

"Maybe." He's not meeting my eyes now. Man, this kid is shy. Have I ever realized how shy he is? Have I ever even had a one-on-one conversation with him before? Suddenly, I can't remember.

"Bacon tuna melt with fries!"

At the sound of Hector calling out my order, Freckles all but bolts. I shake my head and turn to seek out Reagan, surprised to realize how many new customers have flooded the place since Freckles and I started talking. Right now she's taking an order from a family I'm pretty sure isn't seated in her section. Whoops. Maybe I should've let Freckles work instead of asking him a thousand questions.

He returns with my plate, the familiar smells making my mouth water. *Bacon tuna melt, when I leave this place, I think I shall miss you most of all.* I take a big bite, the cheese immediately burning the roof of my mouth. *"Tia Maria!"*

"Cheese burn?" Freckles pushes my soda at me and I immediately take a long, loud sip that does little to soothe the sting. "You never learn, do you?"

Okay, it's possible this happens to me a lot, but I can't help it. They're so freaking good. "Totally worth it," I say, half meaning it.

He grins. It's cute. "Must be. You do it every time you come in here."

"I didn't realize you were noticing," I say without thinking.

The blush comes rushing back with such a vengeance that I'm pretty sure I can feel heat radiating from his skin. If I didn't know better, I'd think I make Freckles kinda... nervous.

Miraculously, he notices then that his coworker is handling an entire diner full of customers on her own.

"I gotta help out," he says apologetically and then

slides out from behind the counter. But before he leaves me completely, he turns and says, "I've got class tonight at six. You're welcome to come with, if you wanna check it out."

My immediate instinct is to say no—what's the point, really?—but I don't wanna offend him after I just embarrassed him. Plus, my mom's teaching tonight, same time slot, and it might be nice to surprise her and then hitch a ride home. "I rode my bike here," I tell him. "Can you fit that in your car somewhere?"

"I've got a bike rack."

"Perfect." I smile before taking a bite of a fry, and I see his eyes move to my mouth.

Okay, it's possible I might've been a tad bit off when I thought he had a crush on Rae.

No matter. Freckles is a local boy, and I'm obviously not gonna be a local girl much longer. I'm just gonna see what's got him so smitten about a community college, surprise my mom, and then hitch a ride back home. No harm, no...whatever.

By the time I take another bite of my sandwich, it's gone cold.

"And down there is the library, and around the corner is the cafeteria." Freckles finishes the grand tour with a flourish of his arm. "And the food doesn't even suck!"

"Well, it's no Joe's, I'm sure."

"Of course not," he scoffs. "Nothing worth burning your mouth over."

I laugh, and he glances at his watch. "Yikes, I'm gonna be late. You sure you don't want to come to class with me?"

"Thanks, but Intro to Microeconomics? Pass."

"It's Macroeconomics."

"What's the—you know what? Never mind. Just go before you're late. And thanks for the tour."

"You've got my number now," he says, waving his phone, "so if you end up needing a ride home…"

"I'll let you know," I assure him.

He smiles, nods, and ducks his head as he jogs down the hall to his class, leaving me alone in what's far more familiar territory than he apparently thinks. Okay, maybe I let him believe I barely knew the place even though I've been here about a zillion times. It *is* my parents' office, after all. I even knew full well that the cafeteria food didn't really suck. But he seemed so happy to show me around, and who am I to rain on his parade?

I wander back slowly in the direction of my mom's classroom, taking my time to look at the flyers on the walls—petitions for new classes, sign-ups for guitar lessons and self-defense… My hands tighten up into fists and I immediately picture myself in one of those karate outfits, facing off against Ashley Martin. I like the way it looks. I picture signing up for it, being one step closer, and I like the way it feels.

The sound of a door slamming in the distance pulls me out of the reverie and I continue on down toward the ASL classroom, with its confusing combination of sign language posters and biblical-themed dioramas, since it's where they teach the Gospels on Sundays. I'm almost there when I hear a familiar trilling.

"Tighter stitching, Kelly! Tight, tight, tight! Don't let that birdie fly away!"

I hide a laugh behind my sleeve and watch from the doorway as Miss Lucy, legendary Fashion Design instructor at CCC for the last gazillion years, flits around the room, tapping students on the shoulder with a stiff measuring tape as they bend over brightly colored fabrics, feeding them through sewing machines. They're shockingly well-equipped for a CCC class, but rumor has it that some rich relative of Miss Lucy's donates something new to the department every year.

I'm about to keep walking when suddenly one of the students holds up what she's been working on and I gasp out loud. It's beautiful. The deep purple-blue shade is unlike anything in my closet, and the complicated beadwork that twines around the single strap and flows seamlessly into the asymmetrical neckline of the Grecian-style gown is nothing short of masterful. A similar, even more complicated pattern belts the drop waist, and just looking at it all, my heart aches that I don't own it, can't put it on immediately and dance around my room.

Of course, the embarrassing sound of my admiration carries, and the whole class looks up to see me standing there, drooling over some stranger's handiwork.

"Sorry," I say, taking a step back, my face growing hot. "That's just…really, really beautiful. The beadwork…it's amazing."

"Maybe from afar," the girl holding the dress says sourly. "Up close, it's a big ol' mess. Look." She pushes it toward me, and I hesitate only a moment before crossing into the classroom and carefully taking the dress from her hands. Yes, up close it's a little clearer that the stitching isn't as even as it could be, that the beads aren't spaced perfectly, but it's still glamorous and glorious and I can't believe such a thing was made in this room, in this community college, in this town.

"Okay, it's not one hundred percent," I concede, "but it's really, really good."

"Michelle is very, very hard on herself," Miss Lucy clucks. "Practice makes perfect, my sweet! Well, practice and a bit more patience. You rushed through the beading here, just as you rushed through the lining. Finishing first isn't finishing best, Michelle."

Michelle bites her lip. "I really thought I had it."

"I know you did, dear, but chiffon is a *very* tricky fabric. We'll practice again next class." As if on cue, the bell rings, and everyone stands and starts putting away supplies, disentangling threads, draping fabrics on mannequins, setting pins, and clearing desks. It's a weirdly pleasant-looking ritual. Michelle half-smiles at me on her way out, and as everyone starts filing out past me, I realize I should leave too. I turn to go, but then I hear Miss Lucy call, "You! Gasper. Stay a minute."

I've met her once, but clearly I'm not all that memorable. Or she doesn't quite have all her marbles. Or both. "I'm sorry if I interrupted."

She waves her hand dismissively. "I've seen you here before."

"I'm Ana and Roberto Reyes's daughter. They both teach here."

It's clear she finds my lineage totally uninteresting. "You've watched my class from the hallway before," she says impatiently. "You're interested in clothing design. Are you considering taking my class?"

She has a slight twang, a little like the accent Reagan's mom puts on, which weirds me out. She sounds sweet but firm at the same time, like I imagine a good teacher should. Like my favorite teacher back in Arizona did, but none of the ones in Charytan do. At CHS, they just sound bored out of their minds, except for Mr. Pratt, my history teacher, who gets really passionate about all the different ways "decent, hardworking folk" (a.k.a. white people) get shafted in this country.

"It's just interesting to see what people are working

on," I say, looking around the class at the half-dressed mannequins. "I'm not…this isn't where I'm going."

She nods, but if she's curious where I *am* going, she certainly doesn't show it. "You don't have to wait until next year, you know," she says over the half-glasses I'm pretty sure are just for show. "We have some high school students take classes here for credit. I'm sure you could arrange something with your school, if you're interested."

Yes, I'm interested! my brain screams, but my mouth feels as if it's been glued shut. This isn't my future. I'm not gonna be one of those CCC kids who never leaves the town, the state, the country. Rae and I have plans. We're gonna see things, do things. We're gonna live together and I'm gonna join a sorority. I'll probably travel some, like Javi. I won't be here forever.

"Thanks," I manage finally, suddenly feeling a burning desire to grab Freckles and have him drive me home. "I'll keep that in mind."

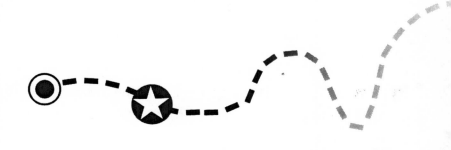

CHAPTER NINE

REAGAN

Things move a lot more smoothly when it's me and Freckles. I like Mitch Macklin okay, on account of he's not a raging asshole like a bunch of other guys in this town, but if he gives a shit about a single thing that doesn't have to do with his band, I have no idea what it is. I'm not sure he's ever even smiled at a customer. He lives in the trailer park next to mine, so I know he needs the cash, but what he's gonna use it for...I have no clue. There's no way he plans to go to college. Mitch is one of those guys who thinks superstardom is gonna pull him out of this place.

Which means he's doomed to stay here for life.

"Little help here?" I try not to snap, but I'm buried under a mountain of onion rings, chili dogs, and cups of pop big enough to use as baby bathtubs, while he rocks back and forth on a stool behind the counter, "manning the register" even though no one's lining up to pay, tapping his fingers in a frantic drumbeat on his ripped jeans.

He stands slowly, as if I've bothered him in the middle of something very, very important to ask his opinion on my outfit, and grabs one dish in each hand, leaving me to balance the remaining four on sweaty palms and in elbow crooks, even though the Krogers are seated entirely in Mitch's section.

Whatever. Not like I have anything better to do. I carefully place all four dishes in front of the respective Krogers, pretending not to notice when Billy, whom I used to babysit for, sticks his nose down my shirt when I bend over to place chicken nuggets in front of his little sister. If I could've felt any dirtier after spending my day running around in grease fumes and cleaning endless blobs of ketchup off of every conceivable surface, that would've done it.

"Can I get you folks anything else?" I ask in my super helpful voice, which has never been used outside these four walls.

"Mayo," Jeff Kroger grunts, not bothering to make eye contact even though he's worked with my dad for at least ten years. Of course, there's already mayo on his burger and in a little cup on his plate, but okay.

"Extra mayo, coming right up."

"And sugar!" the youngest one, whose name I can't remember, pipes up. I can't imagine what on earth she wants sugar for, but her parents don't say anything, so I just nod. "Mayo and sugar."

The girl giggles. "Gross."

"Where are my fries?" Billy demands.

"Fries don't come with chili dogs. If you want them as an additional side, I can place that order for you."

I brace myself for the tirade I know is coming, because it comes every time someone in Charytan is informed that something doesn't automatically come with fries. Never mind that they've all been coming to the same diner for years and should know the menu by heart, since it's all some of them read in a year. Of course, Candy Kroger doesn't disappoint.

"You want me to pay *extra* for fries that should come with it in the first place? Well, isn't that nice," she spits. "Just gouge every hardworking person in this town for every last nickel and dime…"

It's nothing I haven't heard before, and I tune it out like a pro. The chili dog costs a whopping two bucks. If you can't afford fries on top of that, maybe you shouldn't have four fucking children, all of whom have to share a room. My parents may have a lot of faults, but at least overpopulating our trailer isn't one of them. The thought warms me to them a little as I glance around the diner, waiting for her to finish and give up. Joe was very explicit on multiple occasions that we're not to entertain fry-seeking conspiracy theorists.

Then my gaze lands on the couple walking through the door and suddenly I have a burning desire to focus all my energy on Candy Kroger.

The hairs on the back of my neck stand up as Quinn Fitzpatrick and the freaking lumberjack she's with take a seat in my section. I don't know what the hell she's doing here with a guy like Luke Schmidt; she's far too young to be on a date, let alone with a guy who's only a year behind me at CHS. I wonder if she's forgotten I work here.

"I'll get you fries on the house," I say, knowing it's absolutely the wrong way to approach the situation but desperate to get back behind the counter and away from Quinn and Paul Bunyan. "Fries, mayo, and sugar. I'll be back soon."

The fries will have to come out of my own pocket, but I don't even care; *anything* to get away from the back of Quinn's head. How much time have I spent behind that head, braiding the wheat-colored strands as if she were my own personal Barbie doll? I know the feel of that hair like I know my own—maybe even better since I'd never really paid much attention to mine. But Quinn loved having people play with her hair, almost as much as she loved when Johnny—*Fitz*—used to run around, spinning her in the air, making noises as if he were a helicopter.

It's been months since I've seen her, and even that was only from a distance at Christmas mass. The Fitzpatricks don't do Sunday night dinners at Joe's anymore, not since…everything. And even now, it still feels far too soon.

"Where are you going?" Mitch demands as I head into the back room as if mayo isn't readily available in multiple squeeze bottles sitting right in front of my face.

I ignore him. Maybe if I hide out back here for long enough, he'll just go ahead and take my tables. I tell Hector to get another order of fries going and then take my sweet time "hunting down" the sugar packets I know are already on the counter. A few minutes later, he dings the bell to let me know the fries are ready, and when I take them out, it's obvious by the impatient look on Quinn's face and the way Lumberjack Luke is tapping on their table that Mitch hasn't so much as given them menus.

I stalk past where he's set himself up behind the counter again, snatching two menus as I go. I toss them onto Quinn's table without making eye contact before delivering the Krogers' demands. I don't get so much as a thank-you from the family, but as I spin on the heel of my sneaker I hear a rough voice call out, "Hey, Waitress. We know what we want."

Fucking. Asshole. Luke and I may never have spoken, but he's a Charytan lifer too; he damn well knows my name. But it doesn't stop him from snapping his stupid fingers in my direction. I shuffle over, resisting the urge to reach out and crush that hand. Instead, I simply raise my notepad. "What can I get you?"

"Bacon cheeseburger, extra fried onions, cheese fries on the side." AKA the Heart Attack Special, though that could refer to any number of things on the menu. He pokes Quinn in her ribs. "My girl can handle a little onion breath."

His *girl*? Oh, hell no. He's gotta be at least sixteen; Quinn's still in eighth grade. That's…that's…

Exactly how old Fitz and I were when we started dating.

The thought nearly brings me to my knees, and I want to know that they're not doing what we were doing at that age more than I want to take my next breath. I finally force myself to look at Quinn, but she staunchly refuses to make eye contact.

"What about you, Quinn?" I demand, willing her to look at me, just long enough so I can mouth "run" or "stop" or "don't you dare lose your virginity to this finger-snapping asshole" but there's nothing. Literally no reaction to my presence.

Finally, Luke smirks and says, "She'll have a salad."

I snort before I can stop myself. Quinn may be small

but it's completely deceptive; the girl can seriously pack away the grub when she wants to. Though, actually, looking at her now, she's a whole lot skinnier than I remember. Taller too, I think, but who knows; to me, everyone's a friggin' giant. I know after five seconds of waiting for her to jump in and correct him that it's not going to happen, so I just say, "One salad, coming up," and walk back to give the order to Hector, trying to ignore the fact that my notepad is literally shaking in my hand.

"Can I borrow your phone for a minute?" I ask Mitch after I place lumberjack's order.

"Don't you have your own?"

"Not a smartphone. Please. I just want to send a quick e-mail to a friend."

He shrugs and digs his phone out of his pocket, his guitar-calloused fingers brushing over my palm as he hands it over. Immediately, I open up my e-mail and type in Dave's address.

I'm angry at myself for my neediness even as I do it, but I can't help it—I need. I have never felt so invisible in my entire life and all I can think about right now is the way Dave looked at me—really looked at me—that night at the party. The way his eyes raked down my entire body.

I am desperate to feel that again.

Hey, are you gonna be at the Barnaby State thing this weekend?

My heart pounds as I hit Send. A few feet away, Mitch

taps his foot, waiting for his phone's safe return, but then someone in his section calls him over and it gives me another minute to wait. Fortunately, Dave takes no longer.

Yup! I'll be there with a few friends. You going?

Yup, I write back. *Guess I'll see you there.* I'm about to send the response when a wave of boldness washes over me. *PS, I don't have a smartphone (borrowed a friend's to e-mail you) but you can text me at (785) 555-7107.*

Less than a minute later, my own phone buzzes in my pocket, and the very act of pulling it out to read his text—*Is it uncool to bring a Neil Gaiman novel to a frat party?*—makes my palms damp. Knowing Quinn is in the diner, in burger-throwing distance of where I'm exchanging messages with a guy who is *not* her brother, makes me feel like the world's biggest slut.

But it doesn't stop me from texting him, *I think it offends them if you bring your own copy rather than accepting the one they hand out at the door.* Nor from texting Vic, *Looks like we'll have some company this weekend!* It certainly doesn't stop me from smiling as I hand Mitch back his phone with a warm thanks.

But it *does* stop me from feeling like I want to sink into the floor, dissolving into the speckled linoleum for all eternity. So for right now, I'm gonna go with it.

"This is going to be epic," Vic declares for the billionth

time that drive, waving a hand she'd just polished in the bathroom at a rest stop out the window to speed up the drying process. Never mind that I'm practically shivering behind the wheel. "You and Dave reunited, a school with a decent art program, and of course, brand-new boys to meet." She blows on her other hand, and I'm embarrassed to admit that I sort of wish I'd let her do my nails when she offered. Hers are blood-red and look sexy and sophisticated. Mine are so gnawed down to the tips, I look like I got a manicure at Jurassic Park.

"I love that once again, there's no mention of classes or actually seeing the campus."

"Oh, please, as if you're giving a single thought to *anything* about this weekend other than seeing Dave again," she says smugly before blowing on her nails again. "You're fooling nobody, Forrester."

I know I should argue with her, but I can't even get the words out. My brain is mush. It is ridiculous how excited I am to see an impossibly lanky nerd extraordinaire, but so help me God, I am. We've been texting all week about what we're gonna do and see and sometimes just about nothing at all. For someone who didn't even have a cell phone until a year ago, it's crazy that I'm not even sure I could fall asleep now without seeing the words "G'night, Rogue" flash on my screen before shutting my eyes.

Instead of responding, I decide to turn it around. "How about you?" I tease as I switch lanes. "Did you have a wonderful time at CCC? Are you leaving me for a lifetime of bacon tuna melts at Joe's with Freckles?"

I expect her to laugh and snipe back, but the only response is an incredibly loud silence before she finally says, "Ha ha," and then reaches over to turn up the volume so she can sing along with whichever boy band is assaulting my eardrums right now.

I let it go. I'm too wired to care about anything right now. I could listen to these prepubescent boys sing about foreign policy if I had to. Charytan isn't even a speck in my rearview mirror, I'm less than an hour away from seeing Dave and checking out a new school, and I don't have to think about work or home or anyone in the Fitzpatrick family for the next forty-eight hours.

Life suddenly feels pretty damn good.

Even with a little bit of traffic, and a lot of circling to find a spot, we're at registration with time to spare. We give in our names and get packets with badges, a map, a course catalog, and an itinerary of prospective students' weekend in return. Everything is neat and organized and I like Barnaby already. The only problem is that I've yet to see Dave and his friends.

And then suddenly, from a couple lines over, I hear it: "Devarajan Shah." I turn just in time to see Dave get handed his packet. The guy behind him then steps up for his, but he may as well be on mute; I'm still processing Dave's—Dev's—real name and trying to wrap my mouth around the sounds.

He looks up just then and catches me mid-effort, and then, like magic, there's that smile, lighting up the entire room. It is the whitest thing I've ever seen, even whiter than my streak or my arms in mid-January. I couldn't stop myself from smiling back if I wanted to, even though I suddenly feel incredibly shy. I wave just slightly, a meek little flutter, forcing myself to restrain my excitement in the crowd of prospectives eager to get their badges in time for the Mocktails Mixer tonight.

"Is that Dave?" I hear Vic say, and I start to answer when I see the guy who'd been behind Dev in line pull him back by his shoulder. Just like that, he's gone from my line of sight.

"It was. And it really is Dev, apparently." I stand on my tiptoes but I'm still way too short to see over the lines between us. "I don't know where he went. Some guy just pulled him away."

"So let's go outside. Text him to come meet us. I'm getting claustrophobic in this place anyway."

We make our way out, Vic rolling her eyes at me as I pin my badge to the faded Bikini Kill tee she got me for my last birthday, and I pull out my phone to text Dev but then realize he's already beat us outside. He's standing with the guy who'd pulled on his arm—an Asian dude with funky glasses—and another kid who's almost as skinny as Dev but considerably shorter and practically drowning in a mop of brown curls.

Vic starts to walk over, but I hesitate to follow. It's weird to see him in the context of his real life. I didn't really think of him having one, to be perfectly honest. But he does, and it includes friends I don't even know. Friends he's tight enough to visit colleges with the way I'm doing with Vic. How can I think there's anything between us when I don't even know his friends?

She turns, obviously having realized I wasn't following her. "What's with you?" she mouths.

"Nothing," I mouth back, wishing we weren't laden down with welcome materials so we could sign, the way we usually do when we don't want people around to hear our conversations. I square my shoulders and force myself to stop acting like such a wimp. He's just a guy, and we're just friends. There's nothing to stress about here.

Still, I hang slightly behind Vic as she walks over to the guys, knowing her naturally (she insists) swaying hips will pretty much block me out completely. "Hey," I hear her say. I peek out from behind her. "Fancy meeting you here."

The other two guys kind of gape at her, but Dev smiles—not one of his full-wattage ones, just a little one that doesn't even show his teeth. I step out a little more, wondering if maybe he doesn't see me, but he waves just slightly, at each of us. My stomach drops; this so isn't the reunion I had in mind. Where's the dimple? The hug?

"You know her?" the floppy-haired guy asks Dev in disbelief. Judging by the awe on his face as he takes Vic in from head to toe, either he thinks she's a supermodel or he's literally never seen a girl before. Lord knows I do not exist in his vision, even though I've fully emerged now.

"This is…Tori, right?" Dev asks, his lips quirking just a bit. Vic nods. "And this is Reagan." He gestures in my direction. "We met at another prospective weekend, at Southeastern."

I wait for some sort of recognition to alight in one of his friends' eyes, but there's nothing.

"Jamie Goldstein. Nice to meet you," says glasses-wearing Asian boy. The other guy continues to stare wordlessly at Vic until glasses guy jabs him in the ribs.

"Goldstein?" I can't help asking. Not that I know any Jews, but Jamie looks a little…Asian to be one.

"You were expecting something more like Chang?" he asks wryly, and I feel like an idiot.

"I'm sorry," I say immediately. "I didn't mean—"

Dev holds up a hand and rolls his eyes. "Ignore him, Reagan. Jamie's just being a dick because he finds it amusing. He's adopted, though why anyone would voluntarily take in this jerk, I have no idea."

"Ha ha," says Jamie, but he grins, and it's obvious this exchange has happened before. I exhale and narrow my eyes.

"You guys are delightful," I inform them.

"We know," says Dev, and this time his smile shows teeth. "You guys going to the mixer thing later?"

"Of course." Vic flips her hair over her shoulder, and the guy who still hasn't revealed his name looks like he's going to have a stroke. "I never miss the opportunity to down a vodka cranberry, hold the vodka."

"Great, then I guess we'll see you there." The words out of Dev's mouth are friendly enough, but I can't help but feel like we're being dismissed.

"Yup, I guess so," I say tightly, grabbing Vic's arm. "Have fun on your visit." I steer her away and we walk toward the center of campus, neither of us looking backward at the guys.

"What was that?" she whispers when we're far enough away to be out of both earshot and vision. "I thought you guys talked about the fact that you were coming."

"We did." I look up at the trees. The leaves are just turning dappled with the shades of autumn, and they make for an excellent distraction from making eye contact with Vic. "Turns out, we're a lot less awkward via text, I guess." I shrug. "Maybe he remembered me looking different, or something."

"Oh, that is so not the issue. Some guys are just weird in front of their friends. Who knows." She pulls my arm so I stop walking and forces me to turn and look at her. "Doesn't matter. We have hot outfits picked out for tonight, and when we show up to that mixer, either

Dev's gonna fall over himself when he sees you, or we'll know he's not into girls."

"Yes, because those are the only two options."

"Trust me," she says, flicking my white streak with a smile, "they are. Now come on. Let's go get all dolled up for some mocktails."

I still can't believe I agreed to let Vic dress me up for this stupid thing. I'd been high on the attraction I'd clearly been making up in my own head and the thrill of getting out of Charytan yet again, but now, looking in the mirror, I could plainly see the consequences of my temporary insanity.

Not that I looked bad in the dress she'd selected for me. On the contrary, what was a tiny, should-be-illegal, tight-as-a-bandage dress on her is actually a fairly respectable strapless black dress that comes to a couple of inches above the knee on me.

No, the bigger problem is that while she could find a dress of hers that worked on my smaller frame, there's no way to get my size-five feet in any of her size-eights, and I own exactly four pairs of shoes: my holey tennis shoes, flip-flops, hand-me-down red rubber rain boots, and a pair of combat boots I'd bought from the Salvation Army with my very first paycheck. I used to have a pair of heels from Target, for cousins' weddings and the random church visit when my dad gets in one of his phases, but then one of the heels snapped off and damn if I'm gonna pay ten bucks to restore shoes I always hated to begin with.

"I cannot believe you're actually wearing those," Vic says with a sigh.

"I told you I would be." I tighten the laces on the combat boots and tie them into bows as neatly as I can. "You wanted to dress me up anyway."

"You look like Baghdad Barbie."

"Hey, at least the red laces are festive."

"Sometimes I think you might actually be hopeless." She presses her lips together and looks me up and down. "*Maybe* with the right makeup—"

"No makeup. I've told you a billion times, Vic, no makeup."

"Just lipstick!"

"I have cherry Chapstick, thank you very much."

"How about eyeliner?"

"You are not sticking a pencil near my eye."

"Mascara?"

"No."

"Ryan Gosling naked on a sheepskin rug?"

"N—obviously."

"Damn, so close." She walks over to the mirror in our motel room and carefully rims her eyes in liner. "So, we're gonna have fun at this thing even if Dev continues to be weird, right?"

"Right."

"Good. For being a trooper, maaaybe I'll even go to class with you tomorrow."

"You? Class? Voluntarily?" My fake gasp is probably loud enough to be heard through the thin walls. "You are just full of surprises."

"Well, now's a good time to prove to me that you are too." She caps her eyeliner and whirls around. "Don't give up too easily, Rae. I know you want to, that you probably already have in your mind, but don't you dare. I better see a solid effort from you when it comes to this boy."

"What's even the point? We barely know each other, we live nowhere near each other—"

"Oh, hush. When you feel it, you feel it." She unscrews a tube of mascara and sets to work on her lashes. "Besides, you've checked out a couple of the same colleges now; for all you know, you'll end up at the same place next year. And don't even pretend that thought hasn't crossed your mind. You're not that good a liar."

Apparently not.

"You sure you don't want some?" She screws the cap back on the mascara and holds it out to me.

I nod firmly. I'm unsettled enough by the unfamiliar setting, Dev's weirdness, and wearing Vic's clothes. The last thing I want is something else to throw me off my game. Unlike "Tori" and I guess "Dave," I have no desire to be someone else in college. I just want to be me some*where* else.

Plus, I've tried mascara. It looks weird over my white eyelash.

She slicks on some lip gloss, smacks her lips together, and turns to me. "How do I look?"

"Perfect." She really does. She always does. And in those tightass jeans, high heels, and low-cut tank under a blazer, all of which she's added her own personal Vic-esque touches to, I suspect her perfection is going to send Dev's mime friend into cardiac arrest. As ridiculous as I'm going to look in this dress and boots, standing next to Vic is only going to make me look worse. Good thing she makes it worth it.

"Why thank you, Reagan, dear." She wipes a little gloss from her teeth and smiles. "You ready to go?"

I'm tempted to say no, but instead, I check myself out in the mirror. I do look a little like Baghdad Barbie. And apparently like Rogue, too. With a combo like that, how can I *not* kick ass? Dev Shah or no Dev Shah, I'm going to have a damn good time tonight.

And if not? Well, it's a mixer centered around mocktails. If drinks can fake it, then dammit, so can I.

"Tell me again about how fun this is gonna be," I beg Vic in a whisper as we make our way to Prentice Hall with painstaking slowness to accommodate Vic's massive heels. I spare her my mocking because they look awesome and seriously, who the hell am I to be trashing someone else's footwear choice right now?

"*Very,*" she says confidently, grabbing my arm as she wobbles just a bit. "Because if it sucks, we'll just find the guy who's inevitably carrying around mini bottles of vodka and *make* it fun." She tightens her grip around my bare arm, taking care not to muss the red ribbon belt she'd tied around "my" dress to fix the fit and match the laces of my combat boots.

"How do you know that guy will be there?"

"Because that guy is *always* there." With her free hand, she swings the door wide open, and we both point to our name badges, which couldn't look dorkier but are required for entrance. "Do you see Dev yet?"

"I don't see *anything* yet." I stand on my tiptoes, which does all of nothing. "What are you, six feet in those things? You're definitely gonna have to be our lookout."

"Fair point." She cranes her neck and scans the crowd, and I can tell she's either spotted them or found a really hot guy because her lips widen into a sly smile. "Jackpot." She turns to me. "Okay, now remember, play it cool, but don't go down without a fight."

"What does that even mean? Stop mixing messages."

She sighs. "It means *play* hard-to-get but don't *be* hard-to-get."

"I don't want to *play* anything. The reason I *like* him is because we click without any games."

We both freeze, silent, my words hanging over us both. *I like him.* I don't even remember the last time I said those words. But I can certainly guess who I said them about. Icy fingers curl around the nape of my neck and I look away from Vic.

"This was a mistake," I mutter, wishing I'd had the forethought to bring my own mini vodka bottle. I start toward the table of drinks when suddenly a tray is thrust in my face.

"Piña colada? Strawberry daiquiri?" The bright-eyed, bushy-tailed sucker walking around with the drink tray doesn't look as if she'll leave until I snatch a glass, so I mumble thanks and grab a strawberry daiquiri. It's sickeningly sweet and as soon as I take a couple of sips, I start looking around for a place to put it down.

"Hey, you."

I freeze in place with glass in hand as Dev approaches. He's the most dressed-up I've seen him yet, in khakis and a blue button-up shirt. He looks nice. Tall. Respectable. I feel even more like an idiot in my borrowed dress and mismatched footwear. "Hi."

"Interesting outfit."

"Wish I could say the same."

He laughs. "Fair enough. I don't clean up quite as nice as you do."

"You didn't say nice," I point out. "You said interesting."

"Both nice and interesting," he amends with a nod. "The combat boots really do add a special touch."

As much as I hate compliments, they're a whole lot better than his neither-here-nor-there responses to me. Fitz always made sure to tell me I looked good on those rare occasions I actually put on a dress. I can practically hear him say, "You look cute, babe," his words slightly garbled by chewing gum.

"Hey, you okay?"

I don't even realize I've been spacing out until I feel Dev's hand on my bare arm. It's weird and unfamiliar, less calloused than Fitz's hands used to be. Then again, Dev probably doesn't play baseball for hours a day or spend weekends smoothing concrete.

"Yeah, I'm fine." I take another sip of my sugary drink. "It's just really crowded in here."

"Claustrophobic? Agoraphobic?"

"Short."

He cracks a smile. "Well, I'm right here. I'll watch out for you."

Oh yeah? Even when your friends come back? I slip the straw between my teeth so I won't speak the words, and chew on it instead of drinking any more. "Appreciated," I say around the red plastic.

"Least I can do. So is that drink any good? I haven't gotten one yet."

I release the straw. "Actually, it's pretty gross. Like

sugar water."

"Mmmm." He leans forward and captures the straw in his lips, right over where my mouth used to be. It feels like we've just kissed secondhand, except that's idiotic and doesn't exist and why am I sort of turned-on right now? "Totally disgusting." He takes the glass out of my hand, brushing my fingers as he does, and turns to set it on a table. "Better luck with piña coladas?"

I shrug. "Show me the way."

We walk through the crowd, his hand on the small of my back as we search for glasses of frothy white concoctions with cocktail umbrellas. His touch is light, not firmly protective the way Fitz's used to be in similar situations, but it feels impossibly hot through the fabric of the dress. His pinky is dipping dangerously close to skimming somewhere it shouldn't. Well, probably shouldn't. Not that I'd be terribly angry about it.

Someone bumps us from behind and tosses back an apology, but all I can think as Dev's entire body collides lightly with mine is, *Don't step back. Stay right where you are and wrap your arms around my waist and just hold me in place, just for a minute, just like this.*

He does step back, but not before steadying me by the backs of my arms and bending down so I can feel him whisper before I even hear the words, "Are you okay?"

No, my brain whispers back, deafening over the din of the room. *I am definitely not okay.*

VICTORIA

"So I'm probably gonna get a basketball scholarship here, and then it doesn't really matter what I major in, right?" The guy currently fascinating me while he sips from an embarrassingly decorative neon-green drink is named either Don or John, but he's had a piece of pineapple stuck in his teeth the entire time he's been flirting with me and I can't think of him as anything other than Aloha. "I figure I'll probably do English. I mean, how hard is that, right? I speak it and whatever."

"Right, right." My piña colada is down to the crushed-ice dregs. It's not particularly good, but it gives me something to do with my hands and mouth every time another one of these guys gets in my airspace. I internally ream Reagan for leaving me, even though that was obviously always the plan for whenever Dev showed up.

Whatever made him weird before is gone now; he clearly wants her pretty bad, even though I'd bet an entire car ride of listening to Courtney Love that she doesn't see it. Whatever. I know that "any excuse to touch her" move. That used to be Andrew Hollister's favorite move. And it worked for him; he was my first kiss.

"What about you?" Aloha asks, taking another sip of the slime-colored drink. "You majoring in Psychology? Chicks always major in Psychology."

"Astrophysics, actually." I smile sweetly as soon as the

lie is out of my mouth. I may or may not have stolen that from Reagan. Instant conversation killer.

"Oh, uh, cool. Is that, like, with lasers and shit?"

I nod and sip simultaneously. I have no freaking clue what Astrophysics is. I'm guessing it doesn't involve sequins.

"Awesome."

"Yep."

I'm working on an exit line when suddenly I feel an arm wrap around my shoulders and hear, "There you are! I brought you a drink."

It's Dev's friend Jamie, the kind-of-a-jerk guy. His fingers are digging into my shoulder so hard I'd probably mash my heel into his foot if he weren't saving me from the stupidest conversation of my life right now. I glance behind us and see that buddy number three is hanging back, probably checking out my butt. The kid might be quiet but he's not subtle.

"Thanks so much, sweetheart." I don't really know what I'm supposed to do with a second drink so I just let him hold it. Then I turn back to Aloha. "It was really nice to meet you."

He mutters something back and leaves me alone with the jerk and the horny mute. "You're welcome." Jerky Jamie looks seriously proud of himself.

"Yeah, thanks sooo much for saving me from the hot guy!" Okay, my sarcastic gushing might be a little mean considering he *did* save me, but he has total smugface right now. Not that my sarcasm dims it even the tiniest bit.

"Please, if you were so into the hot guy, you would've told me to fuck off."

"There's still time."

He just smiles and sips the frosty blue drink that was probably never for me in the first place. "So, what's the deal with your friend?"

"Hot guy?"

"Blondie."

"She has a name." I nod my head toward Horny Mute. "Does he? Or does he just stand there and stare at boobs all day? Specifically mine?"

Horny Mute blushes, and I feel sort of bad, but my sympathy drains quickly when he fails to actually lift his eyes from the scoop neck of my tank top. I hope he's at least appreciating the asymmetrical abstract embroidery I added to the neckline with metallic thread.

"It's a compliment," Jerky Jamie actually has the nerve to say.

I ignore him in favor of going back to work on my piña colada, scanning the room to see if I can figure out which guy is toting around airplane-friendly bottles of Smirnoff, when suddenly, one is thrust in my face.

Of *course* Jerky Jamie is that guy.

He dangles the bottle in front of me, but I refuse to

grab it. I don't need alcohol to improve this party; I need better company. "Thanks, but no thanks." I push aside the skinny red straw in my drink and down the rest, then wipe my mouth off on the back of my hand.

"Would you rather dance?" he asks as I put my glass down.

"The dance floor's totally empty." *Ouch.* The cold rush of downing all the icy liquid has gone to my head, and I squint against the brain freeze. I regret it a second later when I realize the jerk is actually laughing at me.

Reagan may have the sharp tongue but I've got the look of death. As I flash it at Jamie, I'm pretty sure I can see his junk shrivel up and die. Mission accomplished, I turn on my heel and head away from Dev's creepy friends, curious as to where their leader has taken *my* friend.

I pull my cell phone out of my back pocket and check it for texts. There's just one, from my mom. *How's it going with Reagan and Prince Charming?*

I can't help grinning. My mom is such a nosy gossip. *Trying to see for myself,* I type back. *They disappeared a while ago.* My super-high heels allow me to see over a lot of the crowd, but there's no sign of them anywhere in the room. If they're outside making out…

My phone buzzes again. *Make sure you girls keep an eye on each other! And you better be having fun too, not just Reagan! Love you.*

Love you too. I hit Send and then start a new text, this

one to Reagan. *U OK?* Without waiting for a response, I slip my phone into my back pocket, knowing I'll feel the vibration on my butt when she gets back to me. Then I glance around again for people who actually look worth mingling with at this thing. I see a small group of girls in cute outfits sipping pink drinks and flirting with a couple of decent-looking guys. Perfect. I take a step in that direction, and immediately collide with a drink tray.

"*Tia Maria*, that's cold!" I jump back, just in time to hear at least two glasses go crashing to the floor. And then, as if things couldn't get any worse, I feel a hand yanking me back by my arm and pressing napkins to my now-soaking-wet chest. Of course, the superhero team of Horny Mute and Jerky Jamie have returned.

"Are you okay?" Jamie asks, almost sounding sincere as he swipes at a blob of mockgarita on the lapel of my beautiful—and now ruined—blazer. He turns to glare at the server, who's pushing people back away from the shattered glass, his own bright-red T-shirt miraculously spotless. "Some people need to watch where they're going."

"It wasn't his fault," I tell Jamie, though I'm not sure whether or not it's true. "I'm the one who wasn't watching. Sorry about that," I add to the server, but he's not really paying any attention to me.

Jamie just makes a disgusted face, and then snaps to Horny Mute, "Okay, Max, I think her tank top's probably dry by now."

It isn't, but having Max paw at me isn't really helping. At least I've finally got a name to put to the skeevy face. I yank the napkins from his hand, go for one last halfhearted swipe, and then give up with a sigh. This whole outfit is toast. And of course, just as I find a trash can to toss my soaking wet napkins into, my butt buzzes.

Yes! Sorry! I'm right outside with Dev. Find Jamie and Max and come hang out!

Ugh, all I want to do right now is go back to the hotel, shower this strawberry mess off, and have a little pity party for my once-awesome jacket, which I got on super sale on a family vacation in Scottsdale. I am officially over both mocktails and mingling.

"Is that Reagan?" Jamie asks, peering over my shoulder.

I almost snap that it's none of his business, but considering she told me to find him, I guess it sort of is. It doesn't hurt that when he's not being a jerk, he's not the *most* unattractive guy on the planet, if you like that tough-nerd kind of look, which I hadn't known existed before right this minute. "Yeah. She says they're outside and we should go meet them."

He shrugs. "Cool." He starts to walk toward the door and then pauses and shrugs off his jacket. "Here."

He's wearing nothing on top now but a T-shirt with a math equation on it that I refuse to even attempt to read. It's just as well since I'd rather not notice the fact that he fills it out a *lot* better than I would've expected. Where the heck does a math nerd get pecs like that?

"Thanks, but I'm fine," I insist. What I'd actually love is a different shirt to put on, but there's not much he can do for me there. Frankly, I'd rather he cover back up so I can go back to ignoring his stupid body. He doesn't protest, just slips his jacket back on. Then we walk to the door in silence with Max in tow until Jamie turns to me just before we hit the door.

"Did you say *Tia Maria* when the waiter dropped those drinks on you?"

"Got a problem with that?"

The corner of his mouth turns up. "Nope."

"I try not to swear." Not that I owe him an explanation.

"I gathered," he says with a smile. "Good Catholic girl?"

"Not-so-good Jewish boy?"

The smile turns smug. "Something like that." He pushes open the door then, letting me and Max walk through into the cool night air. We spot Dev and Reagan immediately, sipping drinks and laughing on a bench a few feet away. They're so cute I don't want to disturb them, but Jamie has no such reservations, and he storms right over, leaving Max and me no choice but to follow.

"You shouldn't leave her alone," Jamie says to Reagan, jerking a thumb at me. "Girl's good at getting herself into trouble."

"'Girl' can handle herself," Reagan replies before I can say a word. Then she takes a closer look at me and frowns. "Oh no!" She hands Dev her drink and jumps up to examine the stain on my top with chipped black-painted fingertips. "What happened?"

"Collision with a waiter. No biggie. What'd I miss out here?"

"Just Reagan losing an argument about who's cooler, Hermione or Lyra," says Dev.

She rolls her eyes. "He means that he thinks picking the obvious choice is a safe bet, and he's sorely mistaken."

I have no idea what they're talking about, but they slip right back into their debate and just like that, it's as if they're alone again.

Jamie rolls his eyes at me. "So this is what they're like?"

"Far as I can tell."

"Are you sure you don't wanna dance?"

Not nearly as sure as I was five minutes ago. "What about Max?"

Jamie nods at where Max has made himself comfortable on the bench and is frantically typing away on his phone. "Looks like his Internet girlfriend is back online. Trust me when I say he won't notice where any of us are for hours."

The same definitely seems true for Dev and Rae. Even my obnoxiously loud sigh doesn't make any of the three of them look up.

"Yeah, okay, fine," I say to Jamie. "But first, think we could find me a sink?"

The bright side of mocktails, I realize the next morning as I wake up squinting against the sun streaming the window of our motel room, is that despite the fact that I somehow stayed up with Reagan and the guys until almost 3:00 a.m., I'm blissfully hangover-free.

Of course, that doesn't stop me from wanting to throw my phone—with its blaring alarm—against the wall.

"What time is it?" I groan, reaching out to shut it up.

"Time for breakfast," Rae grumbles back, just barely lifting her head off the pillow. She swings her legs around the side of the bed. "You probably need your energy after flirting your ass off with Jamie until dawn."

"We are not even out of bed and you're making fun of me," I manage around a yawn. "I think that's a new record." The blanket is scratchy as I claw my way out of bed and stretch out every limb. "Plus, I wasn't *flirting* with Jamie. And who are you to talk? You were practically in Dev's lap all night."

She sticks out her tongue as she sails past into the bathroom, shutting the door loudly behind her. From the nightstand, my cell phone chimes with a text. I check it—another text from my mom. *Good morning, sweetie. Forgot to mention last night that you got a letter from Javi. I got one too. He sounds busy! Have fun today!*

The ache in my chest is swift and sudden. I don't want to eat scrambled eggs with a bunch of other prospectives; I want to open a letter from my brother and see what he's up to, see if this letter is the one that finally mentions coming home.

Of course, I also want classic black patent Louboutins, but what I want is irrelevant.

I dig into my bag and find my favorite dress—made by yours truly out of a gray turtleneck and a bunch of vintage T-shirts—and prep the rest of my outfit while I wait for Reagan to come barreling out of the bathroom. As soon as she does, I hop into the shower and take my sweet time thinking about spending the day meeting people who *aren't* obnoxious flask-toting nerds.

"How are you taking so long?" Rae whines through the door. "You *just* showered like four hours ago!"

"Don't hate me because I'm beautiful!" I call back, but I turn off the water and reluctantly step out to get dressed.

"I don't know how you're ever gonna roll out of bed and get to class when we're actually in college," says Reagan as we hustle to the building in which the breakfast is being held.

"I do it every morning now," I point out, struggling to keep up with her in my cowboy boots. Reagan can walk seriously fast when she's in a rush, which makes up for the fact that her legs are half the length of mine.

"Yeah, because either your mom or I practically drag you out."

"Well, you're still going to be there when we're in college. Isn't that the point of rooming together? So you can be my alarm clock forever and ever?" I hook an arm around her neck and drag her close, and she laughs and ducks out from underneath, facing me as she continues to walk backward in her ripped-up tennis shoes.

"I thought we were going to college so life would be different," she teases, darting backward. "Isn't that the point, *Tori?*"

"Well so far, we've had drinks with no alcohol and hung out with obnoxious boys, so it seems just like high school to me." I stick out my tongue and cross my eyes. "Here's hoping there's a little more action at the frat party tonight."

"First things first!" she sings out. "*You* are going to go to an actual class today! Maybe that'll feel a little more like college."

I groan as overdramatically as humanly possible. "What is the point of coming to visit colleges if we're just going to spend the whole time in class?" *Unless it's Fashion Design with Miss Lucy*, I add silently, practically feeling that cobalt gown under my fingertips.

"It's not the *whole* time," she retorts, spinning around to face forward just in time to turn the corner onto the path with the entrance to the building housing breakfast.

"It's one class. And who knows? Maybe there'll even be a hot professor."

"You always know just what to say."

She grins and yanks open the door to the hall. "You're easy. Now come on—let's get this party started!"

I follow her inside and we accept our brand-new name badges, but as we look around for seats and familiar faces, I can't help feeling that so far, this *has* felt a lot like high school—classes I don't want to take, a guy who's no good for me, and reliance on Rae to get my butt moving.

Why do I need to leave Charytan for this exactly?

Chapter Ten

Reagan

"I can't believe we're at another one of these," I muse to Dev as we walk up the front lawn to the Alpha Delta Chi house, where a party is already in full swing. Max keeps bumping into me from behind because he's surgically attached to his phone, and I lost sight of Vic and Jamie I don't even know how long ago. Last I saw, Vic was chatting with some chick who was gushing over her dress while Jamie's eyes rolled out of his skull.

"Amazing, isn't it? Maybe one of these days I'll even learn how to dance." He strikes a '70s move right there on the lawn and I promptly turn my back on him as if I've never seen him before in my life.

"Man, you remain my toughest critic," he says as he takes my forearm and spins me back around. It's the millionth light touch of the past couple of days, and I keep waiting for that stupid little tingle to disappear, but it never does. I hate that tingle. Where does it get off feeling both so new and so familiar? And why doesn't it understand it's not welcome here? "What *does* it take to please you, Reagan Forrester?"

As if I would touch that one with a ten-foot pole. "Clearly you still need some practice," I say coolly instead. "Maybe you should be studying dance instead of science."

He grins proudly. "Liked that, huh? Impressed by my sexy collegiate brain?"

Not even a twenty-foot pole. "Please, you're planning to go pre-med. That question was a total gimme."

"Oh, really. So if the professor of the class we just sat in on had called on *you* instead of me, you would've known that was an example of co-dominance?"

"I'm not going pre-med."

"Ah, yes, I forgot—you are the great 'undecided.'"

"Don't mock me."

"I'm not mocking," he insists as we walk around the house, heading straight for the backyard without so much as a discussion. "I just think it's surprising that someone who has so many opinions about things doesn't know what she wants to study."

"I'm *probably* going to major in English, I'm just not sure. It's not like I want to be an English teacher or anything."

"And what *do* you want to be when you grow up?" he asks with a tilt of his head.

"A grown-up."

He stops walking, leans back against a tree, and slides down the trunk. "That's it? A grown-up?"

"Trust me," I say flatly, looking down at him. "It's harder than you think."

He unzips his hoodie and lays it on the ground next to him. "I can't decide if I'm dying to meet the people who raised you or if I would just regret it instantly."

"What makes you think they're even remotely interesting?"

His chest heaves in a sigh under his Ms. Marvel tee. "You really like pushing the whole mystery-wrapped-in-an-enigma thing, don't you? Well, if I don't get to pry, you don't get to get pissed at me like you did last time."

"What's that supposed to mean?"

"It means that you keep everything to yourself but assume other people can just read your mind. It's not fair."

"Fair to who?" It's weird having this conversation, period, made extra bizarre by the distance between us. Obviously he put out the sweatshirt for me to sit on, but I just can't bring myself to squash it into the dirt with my butt.

"You've been spoiled by Tori," he says, ignoring the question. "It's like…too neat, or something. The two of you." He nods at the hoodie. "Are you gonna sit or what?"

"I don't want to get your sweatshirt dirty."

"I don't give a shit about the sweatshirt."

"Fine, I'll sit on the damn sweatshirt." I drop onto it gracelessly, glad I opted for jeans this time around or I would've just flashed half the party. "Don't be pissed at me."

"I'm not—" He breaks off and sighs. "You're a weird, confusing girl."

"Am not." I think about it for a second. "Okay, I'll take weird, but not confusing. What the hell is simpler than a poor white trash girl who just wants to get the hell out of her life? I'm a walking cliché."

"You really think that's all you are?"

It feels like a trick question. One I'm totally not answering. Instead, I test the waters elsewhere, seeing how the words feel on the tip of my tongue for the first time in a long time. "I want to be a lawyer. I don't know what I want to study because it doesn't really matter what I major in, as long as I get into law school. There. Now you know what I want to be when I grow up."

I brace myself for laughter, but it doesn't come. "I think that's probably the perfect choice for you," he says after a moment. "Arguing for a living? Damn, I should've guessed that immediately."

"That's all you have to say about it?" A chill passes through the yard and I hug my knees to my chest, wishing I weren't sitting on the sweatshirt so he could drape it around my shoulders or something.

"What else should I say?"

"I don't know, something about how ridiculous it is? How no one would ever take me seriously in a courtroom? How I should appreciate that I can just sit at home while a man brings in the money?"

He furrows his thick, dark eyebrows. "Why would I ever say anything like that? Even if I thought it? Which, by the way, I don't. I think you'd make a great lawyer. I hope you're on my team if I ever get sued for malpractice."

I tug on my white curl and watch a guy's massive, barrel-like belly jiggle as he does a keg stand. *Why would I ever say anything like that?* As if it's inconceivable anyone would. As if I haven't heard it a thousand fucking times in every tone from playful teasing to downright rage.

I don't know if it's my silence or my tightened jaw that gives me away, but next to me, Dev makes a disgusted sound, somewhere between a snort and gagging.

"Jesus Christ. Is anyone in your life not a completely unsupportive piece of shit?"

"He's not in my life anymore," I say, far too quickly—and unnecessarily. The truth is, they're my mother's words as much as Fitz's, but his deep, mocking voice is the one that echoes in my brain. Hers flits around, an ineffectual gnat of redneck vocabulary wrapped in faux accent. But his…always his…

Dev jerks back slightly, wincing if I'm not mistaken, though I'm looking everywhere but at him, so who knows. Maybe I want to think the idea of another guy throws him.

Another chill sweeps through, and I close my eyes, imagining the warmth of a decidedly masculine arm around my shoulders. Dev's not budging, but now that Fitz is in my head, it's easy to reinsert him everywhere he used to fit so seamlessly. I can feel his rough callouses brushing the skin just below my collarbone, his steel watch pressing into my shoulder. I know exactly where every hair and bone of his arm would be if he were sitting with me right now.

"So what's the next stop on your epic college tour?"

I open my eyes slowly. A girl is doing a keg stand now, two of her friends cracking up as they hold her by the legs of her bright-red jeans. The foully sweet smell of pot floats in our direction, and I wrinkle my nose. I've always hated that smell. Fitz used to laugh at me about it when I would make disgusted faces as he and his friends lit up in the backyard, Ma Fitzpatrick feigning total ignorance. Said it was a "good-girl gene" that made me hate it.

"I don't know. Vic's the social planner." Red Jeans is a lightweight. She's twice my height and even I could've lasted longer than that.

"Well, what else is on your application list?"

I shrug. "Still working on it. Southeastern turned out not to be a great fit for Vic's academic plans, and Halsing was kind of...underwhelming. I think we're both liking Barnaby though, and at some point, we're gonna check out Chapman State. Maybe Mills. Gas is pretty steep, and I only get so many application fee waivers, so."

"That's it?"

The sharp tone makes me turn and face him for the first time since I sat down. "You have a problem with my list? Why? Where are *you* applying?"

"A few places, but I'm planning on going to KU. You're not even applying?"

"Nope. It's not for me."

"It's not for you," he repeats flatly. "A great school with programs in everything you could possibly want to study, affordable in-state tuition, *and* a law school isn't for you. What, are you scared you won't get in?"

"I'm perfectly confident in my admission abilities, thanks. I'm just not interested."

"I don't believe that."

"Believe whatever you wanna believe."

"Fine. I will. I believe that you're scared." His eyes aren't sparkling the way they usually are; now they glitter with hard determination, and maybe a little bit of smugness. He sits up and crosses his legs, leaning toward me so I can smell the lone cup of beer on his breath. "I believe that you really do think you'll never get out of your town, maybe even your trailer park. I believe you don't think you deserve anything. I believe you have been dealt a really crappy hand and you are so much better than all of it."

There might be another chill in the air. I'd like to think that's why I'm shaking. Why my body is prickling with heat, my arms squeezing my knees so tightly to my chest I can barely breathe. Dev's face is so close to mine I can feel the warmth crackling between his skin and mine, the gentle puffs of air ghosting over my lips from in between his.

He really thinks he knows me. Maybe he does. "Your name's not Dave." I refuse to be the only one on the defensive tonight.

His light laughter surprises me, feels unfair. "No, but it's easier to pronounce, isn't it?"

"Was that you being 'a different person'?" Yes, the finger quotes are obnoxious. No, I don't care.

"That was me having met a whole lot of Kansans who seem to have a lot of trouble wrapping their heads around a name that isn't Chris or Brian," he returns. "I thought it'd be nice to go by something people can pronounce."

"Dev isn't exactly challenging. Dev. Dev. Dev." No chance I could pronounce the full version, but he doesn't know that. "Do I get an A?"

His lips curve into a slow smile, and my traitorous

heart thuds so hard in response it's almost painful. "A-plus."

My arms slide down my legs until my fingers are clawing at the dirt to keep myself steady. He's going to kiss me. And I'm going to let him. No one's lips have touched mine since Fitz's, so long ago now I can only piece together memories of what it felt like. My throat is dry, and I dart my tongue out to moisten my lips, realizing only afterward that there was probably a sexier way to do that. And then…

"We should probably find the guys." He places his palms flat on the ground for leverage to wrench himself upward, then reaches down a hand to help me up. "Have you heard from Vic? Tori? Whatever?" He grins as if we have some inside joke. If I ever found that funny, it must've been a long time ago. I ignore his hand and rise up on newborn pony legs, then reach down for his sweatshirt and shake out the dirt before handing it back.

He starts to reach for it, then hesitates and stuffs his hand into his jeans' pocket instead. "Hold on to it. It's still chilly out."

I shrug, then slide it on. It smells like grass and earth and men's deodorant. I'm sorry I put it on the instant its soft warmth envelops me, because I know I'll never want to give it back, and I'll have to part with it eventually. "Any idea where they are?"

He doesn't respond, so I glance up and see he's looking

down at me, not at my face or even my barely there boobs, but at where my curled-up fists are stuffed into the pockets, unconsciously pushing them out and around with my hands as if I'm trying to make his sweatshirt dance. "Sorry," I mumble, stilling and slipping my hands out of the pockets. "I didn't mean to stretch it out."

"What?" He blinks hard. "Oh, I wasn't thinking that. It's an old sweatshirt. Do whatever."

"Okay." Hands return to pockets. "Everything all right?"

"Yeah. Yeah, of course." He smiles, but it doesn't reveal any of those blinding white teeth. "You wanna take a walk or something?"

With every muscle in my body. But only a few are required to nod, and I use them, and off we go.

VICTORIA

I am never wearing heels again. Or drinking. Yup, I am totally done doing those things. *Done.* No more Jell-O shots or body shots or faux drinks that Jamie turns into real drinks…just done. And heels! Ugh! Why did I ever think I wanted to wear these things? They're torture chambers for the feet! Reagan's got the right idea, with those sneakers I used to wear when I was, like, five. Why would I—oh, right, these make my legs look *really* good.

"Are you seriously staring at yourself in the mirror right now?" The lumpy blanket-covered mass I'm pretty sure contains my best friend in there somewhere shifts on the creaky motel bed. "Go to sleep, *Tori*."

"Man, you are cranky tonight." I slip off the shoes and it feels so good I let out a groan that I'm sure excites the guests on the other side of the thin walls. "I thought you'd have a great time, left alone with loverboy."

"He's not my loverboy." It comes out as an irritated grunt, muffled by the thin, dirt-covered blanket, but even three sheets to the wind I can tell there's something behind it.

"Is that or isn't that his sweatshirt you came home wearing? Giving a girl your sweatshirt is, like, first base."

"Actually, making out is first base, if we're going to be sixth graders again, and *that* didn't happen."

I whirl around to face the blanket lump. "You're kidding me, right?"

The blanket lump moves from side to side in a miserable shake of the head that might be the saddest thing I've ever seen.

"What a loser!" Even I wince at the volume of my voice, but I recover quickly and limp over to the bed on blistered feet, plopping down next to Reagan and feeling an ill-advised cup of beer slosh around in my stomach. "No move at all?"

Another sad shake.

"Unacceptable!" I jump up again, and almost hurl all over my hot-pink toes. "Miss Forrester, we are getting to the bottom of this."

She finally peeks out from under the covers, her blond curls a mashed mess against the side of her face, her anime-character eyes narrowed. "Victoria, go to bed. You are drunk."

"Drunk like a fox!" I have no idea what that means, but I like the way it sounds, so I say it again. Then I get down on my hands and knees, ignoring the wave of nausea rolling through me, and find Reagan's brown canvas bag thing.

"What are you doing, you freak?"

"What you should've done yourself tonight," I say authoritatively, fishing her ancient cell phone out of its pocket. I can sense her arm grabbing out at me before it even leaves her side, and I may be drunk but she's tangled in a mess of sheets and no match for me.

"If you call Dev I swear I will never speak to you again. I mean it, Vic."

"Oh, you drama queen. Fine." I toss her phone at her and reach into my own way cuter clutch—hand-stitched by yours truly out of this awesome '70s-ish-print fabric—for my cell.

"What are you doing?"

"Not calling Dev." I spin even further out of her reach as I search for Jamie's number. I'd laughed at him for wanting to exchange digits last night, but now I'm grateful I have them, even though we spent the entire night purposefully ignoring each other. I find it and hit Send. It rings only once before he picks up.

"Tori?"

"Why didn't Dev kiss Reagan?" I blurt out, jumping back as I ask because I *know* she's gonna jump out of that bed and try to kick my butt. She proves me right, nearly falling on the floor in her rush to lunge at me while still tangled up in the sheets.

"What?"

"Victoria, I am going to *kill* you!"

I hold up a hand in Reagan's face to shush her and dash away again. "You heard me."

"I don't know, because—" He breaks off, and I press my ear even closer to the phone to hear what's happening on the other end.

Reagan pauses in mid-swing of her arm. "What's he—"

I shove a hand in her face again to shut her up.

Because just then, I hear Jamie turn away from the phone and say, "Shah, does Reagan not know about Sara?"

My stomach hardens slowly into a ball of lead, and suddenly, I know I'm going to throw up. I throw the phone at the bed, run to the bathroom, and fall to my knees in front of the toilet, where I then continue to expel every color of the rainbow in liquid form. Reagan dashes in after me and grabs my hair, keeping her other hand on my back until I'm done. When it's finally out of my system, and I fall back onto my butt on the cold tile floor, she says, "That bad, huh?"

I nod weakly. "I'm sorry."

She disappears for a few seconds and returns with a bottle of water. "Do I want to know?" she asks as she unscrews it for me and hands it over.

The water feels so good I drink a third of the bottle before pulling it away from my lips. "No, but you should." I take one more quick sip, this one more to put off telling her than because I need it. "It sounded like girlfriend."

There's a long silence, and then, flatly, "Girlfriend."

"Girlfriend. Sara."

"Sara. Sara sucks."

"Sara does suck."

"Dev sucks too."

"No argument there." I reach out and squeeze her hand. "I'm sorry, Rae."

"Yeah." She sighs. "Whatever. I should've known. Or something. Can we just go to bed?"

"Yeah, for sure. Help me up?"

She stands and pulls me to do the same, and we wash up and get into bed. I expect to have to make myself stay awake for a while to keep Reagan company, but in a matter of minutes, I hear light snoring drifting over from her bed; and just like that, I'm alone, staring at the ceiling in the dark.

I don't know how much time has passed when I hear the chime on my phone signaling that I have a text message. I try to remember where I left my phone, and then I remember that I tossed it onto the bed right before hurling. Did I even actually hang up on Jamie? It takes a few minutes of fumbling around in the sheets but finally my hand makes contact and I check the screen. Speak of the devil.

Everything OK over there?

I glance over at Rae. If she heard the phone, she didn't stir. *Fine*, I write back, tapping angrily on the screen. *He should've told her he had a girlfriend.*

As I'm waiting for his response, I realize that it's not the only text message waiting for me. I'd completely forgotten to check my phone for the last few hours, and even when I'd called Jamie, I'd been too distracted to notice. I check the texts first. There are two. The first one reads, *Hey, it's Steve. Just saw my friend from Miss Lucy's class and thought of you. Hope you guys are having fun.* Seeing a text from Freckles is so unexpected and sweet I smile at the very sight of his name, even though I have no idea how to respond or if I even should.

The other one is from a 913 area code, and says, *Hey beautiful, it's Mark. What are you up to 2nite?* It makes me snort, and I immediately clamp a hand over my mouth to avoid waking up Reagan.

I think you have the wrong number, I type back, and

I'm about to hit send when I suddenly realize with a flash who Mark is. *Oh, holy crap.* I completely forgot that Southeastern guy and I even exchanged numbers. Deleting my original message, I try to think of a clever, sexy message that an actual freshman in college might say.

I got nada.

My phone chimes again. Jamie. I forgot I'd even been texting with him. *It's not exactly like that, but it's something he should've told her. I'm surprised he didn't. But trust me, he's a good guy.*

How good can he be? I type back furiously. *He hurt my best friend, who's pretty much the best person on Earth.*

Another chime a minute later. *Maybe he just doesn't think of her like that so he didn't think it needed saying.*

I glance over at where Dev's sweatshirt now lies discarded on the dirty carpet. Somehow, I doubt that's the case.

Talking to Jamie about this is pissing me off, so I go back to Freckles's text instead. He's so sweet. And, admittedly, so convenient. It's hard not to picture keeping up with dinners at Joe's, followed by rides to CCC, where he'll go to his class and I'll go off to Miss Lucy. Then we'll drive home, holding hands over the stick shift, maybe park somewhere before he drops me off and I tell my mom all about it, signing all the romantic words I've never had occasion to before while my dad occasionally peeks in over the steel rims of his half glasses.

I'm so lost in my visions of this cozy Charytan-centric future that the sound of another text startles me. I look down at my phone. It's Mark again.

Babe, u there? I'm at the Beta Gam party. U should come.

It's exactly the kind of text message I've always pictured filling my phone in college. I mean, isn't that basically the point? Yeah, so they don't have my dream major, but life at Southeastern would be a blast—parties with Sasha, meeting her sorority sisters, going to teas and formals and whatever else they do, having guys like Mark on my arm… Plus, Reagan loved that library, and I know the only reason she's striking it from her list is because of me, which is crazy, right?

Sorry! I text back to Mark. *I'm already out with friends! Have fun! Xo.* No reason to burn any bridges, not if we might be classmates next year.

You pissed at me? I squint at my phone, confused at Mark's response, until I realize this newest text is from Jamie. It's getting hard to keep them all straight. And then I realize I never answered Freckles.

I go back to Freckles's text and reply, *It's definitely been an interesting weekend so far! How are things at home?* Then it's back to Jamie for, *No, I'm pissed at the situation.* Because I am. Because this weekend should've been awesomely fun for both of us, and instead Reagan's depressed and I'm lying here in a lousy motel room trying to figure out what the hell I want and failing miserably.

And just like that, I'm hit with the must-get-out-of-here bug again. I creep into the bathroom, close the door, and dial Jamie's number. It takes a couple of rings before I hear a raspy "Hello?"

"Why are you whispering?"

"Because I don't want the guys to know I'm talking to you," he replies in a *duh* voice.

"Ouch."

"You're whispering too."

"Yeah, because Reagan's asleep."

"Already?"

"What's she supposed to be doing? Staying awake to cry over your friend?"

Jamie sighs. "What's up, Tori? You ignored me the entire freakin' night and now you're calling me for the second time?"

"I didn't *ignore* you. I was getting to know other people. And you were doing the same thing."

"Well, there are no other people around now, so what's up?"

"I wanna go out."

"You wanna go *out*? To where? Why?"

"It's not really a fully formed plan," I admit. "I just want to do something."

"How am I supposed to ditch the guys to come get you?"

His negativity is draining all the fun out of my

spontaneous non-plan. I love Reagan, but as I think about all my options for the future, it's hard to ignore that what might be the best for her isn't the best for me, and vice versa. And this—getting caught up in her romantic drama rather than having fun—isn't what I signed on for with the Reagan and Victoria College Visit Bonanza. Not that I'm not happy to be there for her through it and everything, but, well, she's asleep and I'd like to do something to make the night a little less depressing.

Too bad I seem to be alone on that front.

"Never mind," I tell Jamie dismissively. "I'll just go for a walk around the block or something."

"No, no. Just wait. I'll be by in ten minutes. You're about half a mile up Bunting Road, right? The motel by campus?"

"Yup. Room 417."

"I'll see you in ten."

We hang up, and a rush of adrenaline whooshes through my veins. I have no idea what I'm doing. And I don't care. I'm tired of thinking, and talking, and worrying about the future. All of that will still be there tomorrow.

For now, I'm going to enjoy tonight.

"Do you have any idea where we're going?"

I can't see any street signs in the dark, but the surroundings look familiar. At least, I think they do. "We're not far from campus," I say dismissively, even though we've been driving for a good fifteen minutes. I don't care about knowing where we are right now. I don't really want to know. I just want to get lost and think about nothing.

Apparently, Jamie doesn't feel the same way, because after another two minutes of driving, he pulls off to the side of a road, next to a wide-open stretch of field, and turns to me. "What's up with you?"

"I just wanted to get out. Isn't it nice to get out and do something?"

"Didn't we go to a party tonight?"

The exasperated sigh pushes past my lips before I can even think to tamp it down. "You're a pain in the butt, you know that? Why'd you even pick me up?"

"Because you're hot." The way he says it, it's like there's an "obviously" on the end that he just doesn't say out loud.

"You do everything hot girls tell you?" It's hard not to laugh but he's given me too much power here and I don't want to lose it by cracking. He gets a raised eyebrow and a slight upward curve of my lips instead. It's nice to have the upper hand for the first time this weekend, and even though he's gonna get some either way, I want him to work for it.

"Depends how hot," he says, a little saucier now, as he looks me up and down.

"Drive to Mexico."

He laughs, but he looks half-afraid that I'm serious.

"Where's your sense of adventure?" I ask innocently.

"It got me to lie to my best friends, pick up a girl I barely know, and drive into the middle of nowhere. Doesn't that count for anything?"

"Just barely."

"A peck on the cheek, maybe?"

"Ohhh. So that's what this is about? Hooking up with the hot chick?" I shake my head as if I'm gravely disappointed. A flush works its way up from his neck and it's just about the most gratifying thing I've ever seen. "I just wanted some fresh air." I let myself out of the car before he can say another word and go running into the field, twirling around in circles.

I don't even hear Jamie exit the car, but suddenly there he is, catching my arms in his hands. "You're kind of a crazy chick, you know that?"

I pull my arms free and let myself fall back onto the grass. "So I've been told."

"What's your deal?"

Looking up at him is sort of dizzying. There are stars all around his head, and there he is, all black-framed emo glasses and perma-smug lips. "No deal. Just a little restless."

"I can see that." He straddles my legs as if he's going to offer his hands to pull me up, but he doesn't go that far, just stands there looking down at me. "How's the fresh air?"

I take a deep breath. "Wonderful." I wonder how his glasses stay so firmly on his ears when his head is bent over me like that. "So, this is college, huh?"

"Give or take a full course load and maybe a part-time job and some dorm rooms, I guess so." He smiles. "Not impressed?"

"Not really. You?"

"I like what I see so far."

At that, I grin. "Smooth."

"Give a guy a break."

"You're awfully far away to be making such demands," I reply, because I'm bored of the game and my goose bumps are begging for someone else's body heat.

He needs no further encouraging and promptly drops to his knees, still straddling me. It's quite the interesting position, even with both of us fully clothed. Well, if you can call me fully clothed; in the miniskirt I've paired with a sweatshirt and Uggs, my legs are mostly bare, exposing them to the rough fabric of his jeans. "How about now?"

"Now you're a little closer."

He leans over me, bracing a palm on the grass on either side of my head. His cologne is strong, but it's a pleasant enough smell that I don't mind, even mingled with the cola on his breath. I can see myself in his glasses, and it's so unsettling that I reach up and carefully remove them.

"You know I can't see a damn thing without those on," he says as I fold them up and set them to the side.

"Good thing you don't need to." A second after the words are out of my mouth, his lips find mine or mine find his, I don't even know but it doesn't really matter. I'm no longer cold, and I'm back in control, parting Jamie's lips to tangle my tongue with his, owning this kiss and him like I haven't owned anything in…I don't even know. I made this happen and it's such a good feeling I don't want to stop there.

Jamie's definitely the kind of guy who carries a condom around in his wallet at all times, but I have no plans to do anything with him tonight that requires using it. Still, I feel…I don't know, sexually charged or something. Kissing's not enough, not even the way we're doing it right now, practically devouring each other like starving animals.

I roll Jamie onto his back and wrench myself away, rising up onto my knees and yanking my sweatshirt over my head. I'm about to bend back down to kiss him again when he places a palm flat on my chest and stops me. "What—?"

He grabs around in the grass for his glasses. "I told you," he says, locating them and slipping them on. "I can't see a damn thing without them, and if you think I'm missing this, you're crazy." He whistles softly. "Dammit, you *are* drive-to-Mexico hot."

"You think so?"

His hand skims my skin, then the leopard-print satin of my bra, and he sits up so we're chest-to-chest, nearly mouth-to-mouth. "Yeah, I think so," he breathes before kissing me again. We stay like that for a while, making out, his hands roaming all over the newly bared territory for a while before he unhooks my bra and then it begins all over again. Finally, the cold air on my bare skin becomes so unbearable that I shiver.

"Oh, shit." Jamie pulls back. "Sorry, you must be freezing. I'm an idiot." He slides off his jacket and slips it over my shoulders. "Do you wanna go back?"

I shake my head. "Not unless you do. The jacket's good, thanks."

He nods and kisses me again, first my lips, then my neck, and then he continues southward. I close my eyes and lean back, bracing myself on my elbows, giving him access to whatever he wants. I feel good. *Really* good. There isn't a single person in my life who would approve of what I'm doing right now, and knowing that I'm acting in no one's interest but mine is the biggest turn-on of all.

I relax back fully onto the grass, taking Jamie with me. I don't know if it's him or being at a college or what, but I don't think I've ever been this horny. I'm always the one putting the brakes on things, and even at Southeastern, Mark—who was pretty hot—only got over the shirt, but right now, all I want to do is push forward, do more, *feel* more. I pick my knees up just enough to make my miniskirt swish down around my hips, baring my black bikini underwear to the matching night sky. Jamie's hands are inching toward my waistband, and I know he'll notice in a matter of moments.

It takes longer than I want it to, but I force myself to stay patient. Finally, his fingertips brush where the seam of cotton fabric meets my hip and he looks down, obviously surprised to have encountered skin. He sits up and coughs. "I pictured you as more of a matchy-matchy girl."

"You pictured me in my underwear?" I reply sweetly.

"Can you blame me?" His hands are lingering on the waistband, his fingertips gently brushing the fabric, and I'm not sure what more encouragement he needs from me to get rid of the damn things. Finally, he hooks an index finger in and pulls the tiniest bit before glancing at my face, obviously giving me time to stop him.

I drop my head back and arch my hips up in consent. I feel him hesitate for a couple more seconds, and then he slowly pulls them down my legs with my cooperation before lying down next to me. I've never done anything in that area before, and at the touch of his finger, gentle and experimental as it parts me, I wonder if he's as new to it as I am.

It doesn't take long before his hesitancy disappears, and I'm pretty grateful there's no one around for miles because no one needs to hear the sounds coming out of my mouth or see me writhing around on the grass. The sensations building in my body are from another world, they must be, and I'm sure I can't take it anymore and I open my eyes and tell Jamie to stop.

He smiles. "I will if you want, but you're not done yet." Even though he's kept his smug tone out of it for once, I hate that he knows this better than I do, but I give up my little bit of control and nod for him to continue, because I know he's right and my body is building to *something*, I just don't know what, only that he's moving faster now, and it's getting harder to breathe, and my skin feels like it's lighting up, and—

My entire body explodes. Just…shatters, completely. It's like nothing I've ever felt and it radiates out in waves that wrack every limb and muscle. "Tia Maria," I whisper as I come down from the high, and Jamie kisses me gently in response.

"What the hell does that mean?" he murmurs against my lips. "Can't you just say 'holy shit' like a normal person?"

"I don't swear." I sound as sleepy as I suddenly feel.

"You mentioned that. It's actually kind of cute."

"Cute" isn't really what I want to hear from someone who's still looking at me while I'm basically naked. I brush my arms through the grass until I come in contact with cotton fabric and then motion for Jamie to give me the space to pull my underwear back on and yank my skirt back down.

We're both silent for a while, then Jamie hands me my sweatshirt, and I give him back his jacket. I know this is where I'm supposed to reciprocate but I'm not really sure how many firsts I wanna have tonight, and I'm also not in the mood to have him realize that I don't know what I'm doing. Feeling like the uneducated one in college is getting really old.

He doesn't ask, anyway, and somehow or other we end up lying side by side, looking up at the stars in silence. Eventually, he breaks it. "Would you have gone to Mexico, if I would've driven you?"

I smile at the thought of showing up on Abuelita's doorstep with Asian Jewish Jerky Jamie in tow. "Would you have driven to Mexico, if I would've gone?"

"I'm just trying to figure out who you are," he says, as if I'm some sort of great mystery, some riddle to be solved.

"Join the club," I reply, because maybe I am.

"Do you think you'll come here? For college?"

"I have no idea. Maybe. It's got a lot that I want. You?"

"Probably not. The Computer Science department's not that great. I'm applying early to MIT. We'll see."

MIT? Just when I thought I couldn't feel dumber. "So why'd you even bother coming to visit?"

"Dev said it'd be fun. He wanted to come and

convinced Max and me to come with. He was right."
We haven't been touching until now, but at that, Jamie's
pinky grazes mine, as if to say, *You were the fun part, in
case you didn't catch on.*

"So is Dev coming here?" His name still makes me
bristle. I've been able to push everything with him and
Reagan out of my head for a while, but now it's all back,
full force.

"Nah, he's pretty set on KU. I was surprised he even
wanted to check out Barnaby, but he went to Southeastern
a few weeks ago and had a good time, so…"

Finally, I feel like the smart one again. "Put the pieces
together faster, Jamie."

He's quiet for a moment, and then I hear, "Oh, shit.
We're here because of your friend, aren't we?"

"Oh, yes you are. Tell me again how great a guy *your*
friend is again?"

"I swear he's not like that. He's not even actually
dating Sara. But everyone in the world thinks they should
be—including her—and it's fucked him up for getting
with other girls. Plus, she's also Indian, which makes his
parents happy."

"Do they have something against him getting with a
white girl?"

"Nah, I don't think so. It's just a bonus. Your parents
care if you get with someone who's not Hispanic?"

"They're both Mexican, but I don't think they care if

I date guys who are. Not that I'm in the habit of bringing anyone home, but my brother's dated pretty much every race under the sun. They don't blink. What about your parents?"

"They don't care who I date so much as who I marry. I know they want me to marry Jewish, but otherwise, they're pretty chill. I think they have this perpetual guilt about turning me into a Jew who doesn't look like any other Jews."

For the first time in a long while, I turn onto my side and actually look at him—his spiky black hair, the dark, narrow eyes behind his glasses. The way people treated me for being Mexican in Arizona sucked. It kinda sucks in Charytan too. But at least I fit in with my family. I can't imagine what it must be like to identify as two different minorities and be alone in doing it.

"Does it suck for you?" I ask.

"It did. It gets better the older I get, mostly because I've learned not to give a shit. It used to drive me crazy when people said stupid things like, 'Asian *and* Jewish? Dude, you must be psycho smart!' But the truth is, yeah, I am, so fuck it. I'll own it."

I can't remember the last time I've envied someone this much. Without even realizing what I'm doing, I prop myself up on an elbow and reach out to place a palm flat on his chest, right over his heart, as if it'll allow me to absorb his courage or something. He looks up at me, surprise on his face, and he says, "Does it suck for you? Being Mexican?"

The word "yes" hovers on my lips, but I can't push it out. I don't care that I don't have a thousand friends, or that no neighbors come by to borrow sugar, or that Reagan's mom keeps an eagle eye on me whenever I'm at her house. Nothing that sucks right now has anything to do with my ethnicity and everything to do with me. I'm the one holding myself back right now. None of the rest matters anymore.

"It used to," I say instead. "I guess it doesn't really anymore. Not because 'I own it' or anything. It just sort of is."

It feels like a weak response, especially after his badass declaration, but he doesn't seem to care. He reaches up to cup my cheek in his hand and brings me down for a kiss. It's warmer and softer than the others, and it feels... pitying. I pull back almost immediately.

"What's the matter?"

"Nothing," I say immediately. It's not like I can bust out with, "I feel like your kiss was judging me for being a weak nobody." He's been sweet enough, which I can tell is a stretch for him, but now I just want to go home. It was fun for a while, but now I'm right back where I started, hyperaware of the fact that I have no idea what I want in life. "It's late."

"Did I do something?"

Yes. "No."

He sighs. "You know it's obvious you're lying, right?"

His tone sounds so familiar, and with a flash, I'm back at the vending machine at the motel near Southeastern, watching Dev rake a hand through his hair as he blurts out his frustrations about Reagan. It strikes me just how much I sound like her right now, working extra hard not to open up. I love Reagan, but I don't want to be like that. I take a deep breath and try to pick my words so I don't sound like an idiot.

"I just…feel kinda lost these days. Every day, something new pulls me in a different direction, and I don't even know what I want. My brother's out there traveling and sometimes that seems like the greatest thing on Earth, and I think maybe I should do that too, see the world. But then I go to different colleges, and I have a great time there too, and I think how awesome it would be to join a sorority and go to frat parties all the time and meet new people every day. And then there's a great fashion design program at our local community college, and sometimes I think all I want to do is stay at home a little longer and do that—stay with my family and work really closely with a cool mentor. It's just so hard to figure out what I want, you know? Especially because everyone wants something different for me, and Reagan and I have always said we'd do this college thing together, but what if what's right for her isn't right for me? I mean, we're really different people, and maybe that means we should do different things, but I also can't imagine not being with her next year."

I'm out of breath by the time I finish. It felt so good to get the words out that it takes me a minute to notice the totally disgusted look on Jamie's face.

"That's your issue?" he says as if I've just declared that I don't know what I want for breakfast tomorrow. "You don't know if you'd rather party in another country or at college? Or maybe you just wanna fuck education and go to community college? Or you'll just do whatever your best friend tells you to do?"

It feels like he's just reached out and slapped me across the face. I want to jump up but his cruelty has frozen me into place. The only part of me that still seems to be in working order are my tear ducts, and the feeling of the cold air on my newly wet cheeks finally jolts me into action. Of course, I don't jump up and demand he take me home like I should. Instead, I simply turn away from him and curl into a fetal position.

"Oh, don't—" He stops and sighs. "I'm sorry. I didn't mean to be an asshole. I can't help it sometimes."

It's a lousy apology, but at least hearing it helps put my brain in working order. "Take me back to my room."

"Tori…" I feel his warm hand on my shoulder, and I shrug it off.

"Trust me," I say, shifting into a sitting-up position

before rising to my feet. "This isn't ending any way but with you taking me back to my room right now."

He stops arguing, and we get into the car for a silent ride back to the motel, broken only by the soothing British accent of the woman speaking directions from his GPS. I don't say a word to Jamie before hopping out of the car and slamming the door behind me, but he waits until I'm safely inside before peeling out of the parking lot anyway.

Only after I hear the screeching of his tires do I lock myself in the bathroom and cry.

CHAPTER ELEVEN

REAGAN

I'm surprised at how well I slept, all things considered, but the second I wake up, last night worms its way back into my brain with a vengeance. How is it possible to feel such a strong connection with somebody but miss the most vital piece of information about him?

It's all in your head, a voice that sounds suspiciously, frustratingly like Fitz's fills my brain. *Stop trying to replace me, Babe. It's not gonna happen.*

"Shut up," I mutter under my breath as I lather up with a trial-size bottle of Johnson's baby shampoo. The smell is homey and comforting, and I wish I could use up the entire bottle, but with the amount of money I'm wasting on these stupid trips, I can't afford to take liberties with other stuff. At least breakfast this morning is free, and no matter how badly I want to avoid Dev, there's no way I'm letting him screw me out of complimentary waffles for a second time.

Besides, I can't help hoping that he'll have some sort of explanation that'll sweep me off my feet, or at least something that will make me feel like less of a complete moron. I could've sworn all the signs were there, that there was actual electricity, but maybe I was just seeing what I wanted to see, feeling what I wanted to feel.

Maybe I *am* just trying to replace what I once had.

There's a loud knock on the door; Vic's awake. "You almost done?"

"Yeah, just a minute," I call back. I finish rinsing, shut off the water, flip my hair to dry it with a towel, and then wrap the towel around myself. "You can come in."

She looks like total crap when she does. I've never seen such dark circles under her eyes, her face is creased with lines from her pillow, and her hair's a mess. It looks like I'm not the only one who had a rough night. "Trouble sleeping?"

"Uh huh." She examines herself in the mirror and her mouth twists sourly. She grabs her toothbrush and squeezes on a huge blob of toothpaste.

I step out of the shower and take a closer look at the

back of her head. Is that...grass? "Did you go out again last night after I went to sleep?"

"Ah eh oo a no."

"Uh, pardon?"

She spits and rinses. "I left you a note. On your bag."

"Oh, I didn't see it. Where'd you go? Did you take my car?"

"Nope." I watch her poke and prod at her face. "Jamie picked me up."

"Jamie? Dev's Jamie?"

"If that's what we're calling him now." She turns on the faucet and splashes water on her face. "Are you done with the shower?"

Do I have wax buildup in my ears or something? "Why on Earth would you go out with Jamie? I didn't think you guys were even friendly."

"We're not," she says flatly. "I just wanted to get out, and now I don't really wanna talk about it. So is the shower free for use or what?"

Vic's not a morning person, but I've never seen her quite this pissed off before 9:00 a.m. I open my mouth to press her again, and then I remember all the times she's obviously wanted to push me on the Fitz issue and kept quiet, and I just say, "Yeah, sure," and walk out.

I know Vic, and something is definitely up. If Jamie hurt her, I will disembowel him. I thought nerdy boys were supposed to be safe, but these guys are proving to be anything but.

These waffles had better be worth it.

Our plan is to avoid the boys entirely, but the second we walk in, both Dev and Jamie straighten up. I wonder how long they've been watching the door. If they were hoping to avoid our notice, they chose lousy seats, so I can only imagine we've both got conversations in store. I feel a little cheated that I still have no idea what happened between Vic and Jamie, but then Dev gets up and walks over and thoughts of anything else slip out of my mind completely.

"Can we talk?" he asks, keeping his voice low. His thick black hair is even messier than usual and I hope it's a sign of a lousy night's sleep. I feel just a little bit triumphant that I somehow slept like a baby.

I plaster a smile on my face. I planned for exactly this moment the entire time we were getting ready this morning, and came to the realization that there's just no point. Even if he had a magically wonderful response to why he kept it a secret, what difference would it make? He's going to KU; I'm not. It's time to move on. "Nothing to talk about. Message received. Sorry I got the wrong idea. How are the waffles?"

"Reagan—"

"Dave," I say firmly, and am slightly gratified when he winces. "I really don't want to talk about it. No hard feelings, or whatever."

I forge past him, but he clasps my forearm with surprising strength when I try to pass. I freeze, and he seems to realize how tightly he's gripping my arm because he suddenly drops it as if it's on fire and stuffs his hands into the pockets of his hoodie. "Please."

With one word it's like he's taken a Zippo to the icy armor I've taken all morning to coat myself in. I respond with a jerky nod and we walk outside, and it pisses me off to realize I'm waiting for a hand on the small of my back that will never come.

"It's not what you think. Not really."

This is exactly the conversation I don't want to have, and I huff out a sigh to make that clear. "It's fine—"

"No, it isn't. I care about you. Probably—no, *definitely* more than I should. I want us to be friends, and friends should be able to trust each other."

Friends. I don't have balls, but I imagine that's the feeling of someone kicking you in them. He cares about me as a friend. Sure, me too. That's why even now I wish he'd envelop me in that hoodie while he's still wearing it and I could see if he tastes like the spot of maple syrup that's glistening on his lip.

Instead, I bust out with an uber-intellectual "Yeah."

"I just…I know it's not fair to let you think this was a one-sided thing." He can't even meet my eyes now, which is just as well. "Sara's not my girlfriend, but she *is* a friend who's liked me for a while, and she's someone I don't want to hurt without good cause. You and I aren't even planning on going to the same school…Who even knows—"

"If we'll ever even see each other again," I fill in. "I get it." And I do, actually. Even if he shared my feelings exactly, what's he supposed to do? Throw his life into upheaval so he can have a fling with me on a college visit and then return to spend the next eight months miserable at school and flirting with me via text message?

"It's weird when you put it that way," he says.

Tell me about it. "It's the truth, isn't it? No point pretending it isn't." I know, because I've been trying to ever since he first told me he was going to KU, and it's gotten me absolutely nowhere.

"No, I guess not." His eyes meet mine then, and they look as trying-not-to-be-sad as I feel. "So, we're cool?"

"We're cool." It's all I can get out around the lump in my throat.

"So, waffles?"

"Definitely." We turn and walk back inside, but before we can get through the door, he stops and pulls me aside.

"By the way," he starts, furrowing his eyebrows, "what the hell happened between Vic and Jamie last night?"

By the time breakfast is over, the awkwardness surrounding our little group seems to have broken.

Even Max talks a little bit, since his Internet girlfriend apparently lives in Seattle and isn't awake yet. I'm so stuffed full of waffles I can barely move, and I'm actually aching from laughing at all the stories we've been sharing and jokes we've been muttering to each other during the chipper closing speeches.

Unfortunately, it's the last event of the weekend, and there's nothing left to do but go home, even though we're finally having fun like we should be. "How far's the drive for you guys?" I ask Jamie as we pile out of the hall.

"Just a couple of hours. What about you guys?"

"Three, if there's no traffic. In the other direction," I add unnecessarily, because it's on my mind. Five hours. That's the distance between me and Dev. Even if the idea of a relationship wasn't already crazy, the fact that my job would mean never, ever hanging out unless he felt like driving ten hours just to spend the day sitting in Joe's seals it. And speaking of my job, "We've really gotta head back or I'm gonna be late for work."

"You're going to work now?" Dev's thick eyebrows shoot all the way up.

"Breakfast may be free but gas isn't." I turn to Max and Jamie. "It was really nice to meet you guys." They echo the sentiment, and whatever happened between Jamie and Vic, it doesn't seem to earn a special goodbye. I want to say something else to Dev, but nothing floating around in my head could possibly be said in front of his friends. I settle for an extra brief smile in his direction, and then Vic and I get into the car.

Neither of us speaks until the guys are no longer visible in the rearview, and then at the same time, we both say, "Are you okay?"

Just like that, we both dissolve into laughter. "God, we are pathetic," I say, wiping a tear from my eye when I've finally composed myself. Fortunately, we got out of Barnaby quicker than most and there aren't many cars on the road yet. "Give us a couple of boys and we turn into total messes."

"I know, right? What's wrong with us?" She fishes her phone out of her bag and plugs it into the speakers. "Come on, even you can't deny this ride home majorly requires some sappy heartbreak lyrics."

I roll my eyes. "Same ol' Vic."

"Umm, not quite, actually," she says as she searches through her music.

I pull up to a red light and glance over at her. Her golden-brown cheeks are flaming red in a way they only get about one thing. "Are you telling me that you and Jamie…seriously?"

"Not *that*," she says, but she's reddening like crazy. "But…other stuff."

I bite my lips to keep from laughing. Vic may make out with a lot more guys than I do, but she's such a prude when it comes to talking about it. In fact, she's so hush-

hush on the subject of sex that she's never asked whether or not I'm a virgin, and I know she just assumes I am. I often wonder how she'd react to the fact that I'm not, that I haven't been one since I was fourteen, but there's no chance I'm gonna be the one to open up that conversation.

"Other stuff...that necessitated shirt removal?" I venture, hitting the gas as the light turns green and a warbling teen-girl voice fills the car.

"Among other removals," she mumbles.

"Vic!" I nearly slam on the breaks, I'm so shocked. "Are we talking—?"

"Just fingers," she says quickly.

"Well? How was?"

"*So good,*" she blurts out, and I crack up laughing. Eventually, she joins in. "Why didn't anyone tell me?"

"Because we knew we'd never be able to keep you under control if you knew."

"Ha ha."

"So, if it was so good..."

"He followed it up by being a monumental jerkwad afterward," she says bitterly, sliding off her shoes and putting her feet up on the dash. "He half-apologized last night and again this morning. Whatever."

"We're not talking him trying to force you to do anything, right?"

"No, definitely not."

"Okay, good. Because we're still close enough to

campus that I can turn around and rip him limb from limb if you want."

She grins. "Thanks, I think I'll be okay. How about you? You and Dave seemed to work things out well enough."

"Yeah, we're cool. Just doesn't make sense to be anything more." I figure that if I keep saying it, eventually I'll really start to believe it. Maybe then Fitz's smug smile will get out of my brain.

"Well, that's very rational of you. Very…Reagan."

"Meaning what?"

"Meaning you're good at following your head," she says, turning up the music a notch. "Not everyone can do that. Lord knows I can't."

I know she doesn't mean it to be, but somehow I feel like I've been insulted. "Are you suggesting I'm some sort of robot or something?"

"No! Of course not. But…"

"But?"

"But you're not exactly crazy-forthcoming with your emotions. Don't get me wrong, I respect your privacy and everything, but don't you think it's a little crazy that we've been best friends for years and I know basically nothing about your romantic life? I obviously haven't had a lot of close friends or anything, but this is the kind of thing we're *supposed* to talk about, no? Lord knows I tell you everything when I hook up with boys."

"Yeah, key words being 'hook up with.' If you had serious relationships with them that ended really badly, do you think you'd be that open about them?"

"Yes," she says with no hesitation, and I grit my teeth because I know she's telling the truth.

"Fine," I say on a sigh. I always knew this day was gonna come, and I've already put one awkward conversation behind me this morning, so what's one more? "What do you want to know?"

"How long were you together?"

"Two years—eighth grade and ninth."

"That's your serious relationship? Junior high?"

Already I'm regretting having this conversation. "It's not like this is new information for you," I point out, the edge in my voice obvious to both of us. "You came to CHS in tenth grade and he was already gone."

"Wow, I never really thought about how much older he was," she murmurs. "So when you were in eighth grade, you were with a junior in high school? Isn't that kinda…"

I know what kinds of words she wants to use to finish off that thought, and there's no way I'm going to give her the chance. "It sounds weird when you say it out loud, but it didn't feel that way." My knuckles are going white on the steering wheel, and I count to ten in my head and force myself to relax. "He used to hang out with these kids at my trailer park, and every now and again he'd come over and make conversation, and before I knew it, he was paying more attention to me than he was to his friends. The same thing would happen when he came to pick up his siblings from junior high, and then he would invite me to come back and hang out with them. Their house basically became my second home.

"Then, the night before I started eighth grade, we were hanging out, and he kissed me. He told me he'd liked me for months and was trying to wait until I started high school to say anything, but he just couldn't wait anymore. And that was that. We were glued to each other from then on."

"I can't even imagine you glued to somebody," Vic muses. "Did you have pet names for each other and everything?"

"Sort of. He used to call me Ragin', he said because I got pissed at him all the time. Which isn't even really true."

"And what'd you call him? Fitz?"

"Not when we were dating. When we were dating, I called him Johnny. His real name was John. *Is* John." I don't know if she's heard the rumors yet, but I don't want her thinking I believe them.

"So why'd you break up? Because he wanted to join the army?"

How badly do I want to say yes? To make it that simple and never have to speak of it again? If this were anyone but Vic, I would in a heartbeat. But everything with Dev just drove home the fact that she's all I have, and if I lie to her about this, about anything, then I don't even really have her.

"Not exactly." I hate how quiet my voice gets, but I've never talked about this before, with anyone, and I'm scared to hear what it sounds like out loud, even though this is the part most people know, the part his family made sure everyone knew. "He joined the army *because* we broke up. I don't know if it was revenge or if he thought I'd get back together with him if he'd agree to stay or what. By that point, he was so messed up I honestly have no idea what was going through his head."

Vic whistles. "Wow, that is seriously intense. So why'd you break up in the first place?"

"Ironically enough, because I wanted to get out of Charytan and he didn't, if you can believe that now."

"But you were only in ninth grade when you broke up."

"Yup, but he was a senior, and he wanted to seal the future. He had no plans to go to college or anything. He was just gonna stay in Charytan, probably do carpentry with his dad."

"And you had a problem with that?" Out of the corner of my eye, I see her bend over and grab her bag. She fishes through it and then triumphantly holds up a pack of gum and offers it to me. I decline with a wave of my hand.

"No, I was fine with that, as long as he understood that in three years when I graduated high school, I was getting the hell out of Charytan, with him or without him. He didn't take terribly well to that."

She unwraps the gum, pops it in her mouth, and chews for a few seconds, as if giving herself time to add up the pieces to my story. Or maybe she assumes I'm going to say more. When I don't, she blows and pops a tiny but loud bubble and says, "He broke up with you over that? Who knows if you would've even still been together in three years?"

I smile grimly. "That's...not quite the end of it."

"There's more?"

"Trust me, I wish there wasn't." I can feel the waffles flip-flopping around in my stomach now and I look up at the signs to gauge how far we are from the next rest stop. I feel sick to my stomach reliving this and I need to not be behind a wheel right now. "Okay if we get off at the next rest stop? I need a break."

"From the story or the drive?"

"Honestly? Both."

"Was it really that bad?"

I stare intently at the road, afraid that if I so much as blink, memories will come flooding back, as clear and colorful as the tropical print of Vic's skirt. "He wanted to get married."

There's a strangled sound in response, and I look

over to see that Vic is choking on her gum. I wrench the steering wheel to the side and pull into the shoulder. "Holy shit, are you okay?"

She nods, reaching out her hand and opening and closing her fingers like a claw in a toy vending machine. It takes me a bit to realize she's motioning for me to hand her a water bottle, and I find one and immediately pass it over. She takes a long drink and then sighs. "Yeah, fine. Just... didn't expect that, I guess."

I laugh; I can't help it, even though I know Vic didn't mean anything by it. "You think I did? I was fourteen."

"That's not even legal, is it?"

"With your parents' permission, it is, at least in some states. And guess whose parents were more than happy to give her up when asked?"

"Is that a joke?"

"Fitz had never done more than the minimum amount of research for a school assignment in his entire life, but for this, he had an exact church in Birmingham, Alabama, picked out and everything. My parents loved the idea. I threw up the minute I heard it."

"And you broke up with him on the spot?"

Where the hell is the next rest stop? "Not exactly."

"But if he wanted to get married and you didn't break up...were you *engaged* to him?"

"Give that girl a prize." I swear I can feel the fourth finger on my left hand itching where it used to sport the thin gold band my mother somehow commandeered.

"But *why*? If you knew from the beginning that you didn't want it?"

"Because I was stupid. Because I was completely, totally in love with him and I didn't want to lose him. Because his family already felt like family. And because I thought that maybe, just maybe, if we got married, he'd follow me to college and we'd get out of Charytan together."

"I'm guessing things didn't work out that way."

"You guess right." *Finally.* I spy a sign for an upcoming rest stop, and we remain silent until I pull off the highway with a sigh of relief and slide into a spot close to the entrance. Before Vic can ask me for any more details, I bolt from the car and through the doors.

The bathroom reeks of floral air freshener and isn't helping the horrible wave of nausea wracking my body. I run into a stall and lock the door behind me before dropping to my knees and dry heaving into the toilet. Considering how much I've eaten this morning, I'm somewhat shocked that nothing comes up, but after a minute, I rest back on my heels and let my head fall against the cool metal barrier.

I've worked so hard not to think about this part of it all. I can handle the rest—his family, even his leaving, but not the betrayal that still makes me physically ill. It's the only part no one knows, the only part that might make people understand why I let him go, if it were the kind of thing you could actually tell someone.

The door opens, and then the tapping of Vic's heels sounds on the dirty linoleum. "Rae?" she calls softly.

I stick my hand out under the door, just enough so she can see my chipped black nail polish and the cheap mood ring on my index finger. I stare at the stone, wondering why it's not as dark as I feel, and then there are her toes, and then she's crouching down and squeezing my hand, and then suddenly I am crying, so hard my shoulders are shaking, and she squeezes harder, and then I squeeze harder, and finally I crawl out from underneath and let her hold me and rock me into submission on the floor of a public restroom in a rest stop on I-70.

Eventually, a stranger comes in, a woman in acid-washed jeans and a sweatshirt that smells of baby vomit, and I peel myself off the floor and let Vic escort me out to the McDonald's counter, where she buys us coffee. The warmth seeping through the cup is delicious on my palms, which feel like ice. We sit down at a little table by the window and both of us stare out at the parking lot, blowing on the steaming liquid.

For a second, it almost makes me miss Joe's.

Silence between me and Vic is usually the nice we're-so-close-we-don't-need-words kind, but it's a different kind right now. It feels thick and tense, laden down with questions she's not asking and answers I'm not offering. When she finally does speak, I couldn't be more stunned at the words that come out of her mouth.

"I used to get my butt kicked in Arizona," she says in a faraway voice, her gaze still on the parking lot. "There was this girl, Ashley, who just *hated* me. Hated all the Latino kids in the school, but me the most. I don't even know why. She used to get her friends together and they'd stop me in the hall and demand to see my papers."

My mouth drops open. "What a bitch."

"Yup. She'd make sure I got hit in every gym class, corner me in the locker room…she just made my life a living hell." She taps her forehead, the stripe of a scar I know all too well. "This is from when she rammed my head into a wall."

"And your parents let this go on?" That did *not* seem like the Reyeses I know.

She takes a slow sip of her coffee. "They didn't know. Not until the day I hit back."

I am…stunned. "*You* hit someone?"

She nods, looking so full of self-loathing, I think she'd crawl out of her own skin if she could. "I was just so, so done. Day after day of being treated like I was less than human for literally no reason. It builds."

Oh God, how well I know this. How I hate that I *didn't* know that she was living with this too. Worse, even. She didn't make the choices that got her into this shit. She just *was*.

What a fucked-up world.

"Did you get in trouble?"

She takes a deep breath. "You know how I said we came here because my parents needed new jobs?"

The coffee gurgles in my stomach. "Yeah."

Her eyes squeeze shut. "We're here because of me. Because I got expelled. Because we needed to leave and start somewhere else, and this is where they found jobs. But I'm why they needed them."

Holy. Shit. "Why didn't you just tell me that?" I ask slowly, still trying to process everything she's telling me.

"Because how do you tell a new friend that? Oh, hey, I'm here because I slapped a chick. Don't you wanna be BFFs with me now?"

"I think you know that would only make me like you more."

I expect her to laugh, and feel an unexpected twinge when she doesn't. "Yeah, well, I didn't know that when we first met. They made me feel like I was a psycho for losing my temper like that, and I was afraid you'd think the same thing. By the time I knew you'd understand, it felt weird to admit I'd lied. Anyway, I just wanted to forget about it. Start over." She shrugs, and it is so, so sad. "Same thing we're both hoping to do with college, right?"

I don't even know what to say; I can't imagine Vic

getting violent with anyone. Things would have to be so, so bad for her to lift her hand to someone, and I *hate* that I wasn't there for her then, even though of course we didn't know each other yet. I don't even know what to say, so I blurt the first thing that comes to my lips. "I'm so sorry. I had no idea it was so bad for you there."

"It's weird that you didn't know that," she says, taking another slow sip and letting her gaze drift out the window. "You're the best friend I've ever had, and you didn't know that. And I didn't know you used to be engaged. Doesn't it bother you that for all we know each other, we barely know each other?"

I've never heard Vic talk like this. I feel like a massive oak tree has taken seed in my insides, its roots wrapping around all my vital organs. I flash back to my panic attack, to when she came to see me in the nurse's office, and I take a couple of deep breaths.

And then it's my turn.

"He fucked with our condoms," I say quietly, training my eyes on her even though she's still looking out the window, watching a guy in a flannel shirt examine a dent in his rear bumper. "We started having sex about a year into dating, and I couldn't exactly get hold of birth control pills, especially with no insurance. So we used condoms, and he always bought them because I had no money and he worked on the construction site after school. I trusted him with our birth control; I had no reason not to."

I realize then my coffee's getting cold, and I take a quick sip. "Even when we were engaged, I was adamant about getting out of Charytan when I graduated, and I obviously wasn't crazy about the idea of getting married, either. I was constantly pushing off any wedding talk. Who the fuck wants to be a fourteen-year-old bride, right? I was in love, not completely and totally insane. I agreed in order to buy time in our relationship."

She looks over at me then, her eyes shining with horror as she takes it all in. "You were…you had…you were *fourteen*," she blurts.

"Trailer park fourteen is older than regular fourteen," I say, even though, thinking back on it, I couldn't feel more childish. "Anyway, one day I…" I squeeze my eyes shut and look away. "I miscarried. I hadn't even known I was pregnant. I told John, and he admitted about the condoms. He said he thought if I got pregnant, if we had a baby, it would convince me to stay, to be near our families. And that was it. I broke up with him on the spot."

I glance back at Vic; she looks as if she's about to throw up the few sips of coffee she's consumed on top of this morning's omelet. She tears her eyes away from me and looks back out at the pickup truck. Even though I know it's probably pity she feels for me and not disgust, it doesn't make it all any easier to take. I hate the thought of her feeling either one. I've always known I was too pathetic to have her—or anyone, really—as a friend, but this seals it.

It's too much, sitting there with her, an uncomfortable silence weighing over us. Somehow, I think we were closer when we still had some secrets. I feel like both a slut and a child in front of her now, too stupid and naïve to take control of my own life sooner while she was dealing with shit brought to her through no fault of her own.

"You ready to go?" I rasp, feeling the urge to crush my cup in my hands, if only it wasn't still mostly full. I take a long sip, as if that'll take me closer to some sort of relief. She just nods and we get up and go.

This time, we listen to Fleetwood Mac on the ride home.

VICTORIA

My tongue keeps twisting into a zillion different things to say to Rae, but I know none of them are the right ones. I wish Hallmark made a "Sorry your boyfriend was a freakin' nutjob who tried to trap you by knocking you up" card. Honestly, I'm not even sure what Oprah would do in this situation.

For what it's worth, she doesn't seem to have anything to say to me either, though whether it's because of my revelation or hers, I have no freaking clue. All I want is to go home and talk to my mom or Javi about this, but there's no way I'm telling my mom Reagan's secret, and I have no idea when the next time I'll even speak to Javi could be.

Suddenly, I find myself overwhelmed with the desire to see Freckles; I need to be in the presence of someone who is utterly incapable of judgment. Unfortunately, the only way I'm going to make that happen now is if I follow Reagan to work. I decide instead to text him when I get home and see if he wants to see a movie or something.

"Am I dropping you off at home?"

I'm so surprised to hear her voice in the car that's been quiet for so long that it takes me a minute to realize she's speaking to me, and another to realize that she's getting off at the exit that'll take us back to Charytan. "Yeah." At least I have the letter from Javi to look forward to.

We exchange lukewarm goodbyes and I grab my things from the trunk and let myself inside. There's a note waiting on the kitchen counter informing me that my parents are at brunch with another professor and her husband, and that the letter from Javi's on my bed. I take the stairs two at a time, drop my bag right inside the door of my bedroom, and collapse onto my patchwork sheets, plucking the envelope between my fingertips and ripping it open.

Bula, Little Sis!

Thanks for your last letter. I appreciate that you'd send me one of Mom's messed-up churros if you could. Amazing how much you can miss oil-soaked lumps of dough. (Now, if you can get Abuelita's churros, you send those here immediately.)

I hope you guys are having fun on your college visits! (But not too much fun. Big brother is watching you!) Chase and I took some of the local kids out on boats this week and they loved it, especially since they were way better at it than we were. At least we finally won a soccer game against them, which means they have to honor their promise to teach us a traditional dance. It's cool to do some fun stuff with the kids, since they know us from our school visits where the focus is all on scary stuff about HIV and disease. But it's all stuff we're here for, and it feels good to connect with the kids on multiple levels.

The longer I stay out here, the more I think you might really love doing something like this. Think about all the design inspiration! Plus you'd love working with the kids and getting to see new places—you've never even been to another country except for Mexico! I'm already working on planning my next vacation. Sam wants to go back to Australia, but I wanna see as many different places as possible while I'm here, so I'm trying to pulling toward Samoa.

I know Mom really wants me to come home for

Christmas, but I don't think I can. There's so much stuff going on here around then and I really wanna be here instead of blowing all my vacation days on four hundred different flights to get there. But don't tell her, OK? I wanna break it to her myself.

Love,

Javi

PS—I got a tattoo. Don't freak out and don't tell Mom.

My stomach feels like lead by the time I get to the PS. Mom wasn't the only one who wanted Javi to come home for Christmas. Why does he have to be so far? And I'm glad he says he's having fun, but my heart breaks for him that all the joy is sandwiched between the harsher realities of death and disease.

He's right about one thing, though—I'd love to travel. Every time he goes somewhere new, I pretty much burn with jealousy. I don't even know when I'd do that, though. I'm already a senior, and next comes college, and then comes a job; how do people even do this? How do they get to see and do everything? And Javi has Chase and Sam and his other Peace Corps friends; who would I even travel with? Even if Reagan had the money to go on a trip, I'm not sure she actually *wants* to leave the state, like, ever.

Ugh, just more choices. I don't need more choices. I'm sick of choices. I grab my cell phone and text Freckles.

Hey, wanna do something tonight?

It takes him a few minutes to text back, but I know he's on the day shift with Reagan today. *Sure. Reagan too?*

Well, this is awkward. *Nah, I thought we could hang out just us.* Not that I'm worried he'll say no to that, but I really don't want him to ask why.

Fortunately, he doesn't. *Okay, cool. Pick you up after work?* Then my phone beeps again. *Better yet, let me shower first so I don't smell like French fries.*

I happen to love the smell of French fries, but I'm afraid being too enthusiastic will lead him on, so I just say, *OK, cool.*

Then, because my curiosity has totally been piqued, I turn on my computer and start looking up Fijian fashion.

"How is it?"

I'm in mid-bite when he asks, and I swallow too quickly to answer, nearly choking. "Good," I squeak, though it feels like there's a sprinkle stuck in my throat. "How's the mint chocolate chip?"

"Good."

We're sitting on stools at The Ice Cream Bar, and with my legs dangling free and a vanilla soft serve in a sugar cone in my hand, I feel just like a little kid. I wonder what it would've been like to grow up here instead of in Arizona. "Did you come here a lot when you were younger?" I ask Freckles.

"It's pretty new. Just opened up maybe three, four years ago."

"I'm even newer," I joke.

He smiles, a small one. "I remember." He takes another lick of the bright-green ice cream. "Have you liked it here, so far?"

"I guess so." His smile disappears, and I wonder if I've offended him. "I mean, it's a lot better than Arizona," I add quickly, and I see his shoulders relax. I wonder if he'd still be relaxing if he knew what I'd done, why we're here, but I don't want to talk about that. Now that I know he likes me, I see it plain on his face, and right now, I don't think I could stand to watch it fall away. Besides, what I actually want to talk about is Reagan, but I don't want to put Freckles in a weird spot. "How was work today?"

"Same old Sunday shift," he says with a shrug. "How was Barnaby State?"

It feels like a loaded question, even though he obviously doesn't know anything. Suddenly, I feel guilty for hooking up with Jamie, and paranoid, as if maybe Freckles knows. He couldn't, though; there's no way Reagan would've said anything. I'm sure of it. "Good." My voice is slow and careful, testing. "Went to my first college class and everything. Other than Miss Lucy's, of course."

"My friend Caylee's in that class. She loves it. She's dying to do some workshop with Miss Lucy over winter break and then maybe even intern for her this summer. She's pretty obsessed."

A workshop? An internship? My dangling foot has moved into a full-on jiggle. How awesome does that sound? I'm dying to learn the secrets to the beadwork that girl in the class did, and I definitely need some help with sleeves. Plus, I got this great idea after looking at those websites this morning—

All thoughts float out of my head when I spot a familiar face, and it takes me only a moment to realize that it's Sean Fitzpatrick and nasty Becky Holtzmann from my gym class, who always rolls her eyes when anyone misses a basket or hits a volleyball out of bounds.

"Friends of yours?" Freckles asks.

"No. Definitely not." I tear my eyes away from them and dive back into my ice cream cone.

"I didn't think so. I know he and Reagan aren't exactly..." He waves a hand meekly in the air but doesn't finish the sentence.

"Yeah." I flick a glance over at them again, and then back to Freckles. "Did you know his brother?"

"Fitz? Yeah. He was an okay guy, most of the time. He was already gone before you moved here, no?"

"Guess so. Was it weird when he left?"

"I think everyone was shocked as hell. I know I was. That family's been in Charytan for generations, and as far as I know, none of them plan to leave. Plus, he and

Reagan…" Again with the unfinished sentence.

It didn't occur to me until right now that Freckles had known them as a couple. In fact, everyone in Charytan probably did. What a strange thing that they all did and I didn't, and never will. "What were they like?" I can't help asking. "I can't picture it."

He shrugs. "I dunno. Like a couple. Together constantly. Always holding hands, kissing in the hallway, that sort of thing. If you ever went over to the Fitzpatricks' house, she'd be there, no question. Every baseball or basketball game, she was in the stands. It was weird, at first, because she was so young, but you know Reagan. Wise beyond her years and whatnot."

"He's been gone a long time, hasn't he? If he left right before I moved, then he's already been away over two years. Shouldn't he be home by now? Or did they keep him over there?"

Freckles tips his head and furrows his eyebrow. "You… don't know?"

I don't even know why I'm surprised to hear that I've been left in the dark over something important yet again. And the way he's looking at me makes it clear I'm about to hear something I don't like. "Know what?"

"Fitz is MIA. Has been for six months. No one's heard from him, no one knows where he is, no one even knows if he's alive. I mean, by now the odds are pretty lousy that he is."

Just like that, my entire body turns to ice. I put my cone down on the counter, letting the soft serve smush into the Formica, because if I don't, I know I'm going to drop it onto the floor. Fitz, the love of my best friend's life, the guy who left her heartbroken and secretive and untrusting, isn't even a living, breathing human being anymore. It feels like all the knowledge I had on him has turned into dust in my brain. Like none of it was real.

"Does Reagan know?" I have to ask, because even though I know the answer, I'm holding on to the hope that her "confession" wasn't one big lie.

"Of course. I thought everyone knew, honestly. How could you not?"

"Rae and I don't really talk about him," I say through gritted teeth. *And when you make one person your whole social life, and they choose to hide things from you, you're gonna find yourself in the dark a whole lot.* "Not one of her favorite topics of conversation."

"Can't really blame her," Freckles says with a shrug, clearly oblivious to the fact that he's just sent my mind in some sort of crazy whirl. I can't even tell what I'm feeling now. Sympathy? Hurt? Anger? Mistrust? I want to hug Reagan and shake her at the same time. How could she tell me so much and leave out the most important part of all?

I feel bad bailing on Freckles, but I need to talk to Reagan. Immediately. And judging by the way he's staring between me and my cone as if I'm some sort of crazy person, he's probably okay with ending this "date" early. "Would you mind driving me to Reagan's?" I ask, knowing I don't sound nearly as apologetic as I should.

"Sure." He hops off the stool and takes a few more swipes at his cone before tossing it into the trash while I clean up the mess I've made. A few minutes later, he's dropping me off in front of the trailer park, and I'm shaking as I try to think of what to say. I almost wish I could take him in with me, as if he were some sort of security blanket, but I wave goodbye and then he's gone.

When I first met Reagan, I thought she was a little intense, but I was never afraid to talk to her. We clicked hard and fast, and we've been tight ever since, but now— since we started doing this whole college visit thing, I guess—things keep getting weirder and weirder and I don't know if it's because we're getting older or talking about the future or what.

All I know is that I don't like it, and I want it to stop. Now.

"Who the hell is that knocking at this hour?" I hear her mom yell sourly, annoyed enough that the southern tinge she usually adds to words isn't there. I don't know what the hour has to do with anything—it's only seven thirty—but I'm guessing it has something to do with whatever TV show she's watching right now. She hates being interrupted from doing absolutely nothing.

I hope Rae will be the one to answer the door, but no such luck; her mom's actually peeled herself off the couch long enough to swing the door open and give me her usual suspicious once-over.

Then she points to Reagan's room with a grunt and goes back to the couch without so much as a "hi." Typical visit to casa de Forrester.

Rae's door is partially open but I knock anyway. "Come in," she calls, her voice quiet. Distant. I do, and I close the door behind me. She's bent over something at her desk, obnoxious static coming out of her radio, with only the slightest hint of music in the background. She doesn't look up.

"Rae—"

Her head pops up at the sound of her name. "Oh, it's you." She turns off the radio. "I didn't hear the door. I thought it was my mom."

"Nope." I walk over to the bottom bunk and sit down. "Just me."

"Well hey, just you." She puts down her pencil and turns halfway in her chair so she's sort of facing me, but I still can't see her eyes. "What's up? Have you missed the trailer park so much that you just had to stop by?"

I ignore the joke. "I told you about Ashley. I've never told anyone that before."

"Yeah, and I told you about Fitz. I've never told anyone

that before either. So are we even now?" she snaps.

"It's not a competition."

"Then don't make it sound like one!" She takes a deep breath. "Look, I'm sorry if all the shit about Fitz makes you think less of me. I know I made some stupid decisions when I was younger. I thought I was doing the right thing for me and for someone I thought I loved. I don't know how else to explain it."

"Wait, what?" I genuinely don't know where she's going with this. "Of course it doesn't make me think less of *you*. Why would you even say that?"

"Because this stuff was my fault," she says as if it's the most logical thing in the world. She turns to face me fully. "I know that stuff with Ashley was almost all beyond your control, as opposed to my circumstances, which were my own stupid fault. I get it. I wish I could take back everything that happened to both of us. And I wish I were as innocent as you, but I'm not."

My jaw drops so wide Rae can probably tell what flavor of ice cream I just had. "How can you even think I'm comparing, or that I think this is your fault? Seriously, Reagan, there is twisted stuff going on in your head right now."

She narrows her eyes. "If not that, then what's this about?"

"The rest of it! How could you tell me all that other stuff and not tell me that he's...that he's..." I can't even get the words out, and suddenly it hits me how selfish I'm being. I've never even met the guy and I can't say it, so how can I possibly expect Reagan to?

"Dead?" she says flatly. "So you think that too?"

"I don't know what to think! How am I supposed to know when you keep leaving me in the dark?"

"Oh, I'm so sorry *you* don't know what's going on," she shoots back, her voice oily with disdain. "I'll be sure to give you an exact status on my ex-boyfriend *as soon as I know where the fuck in the world he is.*"

I jump up, and immediately hit my head on the top bunk. Tia Maria! A quick touch of my hand to my head reveals no blood, which means there is nothing to stop me from getting out of there as soon as possible.

So I do.

Chapter Twelve

Reagan

I stare at the door for a long time after Victoria leaves. I know I should apologize, or at least run after her and make sure she has a way to get home, but I feel completely immobile. It's like someone's used industrial-strength glue to keep me in my desk chair.

How did she know? And why can't people just shut up when they don't know what they're talking about? Fitz isn't dead. I know it. I'd *feel* it. I don't care how angry I am, or how much he hurt me—I'd *know* if he were dead like I know my own name or how to fix the fridge door at Joe's when it catches.

The box of letters is all but screaming my name now, and I lever myself off the chair and get the box down from the top shelf, reading one after another after another until I'm surrounded by envelopes. There are so many Fitzes in these letters—angry Fitz and affectionate Fitz and joking Fitz and terrified Fitz. The only Fitz missing is the one who addresses The Incident. That Fitz is conspicuously absent.

Where are you? It doesn't matter how hard I stare at blue ink; it doesn't blur into any hidden messages or clues. It doesn't tell me anything at all.

Slowly and carefully, I pack the letters back into their envelopes and take a step onto the chair when the ringing of my phone startles me and I slip off the surface and fall smack on my ass. The box flies out of my hands and the letters scatter everywhere, heavy oversized confetti covering the linoleum.

"Shit!" I grab my phone from my desk, rubbing my sore butt with my other hand, and prepare to yell at whoever's just interrupted my pathetic evening of reminiscing. Instead, I freeze when "Dave"—I still need to change that—lights up my phone.

Going from thinking about Fitz to talking to Dev feels so...*wrong*. And yet, Dev made it clear there isn't anything between us, so obviously he's just calling for a friendly chat. Just like we used to have before the weekend's weirdness. And if he's trying to keep things normal, I should do the same, right?

Right.

I take a deep breath and pick up the phone. "Hey."

"Hey, you. Guess you got home safe and sound."

"Well, this is my cell, so for all you know I'm trapped in some random guy's attic, but yes, as it happens, I did."

He laughs, and I swear it sounds lower and throatier than usual, making me think things I definitely don't want to be thinking. "Glad to hear it."

"Nice to know you were worried." I don't mean to add an edge to my voice, but it's there, cutting and unmistakable.

There's a pause before he says, "I thought we were okay."

"We are."

"You don't sound like we are."

I huff out a sigh. "You caught me at a bad time, okay?"

"What's wrong?"

The idea of telling Dev about Fitz would be laughable if there was anything humorous about either situation. Instead, I go with the light version. "Just an argument with Vic. How was your ride home?"

"Max was texting with Mia the entire time and Jamie was talking about how he supposedly hooked up with some girl last night. So, literally the same as every other day."

I can't help smiling just the tiniest bit at the fact that

Jamie was at least gentlemanly enough to withhold Vic's identity. "Sounds fascinating."

"Oh, it was. So have you decided yet if you're gonna go visit any other schools?"

"Just to be clear, you're not asking about KU again, are you?"

"Of course not. Though if I *were*, I might point out that the scholarship deadline is the second week of November and if one were even remotely considering attending KU, one should probably pay attention to that."

"If you were."

"Right. The same way I might also point out that my cousin Asma goes to KU and would be happy to host anyone who might want to go visit for a weekend."

"How hypothetically helpful of you."

"Isn't it, though."

It's too much, the playfulness and talk of the future. I need to break the spell. "Is Sara planning on going to KU?" I ask casually.

"She's applying." His tone is a little flatter, but there's no pause, and it's obvious he was anticipating the question. "She's also applying to Northwestern, Notre Dame, Syracuse, Georgetown…"

"And you're not applying to any of those places?"

"My mom teaches at KU. Hard to beat that tuition break."

"Don't you mind?"

"That I can't really apply elsewhere or that I won't necessarily be going to the same college as Sara?"

"Either. Both."

"I like KU. I'm down to be a Jayhawk. And I still have medical school and residency and a fellowship ahead, so I'm sure I'll travel around plenty."

"And?"

"And I already told you I have no delusions of living happily ever after with Sara."

"Even if you end up at the same school?"

His sigh is laden with exasperation. "Reagan—"

"Never mind." I don't want to know. It doesn't matter. *I'm* not going to KU, and he can do whatever he likes with whomever he likes; I'll never see it. He'll be as invisible to me as Fitz.

He doesn't answer, and I'm not sure how to follow up my childish little rant. Finally, I just say, "I should go. Homework."

"Yeah, me too," he mutters. "I'll talk to you later."

I mumble something along the same lines and we hang up. As I set about the task of cleaning up the letters that are scattered across my floor, I can't help wondering when I completely lost the ability to say goodbye like a normal person, to let someone else go in peace.

The next day is about as unmitigated a disaster as humanly possible, barring the fact that I actually ace my

English quiz despite not getting a minute of studying done the night before. Or a minute of restful sleep. Instead, it was just gruesome vision after gruesome vision, from Dev and Sara walking hand in hand on a lush college campus to Fitz showing up at my door minus a limb. Throughout it all, I kept calling for Vic, but to no avail. She didn't even make an appearance.

She doesn't make much of one in school, either. We only have a couple of classes together, and even when we sit next to each other, we only smile briefly and then refuse to make eye contact. It's not a fight, exactly. I don't know what it is. I know I should apologize, but I also know that just saying any words at all will reopen a conversation I absolutely do not want to have. And so when the bell rings at the end of Art, I bolt from the room before you can say "Picasso."

Unfortunately, in my rush to get the hell away from Vic's concern and frustration, I don't pay attention to my actual destination until I collide with something like a car carrying crash test dummies. Only instead of jerking forward on impact, I just gracelessly fall to my ass on the floor.

"Ew, what's wrong with you?" The nasal, high-pitched voice is definitely coming from one of the two bodies currently in my line of sight. I'd put money on the one with the spindly legs and up-to-her-ass mini—which both belong to Kelly Bryce—but I can't count out the hulking beast in baggy jeans for sure. "Watch where you're going." The spindly legs shift into a pose that tells me she's definitely crossing her arms over her tiny chest, and confirms that she's the one making light of my misery.

I have no snappy comeback immediately ready; after all, I *did* bump into them, and I don't exactly have an excuse for it I'm willing to share. I'm certainly not going to bust out with a "sorry" after she was such a bitch, but I gather my stuff up and get to my feet to circle around them as if nothing had happened.

Instead, I catch a good look of the guy's face, and the fact that his arm is around this waste-of-space chick, and I nearly fall down again. It's Luke Schmidt, and he's clearly *with* Kelly. It doesn't look like it's a new pairing, either, despite how recently he called Quinn "my girl" at Joe's. I stand up and hoist my messenger bag higher on my shoulder, knowing I've got nothing to lose right now if I'm guessing wrong.

"He's cheating on you, you know," I tell Kelly, ignoring the meatball completely.

She snorts. I had no idea it was even possible for her to be more piglike, but there you have it. "You don't know anything, you loser," she says with a firmness I can tell she doesn't feel. "Just because you've been single since the second Fitz was smart enough to dump your ass doesn't give you a right to be bitter and make shit up."

Personally, if that were the accurate version, I'd think

it would, but whatever. "The sad thing is," I continue as if Kelly hadn't even spoken, "she's so much cuter than you. You'd think he'd just drop you and be with her fulltime, but she doesn't even go to this school. Which sort of makes it the perfect crime, doesn't it?"

I swerve around them and walk past, knowing at best all I've started is a fight that'll last maybe three minutes, but it feels worth the effort. Until I realize that out there in Charytan Junior High, Quinn Fitzpatrick is on the verge of having her heart broken. I spin back around and storm over to the couple, specifically the stupid hulking lumberjack. "She's only fourteen, you know," I whisper fiercely at him. "She's just a little kid. You can't do something like this to someone like her."

"I have no idea what the fuck you're talking about," he says lazily. He turns to Kelly. "Seriously, babe, she's crazy."

"Would you just stop bothering us?" Kelly spits. "You're crazy. Everyone knows it. Why don't you just go back to keeping your mouth shut like you've been doing so nicely since Fitz stopped keeping you in line?"

I wouldn't have thought Kelly such a bold bitch, but then again, I'm an easy target. There's not a single person at Charytan High who'd come to my defense.

"Shut up, Kelly."

I feel warmth at my back and Vic's words rumbling through my ears. Of course there's a single person at

Charytan who'd come to my defense, even when she's pissed at me. She's not exactly a comeback queen—never has been—but it doesn't matter. My cheeks burn with shame for having thought she'd ever abandon me, no matter how pissed, no matter how much I deserve it.

"Oh, of course, your lesbian lover is here to defend you."

I know I *should* roll my eyes and walk away, that living under the radar is the only way I've survived since Fitz enlisted. But with Vic stiffening at my back, trying to come to my aid even though I don't deserve it, I feel a burning need to prove that I'm worth the damn she can't seem to stop giving about me no matter how much she should.

"Hats off on the *super* original gay joke. You know, just the fact that you think 'lesbian' is an insult is pathetic. What *I* think is that you're all enormous wastes of space doomed to rot in this sinkhole town forever, but on the bright side, it's glaringly obvious you and Luke deserve each other. I wish you the best of luck making each other miserable right until you get knocked up with your ass pressed against the stick shift."

I link an arm through Vic's and together we step around them, ignoring the quiet stares of everyone else in the hallway. "Remind me to stop getting on your bad side," she murmurs as soon as we're free and clear. "What's your deal with them, anyway?"

I explain about Quinn. "This would kill her," I add. "She's so fragile."

There's no response from Vic, and she's not meeting my eyes, just biting her top lip and grazing her fingertips along the cool metal of the locker bank lining the wall as we pass.

"What?"

"Nothing."

"Obviously something."

She sighs. "I just think it's a little...iffy that you're acting like Quinn's your responsibility. I know he was your...I mean, you..." Another huff of breath. "It doesn't sound like she's your problem anymore. Or that she'd even want to be."

The words sting, and I want to tell Vic she has no idea what she's talking about, but after everything, I hold my tongue. "Maybe not," I allow.

We reach the door to her math class, cutting the conversation short. Or maybe it's the perfect timing. "Will I see you at lunch?" she asks as she steps inside.

I appreciated her backup, but I'm still not ready to talk about everything; this conversation proves that. "I need to use the computer for a history paper at lunch. But I'll see you around."

She nods, just once, and slips inside, leaving me alone in a solitude of my own making.

VICTORIA

It feels almost like cheating, but with Reagan continuing to act the secretive weirdo, I don't feel all that guilty as I make my way back to the college office for my study hall period. Not that I really want to have another bonding sesh with Mrs. MacKinnon, but I *would* like to have another look at my options...*without* thinking about what anyone else wants or expects me to do, for once.

The door to the office is partially closed, which means that although anyone can still enter and grab brochures or applications, Mrs. MacKinnon is already with someone. Probably just as well, since I'd rather go on a naked hayride than get any more "advice" from her. I don't so much as glance in her direction when I stroll inside, half-closing the door behind me, and head straight for the catalogs and applications.

It's a sad pile, really. Maybe two kids per year actually go to college outside Kansas, so there's nothing lying around for places like NYU or UCLA, let alone the Ivy League or FIT. There's one brochure lying around for the University of Chicago that's probably been there since the '70s; it's dirty with fingerprints but ultimately, Reagan's one of like three kids in our class with a prayer of getting in, and she's definitely not interested.

The cleanest, newest piles—the ones that have been recently refilled—are for CCC and K-State, though there's a little KU pile that doesn't even look like it's been touched. Of course, KU's been totally forbidden to me by Reagan, but that's exactly the point of coming down here. Before I strike it off my list for good, I need to make sure it's actually wrong for *me* instead of just wrong for *us.*

I reach out for a brochure when a vaguely familiar and brutally obnoxious voice startles me backward. "Wow, I don't think I've ever seen you without your girlfriend."

My hand flies back to my side with a force and speed that could probably kill a man. If only I could test that on Sean Fitzpatrick right now. I know that even if he saw me with the KU catalog, it wouldn't mean anything to him, but I can't help feeling like I just narrowly escaped getting caught hooking up with someone else's boyfriend or something.

"For your information," I tell Sean, bracing myself against the catalog table to hide my shaking hand behind my back, "my *girlfriend* was just getting into it with a guy who's screwing around on your sister. So, maybe you could try to stop being such a jerk to her for once."

He grits his teeth and I can see his jaw popping beneath the tightly stretched skin. "What are you talking about? You don't even know my sister."

"*I* don't, but Reagan does, and she still cares about her a lot, even though your family doesn't make it very easy. Oh, and apparently Luke Schmidt does too."

It's nice to see Sean rendered totally silent, and such

a rare achievement that I take the opportunity to dance right past him out of the office. Only once I'm headed out of the office do I realize that I never even took a brochure.

It's easy enough to find online that night, now that I'm allowing myself to look for it, and the more time I spend on the KU website, the angrier at Reagan I get. Greek life? Check. Multiple enormous libraries? Check. Visual Arts major that's basically perfect for me, and a law school, which is perfect for her? Check. Check check checkity check check check.

So *why* have we been ignoring this glaringly solid option?

My computer dings—it's Javi, looking to chat. I have no idea what time it is in Fiji right now, but it's probably not normal that he's awake. Not that it makes me hesitate for a second before I rush to accept the invitation to chat.

> **FijianPrinceJ:** Bula! What's goin down, little sis?
>
> **Victorius413:** Hiiiiii!!!! What time is it over there??
>
> **FijianPrinceJ:** I'm 17 hours ahead, Vicky. Do the math for once.
>
> **Victorius413:** How many times have I told you not to call me that??
>
> **FijianPrinceJ:** It'll never be enough. How was your trip this weekend?

I debate just how much to tell Javi. Obviously I'm not up for sharing sexual details with my brother, even though he's way too far away to hunt Jamie down. But I also don't seem to be able to talk to my best friend these days, and unfortunately, I don't have lots of other options.

> **Victorius413:** It was fun. A little weird. They've all been fun and a little weird.
>
> **Victorius413:** I think Reagan and I are fighting.
>
> **FijianPrinceJ:** You think?
>
> **Victorius413:** It's not really fighting. But things are weird. I told her about Ashley.

Javi's quiet for a while on the other end, but I can see that he keeps starting to type and stopping. Finally, I lose patience and stab at the keys.

> **Victorius413:** She didn't even say anything. I mean, she said she was sorry and told me her own stuff, but that was kind of it.
>
> **FijianPrinceJ:** What else did you want her to say?
>
> **Victorius413:** I have no idea. It just felt like such a big deal, telling her. It's weird that it wasn't. I was so worried about her reaction and she didn't even blink at the fact that I'd been expelled.
>
> **FijianPrinceJ:** Do you wish she was more

judgmental? Isn't it good that she isn't?

Victorius413: Of course, but it just made me feel so…I don't know. Silly, maybe. That I built it up in my head. That I build everything up in my head.

Now is when I'm desperate to ask—*Was I building it up in my head with you, too? Am I really why you left?* But I don't.

FijianPrinceJ: Maybe you do, a little bit, but things build up IRL too. You know none of us blame you for Ashley, right? Not that it's OK to hit someone, but…

FijianPrinceJ: No one blames you. And you apologized. So stop blaming yourself. It's time to figure out what makes you happy, and just do it. Worst comes to worst, you make a mistake and then you change paths. That's the best freaking part of being a teenager.

Figure out what makes you happy. Like that's so easy. Though, actually, shouldn't it be?

Victorius413: Do you miss being a teen already, o wise one?

FijianPrinceJ: Nope—legal drinking age in Fiji is 21. Happy to be right where I am.

Victorius413: Good priorities, Bro.
FijianPrinceJ: Thanks, I thought so too. Lunch time's over—I gotta run. The kids are calling!
FijianPrinceJ has signed off.

Do what makes you happy. Says the guy who lives in a freaking jungle and can't talk to his sister for more than five minutes because a bunch of kids need his attention. But at least Javi's hanging out with friends, doing some traveling, seeing beautiful things, learning new languages, and getting a sick tan. What am I doing other than getting felt up by some guy in a field?

I click back over to the KU application and check out the admission requirements. My GPA and ACT scores are definitely in the safe zone; my dad would've grounded me for life if they weren't. The Department of Visual Art stuff is a little trickier; I don't have a portfolio. I have a bunch of sketches I've done, but nothing portfolio worthy. Tia Maria, I'm once again hopeless.

Or maybe not.

I pull my phone out of my pocket and text what's quickly becoming a familiar number. *Hey, up for giving me another ride to CCC tomorrow?*

It takes Freckles less than a minute to text back. *Sure, what's up?*

Just want to check something out. No reason to say any more than that until I know what my options are. But for once, the ideas are coming fast and furious, and for the rest of the night, I simply take a pencil and sketchpad and let them flow.

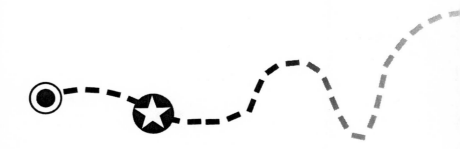

CHAPTER THIRTEEN

REAGAN

What'd the blonde say when she opened the box of Cheerios?

I bite my lips to hide a smile as the millionth blond joke of the week from Dev flashes across the screen of my cell phone. He's been doing this for days, ever since I broke down and texted him *Make me laugh* after that weird morning with Quinn's lumberjack and Vic. Not sure who told him it was a good idea to send blond jokes to a blonde, but he's been at it with a vengeance. For what it's worth, he's got a pretty good arsenal; he's been accommodating my request all week. It's almost been enough to take my mind off things.

Almost.

"What's so funny?"

Apparently I'm not hiding my smile well enough from Sherlock Freckles. "Nothing." I tuck my phone into my back pocket and fill up a couple of thirty-two-ounce cups with cola that table four most certainly doesn't need; the kids are already running around on a sugar high. My butt buzzes with the punchline just as I'm handing them over.

Doughnut seeds!

My barked laugh is loud enough to draw attention from half the diner. Where does he get these? *You are truly twisted,* I text back, away from Freckles's prying eyes. I haven't been responding to most of them, because every time I do, we seem to get into lengthy conversations that occasionally turn into phone calls that make me mad at everything all over again, but with this one, I can't help it.

So I take it this one was your favorite? Cool, mine too.

I'm going back to ignoring you, I text back, praying I'll find the strength to make good on that.

I'd like to see you try. Then you won't get to read my favorite favorite one.

You just said that was your favorite.

Yup, but I still have a favorite favorite. You wouldn't want to miss out on it by ignoring me, would you?

I hate myself for burning with curiosity. I also hate myself for the tiny part of me that wonders if this *is* in fact how he sees blondes. I don't know much about Sara, but if she's Indian as Jamie said she is, then I'm guessing there aren't many jokes about her hair color. Am I just this dumb toy to Dev? Just this blond…thing?

"Rae, can you see what Mrs. Masone wants?" Freckles asks, breaking into my stressing session. "I have to go deal with the triplets' spill."

Ugh, Mrs. Masone may be a pain in my ass but nothing beats scraping globs of mashed potato off the floor, compliments of the now-five-year-old Benning triplets.

"With pleasure," I mutter, sliding the phone back in its spot. Turns out her coleslaw's not sweet enough. She complains about this at least once a week, but it never stops her from getting it on the side. It also doesn't seem to matter that Joe's coleslaw is just about sweet enough to require a root canal on contact.

I do a round on the floor, checking to see if anyone has any complaints—almost everyone does—or needs anything, which, again, is pretty much par for the course. I'm just finishing my sweep of handing out extra mayo, straws, napkins, salt, and "a menu that doesn't have a speck over there" when I hear the familiar jingle of my cell phone ring coming out of my butt.

I quickly silence it and glance at the screen. Dev. No one on the floor seems to need anything for the next five seconds so I flash a hand signal to Freckles to let him know I'm going on a quick break and then dash out into the back alley to where most of the others take their breaks with Marlboro Reds in hand.

"'Lo?"

"You're not really ignoring me, are you?"

I'm so out of breath from dashing into the alley in time to get his call that my laugh in response actually hurts my lungs. Or maybe that's the chilly autumn night air. "You're an idiot."

"Is that a yes? A no? I forgot which one I'm even hoping for."

"I'm at work, so I actually can't answer you every four seconds. These people aren't going to eat an entire cow's worth of ribs on their own, you know."

"Ah, yes, I forgot about your great service to humanity."

"You wanna pay my gas bills?"

"Fair point. So, where are you and Tori"—he always gives her name just enough extra weight to make me roll my eyes—"going this weekend?"

"Well, *Dave*"—because really, I'm not going to let him get away with pretending he didn't do the exact same thing—"we're not going anywhere."

He's silent for a moment, and then, "So, does that mean you decided on a school?"

"No, it means I decided to stop traveling around and visiting them. It got"—complicated—"expensive." Both, really.

"Oh."

"Why do you ask?" I open up the back door and peer inside; Freckles looks swamped. I can't stay out here much longer.

"I just happened to see that Chapman is having a thing this weekend, and I know you mentioned it. Thought you might be going."

"And if I was?"

He exhales sharply. "I don't know. Just thought it'd be cool to see you again. Maybe. That's dumb, right?"

The battery's growing warm beneath my palm. "A little."

His rich, low laughter fills my ear. Such a substantial sound for such a skinny guy. "I'd love to see how you talk to guys you really hate."

"Hang around Charytan for a day and you'll see plenty of it." Speaking of which, I'm pretty sure I see Sean Fitzpatrick's stupid blond buzz cut in there. I let the door close and then lean back against it and close my eyes as a cool breeze washes over me. It's jacket weather, which I always notice weeks too late.

"Is that an invitation?"

"Is what…" I replay my last words in my head. "Sure," I say dryly. "Hang around Charytan any time you like. Nothing will make you happier with what you have than a few hours around here."

"There's a college there, right?"

"Yeah, if you can call it that. Charytan Community College. Where the finest minds of the world's dumbest town go on to rot in classes like Wife Beating 101." Then I think of Freckles, and the classes taught by Vic's parents, and feel a brief flash of guilt. "Well, it's not all bad. Just mostly."

"But not all, right?"

It takes me a minute to see where he's going with this. "Not all," I repeat slowly.

"Seems like something I should probably check out then," he says so that I can hear the smile in his voice. "You know, before I commit to anything."

"Probably." My heart thuds at the word, and I pry open the door for another glance inside. I really have to go. "I'm happy to help you make arrangements and stuff. Ya know, for the good of academia. I gotta run now, though."

"Are you up for it? One last college visit?"

I breathe in deeply. Am I up for it? One more weekend of exploring my maybe non-existent future with a guy who represents everything I don't and won't have? Sure, that sounds like fun.

"I think I can do one last one," I confirm. And then, "Bye."

"G'night, Rogue."

I have no idea what I've just done as I walk back inside to tackle the last few hours of my shift, but I know this:

college had better make me smarter than I am now.

It's been days since I've really talked to Vic, but by Friday morning, all I want to do is find her and tell her about Dev's visit. Not doing so just feels like lying somehow. We don't have any of our first three classes together, but fourth period, we both have study hall, and I know exactly where in the library to find her. Though if she's *not* on the floor of our favorite aisle of the library—the one absolutely no one ever ventures near because it's full of books for classes like physics that aren't required and so no one ever takes—then I know things between us are bad.

I breathe a sigh of relief when I spot her on the floor, though she's so engrossed in whatever she's bent over that she doesn't even notice me until I cough loudly. Even then, she just startles a bit, brushes her long brown bangs out of her eyes, and says, "Oh, hey."

"Oh, hey, to you too." I slide my backpack off my shoulder onto the ugly gray carpet and sit down across from her, resting against a stack of textbooks that probably haven't been updated since Bleeding Kansas. "What are you working on?"

She pulls back from the papers on her lap and immediately the bright fuchsia on the page she'd just been sketching on jumps out at me. I bend over to examine it more closely, careful not to get smudgy fingerprints on the white paper. "Did you design this?" I'm not into fashion—at all—but the dress she's sketched out looks pretty damn awesome. She'd been drawing studs on it when I interrupted, giving a bit of a badass biker look to the otherwise girly floor-sweeping gown.

"You like it?" She sounds almost…shy.

"It's awesome! Are there others under there?"

She nods and flips through slowly, taking care with the pages. The bright colors are a little dizzying, but really cool at the same time. A few of the outfits have a bit of an island-y vibe that I'm guessing are somehow Javi-inspired. A couple even seem to have sort of a Mexican flair. I'm not sure what the unifying theme is, or if there's supposed to be one, but it looks like a pretty kickass collection. I tell her so.

"Thanks," she says, shy again, as she tucks them away into a folder. "So, what's up?"

I feel like I've just stumbled onto something really important and now talking about Dev just seems silly. In fact, I realize with a sinking feeling, I've done a lot of the "let's talk about my stuff over your stuff" thing lately.

"What's that for?" I ask, ignoring her question for now.

She shrugs. "Not sure yet. Applications, maybe. If I get into a design program."

Applications. College. I've barely thought about college all week, but in a weird role reversal, Vic's obviously a lot more on top of things. Meanwhile, I'm wrapped up in a boy. Again. What's wrong with me?

"That's great," I say weakly, because she deserves my support, and it's not her fault I'm a fucking mess. "I mean, I knew you could sew and stuff, but I didn't realize you could do this."

"I'm learning. Slowly." I know she's going for self-deprecating with her smile, but it's impossible to miss the note of pride in it. The note of really, really well-earned pride. I don't even know how one picks up skills in Charytan, but she's certainly doing it, and I admire the hell out of her for it.

"Not so slowly, it looks like."

She just shrugs again.

I sigh and readjust so this one pointy book will stop jabbing me in the back, then focus all my energy on scratching at a crusty patch in the carpet. When a friendship crumbles, there are only really two things that can bring it back: a shitload of time, or a sincere apology. And I am way too impatient to have my best friend back in my life to rely on the former.

"Look, Vic, I'm really sorry about…well, a lot of our conversations lately, I guess. Fitz is just a really bad topic for me. I should've just told you about him from the beginning and then asked never to talk about it again."

"Is that what you want? To never talk about him again?"

I keep scratching. I don't know why; whatever I'm touching is definitely disgusting. At least I'm pretty sure it's not gum. "Yes. I mean, no. I don't know. Not now, I guess."

"Well, whenever you're ready, I guess."

We just sit quietly for a little bit after that, and then she reaches into her bag, but instead of pulling her drawings back out, I glimpse some equations. Definitely calc homework. I kind of wish she'd go back to the sketches so I can watch her work on them, but I feel weird asking, so I just take out my AP Chem notes and we work in silence, the same way we've done a zillion times before, only the vibe is weird.

I try again, finally daring to glance at her face. "I'm sorry about that Arizona bitch. If you want, on our next road trip, we can totally 'visit' ASU or something and go kick her ass. I've been lifting heavy boxes at Joe's lately, so I'm pretty sure I could take her. I'd like to see them try to expel me."

Surprise registers on her face for a moment, and then she laughs, so loudly that I clap my hand over her mouth because I really don't want to get kicked out of the library right now. But I'm laughing too, and she claps her hand over *my* mouth, and just like that, we're best friends and total idiots again.

"She's not worth the gas money," Vic says once we've composed ourselves. "But appreciate the thought. And, by the way, if you ever want *me* to kick Sean Fitzpatrick's butt…well, I can at least leave flaming dog poop on his porch or something."

"Now *that* is a wonderfully sweet thought. He actually came to talk to me the other day, after I got into a fight with that asshole who's hooking up with Quinn. Just to demand what I know. Obviously not to apologize for being a total dick or anything."

"Obviously."

"Well, whatever. Soon enough we're going to college and we'll never have to think about any of these jerks again, right?"

"Right."

Just then, the bell rings—I haven't gotten a minute of work done during study hall, but it was worth it. Only as we're making our way out of the library do I realize I still haven't told her about Dev. But now that things are cool again, I don't feel like getting into it, and anyway, there isn't really time. So I just say, "See ya later," knowing that I won't, and head off to class.

I'm pretty sure I'm going to go crazy as I count down the minutes until the school day ends at 2:37. I'm meeting Dev at CCC at three o'clock, though I don't know whether he needs to believe he's actually on a college tour or if he's just collecting proof for his parents.

By the time the bell rings, I've bitten my nails down

to nothing, decided my outfit reeks of Goodwill (which makes sense, seeing as it was entirely purchased there), and reminded myself a hundred times that we're just friends hanging out and there's nothing to be nervous about. But I *am* nervous and I don't know why and I hate myself for it.

Without Vic's phone, I'm out of luck for music, though I jiggle the radio knobs a zillion times in vain, just because I'm so desperate for it. Finally, I exhale loudly into the car and call Vic; I need some noise to keep me company.

Her stupid phone goes straight to voice mail.

When I pull into the parking lot, I'm singing "Me and Bobby McGee" to myself, which is a terrible idea because I can't hit any of the notes in the chorus and my throat's a little raw from trying. Whatever. I find a spot and sit there for a minute, then rub cherry Chapstick onto my lips. Then there's nothing left to do, but I'm frozen in the driver's seat. What if he doesn't show up? What if I spend an hour standing at the campus map where we agreed to meet, staring at my watch and humming Janis to myself, freezing my ass off in the November chill while he and Sara are sitting at home, laughing—

A knock at my window scares the shit out of me and I jump up so high in my seat I for sure would've hit the ceiling if my seat belt weren't strapping me down, pulling me back to my seat with butt-bruising force. When I finally catch my breath, I turn and see Dev's huge grin on the other side of the window, even more blinding white than I remember it.

I roll down the window. "You know, if you give me a heart attack, you're gonna have to show *yourself* around Charytan, and good luck figuring out what's safe on the menu at Joe's Diner without an insider."

He laughs. "Sorry, I saw you pull in and I couldn't help it. Though I had no idea you scared so easily. I should probably warn you now that I'm going to use that to my advantage all weekend."

"Duly noted. Now can you move away from my door so I don't have to spend the day in my car?"

He sticks out his tongue and steps back, and I unbuckle my seat belt and let myself out of the car and into a warm hug that I force myself out of after a few seconds because the urge to clasp my arms around him in a permanent grip is far too strong. And creepy. "So," he says, jamming his hands into the kangaroo pocket of his scarlet Cornhuskers sweatshirt, "what do we see first?"

"Well, we can consult the trusty map—oh, I'm sorry, is that insensitive? You know, because of your complete and totally inability to read them?" I ask sweetly.

"Phew!" Dev wipes his hand across his forehead as we head in the direction of the map. "I was afraid you might've gotten funnier since we last spoke, but clearly I was worried about nothing."

"Just making sure to keep everything at a low enough level that you can understand everything I'm saying."

"Very kind of you."

"I'm nothing if not a sweetheart." We reach the map, and Dev pulls out a folded-up schedule he printed at home. "So, did you pick a class?"

"Well, you *did* get me intrigued by your mention of ASL, and that's at three thirty, right?"

"I mentioned the class because Vic's mom teaches it," I remind him. "You seriously want to sit in on a sign language class mid-semester? You won't understand a thing."

He shrugs. "Sure, why not? It'd be a cool thing to learn."

"For a future doctor?"

"You never know what'll help you communicate with patients. Do you know where it is?"

I've never been to Mrs. Reyes's class, but with the help of his printout and the map, I find the room easily. We have a little time to kill, so I show him the cafeteria, with its two unimpressive fast food stands and even dinkier salad bar.

"Mmmm." He inhales deeply and his lips curl into a smile. "God, that smells good. I love the smell of delicious fried goodness."

"I think you might be overestimating the deliciousness of the offerings here. This place makes Joe's look like..."

I can't even name any fancy restaurants. The nicest place I've ever been is the Olive Garden, with the Reyeses, for Vic's last birthday.

"That good, huh?" He sniffs in the air again. "Well, I smell what I'm pretty sure are cheese fries, and I'm physically incapable of turning those down. You in?"

I *am* hungry, since I spent my lunch period doing the homework I didn't get done during study hall, but the idea of paying for food at another place when I know I'll get freebies at Joe's later makes me hesitate. Before I can decline, though, Dev says, "Oh, just try one—it won't kill you. Or if it does, at least it'll make a good story," before heading to the counter and buying a paper boat of them.

We sit down at a table, and he looks at me expectantly. "What?" I demand.

"You have to go first."

"They're your fries!"

"They're *our* fries," he corrects as he pushes them over to me, and I dig my nails into my thigh to distract myself from the annoying little ache in my chest that comes with those words. Of course, my nails are non-existent now and serve absolutely no purpose, so I just shove a fry into my mouth and chew.

"Well?"

I swallow. "I'm still alive, and I guess they don't suck."

He smiles triumphantly. "I knew it! Greatest food

ever." He then promptly shoves a fistful into his mouth.

We sit there eating cheese fries while I fill him in on all there is to do in our fair city, from scarfing burgers at Joe's to playing drunk tetherball at the park. "When it's hot out, you can usually find someone in my trailer park making a water slide out of a tarp and a hose, but otherwise, your best bet at recreation is shooting down beer bottles with the construction workers at twilight."

"Have you done that?"

"With my dad, a couple of times, when I was a kid. Then he started smoking again and got afraid I'd tell my mother, so he forbade me from coming. As if he doesn't smell like a barely disguised ashtray at all times."

Dev stuffs another fry into his mouth and scans the room. "I could probably get used to eating this every day."

Subtle topic shift. Though not unwelcome. "You'd be three hundred pounds in no time."

"Hey, I'd welcome the weight gain," he says, patting what is unquestionably a flat stomach through his sweatshirt. "I get cold in the winter."

I roll my eyes. "You make it sound like you're actually considering this place. Nobody actually considers this place."

He glances around again. "I don't know, looks to me like plenty of people have more than considered it," he says, gesturing at the tables filling up around us. "Unless it's just a really, really popular week to visit."

"They're all here for the cheese fries."

"Cute." He pushes the boat toward me; there's only one left. I wave a hand at it—there's no way I'm finishing his fries—and he shrugs and pops the last one into his mouth. "Ready for class?"

"Yes, I'm ready. Are you?" I sign in response, and he looks at me in amazement.

"You can sign?"

"Didn't I tell you that?"

"Yeah, but you made it sound like you only know a couple of words. That looked so legit."

I laugh. "All I said is, 'Yes, I'm ready. Are you?'"

"Still. It looked really cool. Will you teach me how to do it?"

"Let's see what Ana—Mrs. Reyes—can teach you first." I gather up my stuff while Dev tosses out the fry boat. "But I'll cover all the swear words she'll definitely leave out."

"That's all I really want to learn anyway, obviously."

"Perfect." We head out of the cafeteria toward the classroom, just two college students, backpacks swinging, heading off into the future.

VICTORIA

If high school were anything like Fashion Design with Miss Lucy, I'd have a freaking 4.0. Higher, even. She gushes over my sketches, corrects my stitching in a way that actually helps me fix it for the next time, and explains dyeing techniques so they actually stick in my brain. It's been less than two weeks since she let me start sitting in on her class and already I've learned about a zillion things.

I hold out the zipper I've just sewn for Miss Lucy's approval, and feel myself beam as she nods that I've done a good job. We're all at different levels in the class, so except for the half hour of lecture per session, we tend to do our own things. Michelle—the girl who'd been working on that gorgeous dress—is by far the most advanced, and Freckles's friend Caylee is pretty good too. They're beyond hemming and basic stitching and well into just making awesome garments from start to finish. While I've made my own stuff before, I'm definitely happy to go over the beginner stuff with an actual instructor rather than just my abuelita.

With the easier-level zipper complete, I set to work on attempting a hidden zipper, when I see a familiar tiny figure standing in the always-open door to the classroom. *No, it can't be.* But it is. I have no idea what Reagan is doing at CCC, but that is definitely her white-streaked head peering at me curiously from the hallway, as if she's trying to figure out if it's really me.

I pick up my hand to wave, a sheepish smile on my face, when suddenly I hear a faint "What are you looking at?" from the hallway and watch another familiar figure—

this one belonging to Dev Shah—come up behind her. *What the…?*

Now Rae's the one who looks embarrassed, and I have *no* idea what's going on.

"Miss Lucy?" I ask, raising my hand in the air. "Can I go to the bathroom?"

She waves her fingers dismissively in my direction, which is basically her response to everything. I put down my stuff and duck into the hallway.

"What are you doing here?" I whisper fiercely at Reagan, yanking her around the corner. "And what's *he* doing here?"

"I'm visiting a college," he answers, as if it's the most obvious thing in the world that a guy who's goingand has all but moved into KU would check out a random community college five hours from home.

"Uh huh." I turn to Reagan, and wince at the expression on her face. "What? What's that look?"

"That *look* is about the fact that you're taking classes here and didn't even say anything!"

"Kind of like how you invited your *boyfriend* here for the weekend without saying anything to me?" I counter before I can give a second thought to how awkward that statement is.

Unsurprisingly, her face flames, and so does his. "That is *so* not the same, Victoria. You're taking classes at *college* in secret. College in *Charytan*, no less. Our plan was to do this together. To get out of here *together*."

My cheeks feel every bit as hot as hers look, and I hate fighting, but I am so not letting her get away with putting this all on me. "Just because I'm taking classes here *now* doesn't mean this is my plan for next year."

"But you're not saying it isn't," she observes, her eyes narrowing. "Is that why you kept this a secret from me, after we were supposedly done with all those? Because you don't really want to get out of here at all?"

"Or maybe you've just made it clear you think this is a place for idiots, so there was no possible way I could tell you how much I love taking a class here," I snap back. "It's not like I enrolled as a fulltime student, Reagan. I'm working on my portfolio so I can get into a decent design program, period. Now, if you'll excuse me, I'm going back to class." I look back and forth between them. "And don't do anything stupid."

I turn on my heel, lift my head, and walk back into class.

By the time class is over and I've sat with Miss Lucy for fifteen minutes afterward, getting her comments on my application portfolio, Reagan and Dev are nowhere to be found. Not that I'm looking all that hard; I'm not sure I want to be anywhere near that mess when it explodes. Instead, I head straight for my mom's classroom. She just taught three in a row, and I know she'll be happy to hand over the wheel to me so she can relax for the fifteen-minute ride home.

She smiles big when she sees me and envelops me in a hug. "How was class?" she signs.

"Good! I'm making a lot of progress, and Miss Lucy really liked my portfolio." I pull out the sketches and show her where Miss Lucy has made notes, then tuck the folder back into my bag. "I'm definitely going to be working on them a lot this weekend. I need to get that application in next week."

"Good for you, sweetie." She smiles and signs "Have a good night" at a student who's waving goodbye to her, then turns back to me. "It was fun to have Reagan in my class today! You didn't tell me she was coming."

"I didn't know," I admit. "She came to your class?"

"With a cute boy," my mom confirms, waggling her eyebrows. "Indian, I think. Does he go to your school?"

I sigh. "Nope. That's the guy I told you about, that she met on our first college visit."

"What's he doing here?"

"Excellent question." I watch as a couple more students file out and then turn back to my mother. "So they attended your class? Like students?"

"Just like students," she signs with a smile. "Reagan's gotten a little rusty since that week she was at our house every day, but she picked it back up quickly. Is everything okay with you two?"

I hesitate before signing, "I don't know. We're both just…" My hands kinda flop as I think about how to end my sentence. "Focused on the future," I finish after a minute.

I wait for her to respond something about how our future is supposed to be together, but all she signs in response is, "It's nice to see you working so hard. I'm very proud of you, honey."

My mom's not shy with praise or anything, but I *have* been working hard, and her recognition of it kind of embarrasses me in how happy it makes me. "Are you ready to go?" I sign, feeling the need to change the subject.

"I need to run to the administration building to drop off some reports and schedule my mid-term date. Can you sit here for a couple of minutes?"

"Sure, no problem."

She kisses me on the forehead and leaves the room, and I pull out my cell phone to keep me entertained while I wait. Usually I'd bug Reagan to kill time, but that obviously isn't going to happen right now. Instead, I skim through my text messages, wrinkling my nose when I see the chain of texts with Jamie from the night we hooked up. I'd almost forgotten about that argument, and everything that'd preceded it. Closing my eyes, I flash back to lying in that field, to the feeling of power as I took control. God, that'd felt good, the same kind of good I'm feeling now at actually having some sort of direction.

Suddenly, I'm feeling energized, impatient. My toes are tapping frantically on the floor, waiting for my mother's return, and an urge to *do* something is making my fingers tingle. I look back down at the texts and smirk at the screen as I type out a new one to Jamie.

Just to be clear, you were a massive jerk that night. I press Send, and then I move to my texts from Freckles and use the phone number to call him.

He picks up on the third ring. "Vic?"

It's obvious he's at Joe's. He pretty much always is, and the sounds of screaming kids and crashing silverware in the background are dead giveaways. "Hey. Can I come see you?"

"I'm at work. It's actually pretty crazy here—"

"So I'll help. Don't worry, I won't be too distracting, I promise. I just want to see you."

"See me?"

"I'll be there in twenty minutes; I just need to drop my mom off on the way. Can you get a bacon tuna melt going for me?"

"Uh, yeah. Yeah, sure. You sure you wanna come hang out here?"

"Positive," I say firmly. Because I am. About something. Finally.

"Are you sure you don't want to call Reagan and ask her to come in?" Freckles asks for the millionth time as

I snatch a ketchup from the crate behind the counter and throw it to him underhand. He throws me an empty bottle in return, and I immediately set to filling it. Mitch Macklin, a total burnout I know only because his band played junior prom last year and he made a drunken speech that resulted in his being banned from the high school for life, was supposed to do this before the shift. Unfortunately, he *wasn't* banned from the gross, seedy bar that doesn't mind hiring underage kids, and he got a last-minute spot that caused him to bail on work with approximately two minutes' notice.

"I can handle it," I assure him, putting down the bottle and grabbing a handful of menus as a couple of jocks from school walk in with bottle blondes on their arms. "Rae's busy. Trust me." I wait until the foursome sits and then bring over their menus with a smile, as if they haven't all looked through me in the halls of CHS a zillion times.

"I don't need this," one of the girls says snottily, pushing her menu back at me with the tip of a bubblegum-colored fingernail. "I just want fries. I'm on a diet," she explains to the rest of the table.

The other blonde nods sympathetically. "Me too. Just fries for me too."

Jock #1 rolls his eyes. "Chicks. Always on diets." The way he says it, you can tell he thinks it's actually hot. Never mind that French fries are about as dietetic as a bucket of lard. "I'll have a burger special."

"What about you?" I ask Jock #2.

"I'm still thinking," he practically growls.

"Aren't you going to write our orders down?" Blonde #1 whines.

"Fries. Fries. Burger special. Not that hard." God, I sound exactly like Reagan. And I'm starting to understand exactly how she got that way. This job sucks.

"The customer is always right, you know," Blonde #2 informs me.

"Right about what? I didn't question anything."

Before anyone can say another word, a hand on my arm pulls me back.

"Thanks for covering me," Freckles says loudly. "I'll take it from here. What can I get you guys?" He pulls out a pad, which I know will thrill them, and retreat back behind the counter, forcing myself not to give those irritating girls the dirty looks they totally deserve.

I go back to refilling ketchup bottles, pouring fountain sodas, and giving out menus to people who sit at the counter while I wait for Freckles to return with the order. When he does, I expect him to be upset at me, but he seems anything but.

"Sorry about that," he says before handing off the order to the cook. "Some people in this town really rely on the experience of being waited on to feel big or whatever."

"How do you have the patience for that?"

He shrugs. "I'm used to it. And it's not personal. Besides, if I ever want to run my own place, I have to be able to deal with all types."

He says it all so matter-of-factly, like such an...adult. *Boom*—I'm over it. *Boom*—they're the whiny, needy, insecure babies, and I'm just tolerating them. *Boom*—I have a real vision for my future and I'm doing everything I can to make it happen, even if it sucks sometimes.

It is by far the hottest I have ever found Freckles— Steve. The hottest I have ever found Steve.

"What?"

I blink, realizing I've been staring. "What do you mean, what?"

"You were kind of...gawking at me. Did that sound pathetic or something?"

"No! No, of course not. On the contrary—" I'm cut off by the ding of the bell and the shout of an order number. Steve gives me a brief apologetic smile before dashing off for the food, which he expertly balances on bent arms I realize only now are bulging with muscles. I abandon my tasks for a moment to watch him drop off the food, but then Hector calls out another order and I retrieve it. Thankfully, it's only two plates, which I can handle.

The next hour is a total madhouse, and my waitressing skills are definitely not standing up to the pressure. Steve has to utter the words, "I'm so sorry, of course that's on us," multiple times throughout the hour, but he never once loses his cool, never once snaps at me or anyone else. He's like a miraculously unflappable machine.

Finally, the crowd starts to thin out as people head to the movie theater or whatever basement they'll be making out in, and we catch our breath behind the counter. Well, I catch my breath. Steve is totally chill. He offers me to fill me a cup of the watered-down liquid Joe passes off as Diet Coke, but I decline. After a couple of hours in this place, I never want to eat or drink anything here again. He has no such issue, though, and pours himself a cup of orange soda.

"So," he says, taking a sip, "what were you gonna say?"

"When?"

"Oh. Uh. Never mind."

I rack my brain for what he might be talking about, but it's totally fried from the last hour of memorizing orders and table numbers. And then, suddenly, it hits me—he still wants the answer to why I was "gawking" at him. Just when I thought he couldn't melt my heart any more that night...

"You're a good guy, Steve. That's what I was going to say."

"Oh. Okay." The tips of his ears turn red, and he puts down his cup and starts to wipe down the counter. It's not exactly the reaction I expect. But maybe I misread him. Maybe he's not actually into me, or maybe he was, but

I've ruined his night, and now he isn't anymore. Maybe—

"The good guys never get the girl," he says suddenly, his hand pausing on the counter. "Why is that?"

"That's not true," I say automatically, even though thinking about it, he has a point. It took me until right this minute to realize just how much I might be interested in Freckles—Steve—as more than a friend. It took me no time at all to decide I was going to hook up with Jamie, and he was an A-hole. "Well, maybe sometimes it's true."

"Always," he mutters, moving the rag over the countertop again.

I reach out and hold his hand still, then turn his chin in my direction. "Trust me," I say. "Sometimes, the good guy does get the girl."

And then I rise on my toes and kiss him. He rears back almost instantly—clearly I've caught him off guard—but then the rag drops to the counter and he pulls me around the corner to the stockroom and his arms find their way around my waist. He tastes like sunshine and orange soda. I actually manage to forget that we're at the diner until an obnoxious voice from behind Steve says, "Wow, I guess I *really* wasn't needed here tonight."

We jump apart to see—and smell—Mitch Macklin, who's in full rock star mode in ripped jeans, a (fake) leather jacket, and a cloud of pot smoke. I hadn't realized it was raining, but his usually spiky hair is dripping.

He grins. "I thought you might need help with the

end of the shift and closing. I felt bad when I saw Forrester at the bar and realized she hadn't taken over for me, but apparently you found even better help."

"Reagan was at the bar?" I can't keep the shock out of my voice.

Mitch shrugs. "Just for a song or two. She was with some brown guy who looked like he was gonna punch me when I asked her if she wanted me to autograph her boob. They never card at that place."

"You're out early," Steve observes.

"We were just the opening act. So do you want help or not?"

"Yes, we do," I say, because the smell of pot on top of the smell of grease is just too much and I desperately need a shower. I turn to Steve. "Wanna hang out after you clean up?"

"Definitely." His grin is so huge that I can't help kissing him again, just a little peck. "I'll come by after work. Well, after I've showered."

"Perfect." I untie my apron and thrust it at Mitch. "Thanks for the experience, guys. The place is all yours."

As I walk out to the car, bracing myself for the rain, I swear I can feel both guys' eyes watching me leave, and I can't help thinking it's only the beginning of a darn good night.

CHAPTER FOURTEEN

REAGAN

"Welcome to the place where dreams go to die," I tell Dev as I park in the lot of the trailer park he's been begging to see since we left CCC. Usually doing so kicks up a cloud of dust, but it's raining so hard that we're parked on one hundred percent mud. The park is rarely beautiful, but now in the cold, rainy winter, with the trees bare except for some tacky colored lights and the sparse grass a matted mess, I don't think it's ever looked uglier. "Home sweet home."

He looks out the window with an expression of wonderment, but he tones it down when he catches me watching him. "It's got character," he says, cracking a grin, and I laugh because there's certainly no denying that. "Are your parents home?"

The lights are off and the truck is nowhere to be found, so I take that as a no. "I don't think so. Did you want to meet them?"

"Well, I *am* in my parents-meeting best," he replied, gesturing down at the scarlet hoodie he's wearing over a Hulk tee. "Man, are they gonna be sorry they missed me."

"Definitely," I say, though trying to imagine Dev and my mother interacting is hilarious.

"So do I get to see the inside?"

I wrinkle my nose. "Do you seriously *want* to see the inside?"

"Are you kidding? Would I pass up the chance to see where Reagan Forrester eats breakfast?"

"When I do eat breakfast, it's at Joe's," I point out, "and you already saw that this morning."

"Well, where you eat dinner then."

It's not worth explaining that "dinner" in the Forrester home means my mom makes something for my dad that uses up, like, seventy-five percent of our food stamps; she eats veritable rabbit food under the pretense she's on a glamorous diet; and I eat from whatever cans were on sale that week and then nibble on the scraps of my dad's food when he pretends he's too full to finish it. So instead I say, "Fine, you asked for it. But make sure you take your shoes off when we get inside. It's very fancy."

He quirks an eyebrow, obviously unsure if I'm kidding. I just roll my eyes, yank my keys out of the ignition, and get out of the car. For once, I'm grateful for the rain, since it means no one's sitting around outside to hassle us on our way in.

We dash to the trailer and I let us in as quickly as possible, but with no awning over the front door, we're both somewhat damp by the time we enter. I call out for my parents to confirm they're not home, and there's no response but the fervent pounding of raindrops on the roof. I sigh in relief, and then gesture around. "Well, this is it!"

He looks around, and I wonder what he's taking in first—the ratty flowered couches? The chipped countertop in the kitchen that lines one wall? The peeling "tiles" on the floor? "This is one hell of a party house," he says with a grin.

It's such an unexpected statement that I snort with laughter, which makes Dev look inordinately proud of himself. I take him on a brief tour, ending in my bedroom, which is just the bunk beds, my little nightstand, and a little desk with a lone bookshelf over it. I've never really added much of a personal touch to it—it seemed pointless when I was spending my whole life counting down the minutes until I could leave it for good—and I'm suddenly aware of how soulless and boring that probably makes me look.

"I pictured you having at least some posters or something," he says, basically echoing my thoughts as he walks over to look at the books on my shelf, as I knew he would. That one's entirely used books and library loans for my English class this semester, and he seems to realize it because he shifts over to my nightstand to look at the little stack there. When he smiles, I know he's spotted a certain something on the top. "However, I do highly approve of the fact that you proudly display *Lord of the Rings*."

I'd come across it at Vic's house, and she didn't so much as blink when telling me I could borrow it indefinitely. Just thinking of her makes my stomach twinge. I hate that we fought. It's not like I'm gonna call her while Dev's here, though, so for now, I push it out of my brain. "Well, naturally. What collection of literary masterpieces is complete without it?"

"My thoughts exactly," he says seriously. He scans the titles for another few seconds and then asks, "Top or bottom?"

"Excuse me?" I choke.

"Get your mind out of the gutter, Forrester," he says, jerking a thumb toward the bunk beds. "Top or bottom?"

"To be fair, you *were* talking about bed," I point out before walking over and sitting down on the bottom bed. "And the answer's bottom, except when my grandma used to come over, and then I used to have to sleep on the top and I was terrified I was going to fall down and die."

"Valid fear." He comes and sits down next to me, and now we're both on my bed, and I want to stop being conscious of that fact but I can't. "Are you still afraid of the top?"

I shrug, knowing the answer's yes and that he knows the answer is yes, but feeling too stupid to say it out loud.

"I just don't see the point," I say, and at least that much is true.

"Where's your sense of adventure?" He hops up from the bottom bunk and climbs up. The temperature on the bottom bunk drops a few degrees when he leaves, and I watch his long, skinny legs propel him to the bed above me. An instant later, he's out of sight, and then one sneaker after the other crashes to the chipped floor below.

"Sorry," he says sheepishly. "Didn't want to get the bed dirty. It's pretty comfy up here, you know."

"It's comfy down here too," I retort, stretching out on the bed as if to prove my point, even though he can't see me.

"Then we'll both be comfy together," he says, and my mind instantly flashes to what it would be like if we curled up on the same bed, instead of one beneath the other, feet and worlds apart. It's a dangerous thought, and I banish it from my mind immediately.

"So how are you enjoying your first mobile home

experience?"

"So far, so good. It's not what I pictured."

"What'd you picture?" I pick up the threadbare turtle I sleep with at night and start picking at the loose threads.

"I thought mobile homes were more...ya know, mobile."

"Like those RVs you see on TV where pressing a button makes them extend out on the sides?"

He laughs. "I guess. Yeah. I thought we'd be able to drive this thing up to Mount Rushmore or something."

"Well, it can easily be transported to Mount Rushmore on a flatbed, so that's something." I close my eyes. "A trip up to Mount Rushmore sounds pretty great right about now, though."

"Doesn't it?" He shifts and the bed creaks. "Wouldn't mind getting away from everything for a little bit."

"Everything?"

"Well, maybe not everything. You can come. Rest of the world is required to stay behind, though."

I hate how much my entire body warms up at his words. I hate these suggestions of a future that doesn't exist.

"College isn't enough of an escape for you?" I ask tartly, refusing to entertain the other conversation.

The pounding of the raindrops on the tin roof is near deafening in the minute of silence that follows.

Finally, he says, "I don't view college the same way

you do. It's not an escape for me. It's just the next step. I'm excited to go, but…"

"But you don't have anything to escape, because you live such a damn charmed life?" I mean to say it sweetly, and wince as it comes out sounding harsh and accusatory.

He doesn't let himself be baited. "It's obviously not perfect, but I'm not unhappy," he says simply, and it's so confident, so self-aware, that it makes me want to kick the top bunk from underneath. "Look, Rae, I know you've been dealt a shitty hand—"

"You don't know a damn thing about it." My tone is acid now, and the worst part is it's my own fault, because I know he'd listen if I talked. The same way Vic would. I'm the one who won't open up. But he doesn't rage back with that.

Instead he says, "Then tell me."

So I do. I tell him what dinner *really* is at the Forrester house. I tell him how much I live in panic of my GPA dropping because of scholarships, and what a constant battle it is to keep it up because I spend nights and weekends working at Joe's only to end up paying for stupid shit like my mother's manicures. I tell him about the weeks I move in with Vic just so I can get my work done. About how my father's job means he barely exists but he can't manage to put any money away. How my mother and I have not hugged for any reason other than to put on a show for neighbors in as long as I can remember.

He's quiet for another minute, and then he sighs. "This kills me. If you were my mother's daughter, she'd be all over you every minute of every day, and she would *love* you—how hard you work and how disciplined you are." I can't help but notice this would only be true if I were his mother's daughter, and not his girlfriend, but I don't ask if that would still hold true for the latter. I wonder if she loves Sara for this, if she imagines her that way.

"Vic's mother is wonderful to me," I say, pushing the thoughts about Dev's mother and Sara out of my head, "but that doesn't improve *my* home life any." I pause. "I'm sorry. I don't mean to sound like a jerk, but I hate being this…this *thing* that needs to be rescued, but as long as I'm here, that's all I'll be. I just want to rescue myself. And I'm so, so close, I can taste it."

"Does it taste like frat house beer and nausea-inducing scrambled eggs?"

"Mmm, you know? It totally does."

"Sounds like delicious salvation."

"I'm hoping it will be." How can it not be?

"And why can't it taste like that at KU again?"

I stiffen. The KU conversation again. "Because I'm not a KU girl," I say.

"Why not? Is this a Western Kansas thing? You guys are only allowed to go to K-State, and we're only allowed to go to KU?"

I know he's trying to lighten me up, but I'm not having it. "I'm just not."

"But you could be."

"No," I say icily, "I could not be. Because I'm not interested in going."

"I still don't understand why not."

"You wouldn't." I flop over so I'm lying on my stomach. "Of course you wouldn't."

"You're scared. I get that. But I don't get *why*. You're dying to get out of this place. So don't you want to escape to the best place you possibly can?"

"Just stop it, okay? I'm not going to KU because you think I should go to KU."

"Fuck what I think!" he blurts, surprising me enough that I flip back over and sit up straight in my bed. "It's not for me. I think *you*, Reagan Forrester, would shine at KU. I think you would make a fantastic Jayhawk. I think you would love the libraries, and the variety of classes, and being in a bigger city—"

"I'm not ready!" I cut him off, unable to listen to any more, because I want to be who he's describing. I want to love all of those things, but I am terrified. I can barely handle life in Charytan; I don't know how I could possibly handle a school twice its size. And Fitz… "I can't…I just can't do all that."

He sighs. "You have no idea what you're capable of, Rae. No idea what you can handle. And you won't even let yourself try. You carry so much of your family's burden and you think you can't handle going to a class with a few extra kids in it? You think you can't handle a heavy course load when you've got a 4.0 *and* a job? Reagan, there is no one on earth better equipped for KU than you are."

His words make sense, but they don't push the fear away, or shrink the knot of anxiety that grows in the pit of my stomach whenever I think about what going away really means. When I'm silent for a full minute, he asks, "Can you come up here? I'd really rather have this conversation face-to-face."

"You come down here," I say grumpily, still trying to process my feelings on this conversation and unsure I really want to do anything that'll facilitate it.

"I came to Charytan," he retorts, and I obviously can't beat him there. "I think you can climb a few feet to meet me up here."

Reluctantly, I swing my legs over the side of the bed and make my way up to the top bunk, where Dev is lazily spread out, his Hulk tee riding up just enough to reveal half an inch of golden-brown skin. I'm not sure how I'm intended to fit up there with him, and I expect that he'll sit up, but instead he shifts over, and as I'm obviously supposed to lie down next to him, I go ahead and do that. I instantly regret it as waves of heat seem to transfer from his skin to mine, and fix my gaze on the ceiling.

"See?" he says. "Not so scary."

"Not so scary," I confirm, even though this is the closest we have ever been, and I am terrified.

Then there's a hand on my cheek, and my face is turned to face Dev's, and his fingers are still on my cheek, and I have never looked into his eyes so closely. "There's nothing you can't handle, Rae," he says quietly.

This, I think. *I definitely can't handle this.* The pounding of my heart is audible, even over the sound of the rain.

And then... "Reagan? Rae, are you home?"

You have got to be fucking kidding me.

Dev blinks. "Let me guess. I'm going to meet your parents after all?"

I shake my head vigorously. There's just no way. "Definitely not." I scramble down the ladder and indicate for him to follow as I walk over to the lone window next to the beds and shove it wide open. "Come on."

"What? This is insane. Let's just go—"

I don't let him finish. I know several things he doesn't, like that my parents will instantly be suspicious of his brown skin, and it will be glaringly obvious in their expressions and in every word they say. Like that, despite the fact that they never care where I am, they would sooner make me call him a cab than let me take him to his motel, and I'm not ready to send him off just yet— not when he's leaving for good first thing in the morning. I scramble out the window like the practiced expert I am, and left with no choice, Dev follows.

"You're that desperate to avoid your parents?" he asks as we tromp in the mud.

"That obvious?"

He doesn't pursue the line of conversation, for which I am grateful. Instead, we pile into the car in silence and I pull away from the house and head to our final destination of the night.

The rain has eased up somewhat by the time we arrive at his motel. The pouring has given way to a gentle patter, and the effect is softer, sweeter than the pounding had been on the tin roof of the trailer.

Not that that makes me feel better about the fact that I'm about to say goodbye to Dev for what both he and I know will be the last time. Why we'd thought it was a good idea for him to come to Charytan, for us to hang out and "be friends," I have no idea, but in the fall, he'll be going to KU and I will…not be.

"Gosh, it's even more glamorous in the rain," Dev observes as we pull into a spot in the parking lot, making his voice all dreamy.

I whack him on the arm and he laughs. "Sorry Charytan doesn't have lovelier accommodations. Still beats living in a trailer park."

"You underestimate that trailer park," Dev says, unbuckling his seat belt as I turn off the car. The white of his smile contrasts even more sharply against his brown skin in the glare of the motel's neon lights, and the raindrop-covered windshield leaves spots on his reflection. I want to reach a hand up to his cheek, recreate the moment in the top bunk, but I keep my hands in my lap, wrapped around my keys, letting the jagged edges dig into my palm in a way that's oddly soothing given the pain I'm feeling elsewhere at saying goodbye. "No carpet to vacuum, minimal space to keep clean, constant barbecues… If you ask me, you're living pretty sweet, Rae."

He's joking without mocking, and I love that about him. I love a lot about him. But he isn't mine. It was easy to forget that at Joe's, or lying in bunk beds, or sitting here, in the front seat of my car. But I always remember, eventually.

"Good thing I didn't ask you," I tease, but it comes out softer than I intend it to, and I know the thickness in my throat is audible. I hate the way my sadness slowly fills the car in the silence that follows. When I send him back, it'll be to Sara, and the parents that he loves, and a certain future. All I've got to return to is everything I'm trying to escape already.

"We're still gonna talk, you know," he says finally, and I wish he wouldn't. It sounds genuine enough, but it's the kind of statement that never really is. "You're not getting rid of me all that easily. I know I'll never get another one of those legendary Joe's banana muffins if you do."

I know I'm supposed to laugh, but I can't. I can't do anything. This is so much worse than when I ended things with Fitz, and Dev and I have never even kissed, never done any of the talking about forever that was practically a requirement of being John Fitzpatrick's girlfriend. I can't get it out of my head that Dev and I are more than this, more than two people who text each other all day and do strange things in small towns. More than two people who've only actually hung out three times.

I'm not this girl. I turned my back on being this girl. "Forever" is nowhere I want to be at seventeen. But "never" isn't where I want to be either. Especially when I look at Dev. Especially when I think he's looking at me the way I think I might be looking at him.

When it becomes clear I'm not going to say anything, he sighs, rubs his face, and then grabs the door handle, clicking it open. "Come out and hug me goodbye, at least?" he says, and I can tell from his voice that he actually fears I might not, that I might just yank his door closed the instant he steps out of it and then drive off into the night. And a part of me thinks that I should, which is irrelevant because I know that I won't.

I nod once and we both step out of the car. I'm strangely nervous at the prospect, like maybe I won't be able to let go. Like maybe he'll have to scream for help and bring people running from their filthy little motel rooms to pry me off him, and I'll become this story he tells at parties later in life of this crazy girl he knew once upon a time.

I walk slowly around the front of the car, where he's standing with his arms open, looking so cozy and welcoming in his soft scarlet hoodie that even my fears can't stop me from diving in, nestling my head against his shoulder. I fit nicely into the crook of his lanky arm; we're the perfect mismatch of heights for him to rest his chin on my head. Only when he squeezes me do I realize I'm shaking, and while I know the rain is a good excuse, there's no point in trying to pass off my feelings as anything other than what they are.

"It's been fun," I say into his sweatshirt. "Is it weird that I'm gonna miss you?"

"Nah," he says, lifting his hand to stroke my curls, his fingertips grazing the nape of my neck. The gesture makes me shiver just once and then any and all shaking subsides. "I have a feeling I'll probably miss you a little too."

I smile even though he can't see it; my eyes are on our toes, his Adidas and my ever-present tennis shoes. "I have a feeling you will too."

There's a gust of wind then, and I instinctively scrunch even tighter into his arm, which leads him to squeeze me even tighter. We stand like that for a few moments until it passes, and then it's only natural for him to let me go entirely.

There isn't anything left to do but say goodbye, and so we do. He doesn't promise to call or write or text, and I don't need him to. I know he'll want to, and I know he'll know I want to, and maybe that'll be enough. Or maybe things will go back to how they were, and maybe we'll visit each other, and we'll remain great friends.

Or something.

But for now, I've got to get out of there before the tears on my face become too numerous to be mistaken for raindrops. I give one last feeble wave and go back to my car, and when I glance back over my shoulder just before opening my door, I see he's already disappearing into his room. I wait until the last glimpse of his bright sweatshirt passes through the doorway and the dirty tan door shuts behind it. Then I get behind the wheel and strap myself in.

Only I can't make myself do any more than that. Here's where key goes into ignition and gear shifts to reverse and while intellectually I know those things my hands won't do anything but grip the keys. I'm not at all ready to say goodbye. I need to know we'll still be friends, need to know I can freak out to him about college, or tell him when I've just read an incredible book, or count on him to send me the kinds of e-mails that will keep me smiling for the rest of the day. I need to have him however I can have him. And I need to tell him that while I can still do it in person.

I yank off my seat belt and jump out of the car, but my frantic movements are cut short when I realize all the doors look alike and I can't remember which one he just went into. I know calling him to ask is pathetically anti-climactic, but it's the only option I've got. I reach into my back pocket for my cell phone, and I'm just scrolling through for his number when I hear my name and jerk my head up, trying to find the source.

"Reagan?"

It's Dev, standing in the doorway of the room next to the one I would've guessed. I slip my phone back into my pocket and walk up to him. "I was just about to come looking for you," I tell him.

I expect him to say "Why?" but instead he says "Yeah," and I don't know how I'm supposed to take that. We stand there in silence for another few seconds, just looking at each other, neither of us quite sure what we want to say.

The quiet grows unbearable, and I know I need to break it for my own sanity. "I just—"

"Fuck it." He sails forward and crushes his mouth to mine, burying his hands in my hair. The rest of my sentence turns into a muffled groan as I grasp his sweatshirt in both hands, using it to leverage myself onto my toes, to get myself closer, to embed myself in him so that he can't go, can't leave me behind, not fully, not ever. And then my thoughts register and I wrench myself away.

We're both panting heavily when I do. "I can't believe you just did that," I say when I can finally breathe again.

"I can't believe I *didn't* do it before now," he counters, cupping my face in his hands and kissing me again. My knees go slack, and I feel myself being lifted. I wrap my legs around his waist as we kiss and kiss and kiss some more, and I don't know how such a skinny guy manages to walk all the way to the bed with an entire person twined around his torso, but the next time we part lips it's because he gently drops me onto the mattress.

I watch, half-dazed, as he toes off his sneakers and unzips his hoodie, then thinks for a minute and pulls off his T-shirt and undershirt too. Underneath he's all lean muscle, lanky but stronger than I expected. I rise up on my knees to pull him back to me by his shoulders, needing to know if the warmth exuded by his skin is real or just the way I've imagined him feeling more times than I care to admit. I want to experience him with as many senses as possible, and before I even know what I'm doing, I bite his shoulder. His responsive groan sends a shudder through my entire body.

Somewhere in the recesses of my once-functioning brain I know we shouldn't do this. But as his hands caress my hair, my face, my shoulders, I have no idea why. When his fingertips slip underneath the hem of my T-shirt, I barely even know my own name.

We're still kissing, but I feel him growing more

hesitant, his touches gentling, and I wait for him to tell me we need to stop, but the words don't come. Finally, because I can't stand it anymore, I'm the one to pull away.

"It's okay if you want to stop," I tell him quietly, even though it isn't, even though I want this with every fiber of my being.

He shakes his head slowly. "That's the problem," he says, his voice equally low as he rests his forehead against mine, his breath ghosting over my lips as he speaks. "I don't want to stop. I don't want to stop at all. I know that's wrong, but…" He swallows hard. "Jesus Christ, do you even know how beautiful you are?"

My heart pounds in response. "Dave—"

"Dev," he says, his voice ragged. "I loved it when you called me Dev."

I squeeze my eyes shut, feeling as if I'm going to burst. "Dev. I don't want you to be sorry." I won't say Sara's name, or remind him that we aren't going to be together next year, but the words are growing in my vocal chords, waiting to be pushed out into the stale air of the motel room.

"I couldn't possibly be." He kisses each of my eyelids. "But you…"

"I what?"

He tips up my chin to look at me, and his eyes aren't their usual sparkle; they're smoke, and fire, and they make every inch of my skin prickle with heat. "I feel like I'm gonna break you."

"You're not," I tell him, pulling back. *The only way you could break me is by telling me you want to stop.* In a wink I've yanked my shirt over my head, and his eyes go wide. "I'm tiny; I'm not fragile."

"No," he says slowly, his gaze unabashedly raking me up and down. "No, you are definitely not." He leans down to kiss me, soft and sweet but with enough pressure to push me back down onto the bed. I shimmy back up to where the pillows line the wall and he climbs over me, straddling me without putting any weight on my body. "You are amazing. You know that, right?"

I've never taken compliments well, and I can feel myself blush, but I say nothing, instead busying myself with the task of unbuckling his belt.

He smiles when he realizes I won't acknowledge his words, but he doesn't move, letting my hands struggle until finally I've dragged his jeans down his narrow hips, revealing inches of *Star Wars* boxer shorts underneath.

He glances down. "Not my finest," he says apologetically, and I laugh, as if something like the pattern of his underwear or the fact that there are a few tiny holes along the elastic is of any consequence.

"I'm pretty sure I'm wearing Wonder Woman underwear my mom bought me at Walmart," I tell him as he takes his turn with my jeans. "It's not like any of it's staying on anyway." My lips curve in a little smile. "DC-free zone and all."

I expect a joke back, but instead I feel a twitch against my thigh. He'd looked playful before, but now, his eyes smolder, and my body instinctively reacts in response to his. From there, it's mere moments until we're shoving the rest of our clothing onto the floor, frantically kissing and touching each other's lips and bodies with a fierceness I didn't know I possessed.

In all the times I'd imagined this happening between us—and admittedly there were a few—it'd been romantic, slow, a mutual savoring of each other's bodies. Instead, it's fast, and frantic, and I'm shocked to realize I wouldn't want it any other way. I've done enough thinking for the past few months, years, lifetimes. All I want is to feel, to listen, to be.

Smooth, hot skin, damp with sweat and tasting of salt. Puffs of erratic breath—his, mine, ours. Every sense pushed to the extreme. And when Dev arches his back and cries out, I think my heart is going to leap out of my chest.

Afterward, we lie together, tangled up in the sheets and our skinny limbs, until he finally confesses that he can no longer stand the feeling of the cheap motel linen sticking to his sweaty skin. I laugh, and then we roll out of bed and clamber into the shower, cracking jokes about how we're terrified to be alone in the filthy bathroom with God-only-knows-what climbing the walls. He washes my hair and I soap up his skin, and when we're clean and dry we curl up around each other and I fall asleep knowing I am the happiest I've ever been and that will all end when I next open my eyes.

It ends even sooner; my eyes are still closed when the realization slams into my brain that I've just had unprotected sex. The fact that I could be so incredibly stupid as to do that after everything with Fitz rocks me with a wave of self-loathing. Had I thought about him for an even a moment last night, I know I would never have let it happen, but my focus had been on Dev and Dev alone.

Lying there now, I do think of Fitz. And I think I have done a very bad thing. But I don't really have time to dwell on thoughts; I know I need to act. Unfortunately, I have no idea how to go about doing that, but I pray that I know someone who will. Dev is still sleeping soundly when I crawl out of bed, retrieve my cell phone from the back pocket of my jeans, and sneak into the bathroom to call Vic.

She picks up after a couple of rings, sounding sleepy as all hell. "Reagan? Is everything okay?" *Shit.* I'd completely forgotten to check what time it was before calling, and in the fluorescent light of the bathroom I can see that it's well after four. Not the best timing even if we hadn't spent our last conversation fighting.

"I'm sorry to call so late. I didn't even know what time it was."

She yawns hugely, and I can hear her shifting around. "It's fine. Is everything okay?"

"Not really," I say, taking care to keep my voice low. "I did an incredibly stupid thing. Well, I did a really fun and great thing, but—"

"It's like 4:00 a.m., Rae. Spit it out."

"I had unprotected sex with Dev."

"You *what?*"

"I'm just going to assume you heard me and skip ahead to where you tell me what to do. I should pee, right? And shower? But—"

"Tia Maria, Reagan. Please tell me you don't think any of that helps with pregnancy."

"Sorry my parents never gave me a sex ed manual," I retort. "Now help me! Please!"

"Don't think you're going to get out of telling me every detail later, missy," she says, sounding considerably more alert now, "but first things first, you need to get a morning-after pill, immediately."

"And what does that do?"

I can practically hear her rolling her eyes over the phone. "Makes it so you won't get pregnant, but you have to take it pretty much right away. Where are you?"

"The motel."

"Gross. Okay, let me find out some more info on

where we can get one. I'm thinking leaving Charytan is in order."

"Yes, definitely." I take a deep breath. "Thank you."

"Just to warn you, I heard Jane Huntley say that after she took it, she was puking her guts out the entire day. And I'm pretty sure she went all the way to Wichita for it."

"Why the hell would she drive three hours for a pill?"

"Because no pharmacist west of there would give it to her. They don't have to if they have a moral objection to it, or something."

"Fantastic."

"Should I not have told you that?"

I sigh. "Of course you should tell me that. Anything else?" A chill creeps over me. "How much does it cost?"

"I'm not sure," she mumbles, and I guess she's looking it up on her phone. "Varies," she says a few moments later. "How much do you have?"

I curse inwardly for having just filled my tank *and* left a decent tip at Joe's. "Five bucks? Maybe ten?"

"You're definitely gonna need more," she says sympathetically. "Where's Dev?"

"Here. Asleep."

"You haven't even talked to him yet?"

I shift uncomfortably. This is not a conversation I want to have with Dev. It's not even a conversation I really want to have with Vic. I just want it to be over already. "I don't really have to, do I?"

"You sure as hell do if you want to be able to buy it," Vic returns. "Anyway, it's his problem too. Why didn't you guys use a condom?"

"It wasn't planned." The understatement of the century. "It's not like I carry one around."

"Doesn't he?"

The thought nauseates me even more than the thought of taking the morning-after pill does. I know he told me he isn't dating Sara, but that doesn't mean they haven't hooked up. How many times has he loaded his wallet with condoms for nights with her? How many times has he used them with her?

How many times has he forgotten them with her?

"I'm gonna throw up," I announce to Vic, a second before I lean over the toilet and do.

I can't hear her response over the sound of my own retching, and I pray Dev's managed to sleep through all of this as I flush the toilet and rinse out my mouth. Hell, at this point, I pray Dev has packed up his stuff and gone home. I don't think I can stand the sight of him right now.

"I am so dumb," I moan to Vic, sliding back against the bathroom wall.

"You made a mistake," she says firmly. "But we need to focus. It'll take us about three hours to get to Wichita. Do you want to wait until places open so we can see if somewhere closer will dispense it? Or just get in the car and go?"

The idea of not only waking up my best friend at 4:00 a.m. but making her bike over here to then sit in the car for nearly six straight hours is just too insane. Of course, I could just go without her…only I can't. I know I can't. I need my best friend. "I'll wait. Maybe we'll find a place closer. You should get some more sleep. I'm sorry I woke you up." Then I pause. "I *can* wait, right? It won't, like, implant in me or something?"

I can tell Vic's smothering a laugh. "That'll be fine," she says, so confidently I believe it. "Maybe you can get a little more rest before then."

"Yeah, right."

"I'm sorry, Rae," she says softly, and I know that somewhere in her sleep-addled brain she's finally pieced together what a disaster this all is—not just the lack of condom but all of it. "It was inevitable though, wasn't it?"

"If that were true, you'd think I'd have been more prepared," I joke. And then I crumple into a mess of tears.

Vic stays on the phone with me for another few minutes, waiting until I'm all cried out, and then I thank her profusely and let her go back to sleep. I wash my face, which is ten different kinds of disgusting, and then sneak back into the bedroom. My stealth is pointless by then because the first thing I notice when I enter is that Dev has gotten dressed and is sitting on the edge of the bed.

"I'm so sorry," he says, his voice raw, and I know that he's heard if not everything than a whole lot of my conversation with Vic. "I wish you'd woken me up."

I shrug. "Not much you can do."

He sets his jaw, as if bracing for an argument, but a moment later, he relaxes and stands up. "Let me just brush my teeth and then I'll drive you, okay?"

"Drive me where?"

He stops on his walk to the bathroom. "To the pharmacy, obviously," he says, then disappears inside.

I have no plans to go to the pharmacy yet, but I have nothing else to do, so I get dressed anyway. He emerges a few minutes later looking as lousy as I do. "Let's go," he says, hauling his duffel onto his back.

"I have to wait until pharmacies open so I can call and see who'll dispense it. Might be a long drive."

"Oh." He drops the bag and goes to sit on the bed again. "So now what?"

I lean back against the wall, not willing to get too close again. "I wait here until Vic wakes back up and you either go back to sleep or go back home."

"You're kidding, right? You think I'm leaving before you take that thing?"

I narrow my eyes. "You seriously don't trust me to take it?"

"No, I'm seriously not going to leave you alone to

deal with it, when it took two of us to fuck this up," he snaps. "I'm going to drive you, I'm going to pay for it, and I'm going to make sure you're okay. Is that all right with you?"

It's obvious he's pissed, and I know it's obvious I'm pissed. The only thing that's not terribly clear is who we're pissed *at*. Each other? Ourselves? Both?

I don't feel like responding, so I slide to the floor and hug my knees, avoiding eye contact. My head is a mess of incoherent thoughts I have no desire to process. I think I might even be able to fall asleep sitting that way until Dev breaks the silence. "Can you say something?"

I open my eyes. "What do you want me to say?"

"Just...*something*. This was something that happened between you and *me*, and you went ahead and called Vic while I slept. Doesn't that seem screwed up to you?"

"Would you have known what to do?" I challenge him.

"We would've figured it out together!"

"Oh, yeah, like we've done so fabulously with everything else. Because this"—I wave a hand angrily back and forth between us—"has gone *so* smoothly. Why are you even here?"

He winces, and I know I'm being overly cruel, but I can't bring myself to take it back. I'm terrified of what comes next, and I don't just mean the morning-after pill. It took me months to get over everything with Fitz, and even longer to move on with somebody else. And now that I have, all I can think about is how horribly we've screwed this up.

I see him wait for me to follow my last statement with an apology, and when he realizes none is forthcoming, he shrinks into himself, an obvious storm building within him.

"I have no fucking clue," he spits when he finally answers, and I think the depth of hurt and anger in his voice shocks us both. "I had this crazy idea that I had to see you one more time, and I don't even know why. Apparently, I turn into the world's shittiest person when I'm around you. I drag my friends around for no reason, I lie to everyone about my plans this weekend, and I have *sex* with a girl I barely know and don't even use a condom."

He's up on his feet now and shaking with rage, but so am I. Six hours earlier the guy standing in front of me made me feel like the most precious thing on earth, and suddenly I am dirt under his shoe. "I don't know what the fuck is wrong with me, or how this happened, but you know what? You want to go by yourself? Fine. You want to be by yourself forever? *Fine.* That's probably for the best."

He hauls his duffel back onto his shoulder and starts to storm out, but then, unbidden, one last question pops into my mind, and even though I know it's probably the worst possible thing I can ask at that moment, I have no choice. "Dave," I say loudly, stopping him in his tracks. "Are you clean?"

He turns slowly, and I swear there is actual hate emanating from those dark eyes. "Am I *what*?"

"Clean," I say firmly, forcing myself to hold my ground. "Have you been tested for STIs?" Once the words are out, I swallow after them, hoping I won't ever need to repeat them again. "I am, just so you know." I got tested right after I found out what Fitz was doing to our condoms. It's not an experience I'm anxious to repeat.

His entire face transforms, and I know that whatever he's about to say will break me. And it does.

"I assume I am too, since last night was my first time." Then he slams the door, and he's gone.

VICTORIA

Rae picks me up at seven on the dot to drive to what does in fact end up being Wichita. By mutual silent agreement, we don't stop for coffee at Joe's, waiting until we're fifteen minutes outside city limits to get some at a gas station. We don't exchange more than ten words until we're both halfway through our cups. Then Reagan breaks the silence.

"I'm sorry," she says, her voice raw. "I'm sorry I dragged you out of bed for this, I'm sorry I fucked up, I'm sorry I didn't tell you Dev was coming to town, and

I'm sorry I gave you shit for taking that class at CCC. You have every right to do what makes you happy. I just can't stand the thought of losing you. I mean, hell." The corner of her mouth lifts, just for a moment. "Who else would pick up the phone for me at 4:00 a.m. and sit with me on a long-ass ride halfway across the state?"

"Oh come on, you don't think your mom would've—" I break off laughing, then feel bad about it because in reality that isn't funny at all. But then she laughs too, and it sets me off again, and for a little while as we sip our gross coffee and Rae lets me blast Lilah Montgomery, everything feels normal.

And then we get to the pharmacy.

I wait in the car while she uses the cash Dev tucked into her windshield wiper to buy the pill. My hand rests on her back as she takes it, and for a quiet minute afterward. Then she sighs, puts her keys in my hand, and we switch seats. I drive the three hours back to my house, during which she alternates crying with chugging ginger ale to keep the nausea at bay.

She manages not to throw up even once until we get there, but as soon as we get inside, she rushes upstairs while I tell my mom we're home from "studying at Joe's," attributing our early arrival from her full-day shift to bad tuna. Then I head upstairs to find Rae sprawled on the tile floor of my bathroom. "You don't have to stay here with me," she whimpers, as if I would even think about leaving her alone right now. As if, despite all the secrets she's kept from me, I don't at least know her better than that.

"Shh." I hand her a glass of water I've just brought up from the kitchen, where my mother's taking another stab at churros. It's killing me to lie to her, and I think she suspects I am, but she knows not to pry right now and I appreciate it. At least the smell of frying pastry helps a little with the vomit-reek of the bathroom.

As if she knows exactly what I'm thinking, Rae mutters, "Does your mom know? How do you say 'stupid fucking idiot' in sign language?"

"I haven't told her anything but that you're not feeling well," I assure her, motioning for her to drink. "She hasn't asked anything else."

She drinks it in gulps, then instantly takes a few deep breaths before scooting away from the toilet and resting her head against the rim of the porcelain tub.

"Better?"

"Yeah," she says weakly, putting down the half-empty glass. "I feel awesome."

I sit down beside her, stretching my legs out on the cool white tile, which makes the charms on my anklet jingle. "Does that mean you're ready to spill about how the hell this happened?"

Her face twists up sourly. "I don't even know what to say. It was so stupid."

"Hey." I sweep a curl out of her face, brush it back behind her ear. "It wasn't *that* stupid. Not using a condom? *That* was stupid. But you and Dev are crazy about each other. Any idiot can see that. So you guys got a little carried away. It was bound to happen, with all that sexual tension you two have been carrying around."

She groans and closes her eyes, and I wonder what it is she's seeing behind her lids; the way everything in her face suddenly goes slack suggests the words "sexual tension" have been given a whole new meaning in the past twenty-four hours.

"Wow." Even I can hear the awe in my voice, and her eyes fly open. "It was *really* good."

"It was…" She bites her thumbnail while she thinks about how to finish the sentence. It's not often I see Rae involuntarily at a loss for words, and I develop a whole new respect for the tall, skinny guy who apparently rocked my best friend's world. "I can't explain it."

Orrrr maybe she just doesn't want to tell me about it. Again. I look away, focusing at a tiny crack in the paint in the corner of the wall, up near the ceiling. Never mind that I picked up my phone at 4:00 a.m. on only two hours of sleep after a night of kissing and talking with Steve that I haven't even gotten to tell her about yet. No matter how much I think I've earned in this friendship, I'm always a step behind somehow.

I glance back at her, about to impatiently tell her,

"Never mind," when I see that she's leaned forward and pulled her knees up, squeezing her elbows between them, looking like she's mentally preparing her answer, and then, she speaks.

"The first time I slept with Fitz, he went *all* out. We're talking candles, rose petals all over the place, sparkling cider, cheesy music—everything. Granted, it was still in the bedroom he usually shared with Sean, but his parents were away, and he'd gotten Sean and the rest of his brothers to sleep over at friends' houses, and the whole thing was just basically magic."

"Sounds…nice?" I don't mean to sound skeptical, but it just sounds so…not Reagan.

She laughs. "I know. Cliché to end all clichés, right? But it *was* nice. It was nice that he thought he should do that. It was nice that he cared enough to. It was nice that he wanted it to be perfect."

"But…"

"But it wasn't perfect. I'm not candles. I'm not roses. I'm sure as hell not cheesy music. I hated doing something that big while feeling like I was somebody else."

"And last night? Was that perfect?"

She shifts, obviously uncomfortable. "Sort of, yeah. I mean, not in the way you normally think of perfect. We were in a gross motel, and the blanket was scratchy, and we definitely didn't always know what we were doing, and *obviously* we kind of forgot an important part, and we're not even dating! But in the moment, I swear, I wouldn't have changed a damn thing."

I sigh. "You need to talk to him. You know that, right?"

She nibbles at a thumbnail that's already bitten down to the quick. "Trust me, he doesn't want to hear anything I have to say."

"He left you money," I point out.

"Yeah, because he's not a complete and total asshole. Or maybe he is. I don't know." She exhales sharply. "He didn't want to kiss me because we have no future, but then he lost his fucking virginity to me. What does that even mean? And how slutty does it make me that I just slept with someone I'll probably never even see again?"

"Slutty is a BS concept, and you know it. Besides, he slept with you knowing the same thing, and Jamie will probably, like, high-five him for it. No one ever calls the guy slutty."

"Whatever," she grumbles. "This is all beside the point. I should've known better, after everything." But even as she says it I know she's angry with him, too, for the fact that he didn't stop her, that his conscience didn't take over. And I am too, because there's something there. We all know it. After everything, Reagan deserves to be happy, and she came so close, only to have it come crashing down at the first sign of hardship. It's like we keep having to hit some sort of ground zero before we can get to any truth.

And it's terrible timing, I know, but I can't contribute to that anymore. I need to be honest *now*, before it's too late. "This is probably the worst time to say this," I hedge, "but I'm going to schedule a visit to KU, and I think you should come with me."

She narrows those huge brown eyes. "I'm not following Dev to school just because I had sex with him, Victoria."

"This isn't about Dev. Forget Dev. KU is enormous. You can probably go the whole four years without even seeing him there."

I expect my words to be somewhat encouraging, maybe inspire two seconds of contemplation on her part, but instead, her shoulders slump and her face falls even further, as if she's slowly breaking down. I've seen this routine before, during similar discussions, and still, I just don't get it. Only this time, I'm not backing down to give her space to be moody.

"What?" I demand. "What is it about that idea that bothers you so much? Isn't getting out of Charytan and becoming someone new the whole point? Don't you *want* to get lost in a sea of people you don't know? It's like you're attached to this small-town life you supposedly hate with a passion, like for all your big talk about wanting to get out you really just want to make sure someone can pick you up and take you back at any…" I clap a hand over my mouth, watching her bite her lips and widen her shining eyes as much as possible, a superhero effort to keep from crying.

My hand falls into my lap. "Oh my God. That's what this is about. Him. Still."

She's shaking now, silent, her eyes fixed so hard on a point on the floor that I think they might explode out of her skull. One tear is sliding down her cheek, but she's too frozen to swipe it away. I reach out and sweep it from her skin as gently as humanly possible, afraid to disturb her more than I already have.

"Rae," I say gently. "He's not coming back for you. He's not—" I take a deep breath, because saying these words sucks, even though I've never met John Fitzpatrick and I know I never will. "He's not...coming back here at all. You know that, right?"

No response, just a slight rocking motion.

I exhale softly, afraid I'm pushing the limit. Afraid I'm not going to get my message across. Afraid that maybe it's too late for anyone to. I try again, because I can't not.

"Once upon a time, you made the decision not to let your life revolve around him, and that's when you were still together. How can you let it revolve around him now? Especially after what he did to you?"

She surprises me by actually responding. "I need to fix things. He needs to know he has someone to come home to."

"He has a family, Reagan."

"Yeah, and they weren't enough to keep him here two years ago. Only I was, and I failed, and now he's probably…" She sniffles and wipes her nose on the back of her hand. "I owe him something for failing. I owe *them* something."

"No, you don't," I say more forcefully than I mean to, Sean Fitzpatrick's cruel voice springing into my brain. "You don't owe those people anything. Where would you be right now if he'd succeeded? You wouldn't have me to tell you about the morning-after pill, or Dev to pay for it. You would have a two-year-old *child*, and you broke up with him because that isn't the life you wanted. *This* is. And you're blowing it after everything you've worked for to get it."

"Oh, yeah, my life is so fucking glorious," she says, rapping her knuckles on the tile floor.

"Forget right now. You always say life starts when we get out of this place. I just want that to be the right life, and I think we owe it to ourselves to see if KU is it."

She motions for me to hand her a tissue, and when I do, she honks into it loudly. Then she cleans herself up for a minute at the sink before turning to me. "You already applied, didn't you. That's what the portfolio is for."

She doesn't sound angry, just matter-of-fact. "Not yet," I say, "but I'm going to by Friday. The deadline for scholarships is next week. And yes, that's what the portfolio is for. Miss Lucy's been helping me with it. The application itself is quick, no essay or anything. You could fill it out in under an hour. And they take application fee waivers—I checked."

There's no response as she ties her curls back into a baby ponytail with an elastic band from the little tray I keep on the counter, and washes her face in the sink. I watch her in the mirror that hangs over the basin, and when she's done wiping her face with my hand towel, she nods, just once.

I do my best to suppress my smile. "Come on," I say, getting to my feet. "You can use my computer."

Reagan's an impressively loud typist, which doesn't usually bother me, but I need to focus if I'm going to get some more sketches done for Miss Lucy to critique on Monday. The portfolio's not due to KU for another few months, but I need to have one to Miss Lucy by the end of the week if I want to be considered for her week-long workshop during winter break. I leave Rae alone in my room and hide out in my dad's study across the hall, with the door closed to block out the noise.

I'm in the middle of drawing a pattern based on an old picture of me with my abuelo—he's wearing these awesome striped pants I *have* to work into a design— when my phone startles me by ringing into the complete silence I've created. "Tia Maria," I mutter aloud as my pencil goes flying across the page. I push the drawing aside and grab my cell phone, smiling when I see the caller ID; at least it's someone worth messing up for. "Hey there."

"Hey," Steve replies brusquely, sounding all out of breath. "Are you with Reagan?"

"Yeah, why—oh no!" Reagan was supposed to work today. Of course. "I'm so sorry. I swear, it was an emergency. You know she'd never miss work otherwise."

"Is she okay?"

"Now, yeah. I think. I'm not sure." I sneak into the hallway and peer into my room. Her fingers are still flying on the keyboard. I duck back into the study. "She's had a really, really bad day. Are you totally swamped? I could come and help."

"I already called Mitch when neither of you answered your phones the first thirty times I called. He's here."

"Oh. It was an emergency," I say again, because I don't know what else to say.

"I know," he says, his voice dropping. "I'm glad you guys are okay. I was worried."

It warms me up to hear the caring in his voice. He really is, as my mom would say, one of the good ones. "I'm sorry, I should've called."

"It's okay. Is everything fine with you?"

My phone beeps with a text message, but I ignore it; whoever it is can definitely wait. "Yeah, yeah, I'm fine. It wasn't about me. Though I *am* a little tired. For some reason, I didn't get much sleep last night," I say playfully.

He laughs lowly, clearly in hearing range of coworkers or customers or both. "So sorry to disturb your sleep."

"Totally worth it."

"Glad you thought so too."

My phone beeps again. This time it's call waiting, and a quick glance reveals I don't recognize the number. "I gotta run," I tell him with a sigh, "but maybe I'll come by for dinner?"

"I'll make sure I've got a bacon tuna melt ready."

"Perfect." We hang up, and I switch to the other call. "Hello?"

"You're there!"

The relieved voice is familiar, but I can't quite place it. "I am. Who is this?"

"It's Dev. I just texted you. Sorry, I got your number from Jamie."

I shudder a little at the idea of the two of them talking about me, but quickly push past it. "I was on the phone; I haven't seen your text yet. What's up?"

"I just want to check and make sure she's okay." He sounds nervous saying it, his voice quiet and rushed.

"She's fine." I keep my voice down even though I know she can't hear me over her typing. I feel like a traitor for even talking to him after the things he said to her, but it's obvious he's hurting too, and at least he's not a big enough jerk to stick her with the bill or pretend it never happened. "She feels like garbage"—*physically and emotionally*, I try to inject venom into my voice—"but she'll be fine."

"Does she hate me?"

I'm surprised to hear the question; I'd thought it was the other way around. "You're the one who blew up," I remind him icily.

"I know. I...Look, I'm glad she's okay. I have to go."

"Do you want to talk to her?" I ask quickly before he can hang up, though I know Reagan would kill me for asking.

"I can't. I'm sorry. I gotta go." And then he's gone.

I'm still staring at my phone, trying to decide if I should tell Reagan he even called, when I hear a knock at the door. "Come in," I call; I can tell from the quick but light tapping that it's Reagan and not my mother.

She peeks her head in. "All done. Happy?"

I am. But looking at her, and hearing Dev's frantic exit in my mind, I can't help feeling guilty for it.

CHAPTER FIFTEEN

REAGAN

Thanks to Vic, I get my KU application in by the scholarship deadline, and then spend the next couple of weeks finishing off and submitting three more, with a blessing to the god of application fee waivers. Vic and I help each other edit our essays, work together to pick the best of the best for her portfolio, and to her credit, she never brings up Dev or Wichita. Despite the agony of waiting for responses, for the first time in a long time, it feels like I can breathe.

And then Thanksgiving comes.

The Reyeses invite me over, but my mother quickly

nixes that idea, declaring she's "goin' ta make the yummiest southern feast y'all ever did eat." I beg Vic to save me one or twelve of her mother's pumpkin empanadas, and spend the day cooking with my mom instead. To my surprise, it's not a terrible afternoon—we actually laugh together for a few seconds when she pulls the sweet potato pie out of the oven and realizes her affinity for extra marshmallows has turned the entire top into a goopy white mess. But when five o'clock hits, Sheila Black shows up on our doorstep with Jimmy in tow, snapping at full volume about how her asshole ex and his slutty wife screwed them over for the holiday, and that dark, cloying, acrid fog of Myrtle Grove—of Charytan—settles in my lungs again.

"I'm gonna go change for dinner," I say to no one who's listening. My jeans and tank top are fine, but Sheila's probably here for half an hour of ranting, and I really don't need to hear this routine again. I close my door behind me, crash on my bed, and read *Howl's Moving Castle* for the billionth time until the sound of Sheila's ranting subsides and I think they must be gone. Then I throw on my favorite comfy gray cardigan and step back into the main room.

"There you are!" my mother says from the table, where she, Sheila, my dad, and Jimmy are gathered around in its four seats, each at one of our four settings. "I thought you must've left for that girl's house."

Fifty shades of rage bubble up under my skin, but

then Jimmy says "Hi, Rae Rae!" and it makes me smile and say hi back.

"Of course I didn't go to Vic's house," I say calmly. "I said I'd be here."

"Well, our meal just got a little more family-style," my dad jokes, as if it's no big deal that this family doesn't seem to include me at all. He must've come home just after Sheila showed up at our door. "Come on and join us, Pumpkin!"

"Where?" I ask. "And what am I supposed to eat on?"

"Reagan, don't be rude," my mother scolds, helping herself to some green bean casserole.

I'm about to respond when the flash of gold on her hand catches the light. She's wearing it *again*. On *Thanksgiving*.

"Take. That fucking. Ring. Off."

"Reagan!" Of all people, it's Sheila who jumps to admonish me first. I promptly ignore her.

"I'm serious. Take that ring off now. You have *no* business going through my stuff and wearing it."

"Well that's very selfish of you," my mother says. "It's a beautiful ring, and you never wear it, so no one should? It's meant to be seen. You never appreciated it, or that young boy."

This is a joke. It has to be. This is the world's least funny and never-ending joke and somewhere in an alternate universe Fitz is laughing his ass off at my misery.

"You know absolutely nothing about me or 'that young boy,'" I spit. "If you had—if you'd been a half-decent mother when he was in my life—you never would've let me wear that ring in the first place. And you sure as hell don't get to wear it. That's mine, and I want it back. Now."

I'm shaking, and I make the mistake of letting my gaze falter for just a moment, to see Jimmy staring at me in a mix of awe and horror. I quickly train it back on my mother until she pulls the ring off her finger and puts it down on the table with a tremendous roll of her eyes. I snatch it, and my first instinct is to jam it down on my own finger so she can't take it. But the very idea of ever wearing it again makes me want to crawl out of my skin.

Instead, I shove it in my pocket, grab my car keys, and storm out of the house.

I'm just about to step into the driver's seat of my car when I hear, "Pumpkin, wait." I turn to see my dad walking toward me, his broad shoulders in a slump beneath his dusty flannel shirt, and I stop.

"I'm not going back inside," I warn him, "in case that's why you're here."

"I know you're not," he says wearily. "I don't blame you. Your mother loves you, but I know sometimes she's not the best at showing it."

It's what he wants to believe—needs to, even—and because he's the reason I have a roof over my head at all, I lie and say, "I know. I just can't be here right now."

He nods. I hate that these fights break his heart, but as much as I do believe *he* loves me, he's always loved her more, and always will. "Are you going to that girl's house?"

"Yes, I'm going to Vic's house." I don't even really want to—dropping in on them feels both impolite and pathetic—but I can't afford to spend any more on gas this month, so a long drive to nowhere is out of the question. "I'll call if I'm sleeping over."

"Have fun, honey." He kisses the top of my head, and I think he's going to turn back to the trailer, but then he says, "I'm glad you'll be with her next year. She takes good care of you."

I have to clench my jaw to keep it from dropping in shock. I had no idea my father even knew we were planning to go to school together next year, or paid much attention to her presence at all. The way he says it, I wonder if he thinks she's more than a friend, and I'm even more impressed at how okay he sounds about that.

"She does," I finally manage.

He smiles, slightly, and says, "Good. Wish her family a Happy Thanksgiving from me. Or Feliz Navidad. Whatever they say."

So close. "Happy Thanksgiving, Dad." I wrap my arms around him, standing on my toes to do so.

"Happy Thanksgiving, Rae." A quick squeeze, and

then we both take off for the rest of our nights.

Unsurprisingly, the Reyeses welcome me with open arms, even though they've already sat down to eat. I stuff my face with turkey, empanadas, candied sweet potatoes, and churros that taste just a little charred. Instead of talking about Fitz, we talk about Ana and Roberto's classes, where Javi's been traveling, Vic's latest designs. And they ask about me, too—whether I'll miss working at Joe's (definitely not), what I plan to study in college (everything humanly possible), if I've thought about going abroad (if I find myself a generous benefactor, maybe).

They teach me how to say the different foods in ASL, laughing as they recount the early days of Roberto's learning it, and we tease Vic mercilessly about Freckles. We call Vic's grandparents in Mexico City, and sip spicy hot chocolate in front of the fire until we all grow drowsy. No one even asks whether I'm staying the night; they just assume, as if it's my home every bit as much as theirs.

Only as I drift off to sleep next to Vic does it hit me with a pang that if I were her, I'd have hesitations about leaving this life too.

In the weeks that follow, my mother and I avoid each other as much as possible—not a huge challenge when you're working as many hours as I am and also studying for finals. I do stay home for Christmas Eve—after all, it's probably my last one there for a while—and am rewarded with a gift of school supplies for next year, which makes me feel a little lighter. Joe's is closed for New Year's Eve, so I spend the night movie-marathoning with Vic, but otherwise, I work as many shifts as possible over winter break. By the time school is back in session, I'm exhausted as hell and I hate people and mayo and the smell of dried cola puddles more than I thought humanly possible, but I feel *so* ready to move on to the next phase of life, I am practically buzzing with it.

Until I come home one day and am greeted by a big KU envelope on my bed.

Holy shit. There's no mistaking it's the envelope size that screams "Accepted!" but my stomach churns with butterflies as I realize I'm not sure that's actually what I want to see when I open it. It's been weeks since I sat in Vic's room, staring at the website with blurry eyes, my mind and body feeling impossible hollow. I barely remember filling out the application, but I'm staring at the evidence that it happened.

My fingers hover over the seal, but I can't do this alone. I pull my cell phone out of my pocket and call Vic.

"I was *just* about to call you! Did you get it?"

"Yup. Did you get yours?"

"Yup," she says giddily. "Big envelope."

"Big envelope."

"Did you open it?"

"Without you? Are you kidding?"

She laughs. "Good. Put me on speaker." I do, and rip open the envelope as I hear her doing the same on her side.

Congratulations! You have been admitted to…

Oh God, I'm gonna throw up.

"Did you get in?" she squeals, so happily that I know she did, and I can't help but smile. "I did. Did you?"

"I did!" she shrieks so loudly I fear my poor ears will bleed. "Rae! We got into our first college together! Aren't you excited?"

So typical. "Vic, we haven't even seen the place yet. What if we hate it? What if it's not the right place for us?" *What if what we're doing there is just too different and we fall apart? What if I can't deal with the idea of being on the same campus as Dev? What if I just get lost in there and swallowed up and no one cares enough to pull me out?*

Hypothetically.

"We'll never know until we visit," she says cheerfully, obviously not sharing any of my concerns. And why should she? Vic has talent, a plan, and a quasi-relationship with Freckles I don't quite understand but mostly support. I have a half-assed idea of what I want to do with my life and enough ghosts to staff a haunted house. "So, when do you wanna go?"

"Whenever. You choose." After all, Vic's the one who's

actually capable of getting her shit together these days. I'm just the loser along for the ride. "My schedule's free and clear."

"Can do," she says without a trace of stress in her voice, which amazes me all the more because I know she's been busting her butt on her portfolio lately, hoping to get chosen for this winter break workshop Miss Lucy's holding. But I swear, nothing fazes her these days. Maybe Freckles is a calming influence. Lord knows I'm not. "Are you working tonight?"

"Nope, it's my night off. I figured I'd catch up on AP English reading. Say hi to Freckles for me, will you?"

"Sure." We hang up, and I head to my car, knowing that catching up on reading—though not of the AP English variety—is exactly what I'll be doing.

> *Dear Ragin',*
> *I thought I might have a letter from you, with it being my birthday and all, but—*

I toss that one aside and pick up another, skipping past the intro this time.

> *Quinn says she's doing really well in school and wants to know if I'll be home for her graduation. I don't really know what to say about that. It's over a year from now, and who the hell knows where I'll be in a year? Maybe I won't even have all my limbs and shit. Maybe seeing me will just freak her the fuck out.*

A stupid tear slips out of my eye without warning and I swipe it away so fast I almost scratch my cornea. *You're freaking her the fuck out* now, *Johnny*, I want to scream at him. *Where* are *you? Do you have all your limbs?*

Shockingly, the letter doesn't answer back. It just shakes along with the hand holding it, until I drop it onto the floor and pick up another one. The letters are all along the spectrum, depending on what kind of day he had, and my fingers dance around the box like they're searching for buried treasure in a field of land mines. I'm hoping for the letter he wrote the day a sweet kid on the street handed him some sort of candy. That was his favorite day in all the letters.

Instead, I get the worst of the worst.

> *You fucking selfish bitch. I'm here because of you. Would you even give a shit if I died? You'd probably hate me even more for making you stick around in Charytan for one extra second for my funeral. You think you're too fucking good for both our families, that you're gonna run off to a big fancy school and become a big fancy lawyer...Lemme tell you a secret, Reagan Forrester. You ain't gonna be shit.*

I don't even realize I'm crumpling the letter until the words disappear, but soon I'm squeezing it into a ball so tightly my knuckles turn white. Back when we were together, he used to tease me about my dreams of going to college, law school, beyond. I hated it, hated that he didn't believe I could be more than I was, or take me seriously for what I wanted. But it was nothing like this cold, naked hatred. It's a fine line between believing someone won't succeed and actively wanting them to fail, and with this letter, Fitz leapt over. The worst part is, at the time, I assumed he was right.

I remember the day I got that letter. There was a tornado raging nearby, coming in our direction, and I'd saved the note for when the winds really came howling at the walls of the trailer. It's not like we've got a safe lower level in which to take cover, and I thought having something warm and familiar would be comforting when the shit really hit the fan.

What a fucking joke that turned out to be.

The night I read that letter was the only night I could ever remember seeking out a hug from my mother. Of course, she took one look at my snotty, tear-stained face and told me to clean myself up first.

Instead, I left my parents behind in the storm and drove straight to Vic's.

It should've been the night I learned to let Fitz go entirely, but it wasn't. He kept writing for months after, and I kept reading, over and over again. It never occurred to me to stop, even though I didn't write back to a single one. For so long, he was the only person in my life who gave a damn about me. How was I supposed to give that up cold turkey?

But he isn't that person anymore. That person took me in out of a storm and let me pretend I was just upset over a fight with my mom, and gave me hot chocolate with chili powder and cinnamon, and has never, ever stopped being at my side no matter how many times she should have.

I'd been avoiding huge schools for fear of getting lost to Fitz, but we'd been lost to each other since the second I found out how he'd violated my trust. Meanwhile, Vic found me, and I've had a place with her ever since.

I look back down at the letter and whisper, "You're wrong," as I watch it disappear into my fist. Then I toss it into the trash and pick up the KU brochure on my nightstand. It really does look beautiful, and yeah, it has everything I could ask for. Plus, it's five hours from home—fat chance I'll ever come home anytime aside from Christmas, and that's just fine by me.

Of course, it also has one other thing, but the jury's still out on whether the presence of Dev Shah is a plus or minus. Vic's probably right that it was entirely possible I could never run into him again…if I didn't want to.

Do I want to?

My gaze drifts from the brochure to the box of letters sitting on the floor, the few loose papers scattered about.

Once upon a time, you made the decision not to let your life revolve around him, Vic had said about Fitz the day I applied. *How can you let it revolve around him now?*

The answer is that I can't. And I can't let it revolve around Dev either. I've worked damn hard to get out of this town, to get a real education, to go to a school with a beautiful campus, and real professors, and an endless library. Vic and I had wanted to find a place that worked for us both, and now maybe we have. Most of all, I have a ticket out—one I can afford.

I pull out my phone and dial Vic, muttering, "Let's just see who ain't gonna be shit, John Fitzpatrick," while I wait for her to pick up.

And as soon as she does, I say, "First possible day on the KU calendar. Let's go visit us a college."

VICTORIA

"Schedule KU visit...done," I mutter as I cross the list item off in my purple leather-bound planner. "Schedule a silk-screening lesson with Miss Lucy's friend...done. Buy new colored pencils? Done. Aaaand send Abuelita a copy of my portfolio...done." Man, it feels good to cross things off a list.

I still can't believe Reagan's quick turnaround on KU, but it's been two weeks since she called and had me set up the trip and she hasn't backed out, no matter how many times I expected her to. I even held off on actually signing us up, just because I was so sure she'd change her mind. But if anything, she's only gotten more excited.

I'm excited too…and nervous. Freckles and I haven't really talked about the fact that I'm looking at a school five hours away, and my parents clearly aren't having an easy time with it. Meanwhile, I've barely had time to think about it because I've been working so hard to get myself ready for this program. I went through Miss Lucy's winter workshop, but I have to learn all these other things first. It's scary, but it's also pretty awesome.

My phone dings with a text—Steve. *Should I get a bacon tuna melt going?*

Whoops. I completely forgot I was supposed to go in to Joe's tonight to hang out. I glance back at the planner. I still have math homework to do, and a skirt to finish stitching, and my nails need re-polishing…

But I should go. I know that I should. We probably don't have lots of time left together, and he's such a good guy…I'm not feeling up to my usual dinner tonight, though, so I text back, *Maybe a cheeseburger instead. I'll be there in ten.* Then I close my planner, get the keys from my parents, and head out.

He's taking an order when I get there, but he smiles briefly at me when I come in. I take a seat at the counter, where Rae's making change for a guy I recognize from her trailer park. "Hey hey," I greet her when she's done, reaching over to yank her white curl. "Is there a cheeseburger waiting for me?"

"Switched it up tonight, huh?"

I shrug. "Felt like something different."

She tips her head in Steve's direction. "Does Freckles know that?"

"He's the one I asked to place the order."

"Not what I meant, Vic," she says, exhaling sharply.

"Of course he knows." I slide the chunky sea glass ring off my finger and back on again a couple of times. "I told him I got in the day it happened."

"That's not the same as him knowing you're probably going," she points out. "And considering the way he's been talking about our trip there, I'm pretty sure he thinks it's just for fun."

I shift uncomfortably in my seat. "What makes you say that?"

"The fact that he said, 'I love that you guys just go on these trips for fun.'" She crosses her arms. "Why does he think this trip is just for fun, Victoria?"

"Don't ask me."

"I *am* asking you. Does he think you're staying here?"

I shrug again. I'm not lying. I honestly don't know what he thinks. Especially since I've never given him a straight answer about what I'm doing in the fall.

She sighs. "You need to tell him this is for real, and that you're leaving."

"Since when are you so confident that we'll love KU?" I challenge. "What happened to 'we're just visiting' and 'who knows if we'll even like it'?"

"Well, I got turned down for financial aid at Barnaby State, so I really freaking hope we like it." She scrubs at a stain on the counter with a vengeance. "Apparently if you already have any sort of scholarship, you're ineligible, and I have that thing from the English competition."

"Wasn't that, like, a thousand bucks?"

"Yup." She scrubs harder. I'm pretty sure Formica's gonna come off onto the towel soon. "So, I'm pretty much praying KU doesn't suck, because I'm going there whether it does or not. And after you made me apply, you better be coming with me."

Her tone is joking, but I'm not sure she is. Which is okay, because it all works with the plan. We're gonna go to KU together. We're gonna be roommates. I'm gonna do the design thing, and she's gonna do the pre-law thing, and it'll be great. It's not like I'm really thinking of sticking around here for—

"Hey." A peck on the cheek interrupts my thoughts and then Steve is rushing past, calling orders to Hector, putting away menus, and filling up sodas. "Did you get your cheeseburger?" he asks over his shoulder.

"Not yet, but—"

"Hector," he calls out, switching cups and levers without missing a beat. "Is that cheeseburger ready?"

I don't understand Hector's mumbled response, but I guess Steve takes it as a yes because he finishes filling the cup and then he's off again—a multitasking, people-pleasing speed demon. He drops off my burger, takes out the tray of drinks, and is back at my side to hand me the ketchup before Reagan can even grab menus for the family that just sat down.

"So what made you go for the cheeseburger tonight?" he asks with a smile once Rae's gone.

It's a normal question, but after the way Reagan twisted it, all I can hear is hidden meaning. "A girl can only have so many tuna melts, I guess."

He doesn't respond, just watches me eat for a minute, and then Hector calls out an order and he's gone again. I glance around the diner and see Rae narrowing her eyes at me as she takes orders, and I sigh and turn back to my burger only to see Steve has returned to the counter. "How is it?" he asks.

"Good." At least I think it is. I haven't really tasted it. I take a huge bite to make up for it, and end up nearly choking until Steve pushes my glass of water at me. I gulp it down while staring at my fries, avoiding the concern I know is in his eyes. "Clearly I'm very enthusiastic about it," I say weakly.

"Everything okay?"

I nod and take another sip of water. "Yeah, I just—"

"Hold that thought," he cuts in apologetically as the sound of a glass shattering and then a baby screaming fills the air. He dashes off, leaving me with a plate of food I'm no longer in the mood for. Instead, I pull my phone out of my bag and write a quick e-mail to Javi, just to say hi.

He shocks me by responding almost immediately. *Bula, Hermana! I've got webcam access! Can you chat?*

Looking up, I see that Rae and Steve are both too busy to care if I leave. I e-mail Javi back that I'll be at my computer in ten minutes and let them know I'm leaving.

"Already?" Steve looks surprised and sad, even though he's barely talked to me since I got there. "I'm sorry," I say, "but I need to talk to my brother. I'll see you…" I trail off as I remember the list of things awaiting me in my planner. "Friday night? You're off then, right?"

He starts to answer, but Reagan cuts him off. "Right," she says firmly, so I know automatically that A) he wasn't, and B) she was and she'll be covering for him. Just then, the kid starts to scream again, and, wincing, I peck them both goodbye, tell Rae to eat my burger, and head back home.

"Where were you?" Javi asks as soon as we've got our webchat set up.

"Just Joe's with Steve and Reagan."

"Steve's that Freckles kid?"

I roll my eyes, glad he can see me and catch the full effect. "Yes, Javier—Steve is that Freckles kid."

"You're still hanging out with that guy?"

"Apparently so." I sweep my hair up into a ponytail and twist it into a bun on top of my head. "I like him," I add defensively, a little too late, and I know it.

"This is the guy who goes to Mom and Dad's school, right?" I nod. "So, does this mean you're reconsidering going there?" How am I somehow giving this impression off to everybody? I open my mouth to respond, but Javi doesn't even give me a chance. "Because that'd be pretty awesome! Think about it. If you and me carpool to school together, Mom and Dad will basically *have* to get us a car, right? And we can totally take that place by storm. The Reyes sibs, back in action—no one'll know what hit 'em!"

My brain is spinning now, trying to process the words coming out of his mouth as he keeps on going about classes and parties and clubs, and finally I manage to cut him off with a "Wait!"

"What's the matter? You afraid I won't let you pick the car? Don't worry, Vicky, I'll—"

"No, not that." I thrust up my palm to his face on the screen. "You're going to CCC? Like, *this* fall?"

"Yeah, of course." He shrugs like it ain't no thang. "You knew that."

"How would I know that?" I blurt. "You never told me that. You never even told me when you were coming home!"

He laughs. "It's a twenty-seven-month program. How long did you think I was gonna be here? I'm not moving to the damn country. And going to CCC next semester's just the easiest way to readjust. I'm gonna go part-time, catch up on some basic classes, do some more traveling, and figure out where I'm gonna go after that."

The way he says it, it's as if there are no possibilities and all possibilities in this plan, all at the same time. How completely Javi, to simultaneously sound like a lazy butt and a master planner. And even though I'm sort of furious with him for totally failing to tell me until right now, I'm also dying to do everything he says, right down to getting a pair of red-white-and-green fuzzy dice for the car.

But that would mean staying, and I've already decided I'm not doing that, right? Staying means leaving Reagan, and no dorms, and no sororities, and no new boys…but going means leaving Javi, and Miss Lucy, and Steve.

"What's with you?" Javi asks, screwing up his face. "You look like steam's about to come out of your ears."

I had plans, I want to scream. *I had plans and you're screwing them up!* But the truth is, if I really had plans—firm, unbreakable plans—then I wouldn't have run home to talk to Javi; I would've just hung around until I could tell Freckles it was over and that I was set on going to KU. And I certainly wouldn't be thinking about whether our shared car should be a convertible.

"Nothing," I mumble instead, grabbing a pencil and paper from the side of my desk and half-heartedly sketching a motorcycle jacket that'd go perfectly with the new wheels I have in mind. "Just thinking about things."

"Hey. Vic." I look up, meet his dark, concerned eyes.

"It's just an idea, okay? No pressure. You do what you have to do for you. I know you and Reagan have this... thing. I just know you and Miss Lucy have a thing too, and now you and this Freckles guy..."

"I know, I know," I say with a groan. "Trust me—I wonder what I'm doing with myself every freaking day."

"You'll figure it out," he says dismissively. "Meanwhile, just have fun. He sounds like a nice kid, and you and Rae have that visit coming up. I'm sure it'll all become clear eventually."

He juts out his chin. "What's the thing you were drawing just now?"

"Oh, it's nothing. Just sketching." I hold up the jacket to the camera. "You made me think of a new driving wardrobe."

To my surprise, he shakes his head, laughing. "That's your idea of nothing? You don't even know how talented you are, Hermana. Forget what I said. You're wasting your talents in that town as it is. You should be going to that fancy fashion school you used to talk about."

He means FIT, which he knows full well isn't an option; even if I were good enough, there's no chance in the world I could convince Reagan to go to New York. "Javi. First of all, the only reason I can do this is because Miss Lucy's been working with me like crazy, and second of all, stop sending me mixed messages!"

He just laughs again, and I want to yell at him that my

life is not a joke, that my future isn't for his amusement. Of course, that's exactly when he whips around, says something to someone I can't see, and then comes back to say, "I gotta go. Other people are waiting."

I have no choice but to say goodbye and hang up. I know by now I should be used to the fact that no one I talk to has the answers I want, the answers I *need*. But they're out there. They have to be. Because if they aren't, what the heck am I doing with the rest of my life?

CHAPTER SIXTEEN

REAGAN

"No way. This is way too long a drive to spend listening to boy bands."

Vic huffs out a breath. "We agreed, half and half, remember?"

"Hasn't Freckles taught you the value of *any* good music? Almost three months of you guys 'hanging out' and he can't even bring you over to The Beatles?"

"The Beatles are boring," she whines, even as she smiles at the mere mention of Freckles's name. It still takes some getting used to, seeing them together. When I first realized Freckles had a crush on her, I thought he had about the same chances I did of my mom ever looking for a job. But Vic's changed a lot in the past few months, and she's gotten good at surprising me.

Unfortunately, her taste in music remains atrocious.

"Fine, we can listen to your crap as far as Great Bend, and then we're switching over," I concede as I slam the trunk shut on our stuff. "And your nails had better already be polished because you're not doing them on my dashboard again. Five hours is way too long to tolerate that smell."

"Four and a half," Vic corrects me, but she wiggles her fingernails to show that they're already perfectly purple.

It's definitely going to be closer to five, but it *is* a Sunday afternoon and there hasn't been a freak snowstorm in at least two weeks, so I cross my fingers as I get behind the wheel and pray that Vic's right.

In fact, she is: almost exactly four and a half hours later, I pull into the parking lot at the Golden Motel, which is more of a moldy beige, really. Whatever. It's after eleven, I've just driven almost five hours after a full shift at Joe's, and somewhere around Abilene it registered with me that Dev made this exact same trip, all alone, just to see me.

We haven't spoken since the day everything happened, except for one text from him wishing me a Merry Christmas. (If having Sheila Black nearly set half the park on fire with her Christmas lights counts as merry, then sure.) I didn't answer it, and he didn't try again. I thought about texting him to wish him a Happy New Year, but what's the point? Too much has happened and none of it went right. I'm not meant to focus on anything other than figuring out how to get out of Charytan, with Vic by my side, and the night at the motel proved that.

It's been a month since Christmas.

As we pick up our key and then carry our stuff into our room, I can't help imagining bumping into him at the vending machine the way Vic did at Southeastern, even though he lives locally and obviously has no reason to be at a motel. The odds of him even being at KU tomorrow are slim to none, considering there are a billion Admitted Senior Jayhawk Days and he probably won't even go to any of them since his mom teaches Bio here and he's been to campus a zillion times.

"You know you get a look on your face when you're thinking about Dev," Vic informs me as she fishes her toiletry bag out of her suitcase. "I thought you said you didn't think he'd be here."

"I don't. That's what I was thinking of," I admit. "And it's a good thing. Like you said, we can be on the same campus next year without running into him at all. It's not like I'm going to take any of the same classes as a pre-med."

"I still can't get over how you've gone from 'I'd never even consider to KU' to planning your schedule here next year," she muses, pulling her long, thick hair into a ponytail. "You haven't even seen the campus yet."

"Oh, shut it. You know KU ended up being far cheaper than anything else, especially after that scholarship."

"And?"

I grin. "And the fact that it's about four hours further than my parents will *ever* drive doesn't hurt."

"Not exactly what I meant," she says, laughing, "but whatever works. You mind if I jump in the shower first?"

I gesture for her to go ahead, and lie back on one of the beds with tomorrow's itinerary in hand, in addition to the course catalog. I'd narrowed down my major to either English or History or Sociology or possibly PoliSci, and I can't help drooling over all the possibilities for electives, including ASL, or even study abroad. The options here are pretty amazing, and I want to kick myself for ignoring them for so long.

Before Vic even gets out of the shower, I pass out completely, dreaming of the Eiffel Tower standing smack in the middle of Charytan, a mythical giant casting a massive shadow over nothing but rubble.

"I can't get over the size of this place," I whisper to Vic as we turn onto yet another street full of huge buildings and neat patches of grass. We've seen multiple gyms, streets full of fraternity and sorority houses (which of course made Vic squeal like a child, though I'm not even sure if she's still interested or if it's just out of habit), and tons of campus transportation. The place is so freaking big they have *their own buses.*

"If everyone else can learn their way around, so can we," she whispers back, nodding toward a hulking frat guy who's practically busting the seams of his Jayhawks sweatshirt. "If that guy can get himself to class, so can we."

I smother a laugh behind my hand. Her words are oddly comforting, although hearing her be the voice of reason still messes with my head. I don't know how it became such that she's the level-headed one with an actual sense of direction while I'm barely hanging on and routinely obsessing about a boy, but it's been like months of the Twilight Zone.

The student ambassador continues his whole thing, but it's been forty-five minutes and I'm itching for lunch to start already. Plus we saw the library for all of two seconds and I have big plans to go back there and inhale the scent of every single book while Vic meets with someone from the Visual Arts program. A brief memory of Dev's comment about licking books in the library flashes through my brain and I impatiently push it out, turning to Vic to change the subject. "So do you still think you'll do the whole sorority thing?"

She shrugs. "Depends on how it fits with my program, I guess, but I like that it's an option. Checking out a couple of the houses is on my schedule after my meeting with the Visual Arts guy."

Of course it is. Of course Vic has a hundred things planned for today, and I'm not doing a damn thing but sniffing books and thinking about a guy who pretty much hates me, and also happens to be about ten minutes away. The temptation to take my Vic-less time and use it to show up at his door and both beg for forgiveness and demand an apology is strong, but fortunately, there's still a little self-respect floating around somewhere near my spleen.

That doesn't stop me from imagining scenarios for the next fifteen minutes, even though none of them go well. Finally, it's time for the pre-lunch presentation, and I practically mow down my fellow future Jayhawks in my mad dash toward the last barrier between me and sustenance.

After the presentation, we gather to get food and take seats, and Vic and I quickly learn that everyone around us is from Chicago. "Why would you come to school in Kansas?" I can't help asking.

The girl across from me, whose peeling name sticker identifies her as Simone, pokes at the salad on her plate. "It's a whole lot cheaper than school near me," she says, finally forking a cucumber.

"Same." The guy next to her takes a huge bite of his sandwich. His name tag is completely covered up by the huge hooded zip-up hanging only slightly open over his flannel button-down. "Also, fuckin' Jayhawks, man," he adds, spitting crumbs. "Rock Chalk."

"You guys are from Western Kansas? Don't you all go to K-State or something?" asks another guy, Charlie, whose got both the build and appetite of an athlete. "Isn't that, like, a rule?"

"Don't tell anyone," I say conspiratorially. "We're mavericks."

"You're from Dallas?" Charlie asks, furrowing his thick brows.

"What? No—"

"What are you guys studying?" Simone asks, obviously impatient with Charlie.

"Rae's prelaw," Vic declares, with not a little amount of pride, even though it's not an actual major, "and I'm doing Visual Art."

"I am too!" Simone says excitedly, hinting at having a personality for the first time all morning. "I'm doing painting. I just submitted my portfolio last week. What about you?"

While Vic and Simone fall into their own conversation that doesn't really allow for any of us to keep up, I halfheartedly listen to Charlie and No-Name go on about the Jayhawks while trying to figure out exactly how I want to spend the rest of the afternoon. The library seems a little too fraught with memories right now. I know I could go to a KU museum, but I'm just not in the mood. I'd wander, but even without snow it definitely feels like January outside.

"Right, Rae?"

I snap my head up, realizing Vic's just called my name and apparently I was supposed to be listening to that conversation after all. "Sorry, what?"

"I was just saying that you sat in on classes when we visited other schools."

"Oh, yeah, It was fun," I say half-heartedly, because of course all I can think of now is the admiration I pretended not to have for Dev when he aced that question in the genetics class at Barnaby State.

"I couldn't believe it when she went to that class all by herself at Southeastern," Vic continues to Simone. "Like, who even does that? I would've been terrified about being called on. Wouldn't you?"

"Definitely," Simone affirms. She's probably just saying it to agree with Vic, but it sounds genuine enough and it makes me sit up a little straighter. "*Did* you get called on?"

"Nope, thankfully," I admit, "but it wouldn't have been so bad if I had been, I don't think. It was pretty interesting stuff. Not hard to understand or anything."

"Yeah, for you, maybe." Vic rolls her eyes at Simone.

"Rae's, like, top three in our class. It's ridiculous."

"Are you really?" Simone looks mystified.

"It's not a big deal," I mumble. Vic's always been like this, prouder of my academic achievements than my own mom. It gets embarrassing.

But, I realize as I stare at the food I've barely touched on my plate despite having been ravenous less than an hour earlier, it's also true. I *am* top three in our class, and I worked my ass off for it. I also held down a job, paid for my own car, paid for some of my family's bills, and got a solid scholarship to KU. I *do* have a lot to be proud of, and I'm sitting here all miserable, my first time at what's probably going to be my home for the next four years, because of a fucking *boy*?

"I gotta go." I jump up, startling both Vic and Simone, and wrap my sandwich in a napkin. "Do you mind if I skip the res hall thing?" I ask Vic. "I trust your judgment. Take pictures on your phone."

"Are you sure? Is everything okay?"

"Great," I assure her, gathering up my stuff. "I'll see you after your meetings, 'kay?"

"Okay," she says slowly, obviously concerned, but then Simone pulls her back into conversation and I go back out into the wintry day, to take in the library and its thousands of books, to memorize every inch of Wescoe Hall—home of the English department—possible, to remember what it was like to be that girl who lived for nothing but going to college.

Which, of course, is exactly when I bump smack into that fucking boy.

We both freeze. What else can you do? Keep walking like the other one doesn't exist? Pretend we've never spent hours talking and laughing and texting? Act like we've never seen each other completely naked, like he's never suspended himself over me with lean, ropy arms, our eyes locking for one brief instant as if trying to confirm this was real before he lowered himself to press his mouth to mine so intensely it was like he was trying to leave the imprint of my body in the mattress?

He blinks. Opens and closes his mouth a few times before he finally speaks. "How is that you?"

"How isn't it?" I say automatically. I yank my Rogue curl as evidence and then let go, leaving my hand suspended in mid-air for a moment as it springs back up. "What are you doing here?"

"What am *I* doing here? Dropping something off for my mom. What are *you* doing here?"

I gesture up at the colorful banner overhead. "Admitted Senior Jayhawk Day. I'm an admitted senior Jayhawk."

"You."

"Me."

"You said—"

"I know." I readjust the strap of my bag on my shoulder and slip my hands into my pockets, gripping the lining with cold fingertips. "I changed my mind." I thrust one fist weakly into the air. "Rock Chalk Jayhawk."

"So you're coming here?"

"It's not about you," I say quickly, afraid he's gotten the wrong idea. "I mean, it's a big school. You're pre-med. We probably won't even see each other." I don't like the words any better than when Vic first said them, but they seem like the right ones here.

He scratches behind his ear. "I wouldn't want that. I mean, I don't think I'd like...not seeing you. I know I wouldn't," he amends, dropping his hand to his side.

"That's not really how it sounded the last time we talked." Looking at him standing in front of me now, his brown cheeks just a little rosy from the cold, a black knit cap pulled down to his thick brows, his eyes curious and friendly, it's hard to believe he's the same guy who made me feel like a life-ruining slut three months earlier. But the words are burned into my brain; I couldn't forget them if I tried. Which I had.

"I'm sorry for what I said," he rasps, his gloved hands clenching and unclenching at his sides. "I didn't know..." His words drift on the wind, lonely and waiting.

"Didn't know that coming to see me would be such a mistake?" I say coolly when moments pass without him filling in the blank.

He mumbles something under his breath, his eyes on the ground.

"Sorry," I say snidely, "I didn't catch that."

He looks up at me and locks his eyes on mine. "I said I didn't know it could be like that." He swallows so hard it's audible, even with the wind whipping around us. "I didn't know you could feel lucky for getting to hold a girl's hair back while she pukes into the bushes. I didn't know you could look at a girl and think, 'Jesus, I could fall so hard for you if you'd let me.'"

He might as well have hit me with a mallet. "But you—"

"I was a fucking idiot, Reagan. Everything I said—"

"That you turn into the world's shittiest person around me?" I've been carrying that one in my brain, my heart, for months. There's nothing worse than hearing that you make someone's life worse. Nothing. "That you don't know what the fuck is wrong with you?"

He scrubs a hand over his face, and when his eyes meet mine again they're soft, sad. "The thing is, I do know what the fuck is wrong with me, and why I lied to everyone and hooked up with you when I shouldn't have: because I couldn't *not*. I couldn't not know what it was like to kiss you. For a while I could resist it, because it felt so...*inevitable*. I could be patient, because in my head it was just a matter of time. But then suddenly it wasn't, and you were really driving away, and not coming to KU…" He exhales sharply before continuing.

"I am a selfish asshole, but there you have it. I was— *am*—crazy about you. And it made me do some really stupid things. And you know what makes me even more terrible?" He smiles grimly. "For as awful as I feel for everything that happened, I still think it was all worth it.

"I've been friends with Sara for three years," he continues. "All my other friends like her, my parents love her…she should be the perfect girl for me. But I've spent three years waiting to feel for her what I felt after three seconds of meeting you. And I stupidly thought, 'The perfect time will come when we're meant to be more, and we'll know it, and I'll kiss her, and it'll be magic.' I thought it would be homecoming, or New Year's, or prom, but month after month, it never was. And then I opened the door to my room and saw you standing there in the parking lot, in the rain, and I just thought, 'This. This is what the perfect time feels like. It's not about the milestone; it's about the person.' And—"

I throw my arms around his neck and pull him down toward me, pressing his mouth to mine. Even as we're talking about perfect timing and this is decidedly not it, it also sort of is. Because it can't not be. Because it's Dev, and me. Because he's supposed to be at school, and I'm supposed to be at lunch, or not here at all. Because, because, because.

I don't know how long it is before he pulls away to

catch his breath, but he doesn't go far. His hands are on my cheeks, his forehead pressed to mine, his breath gentle puffs of air on my lips. My mind is a swirling mass of gray matter, but after a few moments I finally gather my thoughts, because I know that as simple and easy as this feels, life just isn't that kind.

"What if I don't go here?" I ask, because I have to. "I haven't accepted. I'm just visiting. What if—"

"I don't care, Rogue." He takes the white curl and twirls it gently between his fingertips. "I mean, I care— obviously I'd love to see you every day, and I think this is the right place for you whether I'm here or not—but I don't care. I drove five hours to see you once and I'll do it again and again and again if I have to. Just…I want to be with you. Wherever you decide to go, I'll come find you."

At those words, I burrow into his chest and squeeze him so tightly, I nearly choke the life out of him. He actually has to disentangle himself from my grip, though he laughs lightly as he does it. "Is that a yes?"

I open my mouth to say yes when I realize that once again, I'm jumping the gun. "Can it be? What about Sara and your other friends? Do I have to be some dirty little secret until September?"

Dev looks so confused that for a second I wonder if he's forgotten that I know all about her. Then he narrows his eyes. "I realize I was a jerk, but you don't think I continued to keep you a secret after we slept together, do you?"

I blush and look away, because yeah, that's exactly what I thought. Not because I think he's evil, but because it's admittedly what I probably would've done in his shoes.

"Well, I didn't. I told her."

"You told her? About me?" I squeak.

"I didn't tell her your name or anything, but yeah, of course I told her. Shouldn't I have?"

"I guess." I purse my lips. "I'm kind of impressed. I don't know that I could've done that."

"Well, if it helps, she laughed at first."

"She laughed?"

"She didn't believe me," he admits sheepishly. "Apparently the idea of my meeting a hot girl and getting laid is absolutely hilarious."

I throw back my head and crack up; I can't help it.

"You think that's funny?"

"That obvious?"

"I *did* dream it all, didn't I?" he mutters, and it's just so cute I have to kiss him again.

"What would you have done if I hadn't shown up today?" I ask when we part again. "Would you have just kept this all to yourself until you got over it or whatever?"

He sighs. "I was hoping you wouldn't ask that."

"Why? Because it's true?"

"No, because I had a really, really embarrassing plan

to show up at your school on Valentine's Day." His face is beet red now, redder than I would've thought possible given his natural skin tone, and it's definitely got nothing to do with the cold. "Now can you please stop asking questions with terrible answers?"

"Deal. You just need to do one thing for me in return."

He raises an eyebrow. "What's that?"

I smile sweetly. "Show me the way to the library?"

VICTORIA

I have no idea what made Reagan ditch me at lunch, especially since she hasn't answered either of my texts, but Simone's making for a lousy tour-buddy replacement. "These rooms are so small," she whines as our guide shows us a suite with two doubles that are at least five times the size of Rae's bedroom at home. I'm actually sad she's missing this, though I can easily imagine her eyes widening at the sight.

Fortunately, a tall, chatty redhead named Kimmy with a way better attitude joined us for the residence hall tours in the middle, and her zillions of questions are helping distract me from Simone's whining. She even posed in a couple of pictures for me after the tour, to help show Reagan the dimensions of the rooms.

"Love how many cute boys there are in this place," she observes, her voice tinged with the slightest bit of southern accent. "If that doesn't get you excited for dorm living, nothing will." She scrunches up her eyebrows at me. "Unless you're a lesbian. Are you a lesbian? It's totally cool if you are. There are girls here too."

"Nope, I'm straight." *Though I get that a lot.*

"I never met any lesbians," Kimmy confides as we walk to the common area to take some more pictures. "That'll be cool in college, don't you think? I just wanna meet all kinds of people."

I wonder if meeting a Mexican chick has ticked off a box for her or something. Meeting my mom would probably blow her mind.

We play the "what are you majoring in/where are you from/where else did you apply" game for a couple of minutes, with me declaring myself from "near Dodge City" because no one's ever heard of Charytan, and her doing the same with "near Leavenworth." Then a guy walks past us, T-shirt tucked into the back pocket of his shorts, his chest and back glistening with sweat, and both of us go silent in appreciation.

My parents would probably cross themselves if they could see me now. They're pretty chill and all, but other than the distance, I think the idea of me living with guys who look like that is what freaks them out the most about me going to college. Javi's made clear he's not crazy about his little sister "cohabitating" with boys either, and Steve's been quiet on the subject. Then again, the whole topic of me going away to college is one we've mostly avoided.

I wonder if he'd visit me here, if he'd drive five hours each way the way Dev did for Reagan. Could he, even? Between school and basically working full time at Joe's? Probably not. That seems so...sad.

"So where are you going from here?" Kimmy asks, breaking up my mental pity party.

I hadn't even noticed that the tour was breaking up and we were being guided out of the residence hall. "I've got a meeting with someone from my program in twenty minutes," I say apologetically, even though I'm not sure she was asking to hang out. "Maybe I'll see you later? I'm going to look at some sorority houses after that."

Her face lights up. "Yeah, maybe." We trade numbers, and I realize I just made my first friend at college. And admittedly, I'm a little proud to have done it entirely on my own.

I hadn't made my appointment early enough to nab a faculty member or adviser for a meeting, but the department was nice enough to find me a junior Visual Arts major named Pete, who meets me for coffee in a bright red fleece pullover and a KU cap pulled low over dark brows.

"So!" he says once we've sat down, both of us curling our hands around the steaming cups in defense against the weak heating in the coffee shop. "You're planning to do Visual Arts. Textile Design, right?"

I take a tentative sip of my mocha latte. "Right. I've always been interested in fashion," I say, trying to get the words out confidently even though I feel silly uttering them.

"Very cool. It's a great program. Do you have your portfolio?"

I reach into my bag and hand it over, butterfly wings brushing my stomach lining as I do. No one's seen my portfolio other than my parents, Reagan, Steve, and Miss Lucy, and I've looked it over so many times even I have no idea if it's any good. He's quiet as he flips through it, but my eyes are too focused on his cup of coffee and how quickly I will throw myself out the café's plate-glass window if he spills on my sketches.

"These are really good," he murmurs, closing it to take a sip, then reopening it again once he puts his cup down. "These patterns are so interesting. Can I ask what inspired them?"

"My family, actually." The pride in my voice is audible. "My brother's in the Peace Corps now, in Fiji, and he sent me all these pictures of plants and native clothing and stuff, and I thought it'd be really cool to incorporate that in my designs. And then there's some Mexican influence, inspired by my abue—my grandparents."

"Fiji, huh? That's really cool. It looks so tropical, but earthy. Is there any stuff here inspired by your own travels?" He's flipping through the sketches more briskly now.

Um, what *travels?* Not that I really want to admit to a college guy that other than a couple of trips to Mexico for the sole purpose of visiting my grandparents, I've been all of nowhere. I mean, I guess I could do something with the shades of the Grand Canyon, but…

"Nope," I say, trying not to sound as meek and immature as I feel. "Haven't gotten to do much of that."

"You should," Pete says seriously. "I mean, don't get me wrong—these are good. The colors are really vibrant and the patterns are interesting, but they lack texture. It's obvious they're based on things you've seen but haven't touched." He draws a fingertip over one of the branches in one of my favorite patterns. "In real life, this would probably be knobbly, or at least not completely smooth. Think how cool this would be if it were leather, for example. Or if you'd used shading to show bark."

I rub a fingertip over another of the branches. I see what he means, and he's absolutely right. How could I not have thought of that? I flip through the portfolio, and immediately pick out at least three patterns that are missing the same sort of touches. Suddenly, I'm embarrassed at the lack of depth of color, the flat tones where they should appear three-dimensional, the lack of imagination with regard to fabric choices and textures. What am I doing, thinking I can suddenly jump on board with this whole thing just because I've stitched a few bags and taken one week-long workshop with a community college professor?

Tia Maria, why can't I think anything through? Every time I think I know what I want, I realize I haven't really thought about it at all. I just keep diving in like some sort of blind idiot.

I gently take back my portfolio, even though it doesn't feel like there's anything in there worth saving, and tuck it back into my bag. "Anyway, it's just a thought," I mumble, taking a sip of coffee to hide my stupid quivering lip. "Obviously I'm not married to it. I'm considering other programs too."

"Oh, really?" There's so much pity in his voice, I could die. "Like what?"

"Like…" I think back to the application I filled out not that long ago. Not a whole lot of special skills on there. But at least there was one that had nothing to do with design. "ASL," I say triumphantly. "American Sign Language. I'm thinking of studying that. Majoring in it, I mean." I have no idea if they offer it as a major, but it sounds good.

"Wow, that's certainly a different direction. Hard, too."

"Not so bad once you get the hang of it." I sign the words as I say them.

"Whoa, you already speak it! That's so cool!"

"My mom's deaf; I'd be kind of a jerk if I didn't speak

it. It's cool, though. I like knowing it. I think taking classes in it would be awesome." And as I say the words, I realize they're true. Being five hours away from my mom would be really hard, but video chatting with her about stuff I'm learning in the same kinds of classes she teaches? Why hadn't I thought of that before?

"Let me guess," says Pete, the corners of his lips quirking up as he taps his fingertips on the side of his coffee cup. "You tend to change your mind a *lot*."

"I just don't know how to know what I want, or what I'm good enough at to pursue," I admit. "College is expensive. I don't want to waste my parents' money."

Pete laughs, not meanly or anything, just...laughs. "You don't have to be great at something to learn it, you know. If you were already perfect, taking classes would be a little pointless."

"So what do you think I should do?"

"I think you should do what you *like* to do! Look." He places a palm flat on the table. "You're *good* at design; just because there's room to grow doesn't mean you're not one hundred percent perfect for this program. Learning is kind of the point! And you're obviously good at ASL. And I'm willing to bet you're good at a whole bunch of other things. But what do you *want* to do?"

I shrug. "All of it? Or not?"

"Victoria—"

"I don't want to make the wrong choice!" I blurt.

"Look, I don't want to let anyone down, okay? I don't want to make my family suffer for my mistakes, or my best friend to realize she's too smart for me, or to hook up with the wrong guy because he's too nice or too *not* nice. I'm just sick of not knowing what I'm doing!"

When I'm done ranting, I can feel the eyes of other patrons on me, and I sink down in my seat until my flaming cheeks brush the fur lining of the hood of the coat I've hung on the back of my chair. Tia Maria, I'm a train wreck. "I'm sorry," I whisper, lifting my eyes just enough to see that once again, Pete is smiling. And once again, it's not mean.

"You're what, seventeen?" I nod miserably. "That's what life *is* at seventeen. You make mistakes, you learn from them, you grow up. No one expects you to be perfect or know exactly what you want. There's a reason college students get until the end of sophomore year to pick a major."

"Not—"

"Not with this program, I know," he says, cutting me off, "but if you left it to major in, say, ASL, I bet you could do that." He scrunches his brows. "Is that even a major?"

"I have no idea," I admit sheepishly.

"Well, whatever. The point is, ease up on yourself. Get to know yourself a little better. And forge your own path. You'll figure it out; you're far too talented not to. There's a whole world of possibilities out there, ya know?"

I drop my gaze into the milky depths of my coffee, thinking about the past bunch of months, all the different schools and all the different weirdness at each one. Jamie and Steve. Sorority Sasha and I-Want-to-Meet-a-Lesbian Kimmy. I think about Fitz going to the army, and Javi going to Fiji, and Steve going to CCC, and the fact that unless she ditched me to drive home, I suspect Reagan will be going to KU.

And I think about what I *really* want.

And I finally smile, and say, "Yeah, I guess there are."

EPILOGUE

"Hey, do you want to get Chinese, or—?"

"Hush! It's time!" Reagan dashes past Dev, knocking him back onto her bed, and yanks open her laptop just in time to receive the call. "Hiiiii!"

"Hola, mi amiga!" Vic says cheerfully, shaking a maraca at the screen. "How crazy that we finally convinced my grandparents to get the Internet?"

"Very," Reagan confirms, pulling the laptop off the desk carefully so as not to dislodge the cord, and settles back on to the bed, knocking Dev over again. "How's the Victoria and Javier Reyes World Tour Bonanza?"

"You know you guys just talked, like, two days

ago, when we were in LA," Javi says grumpily in the background, his voice only faintly carrying through the speakers.

"Exactly what I was thinking," Dev mumbles, glancing at his watch.

"Hello to you too, Dev!" Vic sing-songs.

He waves. "Hey, Vic. Sorry, I'm at the cranky point of hunger. *Somebody* was supposed to have dinner with me an *hour* ago, but—"

"But *somebody* was talking to her professor about a competitive tutoring position that would bring in way more money than waitressing at the coffee shop," Reagan fills in, elbowing Dev in the side playfully.

"Hey, that's great!" Vic and Dev say at the same time as he snakes an arm around her waist and plants a kiss on her cheek.

"Get the other cheek for me," Vic commands, and he happily obliges. "Are you sure you want to waste all that waitressing experience? I know Steve misses you."

"Freckles also thinks I'm gonna help out over Thanksgiving break, doesn't he?"

Vic whistles innocently.

Reagan rolls her eyes. "At least Joe's turkey is better than my mom's. How is Steve, anyway?"

"He's good," says Vic, drawing out the words. Behind her, Javi mock-vomits in disgust. "Oh, hush. We're just friends now. We haven't even seen each other in weeks.

But he *did* mention something about applying to culinary school in the near future."

"So at no point will he be joining the Reyes siblings on their glamorous tour of youth hostels and fashion observation?" Reagan teases. "Where's the next stop, anyway?"

"Buenos Airrrrrres," Vic trills. "But first, my parents are coming down here for Thanksgiving. My mom swears she finally made a batch of churros worth bringing across the border down to Abuelita."

"Have you seen photographic evidence of this success?"

"No, but the sign for 'perfect' is just about burned into my brain from all her enthusiasm during our video chats, so I'm gonna trust her on this one." She tips her head. "And how are you guys? You a die-hard Jayhawk yet?"

Reagan rolls her eyes. "Definitely not. People here are crazy."

"*People* just went to their very first game at Allen Fieldhouse and *loved* it, actually," Dev informs Vic. "*People* just like to hate on everything."

"That's my girl," Vic says with a smile. "Don't ever change. Not even for the boy."

"Pssh, for this one?" She flicks Dev in his flannel-sleeve covered shoulder. "Never. So, if I'm not seeing you Thanksgiving, when *am* I seeing you? Christmas? New

Year's? Sometime before we're legally allowed to drink, please?"

Vic bites her lip, her nervousness palpable. "Sooo, about that…"

Reagan narrows her eyes. "Vic. Whatever it is, spit it out."

"Okay, but I'm really excited about it, so you can't be mad."

"Me? Mad?" She turns to Dev. "Can you believe she just said that?"

"Don't be mad," Dev commands.

"You guys are a terrible conspiracy." She turns back to the screen. "Fine. I will not be mad about this thing that will definitely make me mad. Now, what is it? I'm dying of curiosity."

Vic turns to her brother. "Ahem. Javier, the envelope please?"

Javi's eye roll is a thing of magnificence, but he obliges, handing Vic a cream-colored envelope with an insignia in the corner.

"Drum roll?"

"Just read them the damn thing, Hermana."

Vic slides a letter out from the envelope, her hand shaking just slightly even though the envelope has clearly already been opened. Even from two thousand miles away, Reagan can tell she's honestly nervous, and it's contagious. "What is it, damn it?" she demands.

Vic holds it up against the webcam.

Reagan takes a moment to scan it, and then her mouth drops open. "Does that seriously say what I think it says?"

Next to Rae, Dev leans in, squinting at the screen, one arm curled firmly around her waist. "Holy shit. You're going to FIT?"

Vic nods, tears shining in her eyes, her bottom lip pulled firmly between her teeth. "Are you mad, Rae?"

"Am I…? No, Vic, no. Of course not." Tears prick her own eyes, though, and Dev hugs her even closer to his body. "A little sad," she admits as one rolls down her cheek and she quickly swipes it away. "But I'm so fucking proud of you. That's amazing."

"That summer internship Miss Lucy got me helped a *ton*," says Vic, "and I'm not gonna lie—my new portfolio? Seriously awesome."

"Fucking awesome, Vic. Just say it."

Vic laughs. "Even if I were to start swearing, you think I'd even try it in this house?"

"Fair enough," Rae says with a grin. Then the smile falls. "So, this is it, huh? I wish I'd known I was saying goodbye for good the last time I said it."

Vic shakes her head. "It's not for good, silly. And I *will* be home for Christmas." She folds the letter back up and slides it into its envelope. "Things may not exactly have gone according to plan, but they didn't turn out badly either, did they?" She gestures at Dev, who cocks his head as he waits for Reagan's answer.

"Not that badly," Reagan concedes. "But Jesus, Vic—New York? Seriously?"

"Seriously. And you'll come to visit me—finally get out of Kansas for once! Doesn't that sound good?"

Reagan narrows her eyes. "You're really hung up on dragging my ass to big cities, aren't you?"

Vic laughs. "You'll love it. Or at least I'm hoping you will, because I'm hoping I will too!"

"You're not even going to visit before you accept their acceptance?"

Vic glances down at the envelope before looking back at the screen. "Nah. How much can you really tell from just a visit, anyway? When you're headed where you're supposed to be, you just know."

Dev laces his fingers with Reagan's and kisses the top of her head. "I don't think Rae can argue with that."

Reagan blushes at the sight of Vic's knowing smile. "Go get Chinese before this turns into an R-rated movie," Vic orders. "We're not allowed to watch those here."

Reagan laughs. "Fair enough. Talk to you this weekend?"

"You know it. And Reagan?"

"Yeah?"

She leans in to switch off the webcam. "I'll see you at home."

AUTHOR'S NOTE

American Sign Language (ASL) is a visual language, primarily communicated through manual gestures. It has its own independent grammatical structure and mechanics, and does not lend itself well to being directly transcribed (or "glossed") for English-speaking readers. As such, it has been translated into English for this book.

Additionally, *Just Visiting* is set in the very rapidly changing world of college admissions, and uses both real and fictional institutions. All scenarios and characters are fictional, including at the University of Kansas. However, Reagan's financial assistance options are very much based in real options available to low-income teens, and I strongly encourage high school students in need to consult guidance counselors and/or use websites to look into financial options for not just scholarships but test and application fee waivers as well.

ACKNOWLEDGMENTS

If there's one thing I learned from this experience, it's that "the book of your heart" may change, but each one will forever hold the loving labor put into it by the most wonderful and supportive people in your world. This was my most challenging writing experience thus far, but without the following, it would've been wholly impossible:

Lana Popovic, who gave this book her heart and her all (with the fabulous Fancy Allison Singer at her side)— thank you for loving it, polishing it, and fighting for it;

Patricia Riley, for too much to list, and her friendship on top of all of it;

Maggie Hall, Marieke Nijkamp, and Gina Ciocca,

who are forever the brightest stars in my authorial universe, and the greatest critique partners I could imagine; Katie Locke, Sarah Benwell, Candice Montgomery, Ashley Herring Blake, and Sharon Morse—fabulous friends who helped shape a complicated book into its best self; Sarah Henning, for all of the Kansan heart and accuracy; Meagan Rivers and Akchita Singh, for encouraging early reads and love; Erica Chapman and Valerie Cole, for tending to this book when it was just a few baby chapters; and everyone who informed various aspects of my research along the way, including Nita Tyndall, Brooks Sherman, Corinne Duyvis, and Laurie MacDougall.

Thanks and love to Kelly Fiore and Rachael Allen, authors par excellence; Instagram superstar and macaron buddy Natasha Minoso; and the world's greatest book pusher (and brownie maker), Gaby Salpeter—your early love for this book meant the world to me. Huge hugs to the bloggers and booksellers who've supported my work along the way, especially Christina Franke and her eagle eyes, Sara Taylor Woods and her V8 selfies, Nicole Brinkley and the rest of YA Interrobang, Debby (the right Snuggly one), my fellow author-bloggers Eric Smith and Valerie Tejeda, Patricia and Anasheh of the Fantastic Flying Book Club, and my wonderful editor at the B&N Teen Blog, Melissa Albert.

Major gratitude to the rest of my Spencer Hill clan, including Meredith Maresco, Cindy Thomas, Sarah

Henning, Jessica Porteous, Michelle Smith, Karen Hughes, Michael Short, Rebecca Weston, and Maggie Hall, for another cover so beautiful, I can't believe I get to put my name on it.

Love to the writer friends who keep my head above water on a daily basis: Jess, Kelly, Hebah, Sharon, and Tess, for commiseration in moderation (see what I did there?); the YA Misfits, OneFour Kid Lit, and Binders; my co-schmagent, Rick Lipman; my archnemesis, Leah Raeder; Corey Haydu, Lindsay Ribar, Jessica Verdi, Caela Carter, Alison Cherry, Adam Silvera, and the rest of the fabulous and supportive YA authors of NYC; Lindsay Smith, the best vodka-swilling, Stucky-shipping, Knope-abiding accountabili-buddy a girl could ask for; and the real stars in this endeavor: the makers of Gushers and Fresca.

Thank you to my family—Mom, Dad, Mom-in-law, Dad-in-law, Tamar, Jonathan, Aytan, Eric, Orly, Simona, Julia, Eyal, Ben, Liat, Annie, Nili, Besdins, Krauts, Morgans, Adlers, Fisches, Huttels, Weissmanns, and Kanovskys—for your support and your faith, always.

The book of my heart may change, but the keeper of that heart never does. Thank you, Yoni, for so many things, but especially for making food I can brag about on the internet. I love you.

Other Books
by Dahlia Adler

Behind
the Scenes

"Behind the Scenes is sweet,
sexy, and satisfying. Once you
start reading, you won't
want to stop!"
*—Trish Doller, author
of* Where the Stars Still Shine

$9.95 • 328 pages
ISBN: 978-1939392978

Under
the Lights

"A positive, empowering
coming-of-age that lifts the veil
hanging over queerness in YA."
—Leah Raeder, USA Today *bestselling
author of* Unteachable
and Black Iris

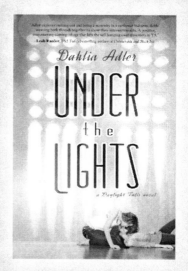

$9.95 • 312 pages
ISBN: 978-1633920170